I0652628

Praise for...

Dreams of the Compass Rose

"A clever concoction of vignettes and short stories knitted into a morality tale about the temptation of illusion and the price of truth . . . an exotic setting reminiscent of Tanith Lee's Flat Earth series. . . . The author's sumptuous language will resonate with Lord Dunsany and Clark Ashton Smith fans. . . . Nazarian's vital themes and engaging characters are sure to entertain."

—Publishers Weekly

"The colorful strong writing style that Vera has worked on for years has come to full fruition."

—Marion Zimmer Bradley

"I love this book. **Dreams of the Compass Rose** is a story-cycle in which we keep coming back to the same characters, except from different viewpoints and different times in their lives. It's set in a land of desert empires that never was, though it could easily be our world—far in the future, or deep in the past. Some of the stories are brutal, some are like dreams. All of them are engaging and resonant, creating a new mythology that feels so right one might be forgiven for thinking that it's the cultural heritage of some forgotten country or people that have been lost to history. It reminded me of those wonderful, dream-laden story-cycles that Clark Ashton Smith and Lord Dunsany were writing around the turn of the last century. **Dreams of the Compass Rose** has a similar stately lyricism, a compelling and visionary voice that speaks to the heart of the reader."

—Charles de Lint

"Nazarian's story cycle treads the borderline between the episodic novel and the short-story collection... her imagery is rich, vivid, and memorable, not to mention being remarkable because she realizes it not in her native language, Russian, but in English.... this is a singularly appealing book by a new voice in fantasy."

—ALA Booklist

"An intricate multi-level story . . . a kind of Aesop's Fables . . . spoken with a voice from the Far East, hypnotic as the desert sands."

—Locus

This book is a work of fiction. All characters, names, locations, and events portrayed in this book are fictional or used in an imaginary manner to entertain, and any resemblance to any real people, situations, or incidents is purely coincidental.

DREAMS OF THE COMPASS ROSE

Vera Nazarian

Copyright © 2002 by Vera Nazarian

All Rights Reserved.

Cover Design Copyright © 2013 by Vera Nazarian

Cover Art Images:
"The Tree of Life," stained glass Louis Comfort Tiffany (1848-1933); "Compass" card. HM 46. Portolan Atlas and Nautical Almanac. France, 1543

Interior: Goody Two-Shoes text divider graphic, 1888 edition.

ISBN-13: 978-1-60762-116-4
ISBN-10: 1-60762-116-9

10TH ANNIVERSARY EDITION
Trade Paperback

March 20, 2013

A Publication of
Norilana Books
P. O. Box 209
Highgate Center, VT 05459-0209
www.norilana.com

Printed in the United States of America

Dreams of the Compass Rose

Norilana Books

Fantasy

www.norilana.com

Other Books by Vera Nazarian

Lords of Rainbow
The Clock King and the Queen of the Hourglass
Mayhem at Grant-Williams High (YA)
The Duke in His Castle
Salt of the Air
The Perpetual Calendar of Inspiration
After the Sundial
Vampires are from Venus, Werewolves are from Mars

Supernatural Jane Austen Series:

Mansfield Park and Mummies
Northanger Abbey and Angels and Dragons
Pride and Platypus: Mr. Darcy's Dreadful Secret

(Forthcoming)

Cobweb Bride
Pagan Persuasion: All Olympus Descends on Regency

Acknowledgements

I would like to thank with all my heart Alan Rodgers, John Gregory Betancourt, the late Marion Zimmer Bradley, Paul Barnett, Jane S. Fancher, Charles de Lint, Diana L. Paxson, Lisa Silverthorne, Rachel Holmen, Paul Melko, Lois Tilton, Stephen Leigh, Beth Bernobich, Lazette Gifford, Linda J. Dunn, Terry McGarry, Roby James, Melisa Michaels, Laura J. Underwood, Mike Resnick, West Flanagan, Modean Moon, Tom Hise, Amy Sheldon, Paul Witcover, Amy Sterling Casil, Tom P. Powers, Kurt Roth, Pat Fogarty, Jeffry Dwight, and at least a hundred other kind friends at SFF Net who tore apart first drafts, slaved over cover art, and in other ways advised, encouraged me, and stood by my side all these years since the strange word "Amarantea" first came to me in a dream.

Most of all, I would like to thank Sherwood Smith, who changed my life.

Dedication

For many friends, and for many reasons:

Steve Algieri, Lisa Silverthorne, Wendi Gansen, Paul Melko,
Jane S. Fancher, Kurt Roth, Lauren Oliver, Sherwood Smith,
William Sanders, Marion Zimmer Bradley, John Sullivan,
Patricia Duffy Novak, James D. Macdonald, and Paul Barnett

Dreams *of the*

Compass Rose

10th Anniversary Edition

Vera Nazarian

Dream One

Amarantea

In the metallic blur of the horizon, below the cumulus cloud skies, lies Amarantea. . . .

It is violet, lavender, or indigo, at dawn, noon, and dusk. It is where the soul flies in search of wonder, when sleep takes you by the eyelashes. . . .

So it was told, in all the lands of the Compass Rose. It was also related, in the late cozy evenings by the marigold hearth, when children settled to absorb the ancestral wisdom of their elders, that Amarantea was a place between worlds, inaccessible.

One such child, sitting at her Grandmother's knee, asked insistently every night to hear the story, until Grandmother nearly went daft with repetition.

"Tell me of the beast that inhabits the island kingdom!" little Learra cried. "The one that has no name, and that can only be seen when it sleeps! Tell me of the king of Amarantea, who has wed a woman with no eyes! I want to hear the words of the greatest Truth that are inscribed upon the coffin of brass—the one that is within the anonymous sepulcher of the unknown one!"

"The beast that has no name does not want nosy little girls to know anything more about it," Grandmother said. "And neither does the king and his poor wife. As to the words of Truth on the brass coffin—why, I've recited them to you over a dozen times."

"One more time, please!"

"It says," Grandmother began to speak with the patience of an antique maple, "that whatever lies within this grave is the only source of evil. And it should not be disturbed by you or me, or anyone with the least bit of brains, for that matter. Nor should silly questions be pursued beyond a certain point."

"No, no!" insisted Learra. "I want to hear the *real* words, please, not your own, Grandmother!"

"Ah . . . What's an old woman to do, when her words are no longer considered real? Very well. It says: 'The soul is a flower, severed from its stem, bearing seed, planted at birth, reaped in death, but never discarded in the bottomless well.'"

"But that says nothing about evil. And what strange words! What does it all mean?"

"How should I know?" said the Grandmother, moving her embroidery needle through cotton fabric.

"Then how do you know the words at all?"

"Why—I was told them when I was your size, little one."

Learra touched a small hand to her Grandmother's sunken cheek, saying, "Then I must find out, before I am your size."

In the mists that form the edge of the world, sleeps Amarantea. . . .

And, all around, an ocean of steel and mauve sun-glitter upon cool waters—for it is an island.

A young woman with a sharp seeking gaze stood on the starboard side of a galley, the only ship that could bring her here, to the end of the world.

After serving twelve years in the cities directly South of the Compass Rose, having drudged away her gleam of youth, her freshest bloom, the softness of her fingertips, Learra had earned enough to purchase one rare pearl of indigo-ebony. And cupping that pearl like her own heart in her thoroughly coarse palms, she had taken it to the one temple in the Southern city that served a true god.

In exchange for the pearl, the god answered her inquiry. Directions were given to her as to the precise location of the mysterious place out of legend that she sought. And a ship was hired, the only ship that would sail there, commanded by an insane captain.

As they sailed through the seas of metallic twilight, through sun-drenched expanses of aquamarine, through haze and mist and downpour, and thunderstorm skies shattered by gods' lightning, Learra sensed her heart take on a certain new rhythm. The rhythm built, so that she could hear her temples almost every waking moment as they drew nearer to their destination.

At sundown on the hundred and seventh day, the needle of the ship's compass lost its magnetism and lost its mind, beginning to float aimlessly in its cradle with every jolt of the ocean waves. Very soon after, they saw the horizon, and with it an indigo shadow on the rim.

Wonder. . . .

When night came, the ship continued, piercing the black satin of the waters and leaving a ribbon of ghost-white lace in its wake, while the moon shone down upon the world from a violet sky.

In the darkness, the land formed around them, volcanic, out of the waters. The ship dropped anchor before a soft ebony shore that arose gradually out of some formless void that was the night.

Learra stood watching the line of surf sweep the black sand like a silver comb. And then she was on a small boat, was being rowed to shore, was stepping upon the soft resilient sand.

The androgynous captain with the fearless eyes would wait for her, three days if necessary, and then, as agreed, would be free to turn around and return home, without any more concern for her fate.

She stood, while the boat returned to the ship, and watched the spray fill her footprints upon the sand with liquid night-silver. She stood, breathing the intense cool wind that carried in it scents of both land and sea, and some unknown soft perfume.

The night wind touched her cheek, and she thought she heard her name whispered, as she started to walk along the rising shore into the unknown. Her way was lit with liquid moonlight.

For a long time there was only a forest of darkness, of trees with winding pale limbs, of leaves rich with succulence, and everywhere living eyes that reflected the moonglow—eyes of those who populated this dark. And then, just as the first lavender shimmer began in the Eastern sky, she came out of the forest into a clearing, and upon the black ruins of something ancient and remote.

The ruins were grandiose. Their nature was that of the fabric of her most vital dream. She knew it, because they stretched for miles in all directions, as far she could see through the encroaching dawn. And yet, as light gathered, pooling onto the sky, it transformed the vista before her. Slowly, very gently, the structures took on a shape, columns shone with clean marble, walls filled out where only moments ago they had appeared to possess gaps of fallen bricks, mortar filled crevices through which the wind had slithered just at the previous heartbeat.

A sensation came to haunt her briefly. She heard ancient sand granules rubbing with a hiss against rock, and breathed a lungful of dry hot air. But quickly it was gone, to be replaced with the quickening sound of the lush forest and the moist cool breeze carried from the sea.

And when at last the first piercing shard of the sun broke through thick growth on the horizon and struck the land, Learra stood at sparkling gates of gold before a fabled living city.

It lay fully formed before her, blazing with the dawn. She saw gold-capped towers and spikes of bronze, all razor-bright. She stared in wonder at perfect veined marble, rose and lapis-blue, and at shingles of sandalwood, painted obelisks and carved winged beasts, and, in the center of all things, a structure of translucent jewel hues.

And yet there was not a living soul within this world. She walked past the gates into a place of fountains, beating in the early morning light like transparent blood from a severed vein. She wandered through streets paved with cream polished stone, underneath arches carved with words she could not read, that had never been pronounced in her lifetime. And she found herself, as the sun swept higher into the sky-dome, at the heart of this dream.

She knew it for what it was, because her own heart pounded within her, and her vision had grown absolute, all her senses having receded to supplement it.

A white luminous structure loomed, wrought with enamel jewel tones—palace, temple, or tomb. And it beckoned her to enter, its delicate archway entrance shimmering with the heat of day, warping like a mirage before her. And beyond it, from deep within—cool lilac twilight.

Learra entered, catching her breath and beginning to cough from the sudden pungent odor of ancient dried flowers. The cloying dust was everywhere, choking her, while the intensifying presence of her dream arose to make her buoyant on the inside. And yet the soles of her feet felt weighted down, heavy like stone.

She was within a domed chamber. The walls were in permanent shadow, but the remote ceiling dome was filled with central illumination that streamed in from a pattern of window skylights high overhead. Razor shafts of sun fell through the skylights upon rows of coffins of brass that reposed upon the mosaic floor.

She did not bother to count the coffins. There were over a hundred, for they filled the grand chamber. Instead, she moved deeper into the room, dragging the soles of her feet, step after step.

She coughed and breathed with distaste, her lungs rebelling at the sickening ancient sweetness. She stood like a thick-minded dull creature, unsure of what to do with herself, with this whole world around her, while long moments flowed past and time blurred.

And then, drunk on time and flowers, she started to read the markings, the incoherent shapes and symbols of an unknown language running like beads of rain past her eyes. She trod heavily and yet softly, letting her vision glide along each symbol, each plaque, striving, with constant repetition, to obtain a glimmer of meaning.

And thus she paced, while the sun slowly traveled the sky towards night, and eventually dipped beyond the skylights. With that came pale violet twilight, and then there was a sudden fall of darkness.

In the dark, she found that she could still see. Vision lost its relevance and she no longer relied on eyes to perceive, but instead the awareness that came through the pores of her skin.

Eventually vision returned. From high overhead, stars poured their remote pinpoint illuminations and gave the chamber a faint form. The coffins stretched in rows of deeper darkness than the air, and, with effort, she could make out the markings upon the brass.

It had grown dull and old again, the brass. Its luster had been stripped away with the night. And for a moment only Learra pulled herself away from her task of perception, and looked around her at the chamber itself. It, the chamber, was now but a black ruin sprawled around her, with missing sections of wall through which she could see the night outside, and hear, from far away, the tumult of forest at the ruins' distant rim. . . .

And then, the moon rose. With the coming of moonlight, ruin receded all around her, and again she could see the glamour of solid refined form. Moonlight streamed into the skylights from above, and the writings on the plaques grew clear again, while the brass glimmered pale and polished.

And as she continued to walk among the rows of brass, she began to decipher some of the symbols, which then wound and turned and slithered into her, making sense at last.

Amarantea. She could almost read the symbols that formed the word, she saw instances of it, etched upon metal, almost like blossoms. Here. And yet again here. . . .

Ah-mah-ran-teh-ah . . . it whispered in her mind.

And she knew, with a surety, with a pounding of her blood, where she was, at last.

What are you, what mystery? My spirit self drowns within you, is consumed. The thirst to know calls, pulls me into you . . .

And for a moment the wind wanted to answer her, swooping down in night gusts from the windows above, whispering, whispering.

There were three coffins in the center of the chamber, somehow distinct from the rest, not in appearance but in their situation, right below the central skylight.

Learra approached this grouping, for something subtle, delicate, intimate, pulled at her. She paused before each, and read the flowing wavering symbols, seeing their pattern in the moonlight, and encountering the *other,* that pattern she had come to recognize and long for. . . .

What was within the coffins seemed to whisper her name. Or was it the wind, cool and insolent?

Open the brass lid—her thoughts taunted her with dream images—open it and release the enigma inside.

If she pried open the heavy lid on that coffin, the one on the right, would she find, within, the decayed bones of an ancient king? And would the coffin on the far left contain what had once been a woman out of legend, a queen without eyes?

And the other one, the coffin that was between them, separating them even in death unto eternity—what greatest evil could be contained within it?

The soul is a flower, severed from its stem, bearing seed, planted at birth, reaped in death, but never discarded in the bottomless well.

What sin had been committed here, in this relic of a sepulcher, within a ruined place at the end of the world? What curse of madness, of unfulfilled desire, slithered about the ruins at night, and revealed their true stagnation only with the retreat of light?

Or—did it thus also show their greatest truth?

Where was it, the beast that has no name, the one that can only be seen when it sleeps?

The ruins stirred in their own bottomless slumber all around Learra. But the beast without a name tugged at her nature, her innards, her fear, urging her and yet pulling her back, seductive in its caution, always but one step away, just out of sight, at the edge of her living dream. . . .

And she knew then, with a sinking, a gentle sadness, that if she were to follow her final desire—the one that pulled at her, that called upon her to open the coffins one by one and thus reveal the final mystery—then she would find out something that was not human, was not hers to know.

Dare to know! wailed the night. *You, who seek, you must achieve that what has driven you all your life. . . .*

And Learra stretched out her hand with its callused work-palm, and trembling, touched the cold bronze metal of the center casket before her.

Do it . . . Whispers came from all recesses of her mind. *Proceed, or you will die in madness. . . .*

The brass handle of the coffin was circular, made to fit her palm exactly. The heavy lid had probably jammed with time; lifting it will require inordinate effort.

Do it . . . This is the one purpose of your life.

And yet she thought, pausing with her trembling fingers locked in an embrace upon brass. And she thought of her life, looked back suddenly, and saw in retrospect something akin to a flower that had developed from a seed, and had grown along a fine stem of experience, and had been cut promptly upon maturation, and now awaited its next stage.

The hand that held the flower was now poised on the brink of a decision. That decision could return the flower back to a familiar place where it could be pollinated and harvested of its seed. Or else the hand could take it far, into a place dark and unsure, into a place without fertile soil, without bottom, or end, outside the world. . . .

The choice was before her, in the form of desire.

Learra looked at the inscription on the coffin of brass, at the ancient coffin itself that lay before her like a lover.

She knew the words that were inscribed there without having to read that ancient tongue. She had known for the greater part of her life, and the words had become a part of her. The words, whispering within her. The words, shimmering like mother-of-pearl in her inner vision, every night before sleep would take her by the lashes. . . .

And the woman let go of the brass, told her fingers to let go, to unclench from their passionate embrace with the possibility of death before her.

While she did so, the moon continued to spill itself softly through the sky window into the sepulcher, over the black ruins, over the island that was half-real, half-desire, over the whole world. And because she had let go, and stepped away, the wind sighed softly, and died in a final echo of a whisper.

Learra never remembered walking outside, nor climbing through the desolate ruins of something precious that had long gone. She only remembered the living darkness of the forest, the tenebrous foliage, and the everpresent moonlight, streaking her path, spilling before her like thick silver honey.

Learra came out of the forest onto the shore just as dawn began to discolor the rim of the horizon over the ocean. Off the shore floated the black silhouette of the anchored ship, a great palm ready to sweep her away, to carry her back to the familiar world.

She paused, stepping into the cold running foam that exuded phosphorescence, that licked the ebony sand. She looked down, seeing again the pattern of her footsteps imprinted in the black sands of this dream shore, a pattern that would fill with eddies of water as soon as the next wave hit, that would soon be dissolved into a furrow, then nothing.

No traces of her would remain here, in this other place. . . .

With the dawn, a wind was rising from the sea. Learra turned around, placing her back to it, and facing for the last time the blackness, then the indigo, then the violet of the quickly lightening land. As she stood thus, buffeted by the gusts, she looked far into the shore line, deep into the forest, where she could see with her mind's eye that which had called her here.

She was leaving it now.

Tears stood for a moment in her eyes, but were soon to be dried by the wind. But then—how to distinguish the wetness of tears from the moisture of sea spray on one's face, from the very mist?

Learra turned away then, and, without looking back, waded into the cold water, black as ink, and swam toward the ship.

On the shore, the light was solidifying, falling all around from the brightening sky. And a form took shape, pale and indescribable in human words. The form moved like a ghost, stood looking out toward the sea's expanse, leaving its own pattern of footprints.

It was growing still and somnolent and alone once again. Its task was accomplished. And so, the beast without a name lay down to sleep, and in its dreams to guard, lulled once again by the silence, lulled by the ocean and the drifting soft black sand of Amarantea.

In radiant glory, bright like the oldest wisdom, exists Amarantea. . . .

It is a dream only, a living memory in the collective consciousness, and yet it beckons the wanderer, always, from its unknown shore. . . .

"Tell the story, please, Grandmother!" the little girl cried, tugging at the old woman's sleeve.

"Yes, please, tell us again of the king and his blind wife!" echoed the little boy.

The old woman, who had once had a sharp seeking gaze but now was almost blind, drew her wizened head closer to the two children.

"Now, now, children," Grandmother said with a smile. "What is there to tell? Why do you pester me so, my little Rinne?"

"I want to hear about the island kingdom!" said the little girl. "And I'm not pestering, please. You didn't finish the story last night, Grandmother."

"Yes, I want to hear about the beast!" Mavion said.

"My, aren't you brave today, Mavi." Grandmother chuckled and continued, "Why, only yesterday, you started to cry when I spoke of the beast. And so I had to stop."

"But I'm not afraid, ever!" Rinne exclaimed. "You can go on, Grandmother, finish the story."

And the old woman proceeded to weave her tale, bright as her own long forgotten dreams. The children listened, while the fire at the hearth burned warm and persimmon gold, long into the deep violet night.

Eventually she was done with the words, and the children were all put to bed, rubbing their eyes and groggy with the sweet perfume of imagination. And Grandmother found herself alone before the fire.

She sat, rocking to herself. And soon, within her mind came the old whispers of intimacy, words familiar and as fine as vapor from that faraway sea. . . .

The soul is a flower, severed from its stem, bearing seed, planted at birth, reaped in death, but never discarded in the bottomless well.

The elusive meaning of it was almost there, just hovering at the edges of her comprehension—as it always must. Just enough to be aware of wonder. But not enough to fathom it to its end.

For, such fulfillment would mean the bottomless well, an endless ultimate night outside the universe, otherwise called the unknown. And who would pay such a price?

Once again from a great distance of memory it came, the voice of the beast without a name. And this time in the twilight of her life she recognized its nature.

It was too late for her. But not for them.

Yes, maybe she would speak these words tomorrow, repeat them out loud before the little ones, so they would know.

The choice must be given, always.

For, one way or another, eventually, all come face to face with it, all hear the music that is Amarantea.

Dream Two

The Miracles of Ris

When sweat, tears, and blood are drawn, truth breaks forth upon the shore.

In the desert, the only god is a well.

—old proverbs in the lands of the Compass Rose.

There are fables, and then there are histories, passed from old to young, that take on the pungent flavor of fable, of the many-hued rainbow, after being re-shaped so many times.

Such is the story of Ris, the Bringer of Stillness and Water, the Bright-Eyed Liberator, the Mad Sovereign of Wisdom.

Incidentally, it is unknown whether Ris is god or demon, messiah or trickster, man or woman or child. . . .

If you were to follow the Compass Rose directly East, across grand stretches of the whiteness that is sun upon sand, you would come upon a place that was once Golden Livais—a town sprawled like a gods' mistake in the middle of the desolation.

No rivers flowed for a hundred miles around, no rain had spilled from the incandescent skies, not in a hundred years. And yet the original settlers had seen scorpions burrow deep, and fat snakes slither, skim the surface of the dunes. And this told them there was to be found a source of water.

When struck eventually, the well pumped cool black water like blood upon the sands, permanently discoloring them with life. The town germinated from this oasis, and after several generations affluent trade routes were established through the desert to the far outlying cities of the South and West of the Compass Rose.

Down one such route, in the wake of a caravan bearing salt and sandalwood, came an old woman and her two children. After an absence of forty years, she was coming home.

"How much longer this desert, Grandmother?" a girl complained. She was slender, with radiant hair the very shade of persimmon in the sun, and with pale freckled skin that was peeling from sunburn. She huddled in the swaying wagon, leaning wearily against the cotton-draped knees of an old woman with nearly black parchment skin.

"Stupid Caelqua," a young voice said. "You know this desert will be all around us forever. It is called Hell."

On the other side of Grandmother, the speaker, Nadir, had attached himself with a grip of misery to the old one's elbow. Nadir was a dark precocious boy-child no older than seven, while Caelqua was possibly fourteen, and they were unrelated, children of two different races.

Grandmother had rescued Caelqua, who had been drudging in a work-board house within one of the distant great cities.

"I take you because of your pretty bright hair, and nothing else," the old woman had said to her, while the smile of her eyes denied the harshness of her words. This implied smile had pierced Caelqua and bound her with ties greater than blood.

When Grandmother had come upon him, Nadir had no name. She had leaned down to pick up a fallen purse from the filth of a city gutter, and had noticed him there, black-skinned as a little demon, crouching against the brick alley wall. The boy had made no attempt to take her possession, and instead watched her with a remarkably clear and wise pair of young eyes.

The old woman left the purse lying, and stared back at the young swarthy thing.

Eyes had met eyes. And after a rich moment of silence, the old woman merely said, pointing to the purse, "Come with me, and bring that with you."

And he followed her like a shadow.

"I take you because you need something," Grandmother had told him as they walked. "And my curiosity will be the end of me if I don't find out what it is. I'll call you Nadir, because we first met at the very bottom—unless you have a better name?"

But the boy didn't.

He thought only for a moment, then shook his head, and followed her from that day on. For the first time acknowledged as an entity, he had been led by this vertigo-filled instant to his first real stab of self-awareness. . . .

And now, here they were. Their wagon jostled over the sands, the last one behind the protection of the caravan. Scalding dry wind came inside through the torn flaps of the canvas, scraped their faces, and took away the precious moisture that endlessly beaded their skin.

"Not much longer now . . ." Grandmother said to her two charges. "Soon, when the sun starts sinking, you'll see the dark shadow of Livais—directly there, on the opposite horizon."

"And then we'll have enough water, Grandmother?" Caelqua said, staring at her with dull ever-parched eyes.

"As I remember, the well is great, and has enough for everyone, child."

"I can wait for my turn after all the caravan drinks," Nadir said proudly, disengaging his grip on Grandmother's elbow. "I don't need water."

"Everyone needs water, even the sand beetle," Grandmother said. "But you are brave and stoic, my Nadir, and I know you will indeed wait for as long as you must."

And thus it was. When evening began to fall, the shape of Livais imprinted upon the dark Eastern horizon, and the caravan moved with the fading sun at its back. Eventually, in the indigo dusk, the many fireflies of gold and amber that were the lights of the town grew into shape.

Soon they were at the gates, were being allowed within, past bored sentries, into a well lit thoroughfare. At the center of Livais was that famous well.

Grandmother stood next to Nadir and Caelqua, among the last in line. When their turn came, surrounded by the loud animated voices of the dispersing caravan folk, orange flames of torches, and vaporous twilight, the old woman stepped forward. With reverence she glanced past the stone rim into the abyss of the well.

She stared, noting the coarse rope of the water bucket. She dipped a pail in the bucket and first lifted it before the muzzle of the animal that had pulled their wagon. Then, smiling, she offered the life-liquid to Caelqua. For the first time in weeks across the desert, the girl was allowed to drink to her content.

When she was done, the water pail was passed on to Grandmother. The old woman took several sips, made a show of having satiated herself, and then deposited the pail into the small hands of Nadir, saying, "And here it is, Nadir, your turn, for you are truly the last."

"Thank you, Grandmother," the boy said with dignity, and then slowly lifted the water to himself and drank in moderate proud swallows.

"Good," Grandmother said. "And now we shall find a place to sleep. Let us go, my children, and find the old house that might still stand, and that was once the place of my birth."

The town was small. After wandering through a dozen streets, turning here and there, they stopped the wagon before a prominent unlit structure. Apparently the old woman's memory or instinct was still intact, for she had found her home.

Grandmother promptly knocked upon the gates, and after several minutes a moving candle shone through the windows.

"Who is it?" came a groggy voice. "Who disturbs the Temple of Ris at this ungodly hour? Begone! Or, if you must, return in the morning."

"What's this?" the old woman said. "Since when have the doors of this house become the doors of a temple? Open up, for it is Ris. I have returned home at last!"

In the ensuing silence, they could hear the night cicadas, and the sharp drawing of breath on the other side of the gates. And then, with a scraping, the gates opened. Nadir and Caelqua saw shadows and a cowled form of a creature, who stared back at them with shocked eyes glittering in the dark.

The old woman stepped forward, saying, "I am Ris. Daughter of Kharaan. Daughter of this house. After traveling the world, I have returned to spend my last days here. Allow us in, for the children and I are weary, and we have come far."

The priest continued gaping. But Grandmother took his silence for a yes, and walked past him into the gated courtyard, leading the pack beast by the ropes, the two children following.

"But—" he stuttered. "But you are—"

"I am a woman, yes. And an old one. But I am Ris, the one who everyone knows keeps the well filled and the waters flowing. Isn't it true, monk, that most recently the water level in the well of Livais has dropped below the normal mark by about the height of a man? That is why I have returned."

"How did you know?" the hooded man whispered. "No one knows this except for three men—myself, Lord Rigaeh, and the old well-digger! Then you are Ris indeed, the Bringer of Water!"

Grandmother chuckled. "How gullible you are. That alone is not difficult to surmise for anyone with eyesight. Anyone who looks closely could see the fresh new length of rope added to the well-bucket. But only Ris the Wise would know that the very nature of the ground water source beneath the well has been compromised. At the rate of fading, there will be no more water left in Livais before two moons pass."

The cowled one stared in the darkness, eyes glittering. "Gods protect us . . ." he whispered, "If what you say is true, then we are doomed. You must speak to Lord Rigaeh immediately! You must tell him of this, if you really are Ris the Wise. . . ."

"You will direct me to this Lord tomorrow," the old woman said. "But for now, allow us to rest in this house."

"As you wish, Wise One. . . ."

The man made signs of obeisance and, bending his old back, preceded them into the shelter of the great dark house. Inside, he took the single thin candle from the shelf where he'd left it to light their way, first within a grand front hall, then up a wide staircase.

The old woman, with candle-born shadows falling all about them, followed him, looking around her with what might have been a look of old wonder and yet a hint of a mischievous smile. Caelqua came immediately after, wary of the flickering shadow-shapes which at times looked like bird-beasts, at times like demons unfurling. And in back of them all came Nadir, seeing the same grotesque forms but somehow wanting to howl with joy at their undulating free expression, sensing the same wildness of spirit unexpectedly within himself.

They were home.

In the morning, the white sun arose with a fury, and began another desert inferno. When the shadows were shortest, and no one dared to linger in the open, the old woman who called herself Ris walked out to the center of town, and stood before the well, wrapped in white cotton to shield herself from the blaze.

She stood heedless of the sun, her exposed skin already blacker than black, her eyes an unusual shade for someone of her race—blue like the remote lapis-lazuli waters that reflected back at her from the long distance down in the stone well.

For over an hour she watched the waters. And exactly three times throughout that time, at even intervals, the mirror surface of the waters distorted, then bubbled, as though gases were rising from the bowels of the well.

And then, satisfied, she simply turned and walked away. She continued walking in the direction of the most affluent side of town. And possibly she didn't even see the small shadow of a boy following her.

At the house of Lord Rigaeh she paused (and from his distance Nadir could see an inexplicable smile pass her wrinkled lips), then knocked, and was allowed within. It seemed word of her had spread—word that Ris had returned to right all wrongs in Livais.

"You claim, old woman," Lord Rigaeh said, "that you are Ris, whose Temple stands within this town?"

Ris observed a man attired in fine silks and wearing wrist- and arm-bands of gold. She did not like his face, nor his unblinking eyes.

"I do not claim. I *am* Ris," she replied in an overly soft voice, using the semblance of old age to her advantage.

Lord Rigaeh leaned forward in his elevated seat, and stared down at her. "Apparently you know more about the well than you should. Who are you really?"

The old one smiled. "Of course," she said, after a slightest pause, "you of all people do not believe in Ris, at least not in the Ris that people savor like an amulet on their tongue."

"Come, both of us know you are an impostor, and that Ris is a figment of my people's imagination," said the Lord. "Let's not lie. Tell me rather, what do you want, now that you are here? What would it take to keep your old mouth properly sealed?"

Besides the surety of death. . . . She could almost hear his thought.

She watched him, unblinking, with her uncanny blue eyes. "Why was the House of Ris made into a Temple?" she asked softly then. "I must know."

"Why?" he retorted, stroking an arm-band of liquid gold. "Are you drawn to the idea of deity?"

At which the old woman laughed, a true cackle.

She is merely insane, it occurred to him then. *A crazy old lizard who would sun herself on my gold. Well, let her hiss all she would, no one would believe her.*

But then Ris spoke words that stilled him. "Why was the House of my father turned into a Temple of Gold? You keep it there, don't you, turning to your advantage an abandoned house with no master? All the bulk of it that you've made off the very life juices of these sad people! Gold, guarded by your minion in the guise of a priest. Gold, made by denying them water periodically. And, only after they pay you their last, you pretend to call upon *my name,* the true name of Ris, to end the charade of water shortage!"

"What madness do you croak, old hag?" Lord Rigaeh exclaimed. "Have you any proof? Who would take the word of a vagrant over the Lord of Livais?"

"Oh, I have proof enough," she replied, her own eyes sparkling angry blue. "Proof of an outlet chamber dug alongside the well, that siphons off the water by means of a clever contrivance of machinery and piping. Whenever you choose to strike fear into these simple people by threatening their water, their very life, you lower the water level."

"Enough!" the Lord cried, his face gone livid. "I will have you thrown into the darkest prison—"

"Is it not too late?" she pointed out. "Most people of Livais know about me, and would expect me to be well and sound when I leave this house."

"True," he spoke then, changing his manner like a serpent. "I cannot have you killed outright. But there are ways to reveal you for what you really are. They will expect certain things of you, I will make sure of that. And when you are unable to satisfy them with the miracles of Ris, they will turn on you. Reverence will become rage. They will tear you apart. . . ."

"We'll see," she replied quietly, this old woman. "But now, I leave you to yourself, Lord Rigaeh who does not believe in Ris. Remember only that in the end truth breaks forth upon the shore."

Outside, Nadir caught up with Grandmother as she left the house. He had waited all this time, hidden in the shadow of the alley, and knew nothing except that this expensive house had a heavy spirit about it despite the outward semblance of opulence, a dark heavy thing of sadness, like stone, like the weight of heartless gold.

"Are you hurt, Grandmother?" he said, walking beside her, easily matching her suddenly old gait. "What did they do to you? What did they say?"

The old woman chuckled, then reached out to touch Nadir gently on the cheek (she never did more than that, knowing his need for dignity). "Let's go and eat, my Nadir. I wonder what Caelqua has in store for us today?"

And thus they returned to the house that was now a Temple, through winding streets, past townspeople who lowered their heads in respect before the old woman, and whispered words of benevolent greeting to Ris.

Inside, the minion of Lord Rigaeh stepped aside, bowing superstitiously, and Nadir followed Grandmother into the kitchen. Here, in the heat of the stone hearth, Caelqua was checking the flatbread and stirring the popping stew. In her zeal to serve Grandmother, she had usurped the place, found stores of onions and potatoes, and had driven the priest to the marketplace, bidding him to return with fresh produce for the table of Ris.

After finishing their meal, Grandmother and her charges cleared the eating area. And then, because the sun was still near zenith, a laziness was upon all.

The old woman sat down in an old chair in the front hall, saying that it had once belonged to her father. Her eyes closed, and she appeared to be sleeping. Caelqua stretched, yawned, and then found herself a place on the fresh pallet upstairs.

Nadir meanwhile, wandered the old house, his spirit wanting to dance for some reason. There was something hauntingly nostalgic in the very walls of this place, a sense of many layers, many worlds. . . . Something intimate.

It was drawing him, until the tips of his fingers tingled, and blood raced through the subterranean caverns of his veins like bubbling spring water. Soon, he would draw near enough to find it.

After several quiet days of sun-washed silence, townspeople came to knock at the doors of the Temple of Ris. They were asking for the old woman. Because in the span of those days the waters of the well had receded like never before.

For the first time ever, the surface of the well-water was too distant to see without the help of a torch lowered down into the stone well abyss. A townsman discovered the atrocity when he was unable to lower a bucket deep enough to reach the water, and had to call the well-digger.

The old well-digger came and tied several additional lengths of rope to extend the bucket's reach. When the water bucket came up full at last, it held a mixture of fine gravel and water, for it had scraped the bottom.

At this, both the well-digger and the townsman let out a keening wail, until more people gathered and picked up the cry. The whole thing might have been humorous except that, as surely as the sun burned overhead, these people were indeed doomed to death without water.

Lord Rigaeh was notified. Upon hearing the news—not to mention the wailing outside—his dark eyes took on an appropriately stricken and sympathetic slant. He responded to the terrified messengers with a pious suggestion that they go find Ris. For, after all, now that she was here in the flesh within Livais, all of their salvations lay with her.

The Lord did not bother telling them of the good store of water that had been hidden in his own house cellar, and that would last him and his household at least two moons—more than enough time to leave the town and scramble across the desert to the closest great city to the West of here.

And thus the townspeople flocked to the Temple and called for her loudly, while the sun beat down with cruelty, and bleached to bone-whiteness the limestone of the streets.

Ris came out, dressed in her usual white cotton. She stood facing them all, then said, "Let us go to the well, friends, for I have something to show you."

She led the procession to the center of town, stopping before the stone well. Here, they surrounded her—women, men, old and young, with one common thing written in their eyes: hope, overlying fear.

"Give us back the water, Ris!" someone cried out. And with that other voices picked up the keening. Some came down on their knees, beating their foreheads against the ground, kissing the sand at her feet.

"Enough!" rang out the voice of the old woman, carrying farther than imaginable out of such a wizened frame. "There is only one here who can return your water to you. It is Lord Rigaeh."

At that point the Lord himself was seen approaching, and the crowd parted for him and his armed retainers. Lord Rigaeh wore a coat of the palest sun-satin and a head-wrap of silk and gold braid.

"I am here, good people of Livais," he said with a look of pasted-on surprise. "Has this old woman who claims to be Ris performed her miracles for you and raised the waters yet?"

"Nonsense. Where is the well-digger?" Ris said. "I ask you all to witness. Have him climb down into the well, and look for any sign of an opening or outlet in the walls of stone."

"What then, old woman?" Lord Rigaeh said. "What would you do even if you find such an outlet? What would that prove?"

Nadir and Caelqua, standing in the front of the crowd, looked with concern at Grandmother.

For a moment, Ris said nothing. And then she motioned for the old well-digger to proceed.

The well-digger dropped in the water bucket filled with stone-mason's tools, climbed over the stone rim of the well, and started to lower himself down along the length of rope. After about five minutes of silent anticipation, high desert wind, and the beating sun, they heard his muffled yell to bring down another person who would serve to verify what they saw, and to bring down a torch.

Someone pushed forward a spindly teenage boy, and someone else came running with a lit torch. Holding the torch in his teeth, the youth climbed into the well like a monkey, and disappeared. Several minutes later, they heard the noise of hammer against stone, and then the sound of released gushing water.

Then the youth's head popped out from the well's opening, followed by the rest of him, while the well-digger still grunted behind him. The boy was wet from the waist down. He began to chatter immediately that yes, indeed, there had been a plugged pipe of some sort, but that, when they opened it, there was only so much water. The inflow did raise the water level, but only so far, to his waist. The rest of the water was nowhere.

"You see," said Lord Rigaeh smoothly. "What do you say now, old woman? It is no secret that there is a reserve chamber, built at the beginning for dire circumstances such as this, to give us just enough water to survive. If you were indeed Ris, as you claim, you would have known that."

The old woman looked at him intently, while voices of displeasure sounded from the crowd.

"We have gold and coins for you, Ris!" someone cried. "We give it all to you if you give us back the well!"

"Fill the well, Ris!"

The old woman turned to the crowd, her eyes quickening with a passion, and she pointed a finger at the Lord. "He has your water, what is left of it!" she said. "And he has the rest of your useless gold! Search his house, and you'll find the water!"

"Halt!" exclaimed Lord Rigaeh. "If you are Ris, then fill the well anew! Show us indeed who you really are. And if you're an impostor, we will punish you as you deserve."

A pause of silence.

Then the old woman said softly, "I cannot fill the well."

At which the crowd wailed.

"But," she continued, "although your well is indeed drying inevitably, there is far more water left than you are led to believe. He truly has your water! And his deceit has been robbing you of your livelihood for all these years. The gold that you bring to the Temple of Ris he puts in his pockets! Ris needs no gold, no worshippers! Open your eyes to the simple truth!"

But they no longer heard.

"The hag is obviously a nothing and a nobody, people of Livais," Lord Rigaeh said. "And she can do nothing for you." And he directed his retainers to take the old woman.

"Come with me," the Lord said to the people. "And we shall go together to the Temple of the true Ris in supplication.

We shall offer gifts to Ris, and once again our prayers will be heard."

The crowd surged around him.

"No!" the old woman cried. "Do not listen, people! How many times must you offer gifts and still lose water? Think! Your water has been fading gradually, even after your so-called prayers are answered. Every time there is less and less of it—"

But her final words were muffled, for she was struck on the face.

A few steps away, Nadir wrestled like an afreet in the grasp of an angry townsman, while Caelqua whimpered, seeing Grandmother's face bleed.

"Bring them also," Lord Rigaeh said, pointing at the children. "They are hers, and all will be punished together for blasphemy."

And with that, the three were taken, and the townspeople followed Lord Rigaeh like sheep to the Temple of Ris.

The sun shone angrily from above upon them all.

"I don't want to die, Grandmother..." Caelqua sobbed quietly in the darkness of the place where they had been thrown. Despite the unmarked passage of time, it must surely be evening by now, thought Nadir. His eyes had been keened to the dark, and he could just barely make out Grandmother and the girl.

"You will not die, child, hush ... I promise you..." sounded the voice of the old woman, stubborn and strong as always, while soft echoes came to dance all around.

Eventually there was only coagulating silence. Nadir felt the slick mildew of the cold stones around them, smelled the rank vapors of this prison.

"I only regret one thing," Grandmother said suddenly. "And that is that I've brought you two here, to this accursed town of my birth. I'd forgotten how it was, forgotten the lies and the fools willing to live with them."

"Are you—are you truly Ris, Grandmother?" The voice of Caelqua trembled. "I believe you are! You can save us then!"

"Oh, my girl," the woman said tiredly, sounding ancient for the first time. "It's true that I was once called Ris. But it was such a very long time ago. . . ."

"Tell us, Grandmother," Nadir said.

"Very well," the old voice responded.

And Grandmother told them of a slave child of the house of Kharaan—a kind man, who, after her mother died bearing her, had brought her up as his own. It was Kharaan who had named her "Ris" in honor of the One who was known to appear to those in dire need, and it was he who had taught her the nature of justice. And as he lay dying, the old man had spoken words that remained when he was long gone: "If truth is ever obscured or distorted, give of yourself in whatever way necessary, to end the injustice." Inspired by these words, Ris had assumed the identity of her legendary namesake.

"But, if you are not divine, how did you know of the injustice of Lord Rigaeh?" Nadir persisted stubbornly.

"That, I did not." The old voice chuckled in the darkness. "It was merely easy to guess. For, anywhere one goes, children, there is injustice. Assume thus, and you will know what to look for, and how to recognize it."

"Then I will fight injustice too, Grandmother," Nadir said. "When we get out of here, I will grow up to be strong and wise like you."

"But I am scared, Grandmother," said Caelqua. "Unlike you, I am not strong, I am not Ris. I am good for nothing. . . ."

"Who or what is Ris indeed, children?" the old one said suddenly. "What do you think?"

"I think," Caelqua said softly, "Ris is either a god, or has the blessing of the gods, and thus a power over waters. You tell us this story, Grandmother, but I know there's more to it that you do not say. You say you are not the same Ris, and that you only pretend to be. But this is what I think. You, who are divine, are locked into this human shape, so that you can be here and love us, for we have none but yourself. . . ."

And with that, Caelqua buried her face in the darkness against the breast of the old woman, and wept with loud rasping sobs.

"My poor child, I wish I were," Ris said, stroking in the dark what she knew to be the radiant hair of the girl.

"Why did you take us in, Grandmother, if it were not for that reason?" Nadir said suddenly.

"I told you already, little demon," the old woman replied. "You stirred my curiosity. Besides, you were filthy as soot, your sweet dark brown skin all covered up by the stain of the gutter, your head full of lice, and I had a great urge to scrub you clean."

"And I?" Caelqua said, quieting her sobs. "Why did you take me?"

The old woman began to laugh. Her chuckles echoed back and forth among stone, and in the dark Nadir felt a tremor, a vibration against the palm of his that was resting on the cold floor.

"Silly, silly questions, my dears," she finally managed to speak through her laughter. "Must there be a reason? Well then, I will tell you. I took you both because I was lonely."

"But Ris is a god!" Nadir marveled. "Can even gods be lonely?"

"Pah! Did I ever say I was divine? Ask the same silly questions and receive silly answers," the old woman said. "Now, enough maudlin nonsense. Go to sleep, both of you, for tomorrow, Ris or no Ris, one way or another we shall be free of this place. And I promise you, no one here shall die."

"I believe you, Grandmother—Ris . . . ." Caelqua whispered. "Whoever you are. . . ."

In the darkness, Nadir thought he heard faraway sounds of subterranean waters. And as he rested his head in Grandmother's lap, they seemed to be rushing nearer and nearer, like blood coursing through his temples, into his very mind.

The morning sun poured its scalding essence down upon Livais. In the center of town, near the well, stocks were erected. The old woman was made to kneel, face down, her neck restrained, her feet bound together, and her hands placed into the wooden contraption. Next to her, the children were tied upright to a wooden post. All three were bare-headed, without protection against the raging sun. And, by the will of Lord Rigaeh, they were to remain thus.

They were to have no water.

Townspeople passed by and spat at the old woman, spat at her gray hair dragging in the dust. They struck and pinched the dark boy, and pulled the radiant hair of the girl, ripping her poor tunic. Urchins kicked and taunted them, bringing cups full of liquid just to their lips, and then drawing away, laughing. Eventually, another old woman hobbled by and shooed the urchins away, shaming them that they were wasting the precious dwindling water in this town with their games. The hag then used her stick to strike another blow at Ris, who remained silent and motionless.

"Damn you," the hag hissed. "They pray even now in the Temple of Ris for forgiveness of your blasphemy, so that Ris will return to us the well, in exchange for all of our gold! Even now, I go to carry the last of my coins to the Temple."

Ris did not argue the illogic of the statement. But Caelqua, sweat pouring down her face, whispered, "Grandmother didn't do anything except point out the truth . . ." only to receive a jab of the hag's stick.

Nadir remained silent, while sweat also beaded his date-brown skin and glistened in the tight black curls of his wiry hair.

At high noon Lord Rigaeh's men appeared, and, grinning, began to untie the children.

"Lord Rigaeh spares your lives. He'd rather you walk through the desert," one of the men sneered, pulling Nadir by the ear.

The old woman was made to rise, her feet unbound, her neck and wrists freed of the wooden stocks. With Nadir barely supporting both his sister and Grandmother, Rigaeh's men drove them past the well, and outside the gates of Livais, unto the burning sand. . . .

It is said that the desert sun brings delirium. And that sand, mixed with wind, tastes like blood. . . .

Nadir did not know how long it was, this burning eternity. He lay face down in the scalding powder, and finally a fire in his mind brought him enough awareness to lift his head and see Caelqua lying in a heap at the feet of their Grandmother.

Nadir crawled. He would not remember how long it took him to crawl those few feet, while the wind howled like a horde of jinn and cut him in the eyes, forced him back every inch. At last, he could touch the two sprawled figures. He drew himself close, and covered his sister's head with his body, acting as a shield against the sun. Next, with supreme effort, he tugged his thin pale tunic from his upper body, baring his dark back, and wrapped the cotton around Grandmother's forehead and eyes, shielding her too from the sun.

He lay thus for an eternity, sinking in and out of this world. And each time as he resurfaced, he felt the hell upon his back, the agony, until the sun began to lean in the sky toward the West.

It was sunset.

They had been denied water for only one day. And yet, because this was the desert, and because they had no shelter against the molten gold overhead, death would be very near. . . .

As the sun bled orange upon the Western horizon and the wind cooled, Caelqua regained consciousness with a shudder. She moved, feeling the small thin body of the boy pressing against her forehead, savoring its odd coolness. Nadir's cheek was pressed against the sand, and he was half-buried by a moving dune. Grandmother lay only a little away, barely breathing. Caelqua burrowed out of the stifling powder.

"Grandmother! Nadir!" She choked on a mouthful of sand.

The two piles of humanity began to stir. Nadir shuddered, resurfacing, while Grandmother barely moved her head to the side and squinted. And almost—just almost—her lips smiled.

And at that Caelqua reached out toward Grandmother, and then began to quake with dry tearless weeping.

". . . Pray, my child . . ." whispered Grandmother's faint voice. "You must pray to Ris . . ."

And Caelqua continued trembling, for as she wept she was also burning up with fever.

They found that Nadir could not move. When Caelqua touched his back, the skin peeled away, and dark blood welled at the place where her fingers had touched. At her touch and its agony, Nadir cried out.

"You too must pray, my Nadir . . ." croaked Grandmother. "It is time. . . . And I will pray with you . . . also."

And then her eyes closed again, and her lips fell motionless in their final soft smile.

The sunset burned and faded.

There were dreams interspersed with prayers, in the darkness of the moonless night.

At some point, Nadir thought he heard his own voice crying, and there were shameless tears running down his cheeks, like needles of broken pride, as he called out hoarsely, mindlessly, the name of "Ris," the Mad Sovereign of Wisdom. And he thought he had crawled forward and leaned his head over the body of Grandmother, and let the boundless tears mixed with his sweat drip down like a burning torrent onto her dry lips, washing her face. . . .

And, at some point, Caelqua felt some other's voice come wrenching from her gut, strong and new, calling upon "Ris," the Bright-Eyed Liberator. And she felt her teeth sink into her own wrists, tasting her own blood which then became water. In a maelstrom of agony and night, those bleeding wrists she offered to Grandmother, held them at the old woman's parched lips, letting her drink endlessly from the vein. . . .

The crescent moon arose briefly after midnight, spilling a silver glow upon the world. And it seemed the very sand dunes were in reality cresting waves of a great ocean, while the desert spilled around them with the cold oceanic currents of the night, liquid and boundless. . . . The waters of the night ocean swelled into giant forms, and they moved all around them, licking the very walls of Livais, scaling them, and filling the town to the very brim with liquid metallic moonlight. . . .

At dawn Nadir awoke just as the sun showed on the Eastern horizon. There was fever in his mind.

Grandmother and Caelqua were gone.

He looked around, thinking that maybe they'd moved in the night. And then he began to dig, clawing at the sand, for he thought that a roving dune had advanced in the dark and buried them with its whiteness.

"Grandmother!" Nadir called, his voice as quiet as a scorpion's, his lungs dry and parched with sudden anger.

"Caelqua! Stupid useless girl, where are you?" He dug wildly, crawling on his knees in the sand.

And yet, as the sun came up higher, beginning to scald, there was no trace of the old woman—his Grandmother whom he knew as Ris—nor of the girl with hair like flames.

Nadir stilled suddenly, and whispered into the face of the morning wind, "She is gone . . . She has left me . . . And you too, my sister . . .

"No!" he croaked then, his little dark face crinkling into a grimace of sand and pain. "No! No! Keep digging! No!"

And then something prompted him to glance away from the sand before him. He turned away, mesmerized, and stared behind him, where only a little away stood the town walls of Livais.

And as the sunlight danced on what had once been stone, it reflected back metallic, for the walls had turned to blazing gold. . . .

The gates of Livais stood open. Nadir moved slowly like a sleepwalker in a daydream, and looked around him with parched eyes at terrifying marvelous gold.

It was everywhere—gold buildings, gold cobblestones, gilded palm and date trees, people frozen to precious statues, and everywhere, golden dust. . . .

In the center of town stood the well, gilded at the rim. When Nadir approached it, staggering, he discovered the rope was also gold, and so was the bucket.

And instead of water there was only solid metal, stilled forever in a golden blaze under the sun.

"I must go from here . . ." he croaked to himself. "There is nothing here, only the judgment of the gods. This place is cursed. I don't want to die here, so let me at least go into the clean desert—"

"Why die, my Nadir?" came a familiar voice.

He turned to see Grandmother, standing upright, with bright eyes and a clean face, with not a trace of sand on her white cotton robe billowing lightly in the wind.

For an instant, Nadir was speechless. And then a wild smile contorted his small dark face, and he rushed forward to hug her.

"Grandmother! I thought you'd died! Or left us!"

"What nonsense! How can I ever leave those who are mine? Come, and I will give you water to drink—water, without which there is no life, and because of which this town perished in their folly."

"But where is Caelqua? And how—" Nadir was speaking foolishly, words just tumbling out of him like droplets of water.

"Come along, hurry now!" the old woman interrupted, and began walking with quick strong young strides. "We will go to my House, the House of Ris."

Inside the old house, there was no gold at all. And the outer walls too had remained gray stone. It was an untouched island amid the golden desolation.

Nadir recognized the strange sensation of immediate intimacy, the feeling of living rushing water. And now he knew whose spirit was within these walls. The same spirit had pulled at him before, had quickened the living waters within him, his very blood, his sweat, his tears—his truth.

Grandmother sat in the old chair that had belonged to Kharaan, and watched Nadir madly gulp down the water from the large wooden cup she had given him, heedless of his manner.

"You have grown and learned," said the old woman, smiling.

"Oh, yes, Grandmother! I have learned abandon! And that water is more precious than gold!" Nadir gasped between swallows. And when he was done drinking, he again rushed forward to bury his face in her old sunken chest, unashamed of his display of emotion.

"Good." Grandmother chuckled, hugging him tight.

"But—what happened here?" he ventured at last. "What odd blight is this? Why are we and this house the only ones unaffected? And what is the source of this new water? For I've seen the well of Livais, and it is dry!"

"This is Ris's House, and you are hers also. You prayed to her, and her blessing rests on you. As for the water—come with me and I will show you."

And then Grandmother winked and motioned with her hand. Nadir wordlessly followed.

They came outside once more, covering their faces from the blaze. As he walked, Nadir wondered that he could no longer feel the agony of his scalded back. As though the very water that he'd drunk had healed him of the last day's injuries.

They walked through Livais, looking about them at the golden statues, at the townspeople frozen in various aspects. At the house of Lord Rigaeh, they paused. The Lord himself stood at the door, frozen to fiery metal, ready to mount a tall pack-beast that was also now a statue. The packs held great filled water flasks that contained water no longer, but shimmering solid metal.

"Some day, people will return here and marvel at the riches of this place," Grandmother said. "Eventually it will all be mined and sacked, and there will be no trace of this town, only a memory. The House of Ris alone will stand, a solitary reminder of Golden Livais."

At the town gates, Grandmother paused. Nadir noticed their old covered wagon unhitched and abandoned. However, not too far away was their pack-beast, loaded with a bag of supplies, standing idly and looking rather well fed and ready to depart this place. Grandmother led the pack-beast out through the gates, and then handed the reins to him.

"What are you doing, Grandmother?" Nadir asked with a sudden premonition.

"Seeing you on your way, of course." The old one smiled, wrinkles crinkling at the corners of her bright young eyes.

"But what about Caelqua and you? And what of the water?"

In reply, Grandmother took his hands and held them tight in her wrinkled own. And then, still holding, she pulled him, and they walked fifty paces through the sand to the place where they had lain hopeless the night before.

There, in the very spot where Nadir had dug with his bare hands, was a welling of blackness, a rich surfacing of moisture, a large flat spot. Already, a number of snakes and beetles were seen scuttling around.

Grandmother reached into the folds of her robe and pulled forth the same cup from which he had drunk. She bent forward slowly, and dipped the cup in the sand, and it came away full of bright, slightly muddied liquid. When the liquid settled, they saw water, fine and radiant like crystal, flashing like mirrors of persimmon fire in the sun.

"This is the new well," said Grandmother. "And *you,* my children, have caused it to be. They, the people of Livais, tried to make water from gold, but only gold comes from gold. And thus Ris gave them the truth of what they asked. You alone brought water to Livais, for you sacrificed your very own water—sweat, tears, and blood—and quenched my own thirst when I was most in need. I drank of you, and now you will always drink of me, and never lack for water. Now, take this cup and be on your way—don't be afraid, it will be full for you always. . . ."

"But what about you, Grandmother, how will you remain here all alone?" Nadir whispered, receiving the cup, while water welled in his eyes, because he already knew the answer.

"I will remain, my beloved, because this is my House. And yet I will always be with you, especially when you dream. Just as you will always be here with me. And this well—*she* is a part of you. . . ."

"Then you *are* Ris, the Bringer of Truth and Water!" Nadir exclaimed.

But suddenly he felt a pang of a different agony come to him, as his soul broke asunder, and he understood and cried, "This well! Caelqua! Caelqua my sister, what has become of you?"

In answer, the old woman—or *someone else*—who had been his Grandmother for so long, only smiled. Ris the Wise, the Just, the Trickster, leaned forward then, and kissed the boy on the brow. And where her lips had touched he felt a seal of warmth, then coolness, like a breath of a faraway ocean.

He blinked, and Ris was gone like a mirage. All around him stretched only the incandescent desert, while to the back of him stood ajar the bright gates of the town of dead gold.

Leading the pack-beast, the boy breathed through his mouth, through his tears, and without ever again looking back, started to cross the desert.

Dream Three

Sailing the Eye of Sun

My name is Lero, and I am insane.

No, do not look askance. For I am quite lucid, and can be charming, if the wind blows from the appropriate direction and billows the sails of my ship.

It is my soul, this ship, the *Eye of Sun*. Together we have sailed around the Compass Rose seven times over, and have been to shores where the volcanic sand is scorched to ebony by the sun, and to others where ice gathers among grand fjords, and glassy shards float upon cold waters.

My men have grown accustomed to obeying a woman captain. They no longer favor me with questioning glances, nor do any presume to hesitate upon my orders. Those newly signed on quickly learn the rumors. For rumor has it that it's wise to fear the look of my eyes.

I am insane, they say, for I dare sail anywhere and everywhere. Truth is, I alone know that my ship cannot sink. It has been thus, a sense within me of its secret invincibility, since the moment I first stepped on deck as a stripling cabin boy who was not at all a boy. . . . This, so long ago. That first moment of profundity, when I felt the solid old cedar wood and the creaking timbers beneath the soles of my feet.

Or maybe that was indeed but my madness speaking from within, this inevitable sense. A link between myself and this floating wooden entity—

It matters no longer, of course, not now.

Gods know, I have stories to tell, so many stories that I am bursting.

I had once taken my ship on a journey beyond all, where dream meets sea, and delivered a woman as mad as myself to the shores of the isle Amarantea, that does not exist—or obviously exists only for the insane. There I waited for her a full day and night, and then she returned to the ship and the *Eye of Sun* carried her home. Her eyes were different when she came back to us, no longer vacant, but full of music, and she looked at me and recognized me for a woman at last. . . .

And once I granted passage on my ship to a haughty Princess with exotic slanted eyes, dressed in precious silk, and accompanied by a silent stately warrior with skin black as night, and loyal eyes warm with wisdom. Theirs was another story altogether. She called him the "lowest of the low." And he was sworn to protect her, this goddess with a petulant mouth. And no matter her inconsiderate disdain of his being, I have no doubt he delivered her safely to their destination somewhere in the Eastern desert. . . .

And now, this. Another story unfolds around me even now.

I must take this young, impossible, self-important pup to a place where he will become a man. He's been entrusted to my care by his noble father, in exchange for a mountain of glittering coin, a priceless cargo of fragrant tea and spices, and goods for my men.

What could I do but comply?

After all, insanity draws me.

And sea salt eats away at cedar wood. Thus, the upper deck of the *Eye of Sun* has long been in need of a fresh coat of paint.

Varian Erae stood outside the cabin, letting the wind billow about him in its fullness, lift him a hairsbreadth above the deck floor—or was it only his disparate spirit?—and carry his essence like a gull above the ocean.

All around, the horizon blurred in vague silver.

So powerful had the forces grown within him, so discordant, clamoring for release, that Varian's father, Lord Erae, had no choice but to send his son upon this journey. The young man traveled now to a far place South of the great continent, an unknown shore, where the sages could be found to train him in the proper wielding of the storm within.

Ah, he wanted to fly! To let go and soar. . . .

But he must not. It was forbidden to allow even the tiniest outlet to the forces or he would lose control, the wise ones told him, and he would strike down all, including himself.

But Varian knew he could control it already. He used it, this power, in the little things. Like making that weatherbeaten sailor blink yet again unconsciously, as he pulled the ropes. Or letting the wind gently open the creaking door of *her* cabin to a sliver of darkness and twilight, and thus allowing him a glimpse of her silhouette within, as she stood silently over the map spread out on the table, and the compass needle floating in its bowl.

He was fascinated with Captain Lero from the start. The fact that she was a woman was revealed only later to him—and him alone, he thought—the longer he stared from the corner of his eye at the tall androgynous form, trying to fathom its very ambiguity.

She was flat as a board, this woman. Taller than any he'd ever seen, taller than most men. She wore plain cotton, just like the midshipmen, and a sword linked to her cloth belt. Her hands were large and callused, agile-fingered and once-fair, like dispossessed princes. Her hair, pale as cream ashes, was gathered in a tail, and her skin deeply tanned and weathered.

When she had welcomed him onto the ship and discussed the terms with his Lord father, only once had she truly looked at him. Her eyes had been like the haze upon the horizon, of inexplicable hue, and ageless. And they pierced him with the sense of the unknown.

Since then, he had watched her, would watch her always. He was searching, he told himself, for a flicker of her insanity.

Sailors moved about the ship doing their tasks, swung like monkeys from the webwork of roping around the sails and the three masts.

"You must promise, Captain, to take my son safely across the ocean," his father had said to her. "Swear that, no matter what, you will place his life before your own, before all else."

"I give my word," she had replied in an earnest voice, watching the great Lord with a steady gaze.

And Lord Erae knew that was all the reassurance he would get. And yet, knowing her reputation, her impossible sense of honor, he could rest easy. His son was in safe hands, and this ship was, they said, unsinkable as magic.

The *Eye of Sun* was a unique hybrid of a galleon and an antique trireme, multi-tiered with complexities of mast and sail, yet punctuated just above water level by rows of closable portholes designed for long mechanical oars that were extended and withdrawn by clockwork, and used exclusively to steer within shallow waters. Upon its main great sail of white canvas was painted a grand golden sun, and within it a dilated human eye—an all-seeing almond with a pupil of azure and lapis blue.

Varian glanced at the great eye, and often vertigo came upon him, a sense of spinning. . . .

They had been many weeks upon the ocean. The wind had remained steady, pulling them along the surface of the waters like a flying lily.

Captain Lero was everywhere, moving silently along with the crew, calling out directions in a loud voice, sometimes steering the ship, sometimes up in the clouds swinging agile upon the high mast. When evening came and the winds stilled, she'd sit in warm camaraderie with the others, and eat the same dry supplies. Often he caught her grins, and the ivory flash of her teeth. Then he'd hear the laughter of the men at her witty casual comments.

Varian, on the other hand, was given a spacious guest cabin, much roomier than the captain's own, and richly furnished. The meals he ate alone each night were served on fine plates, and his cutlery was silver.

His bed was soft and piled high with silken pillows. And yet he tossed sleepless every night, among the sounds of gentle creaking wood, the splash of waves, the humming air, and the thought of *her* lying so nearby, on a poor hard bunk, her body stilled in sleep, her pale lashes resting against her hollow tanned cheeks. . . .

"M'Lord, are ye ill?" said the husky voice of an old sailor, anchoring Varian back in the present reality.

Varian turned, a slim dark-haired youth of slight build— pretty as a maiden, probably thought the old sailor. "I am fine," he said haughtily, his eyes narrowing with irritation that someone would notice how he floated, how disembodied he was. . . .

"Ye don't look it, m'Lord. The wind is cold today, and it bites. Ye'd best go inside. . . ."

Varian reached out with his mind and sent a finger of anger to prick the old man just behind the ear. The sailor reacted by stiffening sharply and, scratching his neck in that spot, instantly forgetting whatever else was on his mind. He turned and went back to his shipboard task nearby.

The ship lurched with a sudden ocean swell, and Varian felt it necessary to grab the railing, so as not to go plummeting overboard. Immediately, from a few feet away the captain approached.

"Careful, Varian," she said, pausing at his side. Her face bore the shadow of a smile. "The deck is newly scrubbed and slippery."

Varian blushed angrily. "No need for your concern, captain, I can stand on my own."

"On land maybe. But it takes quite some time to find the balance of the sea. It took me months, when I first started, before I could run upon the deck with disregard to the swaying."

Unable to avoid it, he stared into her eyes. With a pang of vertigo he surely saw laughter there, a mockery.

"I am different," he said. "And it would do you good to remember that."

"And so I see." With that, she turned away lightly, was once again on her way.

He stared at her back, seeing in it the shape of an insult.

The Lord's son has turned out to be more of a nuisance than I originally thought. He hides in his cabin all day, or else comes out and sulks, standing at the railing, staring off into the distance. I am constantly distracted with worry that the next swell and lunge will send him overboard, for the stubborn pup refuses to take any reasonable precaution. I've informed the crew to watch him closely, to care for him as though he were the child I never had.

For in some ways, he is. Not quite a man yet, scowling with pride, trembling with secret fear of the waters all around us, when no one is looking. And yet no longer a child, for he watches me in a certain way. . . .

He watches me in a way that I do not like. Maybe because I understand it so well, see what beginning thing it portends, see his eyes intense and deep upon me when he thinks I'm not looking.

Only another week upon the open sea. And then we come to the Southern shores, and we are rid of him once and for all. Already the men are whispering, looking at him and then making signs of warding if his shadow falls in a place where it may cross their path. Indeed, there is something heavy, a burdensome dark presence that has been with this ship ever since he stepped on board.

As though we carry an invisible cargo of a giant with us.

Even now, I can feel the ship straining under his weight. It pains me, for as always I feel everything. As the breeze stirs the sails, I can feel with my very mind the canvas unfurl heavily, just as I inexplicably feel the pressing of ocean upon the very fibers of the wooden panels that form the ship, its arching convex spine of antique cedar straining beyond all limit underneath a strange presence.

And today, of all days, as this pressure mounts in my mind, the wind too is rising, cold and serpentine. It is a bad sign for us. For today my wooden love is swaying far too precariously upon the growing waves.

High noon filled the upturned cloudless bowl of the sky. All around the *Eye of Sun,* the ocean blazed cerulean, with razor fragments of sun sprinkled upon the waters, their surface stirred by the cool wind. The ship drove forward powerfully, and the sails swelled full, with the almost living dilated eye bulging on the main sail, surrounded by the sun corona of gold.

"Ah . . . Strong wind and not a cloud in the sky," the First Mate said, raising his ruddy hand to shield his eyes.

Captain Lero neared him as he stood at the wheel. She was silent, and did not want to put into words the sense of unease, the wrongness, that plagued her on this perfect day.

"Captain!"

Behind her she heard the young Lord's son. He stood watching her like a hawk, while the wind swelled and gathered about him, sudden and possibly contrary to the wind billowing the sails.

"Captain, I would speak to you!"

"What is it, Varian?"

She spoke flatly, and did not turn to him, continuing to observe the approaching horizon.

Varian stared at her through a haze, a lightness, floating high above deck, on par with the topmost sail, watching each fiber of the canvas and the highest point of the mast, watching—

But no, he was here, standing on deck before her—she an emotionless post, a thing of wood, an extension of the timbers, a weathered silent entity—

He reached out with his mind and became the sea spray, the microscopic droplets that hung all around them in the violent air and clung to the hollows of her cheek, or sunk into the fine escaped tendrils of her pale hair.

He did not expect it, but Captain Lero shuddered, somehow impossibly feeling the mind touch, and turned directly to him.

"What are you doing?" she said. And then she moved away from the wheel. She came forward, taking him by the shoulder, and with a firm pressure (at which he felt tongues of flame strike him) led him away to the far side of the deck, past staring sailors.

"Now," she said, when they were out of reach of anyone's hearing, "I would like to know what it is you've done. You've touched me somehow, I *know*."

Varian stared up into her cool condescending eyes, and then sneered. "It is true what they say about you, you are insane. I've done nothing."

And suddenly Captain Lero laughed. "Good," she said. "It's good you have a brave tongue. I'll let it go this time. But the next time you 'do' such a nothing, I'll have you put below deck for the rest of the trip. Your father warned me about the untamed powers you wield. Have you forgotten your promise to him not to attempt anything?"

Before he even understood what he was doing, Varian struck her on the cheek. Some madness had prompted him, a violent impulse, a reflex. Maybe because she'd laughed. Maybe because she reminded him of that one thing. . . .

The next thing he knew, he felt an excruciating force against the side of his head, felt pain crack him asunder, and was down, falling under the force of her blow.

No longer was she laughing but towered above him, her face stark like the cold wind. He, meanwhile, scrambled on all fours, feeling the coarse wood of the deck, and hearing from all around the harsh guffaws of the sailors.

He heard Lero give orders to the men, orders to mind their own business—while the world spun around him with shame and incredulity, while below him, the deck rolled with the strong motion of the waves.

Shame was so violent that he dared not even move, only stared at the regular pattern of seams on her boots, felt the rolling below him. . . .

Dissolving, he was the wood itself, the old weathered deck. And then, he was the ship. Finally, seeping through, past the wood, he entered the cold moistness, the great expanse below, reaching out to fill himself with water, with the steady homogeneity, the cool flowing force. . . .

The endless force rebounded in him, filling him like a sail with air, filling him to the brim with urgent energy that must have an outlet. He stood up slowly, and there was a crackling at the tips of his fingers. Sparks landed on the floor of the deck, hissing.

The sailors' laughter died as they watched him, watched the electricity transform his outline with a faint bluish edge.

Only Lero remained impassive, standing before him, looking directly at him with her unblinking eyes.

"You'll regret this, Captain," he said softly in a different voice, one so unlike his childish earlier outbursts.

"Oh, I regret this already, insolent whelp," Lero said. "Allowing you on this ship. But I coveted your father's gold. Not for myself, but for my ship. And I had given my word."

But Varian smiled. And for the first time there was something terrifying in that smile.

An end to childhood.

"Ah, Lero," he said. "I would have you call me by another name. And I would have you covet something else. . . ." And he reached out with crackling fingers, and boldly drew them down her cheek.

At his touch, Lero froze. She was immobilized; not a muscle could she move, only a low grunt escaped her as she attempted to speak. At the same time the First Mate and three other men lunged in her direction, coming to her aid.

And were frozen also.

With the barest flicker of his mind he had reached out, not needing to turn his head to see them coming, knowing all along that they were there, that two had drawn long curving scimitars of steel.

A bluish faint crackle came from his fingers, came to fill the whole ship with stillness—with wax figures of men, living and breathing, yet frozen like puppets. Some were still swinging high up on the mast, marionettes, balanced precariously many feet above. Several were bent from the waist, tying knots, or climbing the stairs down below. Three more were straining under the pull of rope. And another was stuck like an old comical albatross up in the crow's nest.

The bluish force enveloped all of them, all of it, permeating with angry unreleased fury the *Eye of Sun*.

Varian continued to smile, sensing them—their heartbeats, their straining lungs, their diaphragms rising, the pump of their blood—feeling through his pores the whole ship like one being, and at his fingertips, feeling her skin, her. . . .

Somehow, unbelievably, she managed to speak, croaked in a bare whisper, "Varian. . . . You must not . . . do this . . . stop. . . ."

And then, with a mere thought he brought her frozen stiff form to its knees.

She did not crumple like he had done at her feet only moments ago. Rather, she sank on her knees slowly, with odd grace. Her head remained upright, unyielding, in an invisible stranglehold, while her wise defiant eyes continued to follow him.

He stood with a ringing silence in his mind. Looking down into her eyes. Watching her upturned face, the wind dancing in the cobweb tendrils of her pale sun-washed hair. And then he came to lean closer, and his mouth touched her dry motionless lips.

They were frozen, those lips, frozen like all the rest under his touch. And he felt an irrational stab of anger at that, forgetting that it was himself who was holding her immobile thus, unable to resist him or to respond. . . .

"I've wanted you so, Lero," he whispered then, kissing her lips again clumsily, "I—"

But he was kissing a wax doll with dry windblown lips.

And when he released her mouth, there was a fury in her steady eyes. Seeing it, he knew suddenly she could never be his. Because she had given herself already, was taken by a thing of old cedar wood and cypress, was swallowed, and had relinquished her very soul to this ship.

And within him the cold blue lightning suddenly exploded.

Varian was no longer one entity, but the whole cerulean expanse for leagues around, and he swelled below the puny wooden husk, thrust angrily against it from below with his homogeneous liquid mass.

A sudden swell of ocean came to rock the *Eye of Sun*. The frozen immobilized figures of the crew strained with silent cries, the wild expressions on their weatherbeaten faces clamoring for outlet, eyes brimming with emotion, with terror, striving against the force that held them.

Lero was frozen with anguish as she felt the ship and its crew tossed upon sudden unnatural gusts of power, while the cold wind had risen into a gale, and ripped their hair, tore into their skin.

"Varian!" she managed to utter with alien strength. "Release me . . . no one to guide . . . the ship. . . ."

"The ship! That is all you care about, is it?" roared Varian, holding her against his chest as waves rose from all around, starting to crest the rails of the upper deck.

He had to cry to be heard now, for the gale had become a storm, and overhead the sky, only moments ago sun-filled, was now black.

Ocean water poured upon the deck, drenching the frozen figures. Suddenly one of the crewmen, still doubled over in the same pose, was tossed overboard with a last stifled scream.

Lero's eyes were bulging with effort. She fought against the force holding her, fought against the stiffness of her own muscles, the miraculously petrified bones. . . .

Varian staggered away, releasing her, and stretched his hands, glorying in the gale wind, while lightning crackled all around and another two sailors were washed overboard as the *Eye of Sun* rode a succession of impossible cresting waves, each over fifty feet high.

And yet somehow, miraculously, the ship remained afloat. Water went glancing off of it, as though it were oiled. And the great sail, instead of tearing, collapsed of its own accord as the sailors that held it taut were thrown off like ants into the angry black waters.

"No!" Lero howled in anguish, seeing another old friend, a sailor who had been on this ship forever it seemed, ripped from his place near the bow and thrown far out into the churning waters like a still puppet.

"So, you're invincible?" Varian raged, screaming insanely at the mast, at the deck, the timbers themselves, but never at her. "You think that you will stay afloat forever? Watch this!"

A wave began, greater than the others, and as the floor below them gave way—for the deck was now vertical—the *Eye of Sun* began to fall straight down. Lero felt herself tumbling, her stiff body receiving any number of bruises as she rolled toward the railing, knowing that she was about to be removed from this ship forever. At the last moment, something allowed her fingers to grab stiffly onto the wood, the very dear wood of her ship—it was what saved her, the only thing that saved her.

Or maybe Varian's spell upon them all was waning. And no wonder. It took so much power to hold them thus and simultaneously wreak the storm all around.

Even now, he himself was holding onto some roping precariously, mad in his unconcern for his own safety.

"Damn you!" she cried, feeling her lips, the muscles of her jaws freed at last, holding on for dear life, while all around she heard the screams for help of the dying crew. "Damn you, hellspawn, who've come to destroy my ship and drown my men! I wish I've never seen your father, nor his accursed gold, never made this mad promise. I hope you drown in these waves now! I hope to all the gods that you fall like a dead weight and go straight to the bottom! I will not take you any farther on this ship, gods help me, but I would throw you overboard myself! Oh gods, take me! Take all my crew, only let nothing befall my ship!"

And then, with a great pause of silence, *someone* heard her.

The wind screamed, and the waves arose suddenly all around them like a great mountain.

And the *one* that was Ocean came forth from the abyss. And as the maddened form of Varian paused in his own moment of surprise and silence, looking up at the wall of water all around them, Ocean leaned forward with a breath of inner deep, of utter silence, and swallowed him, took him and all of them into itself with a flick of one wave, a finger. . . .

Lero was left alone on the ship, spinning now at the bottom of a well, an abyss of waves and silence.

As the spell came suddenly away, releasing me, releasing my lungs, I cried. Lying face down on the deck, I held onto the railing, and howled, and wept, as though Ocean itself had been in my lungs, in my heart, in my solar plexus.

They are gone, all of them. My men. And he is gone too, the mad one who has brought us all to this end.

Around me, the wall of Ocean stands, obscuring the sun. And as salty boundless tears run down my cheeks, my guts are wrenched by the howling sobs of a madwoman who has nearly lost her love by betraying another.

Lines of choice are blurred. Pride and weakness are intermingled. The madwoman betrays her own self.

My wooden beloved remains afloat. And yet—

My men are all overboard. They sink now, like sorrowful children of the land below, to mingle with the underworld of blue and azure, to dissolve into the boundless place of liquidity.

To what depth will they fall, before their strong weathered hands are gnawed by schools of hungry fish? When will their bones separate from flesh and muscle, and when will water dissolve the innards, the lungs of those whose loud living voices I heard only this dawn, raised in laughter and camaraderie?

The First Mate, Jiand. The one with the loud voice that couldn't carry a tune, and yet was singing daily with boundless laughter. I've known him almost as long as I've known old Hareve.

Hareve. The one who used to tie the knots, and spit overboard, and grin at me, and show me how it's done, one by one, when I was still scrubbing the lower decks. I've called Hareve "father" once, not to his face, but that one time when we fought the pirates, and he stood before me, shielding me from three cutthroats, and got that slash on his neck.

Verig and Bear. Two brothers, who once challenged me to draw steel, and who would've surely trounced me if it hadn't been for sheer luck on my part. They've served under me for years now, and I cannot imagine not seeing their brotherly grins, full of poor missing teeth, and not knowing their unwavering loyalty.

Little Rikah, one of the three cabin boys. I hauled him on-board myself, after he'd picked my pocket in one of the ports we stopped at. I liked his insolent grin then, and he's proved himself indispensable, running like a tightrope walker high upon the lightest webbing of the masts.

My men. My dear old friends. What have I done?

I've traded you all for this old beloved contraption of floating timbers. For the sail with the blazing cheery sun, and the "eye of wisdom"—as I secretly call it. . . .

And I've betrayed a promise to an old man with an ill son who lost control, and whose responsibility I've relinquished to the abyss.

Was it not my own fault, my own insecurity, that let me ignore this youth, ignore his obvious loneliness, the dangerous bent of mind, the obvious first crush of which I was the unfortunate object?

A mere boy, despite all.

And now, he too floats softly, gently, farther and farther down into the waves, and with him sinks the promise of powers fulfilled and deeds accomplished. Somewhere far in the future he might have made a difference, this youth, this boy. With his ability guided properly he might have changed the world.

My friends! For all of you I bleed inwardly where no one can see, and at the same time I bleed overtly before the whole empty universe of ocean and sky. For it does not matter how I bleed, as I am all alone before the gods. Only this is left to me, this floating home. A piece of my own self, a fragment of my being, a splinter. . . .

The *Eye of Sun.* I lean my cheeks against you for the last time, feeling your soft unsinkable eternity, the wood of the sacred ancient groves that was blessed by the gods themselves never to perish in the waves.

I feel you thus, connected to me, for the last time. But for a moment more, we are two eternal souls.

Ocean stands all around me still, like a mountain. It is so close now that I see many faces in it, some like children, some divine, some contorted or wizened with ancient black parchment skin. Ocean is an old woman, reeking of desolation and, for a moment only, distant alien sand underneath a burning sky.

Even now it is awaiting, it seems, my true choice, my final decision. Its hunger may be appeased in different ways.

And now, I make that choice.

If you hear me, Ocean with the face of a hag, if you hear me now, all great gods, then let it be as it must!

Come within my mind, and read me like a chart of ocean ways, and fathom me to the utmost depth.

Great waves shuddered and rocked the *Eye of Sun.* Captain Lero lay, eyes shut tight, face down, lips upon the wood. . . .

A single wave came crashing, like the greatest thunder. In that wave flickered the face of an ancient woman with warm young eyes and skin dried to black parchment by the desert wind, a strange antithesis. And the wave spewed forth human limbs.

The men were moving still. Weakly, and barely alive, they lay, water and seaweed rolling off them, gasping for air, like fish on land.

All fifty-seven of them. Fifty-eight, counting the son of Lord Erae.

Overhead the skies cleared, and the waters receded calmly, allowing a golden blaze of a single eye in the heavens, an incandescent eye that was the true sun.

The ship continued moving, unguided, and along the far southern horizon came a sudden faint glimmer of land.

Varian Erae stepped down quietly upon the black sanded shore of the Southern continent, and was greeted by two men clad in priestly robes of persimmon orange, and with warm humorous slanted eyes. They had known him instantly, here in the Kingdom in the Middle, never having to be told that this was the Lord's disturbed son, the wild power-wielder. They asked him gently to follow, and Varian sensed—without having to reach out a finger of his mind—an instant of homecoming. In that same moment his wild power suddenly settled a notch, settled into a new key.

He looked behind him once only, at the solitary figure of the tall captain. She stood watching impassively from the upper deck, while all around her the cheerful crew, among hollering and guffaws, was busy unloading part of the cargo.

A haze of memory slithered, vague like the horizon.

He looked, and then did not look again, and disappeared beyond the curve of land in the wake of the two sage figures.

Lero stood and watched him absently, watched the curving line of shore only a hundred feet away. She smelled the pungent sweetness of the air that was born of land.

Lero's hand rested lightly upon the smooth polished railing of the old ship, feeling cool silent wood against coarse fingertips.

"Captain! We're done movin' the last of it. And the rowboats are secured. Shall we cast off?" the First Mate cried, grinning at her.

They did not remember, none of them.

Only she would, always.

A few paces away, old Hareve whistled intently, spat, and then started to bind a new length of knotted rope, while Bear winked in mischief to his brother on the far side of the mast, and pulled at the other side, raising aloft the great sail. Somewhere high up in the crow's nest, little Rikah waved his hands in the patterns of a seaman's code, and his thin boyish voice resounded in laughter upon the wind.

"Cast off, then, brothers!" Captain Lero cried. "Let's sail home!"

She grinned, looking at them all. She startled them with the insane fierceness of her smile.

Then she turned, shielding her eyes against an auburn sunset, and walked slowly to take the helm. And only at that one point—only for a moment—the quiet singular emptiness was visible in her eyes.

Beneath them, the ship rolled softly, sweet and ancient.

Her beloved. But no longer unsinkable, no longer eternal. She could taste it now, mortality encroaching, just at the edges.

The *Eye of Sun* would sink someday now, as surely as her heart beat in her breast. And there was nothing she could do about it but live with the taste of its death just on the tip of the tongue. And thus she must, for in all things, Lero madly kept her word.

Taken away, the magical invulnerability. Traded away somewhere, one bit of her soul for another.

For here they were, her brothers, her soul—moving and living and breathing before her, sailing once more aboard a ship called the *Eye of Sun.*

Dream Four

Goddessday

There were two human figures which rode two horses over the craggy hill to look down at the battlefield—one rider per horse. And yet their mounts each labored under a double weight, for death rode at the back of both human figures, skeletal fingers of one silver hand clutching at their saddlebags and the other wrapped around their waists as a vise of emptiness. It was that touch which curled their entrails with cold, corroded the sweet marrow of their bones.

Death also stood at the foothill of the valley, against a crimson sunset sky.

The two mortals were a woman and a youth.

The woman sat rigidly astride a black warhorse, while the last golden rays of the sun fingered the polished steel of her armor, the antique scabbard of her great battlesword, and the ornate visor of the helmet attached to the saddlehorn. A cold evening wind disturbed loose filaments of hair from her unkempt long dark braids. Death's breath kissed the nape of her sunburned neck.

The woman's face was gaunt and lined. Expressionless eyes. She glanced once behind her, to where the other sat atop a russet stallion—a youth, or a boy, also in armor. His hair and eyes were like hers.

He watched her.

"Come," she said, her voice cracking upon its first note as it cleaved the silence. She did not speak again.

He nodded quietly. All that was heard from then on was the sound of hoofbeats against rock, and small stones hurtling away from under the feet of the great horses, chipping and bouncing down before them into the valley.

At the foot of the hill, they paused. The woman looked at the great field before her, covered with bodies. She heard the wind of the wide-open land, a constant soothing hiss.

The sound made by the wind was a major chord.

Between matted grass, steel occasionally gleamed in the waning light, pitch-black with blood. There were movements in places, but as she looked hopefully closer they were revealed to be lurching scavenger birds. Even now, their cries brought more of their kind, black hungry specks against a red sky.

She felt weak. She did not know it, but death shifted its silver gauntness in the saddle behind her, and gently touched her throat, then her cheek, draining her. She was compelled to dismount.

Slowly following the compulsion, the woman entered the field, walking with leaden feet, pulling her black warhorse by the reins. The youth followed her example.

As she walked, she looked at the faces only in order to identify. Her mind was atrophied. Through its placid filter she recognized many of them.

Behind her the youth walked, and stared with hypersensitive eyes, dilated pupils. His hands and jaw trembled, as his reason connected the wounds, mutilations, severed organs and limbs to the faces he knew.

The blood affected him. Amid clumps of ebony silhouette stalks of tall grass, it stained the sand and earth like bits of oasis—a thick congealing juice of over-ripe black cherries, so similar to the dark wine that he was accustomed to drinking. He had known on one level, yet had not known in this reality level of the here and now, that it would be so rich and gelatinous when drying.

Somewhere in the middle of the field the woman paused. She stood dumbly looking at the corpse of a young woman. Having caught up with her, and seeing that corpse, the youth suddenly retched and burst into tears.

She said nothing, did not look at him, vomit and tears dribbling over his face, although it passed through her mind, with a slight irritation, that she had once taught him not to cry at death. But—not his fault now; he had never seen death before like *this.*

Not that *she* had ever seen death at such a scale.

"Mother!" he uttered incoherently. "It's Mideinn! *Mideinn!*"

Her gaze was upon the young girl, whose glass eye-marbles stared, her right hand mangled, encrusted with something that appeared to be so much like a frosting of rust, delicate and dry, and her neck was at an odd angle. Half-slit, a cross-section was exposed, and all around was a thickened pool.

"I warned you when we were still on the other side," the woman said through clenched teeth. "I warned you."

"But not Mideinn . . . No—"

"I warned you on the other side."

Behind them, figures of death stood motionless, hooded, their silver breath curling in the wind, wafting gently over their shoulders, reaching forward with the claws of emptiness.

Eyes of a small boy looked on, blind. They were lost in a haze of remote wilderness; *he* was lost. Lungs shuddered. He muttered the litany of a half-wit, between sobs, over and over.

Suddenly he focused, turned with fury to the woman. "How can you be so silent now? What are you, heartless ice? Your *daughter* is dead!"

She did not look at him but slowly nodded to the rest of the field, her face petrified. "And what of *them?* If I start crying now, I will not stop. There will not be enough tears."

She looked then at the youth. "And you too, Talaq—" Was that a touch of gentleness he heard?—"You must stop crying. It is not the time, not yet."

Through the constant hiss of the wind they heard the distant rich sound of a horn being blown.

Living energy came to the woman's eyes, and she glanced around, searching the horizon. No, those were not carrion birds. Dark moving human specks were noticeable far in the distance, with pennants waving on high. All in black silhouette.

"They surround us," she said calmly.

The youth shivered. The tension of his facial muscles reformed him suddenly into an older man. "I curse them! Burn!" he babbled, while death brushed gentle claws against his hair, "I curse the Gheir, for all their generations, and I curse you, Cireive, High King, *taqavor!* Burn! Burn!"

Her eyes were blank as she replied, "Shhh. Do not waste your breath."

But he continued, his words interspersed with sobs and cackles. "Burn! Oh, gods . . . Not one soul alive! Am I the last of the able-bodied Risei? Gods . . . hear me, hear me, hear me. . . ."

He turned to her, gasping suddenly, his litany coming to a full stop, so that there was a long moment of wind and silence. And then he took in a long shuddering breath, and whispered, "Oh, mother . . . What of the women back at the camp? And the old? The children?"

Her answer was slow in coming. "I don't know. Probably they took them all by now."

And then she too began to laugh.

He watched her, seeing a madwoman.

But she was sane. Oh yes.

"I can't believe," she whispered to herself, while death, standing at her side, pulled the chill edge of an abysmal cloak of night over her trembling shoulders, "I can't believe that all it took was one day for treachery. He promised and I trusted his word. He promised. . . ."

Suddenly she cried hoarsely, raising eerie shadowy echoes, "And all of this, all—it is *my fault!*"

Her head fell forward, as she struck her chest with her gloved fist, while the rest of her was stone. "I trusted his word. I could have been with them. . . ." she whispered.

Talaq's tears had long since stopped. He watched her as she slowly came to her knees before the body of her daughter, who had lived nineteen summers.

With a steady hand the woman closed the eyelids of the corpse, then paused again. She reached out to touch the left hand of the fallen, pale as milk and already stiff, and withdrew a small ring from the index finger. Then she took out a small sharp knife and touched the girl's hair, finding a bit of it that was unbloodied. She cut off a lock, soft and already dust-blown, with the texture of dandelion, and made colorless with the coming night. With jerking movements she wound the hair through and about the ring. And when she was done she placed it in a small cloth pouch and hid it in her armor, somewhere near her solar plexus.

"In memory of . . . you," she said stiffly, relying on ceremony, and incapable of her own words.

Talaq stared at her, this woman his mother. She turned to him, then got up, allowing him his own farewells.

But Talaq shook his head and backed away. "I can't," he said. "I can't *touch* her. . . . Not like this."

The woman shrugged. Her eyes were unreadable. "Then remember your sister however you may." She turned away abruptly, finished.

Talaq was trembling, as behind him death placed its silver finger-bones on his left shoulder and stroked his spine. "Are you—" he whispered, "What are we going to do now?"

"No, I am not going to kill us, if that's what you think. That would be wasteful cowardice. Not to mention, we still have unfinished work ahead of us."

"Then what?"

With a glance and a motion of her head she pointed toward the top of the hill. The sun had bled in red rivulets behind the horizon, and evening twilight distorted the fine contours of the moving figures. They were approaching, so near now that one could distinguish individual moving limbs, all in silhouette.

"There," she said. "The enemy is coming. There is but one thing left for us. We will go to them and surrender."

Cireive's heartbeat raced. It had been like that since dawn, since he gave the command to attack, and his army—the metal-clad legions of Gheir—fell upon the unprepared barbaric rabble of Risei, killing them to the last man and woman.

Only the Risei camp remained. It was situated far away from the rim of these hills, far from the underlying valley on higher ground where the colder lands began, somewhere in the sparse jade forests. There they hid—the old and sick and their whelps, hiding in the silent greenery of the wooded expanses that seemed to have no end.

And yet, they hid all for nothing.

Their camp had been found, among the deeply verdant trees, and it was even now very methodically being taken.

The *taqavor* sat on a silk cushion in a hastily erected tent, surrounded by advisors. He had only one thing on his mind: victory at last over those dregs of humanity that came from the right hand of the setting sun and called themselves Risei—their ultimate destruction. Nothing else now to block his wave of conquest of the cold lands to the right hand of the setting sun.

Gheir legions had come a long way from a distant burning place, the very lotus-heart of the desert. They had come from the glorious right hand of the rising sun, where the hot air warped over the scalding sands, and the skies rained sun fire upon bleached familiar desolation. Beloved familiar inferno.

Here, it was frigid. Even the wind made a different sound in the open spaces of the steppe—a hiss, a constant din. For it honed itself over sharp blades of grass, over heavy stalks of barley and magenta amaranth, instead of grains of sand, and was now singing a savage high-pitched song.

The *taqavor* had tricked her, tricked the legendary bitch-queen Ailsan of Risei, under the pretense of truce. When his spies had reported that she was away from her people—probably to plead for reinforcements from their equally barbaric neighbors—at that time he chose to attack.

He broke the truce ignobly but conveniently, with his customary inevitability. He took the cold land warriors unprepared, with none to command them—just as he had taken dozens of other peoples, many times over, and to all the directions of the sun.

And he smiled, recalling that the queen's young daughter Mideinn had perished in the first attack. It gave him pleasure to know it, because the *taqavor* nurtured several peculiar hates, one such being the hate of everything female. It was no wonder he hated the Risei with their matriarchate.

Thus, only one thing remained. He must have Ailsan herself, living or dead. And now a wild joy was upon him, for he was told she had returned, had been found at the field of battle and had surrendered into his power.

Cireive was not old. It was only his pale hair, gaunt face with its unhealthy fevered stare, and his commanding height that suggested age and experience, and evoked fear from his followers. And yet here was a paradox—he had a son, Lirheas, of twenty-two summers, but they were often mistaken for peers in age, or else for two men unrelated by blood. The youthful fever-energy of the father stood in contrast with the ageless silence that gathered about the son.

The *taqavor* ordered the captive brought in. Seated on the ground at his left hand, Lirheas his son and Prince watched. Unlike the rest of the *taqavor's* advisors, his withdrawn passive face did not contain anticipation.

But the others of the high-ranking Gheir seethed with gossip. At last, they were to behold *her,* the Risei queen. It was always a good thing to see the face of the conquered enemy.

Cireive purposefully looked away. He wanted to see her on his own terms, at the precise instant he himself chose. Oddly superstitious, he did not want to actually *see* her walk in. The *taqavor* appeared composed, but his nerves were on edge and his heart pounded.

He heard her enter, directed forward by the guards. She stopped.

"My Lord," said the guard.

Now. I will look now. And he looked at her.

Ailsan was somehow what he had expected, and at the same time not. He had expected dark intensity, and she was indeed swarthy, a woman in the middle of her fourth decade, her stone face swept by the wind and formed into an insensitive mask.

But he had not planned for beauty, and yet beautiful she was. Ailsan was beautiful beyond belief. Her half-lowered black eyes—no, he realized, they were not black, but dark blue twilight—so haughty, sublime.

Eyes of a queen.

Or maybe it was just his vanity exaggerating her, making her into a paragon for him to topple.

And she was disarmed and in his power.

"You," he said, in a low voice of force, "are the Royal Consort of the King of Risei."

Ailsan looked up, meeting the fevered gaze of the fair-haired man clad in silk and gold. *So,* she thought, *you are Cireive. My enemy. I should hate you. Yet I feel nothing. You are but an empty place.*

"There is no King of Risei." Her answer came in a low quiet voice, startling Cireive. "My Consort died some years ago. I am the Queen."

She had known the intended insult, but had not risen to it. Cireive was purposefully baiting her. Her mate, he knew quite well, had been Consort by title—an ancient tradition of the Risei, and a tradition that belonged to many of the people of the colder lands.

"No matter, Ailsan," Cireive said. Another insult. He used her name.

"What do you want of me, now that you have betrayed a warrior's trust, Cireive?" she said simply, in turn using his name as an equal.

"I want nothing but your obedience and loyalty."

Her gaze on him was unwavering, forthright in its pride. Her lips eventually rose at the corners. "Ah, how simpleminded. Do you really expect this, Cireive? What would you expect of yourself, being in my place?"

"I would not be in your place. I have conquered."

To this, she did not reply.

There were seconds of silence.

He is torturing her, thought Lirheas the withdrawn Prince, watching passively from a few feet away beside his father. And yet an uncustomary restlessness was beginning to stir in him. *My father tortures. . . . Again.*

And had he but squinted in just such a way, the youth might have seen the cloaked form that was death, standing like an honor guard at the woman's back.

Abruptly she spoke once more. It was visibly difficult for her to say this. "My people, back at the camp. I—*ask* you to treat them with mercy in their slavery." She spoke this and then she lowered her gaze.

Cireive's heart jumped again, coupled with an unexpected stirring in his loins. *Observe her reaction now, when she hears. . . .*

"I have been more merciful than you think," he said quietly, so very slowly. "I take no prisoners, no slaves. Their deaths were quick. I ordered my soldiers to be skillful in their slaying, and strike only the throats, or a direct blow to the forehead or the heart. Sometimes it works best when the great vein at the throat is severed with a quick slash."

He ended and observed her.

For the first time there was something on her face, a jerk of a muscle. In an almost surprised voice she said, "You—killed *all* of them? All of my people?"

Cireive's breath caught in his throat. He drank in the change in her, while his loins engorged.

"You killed—the children? So I and my son are the *last* of Risei?"

"Yes," he said, modulating his voice into perverse sympathy. Cireive was a master of appearances.

"*Why?* Why did you have to kill them all?"

"They were a hindrance."

"Oh, gods."

"You, Ailsan, have been brought to this by the will of gods, yes."

She looked away, her eyes alive now and in dismay. "It is my fault," she whispered. "All my fault."

"No!" His voice cut into her. "You were a puppet, and had no choice. Your coward neighbors would not help you. They knew my force and would not. While your insolence made you blind to what I am. I would have swallowed you with your army no matter. Even now, you know it. Look at me!"

"No. . . . If only I had been there, to lead them."

He laughed, beginning to tremble in surges of violent pleasure that he could barely conceal. "Then you would have been dead alongside them. Approach me," he said. "And kneel. I am your proper Lord now."

Her eyes widened. "Damn you, I will not! Never now!" Her speech was quick, fierce. She too trembled now, and he would never know why. He would never see that the death figure, which had not once left her side, now suddenly scrambled forward. Like a horrible parody of a simian creature, death grappled Ailsan, straddled her back, and wrapped cold silver bone-arms around her throat in a chokehold.

Ailsan was now frozen, staring off to the side, no longer looking at him. She had moved on beyond his reach.

A thrill of helpless admiration ran down his back. Inwardly, he trembled to such an extent that he could no longer stop, and in the tremors felt scalding waves, felt oceanic currents of liquid sun race in his veins. He was on the verge of a sensual explosion, and it would take so very little to carry him over the edge of the precipice into climax. Only the added anticipation of seeing her completely broken before him held him back now.

"Take her away, bind her," he said to the guards very curtly, because lust madness was upon him, and he was losing control.

His orders were carried out. With their exit, relief and the cool evening wind from the outside, from the great expanse, entered the tent.

Ailsan spent a painful night, bound with ropes, abandoned on the bare earth floor of a filthy tent. She had been disarmed and deprived of her fine outer clothing, left with only a shift under-tunic. Her well tuned but no longer young body ached after hours of such treatment. Her thoughts, however, were on her son only, an anchor of sanity. Not even death lying beside her like a lover could distract her fevered, singleminded thought.

Talaq . . . she thought, *if you only knew how much my innards bleed for you, how much I know your hurt, despite my outward demeanor. . . . My son.*

They had been immediately separated upon capture, despite mutual protests. She had not been told where he was. She had been told nothing.

At dawn she was roused from a pretended sleep and taken outside into a thick milky gray curtain of vapor.

Eventually the grayness thinned, and a sea of army tents was revealed all around her, stretching to a horizon of nebulous silver mist. Fires were smoking already, small dislocated suns, the giant camp alive.

After several minutes, Talaq was led by two guards to join her. He had been stripped of his finery also, naked down to the waist and shivering, barefoot. His dark, longish hair was clotted, but there was a man's glow in his face, washed by the first morning rays of the sun. His back was straight and stiff as a board. Behind him, death stood with singular pride, today of all days.

"Mother!" he cried, a smile dawning in his eyes. And then he spoke with dignity. "My Queen."

They were not allowed physical contact.

Soon, the *taqavor* himself appeared. Tall and magnificent, he emerged out of his tent followed by guards, while a slow building rumble went up all around as his soldiers saluted him.

He ignored them all. Coming to a pause before Ailsan, his gaze was on her alone. Then he said quietly, without any preliminaries, "I would know if you are ready to bow before me."

"Never."

She looked at him sideways, through slitted eyes. Slits, to hide the razor edge of her anger.

His lips quivered. "Well then," he said. "Well. Guards!" He turned to one of the men holding Talaq. "You, take out your sword and kill him, through the heart." The words were clear, deliberate.

It was all too quick. Ailsan suddenly trembled. She bit her lips, then raised a hand to her mouth, and bit her band. She said nothing.

Talaq, his eyes wide, even now surprised, suddenly straightened. "Mother," he said, in a loud, strangely measured voice, while behind him death slowly unfurled its cloak to its full measure and stepped forward to embrace him at long last. "Do not bow. He will kill me anyway, later. Save your dignity—"

"I love you, Talaq! My *son!*" she then cried, her eyes maddened, while simultaneously a soldier's sword pierced Talaq, cutting off his words. He slowly crumpled to the ground, with a small, no longer human sound.

Ailsan heard the wind blow in her temples. Or was it her blood? Overhead the sun was rising, dispelling the last of the mist.

You did as I told you. You stood and you never cried, she thought. And then, *I have never said this to you, Talaq. . . . Did you hear me? Did you hear, this last time, I wonder?* This she thought while she wailed.

It was the long scream of a carrion bird. So inhuman that Cireive held his breath through it.

Ailsan then suddenly moved. She took a step toward the corpse. Then faltered. Then, slowly, she went on her knees. Silent dry seizures convulsed her body. And, after a while, water came out of her eyes, flowed down her face, endless—all in silence. There was something horrible about this convulsed, sobbing silence.

Then, just as suddenly, she made herself stop.

"You—stupid, *stupid* man," she said to Cireive, her voice steady and hoarse, tears struggling with laughter. "Do you—realize—I would have bowed to you—*yes*, if only you'd waited? You—killed him, and you gave me no *chance!* I am human, not metal, I cannot be plied so easily. I—" She went silent, gulped, still shaking in her paroxysm, then allowed her hands to fall weakly to her sides.

She remained on her knees, having no strength to do anything else. At her side, death also kneeled, waiting.

Cireive's face was stone. "Bow to me now, then," he said.

A few steps away, the *taqavor's* son Lirheas looked down, wiping some dust speck from his eyes.

It would seem that such extended misery deserves a respite, thought the Prince. *What is the gods' will at times such as this?*

"I spit on you now," said Ailsan to the father of Lirheas. And then she said a soldier's obscenity.

Cireive looked at her intensely for a moment, then came forward. His hands closed with grips of iron upon her shoulders, and he literally raised her off her knees. And then, as she stood, he swung his right hand and slapped her resoundingly across the face, with sterile precision.

Ailsan did not resist, falling from his hold like a thing of straw. She bent forward, once more on her knees, her face touching dirt. She was no longer shaking but immobile, a few feet from the still warm dead body of her son.

Then, after moments of complete silence, as guards and onlookers watched with impassive masks of faces, a new trembling came in a wave over her form. She lay and shook with delirious laughter, then slowly raised her face, throwing back her dark filthy hair, and grinned like a skull-mask at the *taqavor.*

"Go ahead, mother-scorned, do what you will, kill me! I *am* the last, now. And what then?" Her eyes were rabid.

For the first time, Cireive's outward semblance of calm crumbled. His mouth narrowed, his chin shook.

What was it that she said. . . ?

"Take her—take the mad bitch out of my sight!" he cried, ending in a falsetto. And then added, as the soldiers began to comply, "Give her thirty lashes, then tie her to a post, under the sun, and give her *nothing* for a day! Let no one approach or speak to her, upon fear of death!"

No, the fever coursed through Cireive's mind, *I can never kill her, not until she breaks. I must see that.*

Ailsan had learned to shut out pain an eternity ago, when she was still a child. "Think *nothing*," she was taught. "Dwell on the things within you, never on the outside world. Listen to sounds in your hazy memories, and never to the sounds at your ears. Look around you with blindness, with the inner vision of unfocused thoughts. And when the pain becomes too great, then lose yourself, and *become* it, enter the heart of pain. Understand it, and above all, never resist."

Her day was a haze of pain, interspersed with nothing. Thinking *nothing,* she did not allow herself to think of her *dead.* Somehow, she knew, for some intangible reason, she had to continue being.

Nothing any longer mattered, except for *being.* Occasionally waking up to herself, feeling silver death finger-bones at her throat, she would say her name in her mind.

Ailsan. I am Ailsan, Queen of Risei. I am . . . Ailsan.

And again, darkness.

Cireive, *taqavor* of all the lands to the right and left and face and back of the rising sun, Lord over Gheir, found no peace that day. Not once did he go to see her, or even deign to inquire of her progress, but nothing else was on his mind. Like an apparition she filled the moments of his daylight. When night came, and he lay in his tent knowing that she was so near, he tossed and could not sleep.

He hated her, hated the queen of Risei, the last one—now, the queen of the dead. Oh, how much he hated. He imagined her bleeding back, imagined how the fine razor-sharp whip had torn into her flesh earlier that day, again and again, cutting, piercing. . . . He imagined how her body had arched at each stroke, pride cast aside, a cry for mercy squeezed from her lips.

When slumber finally did overcome him, he would wake up again in sweat, from a dream of her. Only this time she was inviting him, welded tight in his embrace, her body receptive and infinitely yielding under his, and there was again that familiar fire in his loins. Then, fully awake, he became aware of a real pang of desire, and lay, eyes dilated, through the darkness of night, until another bout of sleep came to plunge him into one more tortured abyss.

This transpired again and again.

J ust before dawn, he woke up. He could no longer endure it. He was obsessed. Wrapping a fine heavy cloak about him against the chill of morning, the *taqavor* stepped quietly out of the tent and into the cold vapor. He made a calming gesture to the guard, who tensed immediately in his presence.

He walked less than a hundred feet before coming upon her. *Superstition . . .* his thoughts tumbled. *I must not. Must not look at her . . . I must not . . . I. . . .*

His delirium was broken abruptly. In the whirling mist, tied to a weathered narrow trunk of a barkless *ghzad* tree—the kind that was to be found everywhere now, for miles upon miles of sparse obstinate growth, as they had moved deeper into this cold region—she stood, loosely tied.

It was an exquisite torture, these loose bonds. She could not quite fall, yet neither could she straighten up. Her figure was twisted oddly forward, black stringy hair hanging in clumps, dampened by the night. A fragile husk. It seemed the wind could carry her away with one single draft, blow her out of existence along with the mist. And yet—

Cireive was delirious again. His eyes did not notice her sorry condition, only the way the part of the rope tied high on her waist emphasized the full curve of breast. Two strong children she had whelped, and yet her body remained flexible and powerful like steel. Once again, a fire crept to his loins, and he hardened.

Quickly, silently, he approached her, reached out for her, and then knew nothing for the duration of that embrace. Apathetic, her head lolled sideways, fell against his chest. He grabbed her by the hair then, to raise her head, and stared at her in the first light of dawn. . . .

In a hollowed face, deathly listless eyes. Lips dry and cracked, parched.

An imprint of thirty lashes somewhere on her back.

Slowly, she focused her gaze, as if only now realizing his presence. Something gurgled in her throat, maybe because death's stranglehold around her windpipe was tightening, as death straddled her wounded back with its silver bone-thighs. "Talaq . . ." she whispered, "You killed . . . him . . . them."

His whisper came urgent in retort. "It is the past, oh Ailsan, the past, now over . . . You are with me, I am your Lord, you hear, you can bear another child, strong, yes, *my* child. . . ."

With a surge of strength she drew away. Then she said in a loud cracking voice, "You slobbering pig. Unbelievable. After all you have done to us, you expect this from me?"

In animal reflex, he grabbed her by the throat, hissing, "Be silent!"

She laughed weakly, so much like the skeletal hag that was behind her. "Ah, yes. Now you are afraid your own men would know of this one small weakness of yours, is that so? Should I scream loudly and make them come running, and shame you before them? No, I don't think it's worth it."

In answer, her arm was twisted painfully behind her torn savaged back. She did not blink, but continued smiling. Indeed, an odd fire had now come to her eyes.

"Go on, break my limbs. It would take more than that to *break* me . . ." she whispered eagerly, with sudden raving energy. "Nothing now . . . Nothing left that can touch me. You've used up your last and greatest bargaining treasure, fool—my son. . . ."

"I will tear you apart, bitch! I—"

"Oh, is that so, brave goat? Then let me tell you—by gods, are you just blind, or a madman? Don't you know, don't you understand, I'm the one with power over *you,* can't you *see?*" she went on fiercely.

"A rabid bitch—"

Her teeth bared. "No, a jackal! Wild, yes, the last of my kind—you made me so—can you for a moment conceive it? Can you conceive being the last, the *only*—"

She broke off, just as suddenly becoming again like stone. "I am wasting words. Leave me," her voice said tonelessly, oddly commanding, and she went permanently silent.

He slapped her again. And again. He tore the remainder of her clothes and his own, and with a grunt of fury he impaled her upon himself. He thrust his loins repeatedly in madness, while his teeth closed upon her throat, then crushed her lips, then his mouth kissed them, then again, wounded.

Only—it was like wounding mist. Or some other such insubstantiality.

She knew searing fire, a universe of pain, but she was a dead weight, already retreating inward, deep, to a place where even the death embracing her with sepulchral silver could not reach.

I am not here. I am. . . .

Dzieru, Archpriest of Gheir, was told to perform the Sacrifice before the sun set. Early that morning the *taqavor* had stalked madly into his presence, unusually disrespectful, and commanded the Full Ceremony before all the great armies of Gheir. The Risei bitch-queen, he cried, was to be deprived of her heart, the organ was to be cut into seven pieces, fed to camp dogs, and her body burned to a crisp, dedicated to the god of Conquest, Margh-Qa, the Apex One.

Dzieru took all this in calmly, noting the odd disheveled state, Cireive's feverish eyes. It was true then, Ailsan, the fabled queen, had more power than he had expected. Already Cireive was thrown off balance, irreversibly changed.

He, Dzieru, must now go about it very firmly and dispose of her for good. It was not healthy, this effect on the *taqavor*.

W hy do I bother? thought Ailsan. She was an empty husk left to wither, tied to the torture instrument.

The sun rose higher. *He* had abandoned her quickly after the rape, fearing to be seen, fearing to display weakness.

Here was peace. Long moments of it.

Why do I continue being? What does anything matter? Who am I? I no longer know.

Why? Why?

L irheas, silent Prince of Gheir, touched a dull cold hand against the leather-wrapped handle of a tiny dagger in the secret lining of his trouser leg.

In his tent, alone, he brooded upon the justice of mercy killings. He had seen mares in pain, had himself put them out of their misery. It had not been easy for a youth, but it had been infinitely easier than watching them convulse. . . .

Now there was another in need of this. He looked out, moving the flap of the tent, at the slumped, no longer human form in the slithering daylight under the sun.

High noon over a great cool expanse.

No, I cannot. Not her.

T he *taqavor* rode arrow-straight, magnificent in his armor, in review of his legions.

The sun rode high. Pennants and banners of deep crimson, white and gold shone in aerial glory among the ranks of glittering steel. . . .

The wind blowing in his face, caressing the pale strands of silk, his hair, caused his eyes to tear suddenly. His leathered glove tensed, gripping the war stallion's reins, and he blinked only once.

Show no weakness. Show no. . . .

W hen the sun came lower to the horizon, and the farthest reaches of the sky ripened to the color of persimmon and burned, Ailsan, once a queen of Risei, now queen of the dead, was escorted by guards to the small rocky hillock. The Gheir army stood tense all around, covering the plain as far as the horizon flowed unto fiery eternity.

As she walked, staggering, they opened ranks to make way for her in awed silence. A million staring eyes. Whisperings of "she."

At the top of the rising stood the Archpriest. A few steps away, Cireive himself. All in black silhouette.

Drums rolled, and a low eerie wailing began. The entire army then seemed to sink, a field of black grass cut down, as the soldiers of Gheir went on their knees before the Sacrifice of Margh-Qa.

Ailsan gathered herself with a supreme act of will. No longer staggering, she now walked without weakness, a stone among stones. Cireive, his fine pale hair moving in the wind, was another stone. Impassive, he watched her stop.

The low monotone voice of Dzieru began a hypnotic incantation. Clad in voluminous dark, in a multiplicity of illusory veils cast before the eyes, the Archpriest was terrifying to the Gheir.

Out of nowhere, a sudden force, inevitable like the wind, compelled Ailsan to fall down on her knees, her head lowered before Cireive. She lay at his feet swooning, and death lay on top of her, covering her back, shifting its infinite gray weight.

A rising sigh of satisfaction coupled with terror moved among the army. All things were as they should be.

Dzieru spoke in a ringing voice, and every entity heard. "Behold, my Lord, the vanquished Queen kneels to you."

Cireive's heart quickened. He looked at her. "You kneel," he repeated almost in surprise, his voice also heard by all. "But that is not enough. You know it is not. Tell me you *serve* me! Tell me I am your *Lord*."

Ailsan's figure appeared to shake, and her lips moved silently. A whisper came. "My . . . Lord."

And then, with even greater difficulty, "My soul . . . cannot . . . kneel. It . . . will *not* . . . kneel."

She was visibly fighting the compulsion. Only Cireive heard her weak words.

Dzieru meanwhile, took out the sword.

Fire was in the mind of Ailsan. She was being torn apart. Here was her Lord before her, to be worshiped. Something around her cried loudly, 'Submit to him.'

And yet some strange other part of her—one that was inside, one that was stubborn and raw like an open wound—refused. And out of all her collective memories, one thing only kept surfacing—eyes of glass.

Eyes of the *dead.*

First there was Mideinn, frozen in death, then the thousands of slain on the field, their eyes all bulging, silent, and in their silence strangely childlike, forgiving her. Death had renewed their innocence in that last moment of embrace. There was no accusation, only a soft memory flower unfurling its petals of silver.

And it broke her at last.

Ailsan died in that moment, or maybe not. Maybe she was only thrown with the force of her agony into a bottomless abysmal well outside the universe, fleetingly to know the nature of true death. And then just as violently she was wrenched back into the mortal fabric of the world by the memory of the wild, living, *beloved* eyes of Talaq, that last instant before he had died—

"Enough!" she cried abruptly. Her voice came piercing the silence, a hush of thousands, as thunder gathered in her mind.

Deliberately, she stood up and looked at the Archpriest, who paused in surprise, the ceremonial sword still in his hand.

"Damn you to the Skies!" Cireive exclaimed, trembling. He pulled out his own great sword of polished metal. "Enough, yes, I shall kill you myself! No more!" The blade, a senseless thing, rose high in the air.

Sitting upon Ailsan's back, death became very still. Its skull-mouth was suddenly visible in the hooded darkness, jaws parted to reveal a hungry void. The crimson light of sunset gleamed acutely against the bone-whiteness of death's teeth, turning it to rose.

And then the sun swooned. Or was it that all of a sudden a great dark cloudmass appeared out of nowhere in the volcanic sky? And with it built a rumble of gathering thunder.

The violent thunderclouds gathered from all directions— from the right and the left hand of the setting sun, from the sun's bright scarlet face, and from the sun's obscured rose-tinted back.

A heartbeat. . . .

Then a hair-thin line of white celestial fire split the boiling red heaven into shards, like broken bloodied glass, and fell upon the figure of Ailsan. And in that moment the woman glowed.

Panic started everywhere. The Archpriest began to make violent ritual gestures in the air, and electric currents jumped from his fingers. Cireive paused, sword held over his head, gripping it with both hands, in the stance of an executioner.

And then her voice came. It was no longer even remotely human in essence, but thunder and raging wind.

The Skies heard you, Cireive. I am—Damned.

She stood before him, monumental. A silhouette against the madness of heaven.

She did not need to raise a hand to meet the crashing blade. She parried it, instead, with a look of her eyes.

On one side of her, the Archpriest's sword went up in flames. On the other side, the sword in the hands of the *taqavor* splintered, never completing its down-arc, while the *taqavor* himself gave a horrible cry, and for one fraction of an instant also glowed.

And then Cireive dropped what was left in his grip, still attached to shards of a broken blade, watching the hilt burn in his fingers. A moment, and the black charred remains of metal turned unbelievably not to liquid but to solid coal, which then crumbled into ash-dust.

Stand back, priest and king, from my wrath, boomed the voice of no woman but a goddess.

She was a torch. She burned and turned to black parchment, and time swept past her, accelerating, then spinning at last in a circle so that she was at the same time a child and an old woman with a wizened face.

Dzieru, finding no more ritual force in him, cringed, retreating down the hill. Cireive faltered for a moment, and then he also ran—ran like a possessed coward madman, clutching his burning hand and leaving behind his pride.

She stood watching them retreat both from her sight and from her memory—for her memory no longer held a place for such trivial things, swept as she was with time.

I am Ailsan, she said, *I have been Damned to bear the burden of being the* last *one.*

And then, from the sky, another Voice sounded.

She is the last, it said, louder than thunder, and suddenly the people knew the sound of Margh-Qa.

Through that storm, a vague, giant shape moved, flickered for a moment—a divine shadow the size of heaven. Then, for the second and final time spoke the god, the One who had possibly never been heard to speak before.

A new one comes in our midst.

And more thunder.

I am Ailsan. The soul and spirit of Risei, my people. There was a legend among my people that never should there be an end to Risei, but that if it did come then their soul would not die but be preserved with the gods.

She stood looking at the last moments of sunset, while tiny specks of remote humanity, the army of mortals, ran like ants upon the hillside.

They ran from her, leaving her all alone.

But she was not yet alone. Not quite.

Ailsan turned around, and for the first time felt an immense burden of shadow leave her shoulders, ease her back. Something cold and eternal left her, stepped away.

Something.

Ailsan stood and faced the form of gaunt silver darkness, clad in a cloak of night. Death stood before her, tall and insolent, and yet locked in a paradox of simultaneous remoteness and tangibility.

Ailsan knew this entity at last, knew it in a physical sense, because now she could reach out with her hand and touch the cold folds of death's eternal cloak.

And, as she did this, death was the one who recoiled.

"You," Ailsan said, her inner vision opening to the truth. "I know you. You damned bitch!"

And with a scream of divine thunder, Ailsan swung her hand and landed a blow at the side of the skeleton's right cheek, a blow that sent the shadow form reeling, thrown to the ground with a violence that held in it all the pent-up agony of cumulative human loss belonging to a whole people.

Death lay for a span of timeless moments on the cold earth, made oddly corporeal by its proximity to ethereal immortality, by comparison.

At the feet of death, a little away upon the cold rock, lay a curved scythe blade of strange nameless metal shimmering with its own eerie light in the twilight.

"Receive the Blow for all that you have taken from me," Risei-Ailsan said. "Receive it, and remember."

And then the new goddess nodded in the direction of the shimmering blade and said, "Pick it up. Take your scythe, and hold onto it well. And yet I promise you, you will lose it again, Hag. That, as a reminder—for I damn you to remember always what you do and who you are."

And the manifestation of death reached forward with its silver finger-claws, slowly took hold of the scythe, and then crawled away, leaving the goddess this time unto eternity.

Risei-Ailsan was alone at last.

And as she too started to fade into the dusk of the night air, the goddess softly wept.

L irheas, Prince of silence, observed with awed awakening, from a distance, the coming into being of the goddess Risei-Ailsan. And suddenly it all burst through his skull, and he could hear and see and sense all the earth and sky, all at once.

And thus as he watched the Gheir and his father run in madness, he *heard* her immortal voice thunder in the plain, rioting the army, and he also heard her voice whisper to him, yes, a soft private voice.

I am a jackal torn away from her cubs. I am the mother you recognized in me, the mother you never had. Lirheas, Prince of Gheir, you will remember me always. Not because of what I am now, not because of pity, although that too you've felt. No . . . Remember me only as that which your father loved, hated, and feared. For I revealed to him the truth of himself. And he will bear the burden of the truth now, unto madness.

Know that loyalty is the most precious thing. To be gifted in trust, not taken by force.

Know that a mother's desperation is the strongest force, and a mother's forsaking is the greatest loss. I now bear one secret guilt within me always, a guilt of pride. My son might have lived, if only—

And yet my spirit cries! I could not do otherwise! For now I am paradox. I am pride unfurled, coexisting with humility. I am Risei. I am Ailsan. I am the vast desert and the deep ocean. Remember me, for a goddess speaks within you now. And forget. . . .

Thus the young son of the *taqavor* was for one instant only inside the soul of Her who was from then on worshiped under the name of Risei-Ailsan, Bringer of Stillness and Water, the Bright-Eyed Liberator, the Mad Sovereign of Wisdom, and then simply Ris. He knew her and then knew not, only remembered in hazy musings a shadow, understanding for the first time an old legend among his own people.

The gods, it said, are all the *souls* of different peoples. When a people dies, the last woman or man among them is always something more, always sacrosanct. It is the last that bears all the responsibility for a people, and is never to be dishonored.

Or else, the gods hear. And they elevate the *one* in misery, so that a new deity joins the pantheon, forged, like all the others, from the collective spirit of a people.

That is the secret of deity.

And he knew it. Lirheas the Prince of revelation knew the lore as he witnessed the Change taking place, and he too was elevated. Later it was he who would look upon the rising and the setting sun, observe its burning face, its scalding back, its left hand and its right—from all directions.

And in the wide expanses of the wind, the ocean, the desert sand, and the glimmer of daylight, he would observe the Compass Rose.

Dream Five

Tale of Nadir

The boy came out of the desert, leading a pack-beast and carrying a cup of water.

His skin was dark like the rich soil underneath the sand; his hair midnight-black and wiry, short against his scalp; his features rounded, flat and soft, malleable like sweet brown clay and belonging to a darker race of humankind.

His eyes were startling. They were like an ocean at night, without a horizon line and without bottom. Lurking inside were experience and sorrow.

No one would question the boy's facial expression, nor his solo emergence from out of the desert, nor the fact that his pack-beast did not look nearly as parched and weary as was customary after a long crossing of uninterrupted sands.

However, one thing unexplainable was the cup filled with fresh water, seemingly boundless, that the young one carried in his dirty palms.

The water was clear and stood so very near the brim. It sparkled in the sun with an added brilliance of a peach sunset, or maybe a hue deeper than gold and rosy with persimmon. Whence did this color come? For the cup itself was faded brown, old polished wood without a hint of embellishment.

The boy came to the outskirts of the sands, to a place where sparse growing shrubs crested the dunes, and rock formations hid occasional spots of oasis. Here, nomad tribes would stop and set up their tents, and here caravans often met to exchange wares and transfer news of the greater world to all the corners of the Compass Rose.

At one such spot of oasis a dozen caravans had come together—a horse trader, several gemstone merchants, a wood importer, and other lesser vendors. The temporary market was erected for a matter of days only, after which all would proceed their own ways, having acquired and sold new property.

The boy paused before the clearing, hidden by an outcrop of rock. His heart started to beat loudly in his temples, and internal waters went coursing wildly through his flesh. There was fear, uncertainty, hopeless despair. Dared he enter this camp?

He considered for a moment, standing in the midday sun, while the liquid at the rim of the cup that he held trembled in the wind. Eventually he pulled the pack-beast gently closer to him and absentmindedly lifted the wooden bowl to its muzzle.

While the mangy old creature drank, he watched the scene before him, the moving people, braying mules and loaded camels, the mayhem near the watering hole, and the fine expensive tents. This was no ordinary market scene, for he could tell there was old noble money here, in the very manner of cloth draping the tents, and the rich woven blankets of the beasts.

And then he looked to the side, to the edge of the tallest tent, and saw a wonder.

A horse with skin of mother-of-pearl.

To say this is no exaggeration. The colors moved and rippled in the sun from the palest cream pearl to sudden flows of lavender, then tints of lapis, and a wash of metallic green, and then sudden rose. And then, the next second one blinked, the pearly hue returned, like a scene prior to a dispelled mirage. The beast moved gently, milling from one foot to the other, and its flanks and back glittered in the light as though oiled with the thick flammable material that is sometimes found seeping through the earth in certain faraway Western places, and creates filmy rings of rainbow upon its liquid surface.

The horse was tied with at least three long ropes to different poles that had been driven into the sandy ground, and was guarded by two well armed soldiers.

It was not particularly unusual in equine size, neither large nor small, but rather of a more refined and aristocratic shape, with a quick wiry frame and nervous delicate features. The mane of the horse and its finely groomed tail were as pristine white as the sun upon the sands of the desert. The whiteness stood out in a shock of perfection against the skin with its mere hint of rippling rainbow of mother-of-pearl.

The boy knew then that he had to come forth. He had to be near that creature out of an unbelievable dream.

And so with a gulp he stepped away from the safety of the outcropping, and said distinctly, "Come," to the pack-beast. The boy wanted to announce himself to the world at large. He wanted to announce his emergence out of the dream that was the desert into the reality that was the world of men and caravans, and—the creature of mother-of-pearl.

It was obviously there among them, and *it* had to be divine, so of course he could find himself a place among mortals once again.

The boy walked forward upon the sand and rock, barely moving his gaze from the beautiful horse, until he was in the clearing and someone nearly ran into him.

"Watch yourself, boy!" The man spoke harshly and was on his way past him, pale cotton robes moving in the strong wind, features obscured by his head wrap, except for a dark flash of beard.

As the man went by, the boy smelled a whiff of camels and spice and humanity. It smote him with the power of the present reality, of the here and now, and dispelled the last vestiges of his desert dream of solitude.

He was back among mortal men. And he was completely ignored.

The boy stood holding the reins with one hand and the cup in the other, while around him passers by moved quickly, emerging from tents and carrying wares.

He was an island.

And less than thirty feet from him stood the fabulous beast.

"What are you gawking at?" said one guard, noticing him standing so near. "Even staring at Tazzia for the likes of you is forbidden. Scram, dark boy! Before the Lord sees you despoiling his greatest prize with the lust of your unworthy eyes."

"Ah, let him be, Grego," said the other guard. "Tazzia is on display for all, and lust is but in our mortal nature."

The boy looked directly into the warm eyes of the man who had spoken last, and was emboldened to ask, "What manner of horse beast is this Tazzia?"

The guard laughed. He was handsome and confident. He had olive skin, and his infectious grin revealed strong healthy white teeth. But on second glance his eyes were not warm, but pale azure like the water of the sky or the air of the wind—things cool in themselves that only reflected the heat of the sands below or the sun's fire. Warm only by association.

And the dissonance made the boy confused.

"Tazzia is like no horse you have ever seen, little man," the guard said. "And you will never see one such again, for as long as you live. That I can promise you. Tazzia is rumored to be a god."

"What kind of god?" said the boy, continuing to stare. "I have seen a god in the flesh, and it wasn't a strange thing at all. Not like you'd think. Gods can appear to be exactly like us. But I believe that this here is a marvelous creature."

"Well, what have we here, a little wise man who knows gods in person? Tell me, little man, what is your name?"

The boy grew still for a moment, remembering in odd silence. "The god," he said, "named me Nadir."

At that, both the guards guffawed. "The god! The god, he says! He's been named by no less than a god! Does it make him a proper priest of that blessed god? Well, are you a priest, boy who has been named Nadir?"

But in that moment there came a rather sharp snort from the direction of the fabulous horse.

The creature of iridescent cream and rainbows stomped on the ground angrily and tossed its head, white mane flying in the wind. And immediately the guards dropped their mockery and the cynical expressions, and turned their full attention to their equine charge, forgetting altogether the boy named Nadir.

Nadir stood thus, and watched a maddened rolling eye of Tazzia follow him sideways, like a malevolent violet gem. If this was a god, then it was surely not a pleased one. And it had seen him, the boy, as surely as the boy had seen it.

"Stand clear!" exclaimed Grego, "Woah! Hold that other rope, Zuaren, damn this beast . . ."

And in the instant that he spoke thus, Tazzia stood up on its hind legs, looming suddenly fully twelve feet tall, throwing its mane back, shaking his beautiful head madly, and kicking with its front legs in a flurry of sand dust.

The pale-eyed guard named Zuaren moved faster than anyone Nadir had ever seen and snatched the torn piece of thick coarse rope still attached to Tazzia, while the other end fell limply on the ground near one of the wooden posts.

"This is the second broken rope today," he grumbled, pulling up sharply and jerking Tazzia's lovely neck.

The horse neighed in fury and was back on the ground with all four legs.

"I think he thirsts," Nadir said suddenly. And just as suddenly he left his own pack-beast standing several feet away, stolid and undaunted by the passion display of the greater horse.

And Nadir approached the creature of mother-of-pearl with his cup of water.

"No, boy, get back!" cried Zuaren, but then his words froze to silence, for Nadir had raised the wooden cup and lifted it before Tazzia.

The wind of the desert all around them was the only sound, as Tazzia became still and put its slender muzzle forward.

The creature of mother-of-pearl drank the water from the wooden cup.

And drank.

Long minutes later, as its lips were still moving thirstily and its throat muscles contracting in rapid swallows, the two guards stared in amazement, for there seemed to be no end to this water. Nadir's hands tired from holding up the cup.

At that moment, from the ornate door flap of the grand tent behind them came the Lord himself, followed by several retainers.

"What is going on here?" said Lord Urar-Tuan. He was a short and slender nearly hairless man with an ocher tint to his skin, and weirdly slanted eyes. His hair was oiled, black, and gathered in a tail in the back of his scalp, while the front half of his head was shaved. He was clad in bright glistening silks, finely embroidered with ornate, delicate designs.

Nadir, as he continued to slake Tazzia's thirst, couldn't help but stare at its master. He had never seen such a smooth hairless man before, such slanted eyes, such yellowish skin.

Maybe this was another god?

"You!" exclaimed the Lord in a rather un-godlike shrill voice and with an oddly slurred accent, seeing the boy. "What are you doing there? Get away from my property!"

Nadir gulped and drew the cup away from Tazzia's soft, dripping, still-moving lips as he met the sudden intense cold anger in the slanted eyes of the man.

And then the Lord motioned for his retainers to take Nadir and bring him forward.

Nadir felt himself grabbed roughly by the elbows and literally picked off the ground, carried several steps, and then thrown at the feet of the exotic Lord.

As Nadir fell, his wooden cup came away from his hands and landed at the feet of the Lord. As it landed upright, splashing a little, then settled, everyone could see that it was filled to the brim with clear water. . . .

Lord Urar-Tuan drew his thin dark brows together and stared at the wooden cup at his feet, its oddness registering in his mind just for a moment. But then his awareness passed, and he turned away to stare impassively at the dark boy scrambling to rise before him.

"I can have you whipped, boy," Lord Urar-Tuan said. "What manner of filth did you try to feed my horse?"

"Forgive me," Nadir began, "I could see that the creature was thirsty, and this is perfectly good water, so I gave—"

"My Lord Urar-Tuan," the guard called Zuaren interrupted suddenly. "The boy indeed meant no harm, and Tazzia was once again bent on madness. We have noticed that drinking has appeared to calm him down—that is why we allowed this. In fact, there is something rather unusual about that cup. . . ."

"Guard, I can have you whipped also," the Lord said, cutting him off in an icy tone. "Indeed, I will have both of you punished for allowing a stranger to even approach my Tazzia."

And, saying those words, Lord Urar-Tuan kicked the wooden cup at his feet with the toe of his embroidered shoe.

The cup rolled only a couple of feet, hindered by the sand, and then landed once again upright . . . and filled to the brim with water.

This time there was no mistaking the oddity.

As everyone stared—truly, a small crowd was beginning to gather near the tent—Lord Urar-Tuan glared at the cup intently, then walked forward and picked it up.

Nadir's hands clenched involuntarily as he watched the Lord roughly handle the cup.

Lord Urar-Tuan paused for only a second, holding the full cup in his right hand. Then with a sharp gesture he tossed its contents to the ground below.

Everyone watched an exact cupful of water violently drench a spot on the ground, discoloring the sand.

And then everyone watched as the Lord brought the cup back upright, and it was ... full to the brim with liquid, glittering persimmon in the sun.

And in the general silence a young boy's defiant voice was heard.

"This cup is blessed," said Nadir, rising from the ground. "For it has been given to me by Ris, the Bringer of Stillness and Water. Ris the Divine has made it so that the cup remains full always, bottomless. I have crossed the desert with no other water than what is contained within, which has been enough for me and my pack-beast. And the boundless water itself is my sister, also blessed by Ris."

And then he outstretched his hand and said bravely, "Please return the cup to me, my Lord, for it is mine."

But no one was ever to know what Lord Urar-Tuan would have done on his own—whether he would've conceded to the noble or the greedy act; whether he would've surrendered the wondrous cup to its rightful owner or tried to keep it for himself against all the gods' justice—for in that moment a little girl came forward from out of the shadows of the tent.

The little girl was like a porcelain doll, a weirdly beautiful replica of the exotic Lord, and was wrapped in the same expensive grade of silks. Pearls and glittering stones lay in close rows upon her brow and over her sleek black hair, and hung like grapes from her tiny earlobes. More strings of jewels cascaded from her temples in garlands and fell to her neck and below, to her tiny silk-wrapped waist. She wore soft embroidered slippers also trimmed with pearls, loose pants, and a fancy caftan on top of it all, like a many-layered inverted rose blossom with drooping petals.

The girl had the same slanted eyes, thin slivers of almond. The eyes stared unblinking at the boy, then moved away.

And then she pointed at the cup, speaking to the Lord in a strange lilting tongue, tones rising up and down like waves of water, or dunes sliding in the wind. . . .

An involuntary smile came to the previously impassive features of Lord Urar-Tuan. He chuckled softly, then nodded and gave the cup to the little girl, and patted her cheek. Then he glanced at Nadir and said in the more familiar tongue, "How much do you want for this magical trinket, boy? My daughter will have it for herself."

Nadir stared back and forth between the tiny animated doll and her imposing father.

"No," he said. "You don't understand: this is my cup! My grandmother—that is, Ris—gave it to me and none other, and I demand it back!"

"Demand?" Lord Urar-Tuan said, this time laughing darkly. And then he added, "Someone, bring me a small purse of gold coins. About twelve should do it."

"No!" said Nadir, but his protest was unheeded.

A servant went to fetch the gold.

The beautiful little girl meanwhile moved a few steps away, and held the cup with both of her tiny hands, shaking it a bit, and making the water slosh back and forth and spill past the brim. Soon her tiny face glowed with a smile that was hard to describe because of its oddity, and then she giggled to herself. Muttering in her lilting tongue, she swirled the water in the cup with her finger.

Next she started to upturn the cup and spill endless cupfuls on the dry white sands around her, spinning in place, splashing herself and making gurgling sounds of wicked glee. Seeing that, some of the nomads who had gathered to watch shook their heads. There was a swell of displeased mutterings in the crowd.

"Spoiled girl . . . Have respect for the water," they were heard to say. "Water is a gift of Ris, especially in the desert, and especially from the blessed vessel."

"Egiras!" called Lord Urar-Tuan, noting everyone's displeasure.

The girl turned quickly, and her laughing face transformed into a petulant frown.

The Lord said something stern in their alien tongue, and the little girl frowned even more, but stopped playing with the water.

At that point the gold purse arrived.

Lord Urar-Tuan made a great show of opening the silk bag, and spilling twelve shining gold coins upon his palm. He then put them back in the purse and handed it casually to Nadir.

"I don't want anything from you!" the boy said in outrage. "I want my cup back! Give me back my cup!"

A knot of pain intertwined with anger was building in Nadir's throat. He wanted to collapse and weep, to allow his facial features the freedom to convulse into a spasm, but he would not. The boy's face was immobilized with the effort of holding himself back, and he glared at the Lord.

"You refuse this fair payment?" said Lord Urar-Tuan, smiling thinly and ignoring the boy's fierceness. "Well then, you will have none. I count to three and if you will not take the purse then it returns to me, and everyone will have seen that you refused it. I still keep the trinket. One!"

Nadir trembled.

"Take the purse boy, don't be a fool," Zuaren said quietly, "Go on. . . ."

In Zuaren's hands at the other end of the rope, the creature Tazzia began to snort, nostrils flaring.

"Two!" Lord Urar-Tuan said. The little girl Egiras giggled, looking at him with wicked laughing eyes.

And Nadir stared back at her, stared at what he saw now as a beautiful demonic doll, and in her eyes a challenge.

And, staring, he drew his hand forward and accepted the bag of coins. He was not sure why he did it, only that it felt like the right thing to do in that moment of surreal intensity.

Everyone in the crowd breathed a sign of relief.

"Good decision, boy," the Lord said. "I like your prudence. You can come to the back of my tent and eat with the servants. Go on now, take your old donkey or mule or whatever this sorry creature is, and go to the back. You—show him where the cook works the fire. . . ."

And Lord Urar-Tuan turned away without another glance at Nadir, and went back inside his tent.

The little girl followed him, no longer frowning but impassive and with a very adult expression of disdain. She held the wooden cup of water close to her chest, and then, just before disappearing behind the doorway hangings, she threw a quick icy glance at Nadir. She purposefully allowed the cup to tilt in her hand so that its contents spilled endlessly upon the sand for several long moments. . . . And then, with a final toss of her bejewelled head, she too was gone.

The crowd began to disperse. And yet some people were still shaking their heads, for all could see injustice wrought before them.

"Poor foolish boy," whispers came. "Lord Urar-Tuan has tricked him out of a treasure. . . ."

In the meantime, the servant who had been singled out by the Lord motioned for Nadir to come along.

Nadir stood petrified, unsure of what to do next and confused by what he'd just conceded to by accepting the coins.

The desert sun beat down from on high, and air pulsed with heat in the middle of the clearing in front of the great tent. Before following the servant, Nadir threw one wistful look at the closed tent flap where the Lord had disappeared once more inside. And then he stared grimly at the two guards milling about and tightening the ropes around the odd iridescent creature Tazzia.

In the warping air, Tazzia seemed to waver in and out of this reality, and Nadir blinked, unable to focus his eyes properly upon its suddenly unstable form. It was as though the trembling spouts of heat rising from the sands were fueling its existence.

"Don't forget your own mangy old beast there," Grego said, noting the boy's once more mesmerized pause.

Nadir emerged out of his reverie and guiltily went back to take the reins of his poor complacent pack-beast.

"Look at its foaming mouth. Now, *it* needs water," said the other guard, Zuaren. "So, then, what will you do, boy? You've lost your miraculous treasure, but you've gained in coins. Will you part with some now for a bit of liquid nourishment and a bit of advice?"

"Stop your foolery," Lord Urar-Tuan's servant said to the guards as he paused, seeing that Nadir was not moving. "And you, boy, once and for all, come along. The midday heat is unbearable, and I have no time to tarry."

In that instant, Tazzia neighed, shaking its head lightly. Its intense eyes suddenly met those of the boy, and he was sure he heard words spoken in his mind.

Do as they say. Go inside, and wait.

Nadir froze, then suddenly felt the dry heat of the desert wind lick the nape of his neck as though an invisible hand touched him and pushed him forward.

And thus Nadir took the steps toward the tent.

He was sure now, a god was watching his back.

Nadir sat cross-legged on the floor of a poor smoke-filled tent, at the outermost edge of a meal-circle. Regular servants of the Lord Urar-Tuan sat closer to the middle where the hot coals were maintained. On top of the coals reposed a large flat slab of stone, upon which meat and vegetables were being grilled, stewing in their own juices, and sprinkled with newly traded spices.

"Put the best pieces here on the Lord's tray," said a shawled woman servant to another. "And take them to the Lord's tent. When you serve them, be sure to put the sweetest palest chunks on the little one's plate, since she likes them lightly browned only. Do it exactly, now."

The second servant proceeded to fill the tray with the choicest bits, while the others chewed in hungry absorption. There was little conversation.

Nadir held his own piece of roast wrapped in fresh steaming flatbread, and was done with eating it in two hungry gulps. But he was too shy and too proud to ask for more, although his stomach continued to growl in emptiness. It had shrunk accordingly, after his endless days in the desert, for he had had nothing to eat most of the time except for occasional bits of sparse growth and fallen date-fruits and the endless supply of soothing water that had nearly fooled him into satiation. In this mortal place of human and animal smells, his stomach had re-awakened and was making itself known to Nadir.

Something was not exactly right, and he could not quite pinpoint it, not at first. And then it occurred to him: he missed washing down his meager food with the clean water from the wooden cup. The cup had kept him company for so long that it now seemed forever. He missed its familiar liquid balm.

And with that thought taking hold of his awareness, Nadir brooded, his intense little features forming into a menacing frown.

Sitting nearby, one of the Lord's guards noticed the boy's dark demeanor. "What's the matter now, little man?" asked the blue-eyed guard called Zuaren. He was chewing his food with animation and with a show of healthy white teeth.

Nadir glared at him, then said, "I have to get back my cup. Ris gave it to me, and it belongs with me and none other. It is my sister, the water that flows from it! I must have it back."

"Or else, what will you do?" Zuaren said, moving closer to him on the floor. He settled just alongside the boy.

"I don't know," Nadir said. "But I must do something. Grandmother—that is, Ris—told me I must always fight injustice, and this is my first test. I cannot fail her."

"Amazing, isn't it," said Zuaren, looking into space in front of him and ripping off a piece of flatbread, "to have a goddess for a grandmother? You must be a lucky little man indeed. Tell me, what is it like?"

"It is like nothing," Nadir said sullenly. "She was just Grandmother. And why do you care?"

"I don't, actually. But I am curious as to what it is about you that made Tazzia grow meek and obedient, even for the little time it took you to feed it the water. Maybe it was that cup of yours. They say gods can sense each other, and each other's handiwork."

Zuaren spoke quietly and did not turn his head toward the boy.

Nadir watched his profile. "How did you end up with the job of guarding Tazzia?" he asked. "And how did Tazzia end up where it is now, bound and helpless, and under the Lord's whim?"

Zuaren laughed. "And how did *you?*"

"I am not bound and helpless! And I serve no one!" Nadir exclaimed.

"Shhh, not so loud," the guard replied in a level soft tone. "The first thing you need to learn is not to react. That is your first lesson. When you flail out in passion, you become vulnerable."

Nadir stared at him, but kept his silence.

"Good," said Zuaren. "Now we can talk like men."

He touched the shoulder of someone from the Lord Urar-Tuan's household sitting on the other side of him, closer to the hot coals and the food stone. "Hand me some more of that bread and meat, will you?"

The other man turned around with the intent to grumble at the interruption. But, seeing who it was that spoke, he suddenly drew in his breath and, nodding, proceeded to load up a piece of flatbread with the fried food. This he passed to Zuaren.

"Thank you, friend," the guard said in reply, grinning, showing once more his teeth. He took the food and, as Nadir watched in surprise, he deposited it in the boy's lap.

"Eat," Zuaren said. "For someone who's come out of the desert after consorting with gods, it looks like it took the flesh off your bones, in addition to other things."

"I would rather not eat more of *his* food than I have to. His charity is already gagging me because I know what I've traded away for this sorry bread and meat—my honor."

The guard chuckled.

"It took you all this time to come up with that, eh?"

Nadir stared at him, and then in peculiar silence took the food and started to put pieces of it in his mouth.

Zuaren lifted one dark handsome brow. "You learn fast," he said. And then added, "Good for you, little man. You did not react, and you proceeded in wisdom by not wasting a good meal when you need it for strength. Therefore I will help you."

Nadir stopped eating.

"Yes," said the older man. "You heard right, and I will tell you what I mean, but later. When the sun sets and it is time for sleep and darkness."

And then he drew his head close to the boy's ear as though leaning forward to adjust his clothing and his prominent daggers, and uttered in a voice that was barely above silence, "I will help you get the cup back. Do not leave here, and wait for me."

And then Zuaren rose, silent like a large cat-creature, and was out of the tent. No one turned to look at him leaving, though there came a tensing in many backs.

Nadir remained eating in the corner, in suddenly relieved, ravenous silence.

The night in a desert oasis comes quickly, like the falling cloak of a swarthy god. With it the temperatures plummet, for the desert knows only extremes, no middle ground.

Nadir shivered, sitting outside the small cooking tent belonging to the servants of Lord Urar-Tuan. All around him, bluish dusk. A few steps away stood his patient pack-beast, tied to a spare tent peg driven into the ground. It was starting to fall asleep, having just eaten its fill of dried grain that Nadir had traded earlier in the day for one of his twelve gold coins. Since he had no lesser currency and the grain vendor had no change— or pretended to have none—he ended up paying exorbitantly. Then, to water the animal properly, Nadir had to stand patiently in a long line at the common well, waiting his turn. How odd it had been for him thus, not to have immediate access to water.

Water is a treasure in the desert. . . .

Nadir knew with every passing moment that he lost something irretrievable, something that had no price in human terms. He had lost it in exchange for twelve gold coins.

Gold for water. . . .

A sudden acute memory pierced him like a clap of thunder. In the rapidly cooling dusk, in a state of amazing mental clarity, Nadir shivered with terror, shivered with self-hatred at what he'd done.

He had done the very same thing that those others had, so long ago it seemed—they who had tried to barter for water with cold metal.

And Ris had given them what they asked.

"Ris!" Nadir exclaimed in an agonized whisper, having a sudden insane need to speak out loud, or else internal waters would come bursting. "Grandmother! Forgive me for what I have done! How could I? How?"

And in that same moment in the darkness, he heard the soft neighing of a horse, only a little away. It came from the other side, from the front of the greater tent.

The moon was rising.

Nadir crept around the side of his dozing pack-beast and then made his way on tiptoe around the tent. Just as he was about to come to the very front, he felt something sharp poke his side, and a strong hand came around his mouth from behind in the darkness.

"Halt . . . not a sound."

Nadir's outcry happened only in his mind, because he recognized in the hissing whisper the voice of Zuaren.

The hand released him, and Zuaren turned the boy by the shoulders to face him, turned his little dark face to the moonlight.

"Make no sound, little man, I don't want Grego to hear us," Zuaren said. "He is over there, next to Tazzia, nodding off as usual."

"What—" Nadir began, his dark eyes wide open and glistening in the moonlight.

In reply, Zuaren, his own face fathomless shadow, put a finger to his lips and motioned with his hand for the boy to follow.

They moved in silence for about thirty paces until they were on the other side of the tent, and Nadir could see the shadow form of the fabulous horse standing silhouetted against the ichor-dark sky and the even darker foliage of the oasis.

And then, as his eyes got accustomed to the intensity of looking at the shapes of night, Nadir saw a wondrous sight.

Tazzia was translucent.

Half corporeal, half ghost, the horse stood with its head lowered in sorrow, while with every smoothing caress of the moon's glow its mother-of-pearl form fluctuated in solidity, like a swaying forest of water vapors. And at times, like clouds passing through its insides, the mists thickened or thinned so that in snatches one could see the opposite side, see right *through* the creature.

And then Nadir could feel a faint vulnerable touch in his mind, a *presence.* And yet it was so insubstantial that he was not quite sure if it really happened, was not sure—

"Look at him . . ." Zuaren whispered. "The night is cruel to him, for his nature is that of hot warping air, and the cold saps his strength. He is an immortal and thus cannot be relieved by death. And yet he suffers the agony of the dissolution of his flesh every night. Sometimes I try to light a small fire near his feet, but the Lord saw me and would not allow it, for Urar-Tuan wants him to feel the agony, wants him weak and pliable. And so I bring hot coals or rocks wrapped in cloth, and lay them invisibly nearby to relieve him. . . ."

"But why?" Nadir whispered. "Why does the Lord want this to be? What has this beautiful creature done to deserve it?"

"Why should its beauty be a point of consideration? Few living beings deserve such treatment," Zuaren retorted, and Nadir was instantly shamed.

"What will happen? This is not right!" the boy whispered after a long silence, as he watched Tazzia shimmer in and out of existence.

In answer, Zuaren leaned forward and looked closely into his eyes. "Promise me, boy, that you will say nothing of this to anyone . . ." he whispered. "Promise me!"

And after Nadir nodded, his little face very serious, Zuaren said, "I will soon take Tazzia away from here."

Nadir's face glowed in animation.

"But," Zuaren continued, "I will need your help. Can I count on you, little man?"

"Yes!"

In the moonlight Zuaren grinned, baring his teeth like ivory. "Good," he whispered. "Now come with me, away from this place where we may be found, and I will tell you more of Tazzia and of how he was bound to Lord Urar-Tuan. You want to hear more of him, do you not? Yes, I know you do . . . you are under Tazzia's thrall."

As the moon rode the vault of heaven near the zenith over the desert, Nadir settled near Zuaren at the foot of an old palm.

The older man handed him a piece of bread and some hard cheese made from camel's milk, and then told the story of Tazzia.

When Zuaren was hired by Lord Urar-Tuan to guard Tazzia, the creature had already been in the Lord's possession for quite some time. What he knew were things disclosed by other servants, and much of it had been exaggeration and the result of fearful overactive imaginations, so that he had to wade through the fabricated morass to establish the truth.

It seemed that back in his own distant land somewhere in the great Middle of all places, Lord Urar-Tuan had dabbled with the powers of the world that are normally left unpronounced—those ancient half-formed lurking forces that permeate the fabric of night, the energies that are released in the slow decay of sunset into indigo dusk, the essence in the wind that comes forth only with cold, as the two greater shining celestial entities and the lesser pinpoint ones hide beyond the horizon. . . .

For, in the things that reside between day and night, at the moments of dawn and sunset, hides the One who is known as the Lord of Illusion. *He* can never be seen at times of great clarity—which usually happen when there is great celestial light—but only during twilight.

At such in-between times, the Lord of Illusion slithers in like one's shadow, and begins a slow interplay with one's greatest weakness.

For most that weakness is lust.

For others it is self-delusion. That is the downfall of the cleverer stronger ones, the ones who cannot be tempted.

Instead, they can be deceived.

And that is what had happened with Lord Urar-Tuan. In his great intelligence and learning, Lord Urar-Tuan had conceived the idea that he could bind the Lord of Illusion Himself like a personal servant. He had read the most ancient books of wisdom, filled with symbol-writing that he had to learn first—symbol characters that were like flowers or like tiny marks of a brush.

And from them he gleaned the secret rituals that were needed to invoke the Lord of Illusion into this reality.

It had taken him many moons and the cycles of many seasons. During that time Lord Urar-Tuan had become an esoteric man. In the course of this, he had also taken a herbal draft of ancient ritual potency and impregnated a wife who bore him a very extraordinary child.

That child was human but on the verge of *otherness,* and that child was his means of calling forth Illusion. She was none other than the little Egiras, a thing of wicked beauty and a creature bound to the Lord of Illusion from the moment of her conception.

"I hate her," said Nadir, interrupting the tale. "She is the one who caused Lord Urar-Tuan to mock me and take away Ris's cup from me. She is a horrible little beast!"

"Ah, but she is much more than that, and she is worse than you think," Zuaren said with a rueful smile. "Be wary of her, boy, even more so than of her father. For she belongs not to her father but to *Him.*"

And then Zuaren continued to tell what he had learned.

After Egiras was born, and when she was old enough to walk—a mere toddler with precocious eyes—Lord Urar-Tuan began the ritual of seducing the Lord of Illusion.

What one thing could there be that would tempt Illusion Himself? What would draw *Him* into the mortal world to fully manifest in the flesh, and to remain thus, bound?

It is said that Illusion is drawn to more Illusion out of curiosity, for it recognizes itself and wants to look and admire and fathom it from the outside.

Lord Urar-Tuan had observed during his sometime travels through the deserts of the South that upon occasion, when the temperature of the air grows to a nearly unbearable point, the air begins to take on a translucent form. It shimmers, warps, and often acts like a great wondrous mirror standing upright in the desert and reflecting from afar places and objects that are not really there but hundreds of miles away.

The desert nomads call it a mirage.

For many it is a true Illusion.

And Lord Urar-Tuan had a marvelous moment of insight. He would create a unique mirage that would be irresistible to the Lord of Illusion, even in the middle of day. That mirage would seduce and trap *Him* in the mortal world, and then Urar-Tuan would have at his disposal terrifying wonder. . . .

And thus the Lord traveled with a richly laden caravan from his distant homeland to the deepest desert, here. And he had brought his daughter with him on the journey.

Egiras, the little girl of five summers, had come eagerly, paying not a moment of heed to her weeping mother, who was sure she'd never see her child again.

At some point among the scalding sands, when the sun stood mercilessly at the zenith, Lord Urar-Tuan determined that this was the precise location and moment that was pointed to in his esoteric calculations.

"Stop here," he told the caravan leader and his men. "And now, I want you to build me a fire."

The Lord's retainers looked at him with confusion, but obeyed nevertheless. They selected a flat place on the sands and set out in a particular arrangement the specially prepared logs of wood painted with a resin that contained in it bits of divine sorcery. Then they poured a flask of pure distilled alcohol in the center of the woodpile.

When all had been made ready according to the meticulous instructions, Lord Urar-Tuan stepped forward, leading his small daughter by the hand, and took out a tiny dagger—as tiny and sharp as a needle. This he used to prick the little index finger of Egiras, at which she cried out once in anger, but then was oddly silent and unlike a child of her age.

Lord Urar-Tuan guided her forward and extended her hand over the center of the woodpile. He squeezed her finger until several drops of dark blood came falling and stained the amber resin coating of the wood.

One last drop he directed to the very middle of the woodpile, to fall upon the alcohol-stained sand.

When he was done, Egiras stood back and sucked her finger with a blank expression on her face, and her lips were colored with a bit of her own lifeblood.

Then the Lord motioned for all but his daughter to retreat, and they obeyed so that Urar-Tuan stood alone with her. Hiding in the wagons of the caravan, they watched from a distance, seeing their Lord take out something pale and glittering from the folds of his clothing.

Some swore it was a rare transparent diamond. Others claimed it was nothing but a piece of ordinary glass brightly polished and shaped by artisans into a plump convex shape.

No matter. Because Lord Urar-Tuan raised the object before him at arm's length and pointed it between the woodpile and the sun.

Within seconds the wood began to smoke. And as the ordinary caravan folk watched in wonder, a bright orange-gold flame burst forth from the wood.

And then the flame took form. . . . The form was vague at first, a bare flicker of deviation from ordinary fire, a merest hint of otherness. But then it began to solidify, and in moments it took on the distinct shape of a horse.

It stood before them, the fire horse, wrought of licking flames, semi-transparent, elegant and menacing. For it had the same dark eyes as did Egiras. There appeared to be two spots of dark deep crimson akin to her blood in the eye-sockets of the flame-creature. And though in reality the girl's eyes were jet, they bore a resemblance to the fire eyes in slanted form and expression.

"Behold the Fire Horse! She is your kin spirit, Egiras!" exclaimed Lord Urar-Tuan in his native tongue. "Can you feel the bond?"

But Egiras stared coldly at the creature of flames, and she replied sullenly, also in the language of their homeland, for it was the only one she knew as yet, "No, father." And then she added, "This thing is nothing, temporary and fickle—while my own fire burns forever."

And saying that she turned away from the marvelous sight of flames in living form, the streaming warping air currents all around. And she was thus to miss the soft fluctuation in the fabric of the air just behind the flaming mare.

For, beyond the smoke and the licking flames, another equine form began to grow. . . .

They say that Lord Urar-Tuan was heard to gasp in that instant, the only time he had shown emotional vulnerability. He took several steps forward and reached out with his hand in an almost pitiful gesture of longing.

Here before him was the moment of fulfillment, the point for which he'd been studying the most ancient wisdom for endless seasons. Before him, Illusion Himself wavered in and out of time and place, *His* bluish equine form—chosen to complement the golden form of the mare, which was a mystical representation of the year of birth of Egiras, and which was incidentally known to be a particular temptation to Illusion—*His* form was burning with a different, cooler fire than the flame that had created the fire-mare out of the blood of Egiras.

And, seeing Illusion Himself at last, Lord Urar-Tuan howled.

He cried out his exuberance, his glory, to the incandescent skies. And then he spoke ancient words that he knew were the most powerful kind of mortal-wrought binding.

"I attach you to me!" he repeated in all the languages known in all the lands that rimmed the horizon. "With the strength of my desire, my spirit, and my very life! In the same way, I bind myself to you—when you breathe, I breathe, when I die, you die!"

He spoke thus, knowing that what he was creating was a paradox, for a god could neither die nor need to breathe.

And thus, neither would he.

Because from this moment on, bound to the Lord of Illusion, Urar-Tuan knew he would become immortal.

The stallion in the form of electric blue flame stood at the side of the fire-mare. And then *He* approached with his muzzle to caress the mare which turned its Egiras-eyes of fathomless darkness to the Lord of Illusion.

You have what you asked for, mortal, said a voice in the wind, like a great void, and was miraculously heard by all—to which they later swore—from their hiding places around the caravan.

And in the balance, I have you. Do you understand the arrangement?

"I understand, oh yes!" exclaimed Urar-Tuan, an insane smile breaking out on his normally composed fine features. He took another step and reached out with his hand to touch. . . .

"No, father!" came the thin voice of little Egiras. She still stood with her back to them, and would not turn. And yet she knew what was taking place.

"Do not try to hold him, father. . . . You cannot hold Illusion, no one can. . . ." she whispered.

"What do you say, foolish girl?" hissed Urar-Tuan, whipping his head to stare at her, his face a roil of madness.

"You think you do, but you do not understand." She finally turned around, slowly, and now the Lord could see that she was terrified but had been hiding her child-eyes.

And still looking at his daughter, Lord Urar-Tuan put his hand upon the bluish flame of Illusion.

And felt nothing.

For there was nothing to feel or to touch.

And in the burning wind, out of the void came laughter.

You have bound yourself to quite another thing, mortal. Unlike me, this is a corporeal being, and its nature is incandescent air. And while I am nothing but directed thought, he is shaped by the matter of your mortal world, and in that form he can be destroyed.

"What . . ." whispered Lord Urar Tuan.

He is Mirage, and his true name is Tazzia. Take him, for he is my poor distant brother. Mirage often pretends to be me, and yet Mirage is the one I mock, for he is ruled by the forces of your world, and has little control over his manifestations.

But now, you've changed that. You have given him a ridiculous mortal form, and anchored him in the corporeal reality by the very nature of your being. Behold!

And as the voice of Illusion spoke and was somehow heard by all, a third equine shape began to shimmer into being at the center of the fire.

He was translucent at first, and then his hide acquired the gleam of mother-of-pearl and his mane and tail streamed incandescent white in the flames. He shook his head and neighed in amazed protest, and then stepped out of the flames and onto the white desert sands.

"No!" cried Lord Urar-Tuan, "This is not what I want! I must have you, Illusion!"

In a manner of speaking, it is exactly what you have, said the mocking divine voice, as the blue Illusion-stallion began to fade. *Enjoy Tazzia, foolish mortal. Torment him to your heart's content, and thus give me my pleasure. Because now you are fully mine, and in your final hour I will come for you to lead you into the ultimate Illusion. . . .*

And Lord Urar-Tuan howled once again, this time in fury, and he struck the beautiful creature Tazzia on its fair noble head. And the divine horse of mother-of-pearl cried out in pain, yet could do nothing but stand before him in shock.

Egiras turned away and began walking to the caravan. She did not watch her father call for ropes and roughly harness and bridle Tazzia, nor did she care to see that the fire continued to burn unattended, and in it still stood the golden mare of flames—an empty husk of illusion and her own drops of blood, on the border between existence and dissolution.

"How do you like the story?" said Zuaren, as the moon began to dip to the horizon. "I tell it well, and the telling inflames my blood also, to be reminded of this. For, as I serve Lord Urar-Tuan, every moment I spend with Tazzia I have to pretend cruelty. That is his way with Tazzia, and he expects no less of his hirelings. He has no use for Tazzia—he cannot sell him nor make him do his bidding nor even gain pleasure from his divine beauty. But he can cause it pain and delude himself that it is the Lord of Illusion and not Mirage that he tortures in useless revenge. . . ."

Nadir sat thinking in silence. He thought of Tazzia dissolving in the cold of night unto eternity, and yet unable to, and of its pain. He thought of this man before him, a soldier-guard who was yet oddly merciful and wanted justice.

Or did he?

Should Nadir believe this one, this Zuaren?

Who was he, in truth? What did he want?

And yet what did it matter, thought Nadir, when he had no other real choice but to accept his words. At least this one offered him a promise—he would help him get the cup back somehow.

As though Zuaren could read his mind, he said, "Now, remember what I told you earlier, that I would help you regain what is yours, what has been taken away from you?"

"Yes. . . . But how would you do that?"

Zuaren drew close to him, and suddenly grinned. "Tomorrow," he whispered. "You will see. But in return you must do something for me."

"What?" Nadir asked suspiciously.

"You will know it when I ask you, and not any earlier."

"But—"

"If you cannot do this, then admit it now, boy. I will not hold you to anything. We part our ways, and you pretend I never told you any stories."

"Why are you so eager to help me? How do I know you will not rob me and take the cup for yourself, just like the Lord Urar-Tuan?" said Nadir, his eyes intense. "How do I know anything? Why should I believe anything you say, or trust you?"

"To tell you the truth, I don't know. Why should you trust me indeed?" Zuaren said, pulling back and taking another bite of bread, and then opening a flask of water to wash it down.

And then he pointed at the horizon and at the moon, which was almost hidden away. "My turn for the night watch is coming up, little man. I need to go and wake Grego, so that I can officially tell him to go back to sleep, and then, as soon as he does, I can get some sleep myself. Tazzia will not go anywhere, not in his condition, nor is he able to, because of the Binding. The only reason the Lord has us guard him is so that other idiots do not attempt to steal him. It has happened before. If it happens again, it will only wake everyone up, since Tazzia cannot venture more than one hundred feet from Urar-Tuan without beginning to scream in pain like a divine minion of hell."

Nadir listened to this with interest.

"Why don't you sleep now, boy, and think of what I've told you? Tomorrow let me know what you decide. But once you promise, there is no turning back. You will do what I say when I tell you."

Nadir nodded, and then got up in silence. He crept in the darkness back to his pack-beast and fell asleep soon after, curled up in an old cotton blanket on the bare cold sands.

The next day, as the brilliant sun rejuvenated the desert, Nadir had made up his mind. There was something about Zuaren that he did not quite trust, something peculiar that made him pause in doubt.

As he passed the Lord's great tent and saw once again the iridescent creature Tazzia which he now considered only in pity, and then saw the pale-eyed guard's handsome face, he hesitated.

Nadir stood impassive as Zuaren greeted him and winked at him. And then Nadir said one word only. "No." With that he turned away.

I will get the cup back myself, he thought. *I will do it my own way.*

When the heat grew more intense and it was nearly noon, Nadir came up to one of the merchant caravans, leading behind him his pack-beast.

"I want to sell this animal," he said to the old bearded man, dressed in fine cotton, who stood next to a number of beasts herded in an enclosure of wagons. There were camels and dromedaries, and some mules and donkeys, not to mention some small wiry ponies. They were being readied for auction. All were full-bodied, with glistening hides and brushed manes and tail-hair. Some had been sold already.

The old man took one look at Nadir's pack-beast, and then back at Nadir, and said, "What? Are you crazy, boy? What have you got there, an ancient donkey or a pony? This creature is useless to me. It is too old, with a poor skin condition, and I could never resell him to anyone."

"What would he be worth then, sir?"

The old man began to laugh. "What would you pay me to take him off your hands?"

And Nadir turned away sadly and walked slowly back to Lord Urar-Tuan's tent.

"What now, boy?" said Lord Urar-Tuan, watching the dark glitter of Nadir's intense eyes.

Inside the tent it was cool and dark, and the Lord's chiseled face was in shadow.

"I have brought back your gold coins, my Lord," Nadir said. "All except one. Please take them back and give me back my cup. I will work as much as needed to repay you the one coin that I have used and cannot return."

Lord Urar-Tuan considered him. And then he said thoughtfully, "If something different had not happened overnight, I would not even be listening to you now. But it did happen. My daughter Egiras tells me that wooden cup of yours has gone dry. She woke up, and it stood near her pillow completely empty—nothing but dry old wood."

"What? What do you mean?" Nadir said.

"Yes, very peculiar," said the Lord. "It seems that the cup worked its miracle only for you, or merely when it was in your presence—if it ever did. And now that I think about it, I wonder if the whole thing was not a trick to swindle me out of some gold coins, eh, boy? Was that water trick just some illusion work?"

"No, my Lord!" said Nadir in outrage. "It was all real! The cup saved my life in the desert! Oh, please, I must have it back!"

"Very well," said Lord Urar-Tuan unexpectedly. "Now, give me back my gold—all twelve coins. And you can have it."

"Here are all but one. . . ." Nadir handed the Lord the silk pouch.

Lord Urar-Tuan shook his head, as he accepted the pouch and hid it in his clothing. "Then you owe me one gold coin. Until you repay it, that wooden trinket is mine."

"I will work for you, my Lord!" exclaimed Nadir, bowing his head in gratitude. "I will do whatever you require!"

And then Lord Urar-Tuan smiled darkly. "Good boy," he said. "I knew there was a reason I liked you. Well then, I need no more cooks or servants, nor any other domestic hires, for now. Therefore, your task is to be my daughter's obedient companion and plaything for seven days or so while we travel the desert toward the East. My Egiras gets lonely and bored when she has no one to play with, and on this journey she has had no adequate companions. You are the only one near her age, so you will do well."

"Oh . . ." Nadir said. As the Lord was speaking this, he began to feel a sudden cold rise inside of him, a clamoring dark fear, a sense of impending fate.

And when it was over, because he had no other choice that he could think of, he slowly nodded in acquiescence.

"Excellent," said the Lord. "Now go on, and keep her well entertained." And then, just before Nadir had turned to do as he was told, Lord Urar-Tuan added, "But remember, boy, if she complains about anything, our agreement is nullified and I keep the cup."

Hearing that, Nadir went still and felt his insides drain of all emotion, becoming like stone.

L ike her father, Egiras was an excellent tormentor—maybe even more so. Nadir had learned it after no more than half an hour in her presence.

Egiras, the pretty porcelain doll, had her own cozy little room inside the great tent. Delicately painted cloth divider walls were put up to create partitions. The floor was lined with bright rugs, and there were jeweled trinkets and pillows strewn everywhere.

"You," said Egiras, barely able to speak the tongue of the desert peoples. "Pick up!" And she pointed at all the items on the floor, all the while staring at Nadir with a frown.

The boy glared back at her and then immediately remembered that he was supposed to be an obedient companion. Besides, he knew that his cup was somewhere among her things, and he had to know its whereabouts even though he would not try to take it, being peculiarly honor-bound.

Thus, swallowing his pride and casting his gaze downward, he started to pick up the sparkling items on the floor, and to straighten the pillows and rugs.

He was done in less than five minutes, while Egiras sat on a pillow in the corner, like a little queen, and picked at her tiny painted nails, watching him work from underneath the pearl fringe of her headdress.

As Nadir stood aside, she got up and made a great show of looking closely at the neatness of his handiwork. And then she stomped her little foot and screamed, and started to throw all her jewelry and pillows, so that once again the room was a disaster.

Nadir watched her in silent horror.

"You!" screamed Egiras. "Pick up!"

Nadir's jaw fell open, and he clenched his fists. But then again he looked down, thinking, *Ris, Grandmother! Help me, forgive me, for I deserve this, having taken gold in exchange for water.*

Gold for water. . . .

And he began to perform the thankless task once again, in silence.

For two days Nadir had been for all practical purposes a slave of Egiras. She had forced him to do ridiculous tasks and to run errands for her, so that the boy did not have a moment to sit down. Nadir had been sent to fetch fruits for her from the vendor, and when he came back with a large bowl of succulent dates, Egiras tasted one, scrunched up her evil doll-face, and threw the rest on the ground outside the tent.

Then Egiras was in the mood to play, and she took out her colored semi-precious rocks and a delicate game board of sandalwood trimmed with ivory. Nadir was shown, with many gestures and many uses of the words "no, idiot" in his language, the basic rules. He went through the moves in sullen resignation, and when Egiras won the first time, she laughed in sheer pleasure, but when she won the next time and the next repeatedly, she started to frown and chattered angrily in her tonal language. Finally, when he lost yet another time, she screamed like a wild carrion bird and slapped Nadir on the cheek, raking him with her sharp little nails and leaving a bleeding mark and an imprint of her metal rings on his dark skin.

Nadir's eyes were murkier than night with intensity, and yet he did not move or flinch, and continued to stare in front of him.

Unfortunately, this made Egiras even more angry, and she struck him again and threw the game pieces at him in a sparkling jewel shower. And then she got up, her mood changing mercurially, so that she was suddenly remote like ice.

"Go . . ." she hissed, and pointed to the exit.

And Nadir could do nothing but obey—until he was called back again the next time.

As he ran about on his various sorry errands, Nadir would pass occasionally near the place outside where Tazzia was tethered, and he would catch the fleeting gaze of Zuaren's pale eyes. It seemed the man laughed at him now.

Or maybe it was only Nadir's broken remnants of pride.

In the evenings and mornings, Nadir was sent to eat with the servants, and that was his only time of peace. He would eat hungrily, shaking with stress and exhaustion, and occasionally would feel Zuaren's piercing gaze on him.

It seemed the guard was waiting.

After the evening meal Nadir had to return for another two hours or so to entertain the little wicked monster. Egiras had an odd ability not to sleep, or at least never seem to be tired, while the boy would be barely able to keep his eyes open. Finally Egiras got tired of his dullness, and she sent him off to sleep, in disgust.

As Nadir crept to his usual place outside near the large tent, he saw a shadow move, and then recognized the form of Zuaren.

The guard came before him, emerging suddenly out of the thick night like a peculiar god, it seemed, rather than a mortal man. Or so it appeared to Nadir, who was possibly hallucinating in exhaustion.

"How are you surviving, little man?" whispered Zuaren. "Maybe now you have changed your mind? Is your answer still 'no,' or do you want your cup back and to be free of your fate?"

"You . . ." whispered Nadir in return. "I don't know. I—"

"All you have to do is a very little thing. Come now, boy, do it for yourself, for me, and for Tazzia. . . ."

And in the cold darkness of the desert night, Nadir frowned, torn with indecision. Torn, and he did not even know exactly why.

Finally, after an eternity had come full circle in his mind, or a mere blink of an eye, Nadir nodded tiredly.

"Yes," he said. "I will do it. I hate her so much that I will do it. But only if you tell me what you plan to do. I do not trust you."

Zuaren grinned. "I am glad, boy," he said. "You can trust me or not, but I will indeed tell you, and thus reassure you that it is a harmless but clever thing that I plan."

"Go on . . ." said Nadir. "But hurry, for I am so tired that I will fall asleep before you are done."

"Tomorrow, at the height of noon, for that is the time that Tazzia is at the height of his powers, when the heat is greatest over the sands, and the air swims thickly—tomorrow, you will manage to get near Lord Urar-Tuan's tray of midday food. I want you to take a tiny snippet of powder from this bag, as little as would fit on the tip of your nail, and drop it in his drink."

Nadir began to frown, but Zuaren put his hand up, saying, "No, it is not what you think, it is not a poison, boy. I would never ask you to kill anyone on my behalf. Rather, it is simply a substance that will relax his muscles and pattern of thought, so that I can break his Bond to Tazzia."

"Why can't you do it yourself? Why must I do it?"

"Ah, it's a complicated thing, little man," said Zuaren. "I cannot do it myself because Lord Urar-Tuan is so powerful in sorcery that he could possibly learn my plan for Tazzia when he *sensed* my touch upon his drink, and I cannot risk that. But if you do it, he would sense only you, and it would throw him off sufficiently, for in his pride he does not think much of you, much less think you capable of deceit."

"It's true," Nadir said. "I don't like deceit, and I don't want to do this dishonorable thing."

Zuaren smiled. "I thought you disliked Egiras even more than deceit. What will it be?"

The boy frowned but said nothing.

"Now then," continued Zuaren. "Once that infernal sorcery is broken, Tazzia will be free to go, and no ropes will be able to hold him at that point. You, in turn, can simply take your cup from the little bitch's quarters—since after all that drudgery you owe her father nothing—and the two of us can travel through the desert far away from here."

"Sounds much too easy," muttered Nadir. "How will you break the Bond?"

"Ah, you must leave that to me."

And with that, Zuaren slipped away into the night.

Nadir woke just after dawn, trembling. He forced himself to rise, quickly ate in the servants' tent, and then presented himself before Egiras, who was awake already and looking bright and animated as always. His first task of the day was to collect cactus flowers for her, since it was time for many varieties to bloom, and this would occupy him well until noon.

As the sun scaled the dome of heaven and positioned itself straight overhead, Nadir found some pretense to end up in the kitchen tent near the tray that was being sent up to Lord Urar-Tuan. Since he had had the chance to observe this for a number of days now, Nadir knew exactly how the food tray was assembled.

When the goblet was placed and filled with cool drink, Nadir asked the servant some question to distract him, and then edged so that he could stand just in the right place. His fingers had been holding a pinch of the powder for so long that they had grown stiff with tension, and when he finally let go of it he was more than relieved to notice a nearly translucent substance immediately sink and dissolve into the dark liquid.

And then his luck doubled.

"Since you're here, boy," said the servant, "take this tray up to Lord Urar-Tuan, before it gets cold."

"Yes . . ." whispered Nadir, and had to lower his gaze to hide his eagerness.

Clutching the tray with more care than he had ever given anything, Nadir walked slowly into the great tent, and then placed the tray on the small table near Lord Urar-Tuan's private quarters. He lingered just long enough to see the Lord come out and sit before the midday meal tray, and take the goblet in his hands, then raise it to his lips for a long draft.

And then Nadir slipped out of the tent and walked by the place where Tazzia stood in expectant silence. Tazzia's eyes were violet and intense.

It was as though Tazzia knew their plans.

As he walked past Zuaren, Nadir made eye contact and nodded briefly. Zuaren understood only too well.

"Wait a little, then go get it . . ." he whispered. "Then return here."

And Nadir was on his way.

He sat in the back of the tent, his heart racing so loudly, internal waters running so swiftly in his temples, that he could not hear the wind nor feel the heat of the sun for the cold inside of him. He sat and counted his fingers, over and over. And then he arose and slipped into the Lord's tent, and made his way into the little quarters of Egiras.

He knew exactly where she kept the cup. It was inside the small wooden chest where she put all her trinket toys, and which he'd had to clean and organize on a regular basis. Why had he not tried to take it before? It was an odd stubborn sense of honor inside him that had made him leave it be, as though a debt on his part had not been paid—more than just a debt of a single gold coin.

But now, things were different somehow. Urgency was in his mind—and yet he was cold, oh so cold—and nothing mattered any longer.

Luck was still with him, because Egiras was not in the room. Nadir took the cup—dry and brittle indeed—with his trembling fingers, and he hid it in the folds of his poor clothing, near his heart.

And then, at the same instant that he felt its soothing familiar touch upon his skin, there came a horrible human scream from the inside of the tent, from somewhere *else*.

It was the voice of Egiras. He could never mistake it, the hateful screech, for he knew it like his own breathing now, knew and hated it. . . .

And yet, this time there was something different.

For Egiras was crying not like a mindless beast, but with true intense anguish, with a piercing agony that tore through Nadir and reached all the way to his soul.

Without a moment of doubt, Nadir raced. He tore around the corner, went past the many room partitions as other servants came running from all directions, and was soon in the main area of the tent, in the Lord's quarters.

In the corner near the food table, Egiras kneeled before the upturned form of Lord Urar-Tuan, her father. Her face was inhuman, a roil of tears, and she was keening in a voice of madness.

And as Nadir drew closer he saw a pool of blood had gathered around the motionless body of the Lord, and was seeping from a small but deep and masterfully precise gash directly in the left side of his chest, in his heart.

Lord Urar-Tuan was dead.

And at the same time from the outside of the tent came a great neighing sound, a divine *voice* screaming in exultation.

Nadir's mind spun in a horrible cold void, and he walked quickly outside, past the running horrified servants, and paused before the sight of Zuaren cutting Tazzia's last rope.

There was a feral, different look in the man's pale eyes, and a few steps away Nadir saw the slumped dead form of Grego, also stained with blood, and stabbed in the chest with equal precision.

"Murderer!" cried Nadir. "What have you done!"

Zuaren threw him a sideways glance, saying, "Are you daft, boy? What did you think I'd do? How else to break a Bond that can only be broken by death? I killed the monster Urar-Tuan, as he deserved. And now you have your precious cup of Ris. So you can either come with me as we had planned, or you can scram to hell for all I care!"

"You murdering liar!" said Nadir. "I will not let you go!"

"What will you do, little fool?"

"I will stop you!"

In reply, Zuaren laughed. He took hold of Tazzia's shining mane, and cut the last of the harness, and the equine form was now free.

"No one can stop me now," he hissed, patting its lovely neck. "Forgive me, Lord Tazzia, for hurting you even under a pretense."

I forgive you and thank you, mortal! replied a sudden deep voice of scalding wind, and Tazzia spoke in their minds, as all gods do.

"Do you know who I am?" said Zuaren to Nadir.

And as the boy watched in terror, he demonstrated. Three of Lord Urar-Tuan's men came running from the tent, armed with swords. But before any of them could strike a blow, Zuaren moved like lighnting, and then two swords sprang forth from his hands also. He cut and pierced with both hands simultaneously, and retracted his blades within an instant—so quickly that one man was down immediately, bleeding profusely as he fell. The other two men attacked from both sides, but were repelled immediately, and, one after the other, followed the first one's fate. All were stabbed in the same methodical way.

"Assassin!" whispered Nadir. "I have seen such moves only from the best, back in the great city! What are you doing here? Why pretend to be a guard?"

"I was sent here to destroy Urar-Tuan, and I have succeeded," replied Zuaren. "Now you know me, boy. Do you still want to stop me? Do you think you can?"

"Yes!" cried Nadir. "I can and I will!"

And Zuaren laughed again. "Maybe," he said. "You are brave, little man, and you have a bright heart. Maybe you will, someday."

And then, surprisingly, Zuaren leaped and pulled himself over the iridescent horse's back. Tazzia did not protest, and instead immediately accommodated his rider.

I will remain in this shape long enough to take you to the City, mortal, said Tazzia. And then he turned his horse's head to look intensely at Nadir.

And you, my child, I thank you also. But you I cannot take. You must stay behind and fulfill your fate.

And with that the horse the color of mother-of-pearl bounded forward and was suddenly ten feet above the ground, and then above the trees, rising like a burst of hot air. On his back sat the pale-eyed assassin with the grin of ivory teeth.

Like a burst of living flame, a moving illusion, they receded. . . .

Nadir did not linger to look back at the dissolved mirage. Instead, he turned and stepped over the fresh bodies to enter the dead Lord's tent.

Inside, there was panic and mayhem. Egiras was surrounded by a dozen servants, and a physician had been brought in, but obviously nothing could be done for the murdered Lord.

"It is her fault . . ." came some low whisperings. "She killed her own father! We know her kind, the little witch!"

"Leave her alone," spoke others. "She is but a poor child, orphaned now. . . ."

"No, she must be guilty!" others retorted. "Did you know that Lord Urar-Tuan was nearly invincible? No assassin could have taken him this easily. Obviously he must have been drugged to dull his sorcerous reflexes. For the Lord could fight like a demon. And who else but the little witch could have drugged him?"

"Nonsense," said the old physician. "The Lord is dead, and it is too late to speculate what killed him. Leave the poor child in peace, for look how she grieves."

But suddenly among the tumult—before there could be any more suspicions or accusations of anyone—Egiras raised her contorted little face and cried out one word, "Tazzia!" And she pointed with her hand outside. And soon enough, others came into the tent to report multiple murders outside and the missing magical horse creature.

And in the ensuing greater panic, Nadir stood like an island. The guilt of silent responsibility weighed heavily on his shoulders, for he had been the one who had drugged Lord Urar-Tuan, and thus precipitated this whole tragic end.

And yet, was it tragic? Certainly not for Tazzia.

Or was it fate? Certainly it was, for Nadir.

And Nadir came forward then, humbled and cold and dead on the inside. Egiras had been once again forgotten as everyone was now outside, looking for the assassin among the many caravans of the oasis.

Egiras sat crouching in the corner, with the vacant eyes of a wild animal. When Nadir came down on his knees and leaned forward to touch her on the shoulder, she started, then glared at him with eyes of evil.

Nadir sensed that she knew.

He reached out and took the wooden dry cup full of nothing but air. And with a load of unrelieved guilt, he surrendered it back to Egiras, placing the empty wooden object in her cold palms.

Egiras stared at the heartless thing in her hands, then took a good aim and threw it hard against the wall of the tent.

The cup struck something hard, maybe a ground pole of the tent. And yet it did not shatter, being simple wood. It lay there, rolling about, then went still and silent, and Nadir did not look at it, putting it out of his mind, for it was no longer his to have or to give or to regret.

"I will help you . . ." he whispered to Egiras. "I promise, before all the gods, before Ris. . . . While you need someone, while you are alone, I will never leave your side. I know you do not understand my language yet, do not know what I say, and thus I can say this. Forgive me. I will serve you now, in truth, and honor."

"Idiot . . ." said Egiras, like a cold serpent, never blinking, looking into the boy's ebony eyes. It was one of the few words she knew, but Nadir was not sure what else she understood.

And really, it did not matter.

He had Bound himself, as surely as anyone, without any magic or power, and merely by the promise of an honest word.

His only witness was the fiery wind blowing from the East of the Compass Rose.

Dream Six

Shimmering Scythe

It is rumored in the lands of the Compass Rose that death is a chameleon. But in truth that is not so. For death is, has been, and always will be forthright.

It is only death's scythe that shimmers. . . .

The man ran.

I saw a glimpse of him as I rang the midnight copper bowl while walking slowly along the curving street of my route.

He, the man, was cloaked in deep indigo, his outlines blurred into an illusion of metal created by the moon and motion. And he was moving as infernally fast as the shadow form directly following him. They ran, always equidistant, neither one human in my reckoning. First they moved along the cobblestones of the street just ahead of me, then, like sudden upswept gusts, they were up on the rooftops, barely skimming the shingles, jumping from one housetop to another, lighter than cats.

Another heartbeat and they were gone.

And that was that.

No, I never drink on my route. I promise you I did see them both, and they were none other than death and the thief who stole its scythe.

And damn you if you don't believe me. Ask any other night guard in this great city, for these two are a rather common sight.

In a nameless tavern belonging to Belta Digh, the roof of which was inlaid in fine glazed cedar wood, and the sign of which was but two unknown glyphs, people gathered to drink and tell stupid tales. At least, Belta felt they were rather idiotic after cups of her usual brew had made the evening rounds.

Belta Digh was a giant middle-aged woman, once a stranger to this city but now quite a landmark herself. What would these fools do every night without Belta's tavern and potent drink? And what other tavernkeeper would have the heart, not to mention the muscle clout, to personally drag one home after a long night?

"I saw death last night, chasing the thief," said a solid woman guard, dropping in after sundown.

"What else is new?" Belta lifted one dark eloquent brow as she arranged rows of newly washed mugs behind the counter.

"What I don't get is, why would any man want to tangle with death itself?" said someone.

"Possibly because he is a half-wit?" put in Belta.

"But even more curiously, why doesn't death catch up with him once and for all?"

"Aha!" spoke up Belta again. "But the thief has the scythe. It gives him a measure of death's own powers, and allows him to keep just enough ahead to remain out of reach. Or so I've heard."

"You've heard? Who told you, Mistress Digh?" they all clamored.

"Why, death itself, of course. Believe it or not, upon occasion it also visits this tavern."

S eert ran. The darkness of the night flew by, stars spinning out of their celestial sockets, edges of clouds torn asunder by the accompanying winds that arose on both sides of him.

Always, that hiss of air, all around, and the universe spinning.

And always, that relentless shadow only fifty feet behind him.

Death.

He had learned its smell, could recognize it now, like a hound. And yet Seert continued running, clutching in his hands a fine slim crescent of silver metal—unknown metal, to tell the truth. He had never had time to slow down, to look closely at the impossible perfect thing in his hands, at its razor edges, fine like rice paper, and its surface, like rose petals. . . . Deceptive.

He had not slowed down for one moment, ever since that day—or was it night?—that moment when crouching by *her* deathbed he had waited for the soft breath of the shadow, waited until death grew prominent. And then, as it leaned over *her* pale sweet dying brow, then he pounced forward with a cry of madness and took hold of the crescent blade that had drawn just near *her* soft slender throat. . . .

He tore the scythe blade off its handle, and in that moment his fingers bled, for he had cut himself.

Why did he not die then? Maybe because he fathomed the mystery, the truth of it.

This scythe had not been meant for him. Thus, it would not harm him.

But yes, like all sharp things cutting skin, it made him bleed, and what came softly from his vein was pale and colorless, and unlike what he'd expected—for by touching the scythe he had been changed. Thus for an instant he looked down upon his barely stained fingers, and wondered madly if indeed vapor had always run in him, not blood. . . .

But no, he remembered. It was merely apathy, death trying to paralyze him in that moment of insolence. And the thought of blood made him remember *her* name, the name of the woman who had lain dying, and now would not.

The ancient meaning of the woman's name was "blood," Ahiroon.

And he was on the run now, and always would be, because of her.

"One cool evening," Belta Digh said, "a tall stranger came into my tavern."

"Who was he?"

"Not he. A woman. She was as tall as me but thin. And I never got a chance to see her eyes, only the silver sheen of her skin. Well, death has no eyes, they say. But death does appear to drink a mug or two."

The listeners made avid noises of appreciation, and Belta continued with her tale.

The strange woman, it appeared, had come in for but a moment, planning to drink her mug and leave. But something cozy about Belta's establishment, not to mention the pungency of her brew and the lateness of the hour, made the stranger linger, and finally spill her own unbelievable confession.

The woman was death. And death, cursed ages ago by the goddess Risei-Ailsan, had been robbed of a certain scythe. The potent curse of Ris caught up with her at last, and this scythe was taken by a young man, crazed by tragedy and an overabundance of love for a young dying woman. And because of the nature of it, now the young woman would never die, and death could never catch up with the young man, were she to chase him until the end of the world.

There were oohs and aahs of awed wonder, as the listeners settled in closer to hear Belta Digh's mesmerizing voice.

"Poor death . . ." someone said.

But then someone else boxed the first speaker on the ear.

"Poor nothing!" said Belta. "Poor us! Woe to us all! For while death has many scythes, one for each and every one of us, only our own scythe can bring our blessed end. We will all continue dying in our own time—that has not been changed. However, by withholding that one young woman's scythe, the whole world will be delayed in the final accounting hour. Or so said death to me."

"Seert! Stop running. Seert . . . Let me speak to you!"
He heard death's cries continuously in his head now, memorized the very timbre of her haunting voice.

And he ignored it firmly, while his legs continued pumping, endlessly, tirelessly, as he skimmed lightly over the earth.

How much time had gone by, he did not know. And in truth it no longer mattered. He had ceased feeling anything, lost track of his very pulse, the feeling of breath being drawn.

There was only that wan razor-sharp crescent of unknown metal, held firmly between his fingers. . . .

That, and the knowledge that Ahiroon would live now, forever.

"Seert!"

The eternal shadow was just behind him. He could see the billowing edges of its cloak, rolling in the wind like storm clouds racing upon the sky.

He turned his head, and deliberately laughed, his mouth open into the wind, laughed at it. There.

"Seert. . . . You, whose name in the ancient tongue means an intense loyal heart. . . ."

Death's voice continued, pleading with him softly, always pleading.

"Don't you know that you also will never die now? And yet neither will you live. Only continue running from me. . . ."

He ignored her, his arms pumping back and forth in a rhythm of magic, while the world around blurred with motion.

"And neither will *she* live, truly, the woman you love . . ." whispered death. "It was her time, and her body had been wrecked with illness. Give her peace, Seert! Both of you are only deluding yourselves and postponing the inevitable!"

"Shut up, dark Hag!" he exclaimed. "Nothing you'll ever say will change my mind. I will run thus until the universe falls around me! If that is what it takes to buy life for my Ahiroon!"

In answer, death once again moaned sadly, and continued calling out his name.

Somewhere in the part of the city where gold was not uncommon, a bedroom window was opened to the sweet air of night, and orange candlelight streamed out like a fan of brightness.

Death came into this bedroom softly, and leaned over the shoulder of a pale emaciated young woman, propped up by a mountain of pillows and reading a thick old book.

"Ahiroon . . ." whispered death.

"Why hello again, pathetic Hag," said the young pale woman in a strong living voice, raising but one brow archly, and continuing to read.

"At least look at me, Ahiroon!" said death sadly.

The young woman put down her book, and then looked up with exasperation. "What now?"

Death sighed, then took in the appearance of the young woman. "You look very thin and pale, Ahiroon. Skin and bones. Have you been eating, at least?"

"And what is it to you?" the young woman snapped at her. She then lifted an extremely bony wrist and with surprising strength yanked death painfully by the vaporous hair.

"There," said Ahiroon. "How do you like that, ugly Hag? Do you realize I can do anything to you now, and you could never do anything to me? How does it feel to have the tables turned, for once? Oh, and would you like a cup of tea?"

"Tea will be fine, thank you," said death, settling down at the woman's bedside while Ahiroon rang for a servant. "Yet this is all an illusion, Ahiroon, you must realize. Your strength is not real. Your poor ill flesh has been frozen in a moment of time, that is all, and you will never again get better."

"Hrumph!" said Ahiroon.

"Would you like to spend eternity in this bed, reading books?" continued death. "Seeing endless sunsets and dawns and afternoons displace each other until boredom eats you alive? Your cheeks will never be pink again, and your eyes, lovely though they are, will be forever glassy. The hands that lie on the coverlet will always shake slightly as you turn the pages. You will always rely on others to help you walk even a few steps. Is it worth it, to exist like that?"

"There'll be time to read a million wonderful books," said Ahiroon with a shadow of a smile. "More books than any single person in history has ever read or will read. I will read them all!"

"And what then? After the last book is written, then read, and the world comes to an end, what will you do with your existence?"

The servant came in bearing an aromatic pot, and Ahiroon personally poured a cup for her unwelcome visitor.

Death swallowed a bit, then moved a shadow lock from her pale grand forehead. "Ahiroon. . . . Don't you feel sorry for poor Seert? He loves you so much that he has in all effect given up the rest of his own existence. Even now, he is running from another manifestation of me, holding tight your scythe. He stole it to give you life, and yet you can never be together, you and he. . . ."

For the first time, Ahiroon put down her own cup and stared at death, a kind of intensity beginning to brim in her glassy eyes.

"Once again, I ask you to reconsider . . ." said death softly.

"Never!" exclaimed Ahiroon, with more angry passion than death thought her capable of.

"At least have pity on him, the one you love! For love of you, he cannot and would not stop running!"

And then Ahiroon began to laugh. A terrible wheezing sound, as from an animated corpse. "I, *love* him? I? I never said I wanted to be with him, not for a moment!" exclaimed the young woman, laughing wildly. "I simply want to live, and he— the fool who can't take no for an answer—he wants to love me! A great arrangement, I say! Let him love me and run for all eternity! Don't you understand, Hag, that I just want to be free? Free of him, free of you! Not to be loved, but to be *free,* and to be my own!"

Death stared in sudden quiet understanding at the young woman. Stared at her blazing glassy eyes, her trembling hollow cheeks, her mass of cobweb hair. . . .

"Very well . . ." said death then, and was gone.

And Ahiroon, whose name meant blood, was left laughing hysterically, book forgotten, pale and bloodless as the sheets beneath her.

"What a terrible young woman, this Ahiroon!" several exclaimed, while Belta poured another round and collected their coins.

"And what a noble loyal youth, this Seert! No wonder his name stands for 'heart.'"

"Yes, well . . ." mumbled Belta Digh. "I'd hold back judgment, if I were you."

"What happened then, Mistress Digh?"

And Belta told them the rest of her tale.

"What happened? Why, death was so unsettled by this turn of events that she again came to my tavern. And I, of course, gave her advice. Very simple, I told the silver-skinned one. Once and for all, you need to stop chasing the thief."

Seert ran through the blazing golden desert. Straight ahead, the disk of the sun floated like a great apricot in the liquid honey that was sky. And beneath the soles of his feet air warped, as heat rose from the white sands.

Was it only a mirage, or had the ever-present shadow trailing him disappeared somewhere behind, in the swirling waves of dunes?

And what of the voice? There was now a silence in his mind. And the whispers had quieted into the hum of the wind. . . .

Seert skimmed lightly over the sands, leaving no trace, lighter than the scampering legs of a scorpion. He continued to move into the disk of the sun, and looked behind him once only.

Strangely, he saw nothing.

A trick, he thought. *The devious Hag is playing hide-and-seek with me. What if I oblige her?*

And for the first time, Seert allowed the rhythm of his pumping heart, his flailing limbs, to differ. He slowed down after some time, and suddenly, like a shock, was back in the living cradle of the world.

Desert heat swept over him. The soles of his feet finally made impressions and sank into the sand. Seert walked for some time, stumbling, and then stopped altogether, while sweat ran down his clammy flesh.

He sat down then in the partial shadow of a roving dune, and stared at the bundle clutched in his arms.

In his grasp, the metal claw that was the scythe flashed like a razor in the sun. And as he blinked; once, twice, it shimmered, winking back at him, beckoning like mother-of-pearl.

Honey waves of sunset flowed outside the window. Ahiroon put down the tome of riddles and ancient mysteries, and lifted her wan gaze to see him enter her bedchamber.

"You!" she said.

Seert stood silently before her, his eyes ghosts, and his whole demeanor not much different from that of the Hag.

"I suppose I should thank you," she said. "Idiot that you are. You've bought me precious time."

"Ahiroon . . ." he whispered, his voice hoarse like the desert. "I think I've won. . . . I've outrun her, you know. For you, Ahiroon. . . ."

She looked at him blankly, strangely. "Where is it?"

"The scythe? I still bear it. I'll bear it for you always."

"Give it to me."

"What?"

"I said, give it to me!"

He stared at her in sudden horrible grief. "But—" he said, "If you touch it, you will die, my love!"

"I'll do no such thing, and I'm not your love! Now, give it to me."

"But—"

"If you truly care for me, for once, do this one thing right, Seert! It's the only thing I've ever asked of you!"

And Seert stared at her, tears pooling in the corners of his eyes, muttering, "I looked at the scythe, and things seemed so clear to me then. I thought, if I came back, you'd feel differently. . . . After all that I've done for you, after all that came to pass. I conquered death itself! And for what?"

"Good question," said the emaciated young woman.

And he saw the pale metal of the crescent shimmering in his hands again, and the glaze of her eyes.

"Take it!" he said, while the shimmering came to permeate him. "Take it then, and damn you!"

He reached out to her, and placed the gleaming pale thing right in her lap. It rested there, colors swimming against the pale cotton coverlet next to a book with an old tattered spine. And he turned around then, and was on his way out.

"Thank you, Seert. . . ." Her voice came shadow-soft from behind. "Maybe you do love me, after all. That, I will not forget now."

Hope surged in him, like a sudden waterfall. He turned, eyes igniting, was about to speak, implore once again—

But she lifted her thin bony wrist, and stopped him with one undeniable weakling gesture. "No, no more. Go, gentle heart. Go to your own well deserved peace."

And he knew it was to be thus, at last.

"Is that all?" asked a thoroughly drunk tradesman, hiccuping loudly. "So, did she die in the end, Mist—hic—Mistress Digh?"

"Now, now.... I believe I'll tell you more of this tale another day, good folk," said Belta, seeing many other inebriated eyes, not to mention a goodly stink of belches. "The hour grows late, and I'll be closing the bar now. Off to bed with you all!"

"Oh, you gotta tell the rest, Mistress Digh—"

Their drunken clamor was incredible.

"Closed! Off with you now!" roared Belta, striking the small copper closing bowl that hung on a string near the counter.

And that was that.

Everyone knew the sound of that bowl, and the powerful alto. In about five minutes, the drinking room was cleared, and thankfully no one had to be carried out tonight.

Belta helped a slightly staggering man to the door, the last of the poor idiots, and then shut and locked it firmly behind her.

She then blew out the candles near the window, leaving only the ones burning at the counter, and started to put away the dirty mugs and scrub the place down.

In the corner, a shadow moved.

Belta swung around, her apron splattered, a dish rag in her hand, and then, recognizing the shadow, let out a sigh of relief.

"Ah, it's only you, death. You scared me there for a moment. I almost pelted you! Thought you were old drunkard Givas, who often hides here around closing time. Or, worse, I thought it was the girl, here already...."

"Not yet," said a voice like dusty cobwebs. "It is only I."

"Good," said Belta, and handed death the dish rag. "Then start scrubbing. It'll help you pass the time."

"I am worried . . ." whispered the shadow, taking the rag with possibly trembling silver fingers, and rolling up sleeves of darkness to expose pale wrists, arms and elbows.

"Hrumph! Don't be, I'll take care of it, don't worry," said Belta as she proceeded to clean like she meant business.

Eventually, as they got the tavern in order, there was a knock on the door.

Death and Belta froze simultaneously.

The candles sputtered soft and golden in the silence.

"You realize that I can't lie?" said death. "I never could."

"But I can," retorted Belta. "Now, go sit still, there in the corner."

And she went to open the door.

Ahiroon, pale and staggering like a wraith, entered the tavern slowly. Her eyes burned with an unholy intensity, while her fingers clutched a shimmering blade of unknown silver metal.

"Are you Mistress Belta Digh?" she said in a surprisingly strong voice of passion. "I am here to make a deal with death. Is the sorry Hag here yet?"

"Come in, girl," said Belta, showing her customary robust smile. "Yes, death is here. There, over at that table. But never mind her, you'll be dealing with me."

"Is that so? Then pour me a mug. I've discovered that I can neither die nor get drunk."

After the brew was poured, and everyone settled at different ends of the long table, Belta cleared her throat and began to speak.

"So," she said. "It appears that you, death, and you, my dear Ahiroon, are at a quandary. And I was asked by both parties to mediate between you—glad to oblige, by the way."

"Go on," said the young woman, never glancing at the shadow. "Tell Hag that I have the scythe, here in my hands. And

I know its secret. This scythe in her hands will end my life. But in the name of Risei-Ailsan, in my own it will end *hers,* if she gets anywhere near me! That's the real reason she's so desperate to get it back!"

"You can please talk to me directly, you know. . . ." said death, folding bony silver fingers together in front of her.

"Silence!" snapped Ahiroon. "I choose to have my dealings through Belta."

Silver fingers drummed on the table.

Belta Digh leaned back in her chair comfortably, and took a swig of her own brew. She looked back and forth from one to the other. And then she took another deep swallow, while they waited, death and the young woman, in nervous tense silence.

"Technically speaking," said Belta, "death has no life—no offense—that could be ended. But it does own up to an existence of sorts, will you agree?"

Death nodded, and Ahiroon snorted.

"Then I propose a trade, a standard contract between the two of you. So that death can exist to do her necessary job on all of us—sooner or later, yes—and Ahiroon can go on living until she is old and gray, quite a bit more so than me."

"What?" said death. "You didn't tell me that was part of it!"

"And you promised I could have a go at her with the scythe!" said Ahiroon angrily. "I'd like to chase her down and give her a prick or two before I agree to anything! You promised!"

"Now, now," said Belta. "Simmer down before I box your ears, both of you. Or else, out you go from my tavern, and you can handle this yourselves!"

Silence came quick as anything.

"Now then," said Belta, leaning forward against the table. "There's one thing that only I know about each of you. Death, despite what everyone thinks, is incapable of telling a lie. Hence she is incapable of making a false promise. And you, Ahiroon, my proud intense girl, are also incapable of lying—that's why you were always honest with Seert, up to the very end. Now, knowing that about both of you, it's quite safe for each to trust the other's given word. After you make your mutual promises, Ahiroon will hand me the scythe, and I will pass it on to you, death. And then the two of you will never see each other again for at least forty years. After which you, death, may come to her at last, but gently, so that she'll never know or feel the blade of silver against her neck. . . ."

And, saying that, Belta sat back again, and lifted her mug.

After a long silence, death spoke first. "I promise," the shadow said, "to leave you alone, Ahiroon, until you read five hundred books."

"I read fast," said Ahiroon, looking death boldly in the eyes.

"Then maybe you should slow down and take time for long walks in the garden, and playful afternoons in the spring?" suggested Belta. "It'll put color in your cheeks. Besides, that gives you at least a book a month."

"A thousand," said Ahiroon.

"You drive a bitter bargain. Done," said death softly.

"Well then. I too promise not to harm you, Hag, and to give up my scythe unto your keeping."

And with those words Ahiroon took a big breath and fearlessly offered the curved shimmering blade to Belta Digh.

Looking from one to the other, Belta took the scythe.

Here it comes, she thought, *the moment of truth. Now we'll know for a fact whether death lies. And it's a good thing to know.*

The scythe was a cool rainbow of light in her large palm.

Taking a deep breath, and secretly invoking long-forgotten gods from her distant homeland, Belta reached out and placed the shimmering blade into death's silver fingers.

There came a bright flash.

A shadow sigh. . . .

The candles sputtered and went out, while dark rushed in.

Ahiroon gave a small shriek. And Belta felt her own heart sink, then make a wild jump in her ample breast.

Silence.

After minutes of hammering temples and held breath, Belta finally moved. She got up and by touch only relit a candle.

Death was gone.

Instead, there was a loud hiccup. There she was, Ahiroon, pale as parchment, but grinning, calmly sipping her mug. The young woman was now as drunk, as mortal, and as free as anyone else in Belta's tavern.

A s I make my rounds each night, I admit I no longer see the two shadows, death and thief, racing through the midnight city.

Ah, I sigh, for in that velvet ebony hour, I miss them. There's now one less good tale to tell at Belta Digh's tavern. . . .

They say Belta's tavern finally has a real name. Belta made it known one night, to the inebriated amusement of all.

"Tsaveh Dahnem" she calls it, pronouncing those two foreign symbols that are painted on her sign. What does it mean? I think it means "I take your pain away."

And so she does, our Belta. She can take care of it all, solve your problem, as she pours you a mug and calls you a fool.

Why, even death knows that.

Or, at least, death must surely speak and read her native tongue—all tongues for that matter—as it reads and knows the hour of our parting. Surely, it had recognized the meaning of those glyphs when it first paid its needy visit to Belta Digh's tavern.

Dream Seven

City Of No-Sleep

If you ever get lost, somewhere West of the Compass Rose, look for a city called No-Sleep.

The city is ancient yet young—as each new day is young. And it's filled to the brim with miracles.

But the king here is old and mad like a mangy goat. They say his mind is broken; a fractured mirror, filled with disjointed, ever-changing images, which are his dreams. They reshape the fabric of the city every night.

The old madman spends his waking hours attempting to put together the shards of the mirror in order, and then sleeps erratically, during which time chaos returns to him. And the residents are known to keep themselves awake for as long as possible, so as to delay the inevitable changes, for they come only after sleep's oblivion.

You are welcome to visit this place if you like, to marvel at the wonders.

Only, whatever you do, don't fall asleep here. For, the next time you wake, the city will have rearranged itself.

Ierulann stood above the woman. The woman was prostrated at her feet, groveling, and her tears were watering Ierulann's boots.

"Please forgive me, Guard of Law, grant me mercy! I wouldn't have been driving my wagon so fast if I'd realized I was on the King's Road, for it wasn't here yesterday! And my employer will pay me a pittance for tardiness! I must deliver these goods, or lose my job, and I have children to feed. I beg you not to judge me by the letter of the law! Mercy, just this once!"

"It's true, the King's Road was to be found two and a half leagues to the South of here, last night. But so what? You should've known better than to be late in the first place," said Ierulann impassively, holding her tablet, and about to mark down the woman's name and today's place of residence. Guards would be dispatched there in a hurry to collect the Fine before the King Dreamt and the city was rearranged overnight according to some new chaotic pattern that lived in His mind. A day later the woman's residence might no longer exist, and her meager possessions that now belonged in full to the King wouldn't be there to be collected and deposited in the Treasury. No doubt, these worthless items will likely disappear from that very Treasury again on the morrow—indeed, the woman herself may end up on the opposite side of the city, and her children who knew where else—but that was not the point. The Law was to be upheld.

The woman continued weeping, her sobs turning into dry heaving shudders of desolation. She was one of thousands.

There were so many of them, thought Ierulann, each one often having gone without sleep for days now in a hopeless attempt to curtail the changes. This one's reason was obvious—one of the starving multitudes, she was attempting to keep her family together, but was slipping up due to exhaustion, and had committed the trespass of carelessness.

For everyone knew to drive slowly on the King's Road. It was his earliest—and possibly most irrational—decree, and one he expected to be followed unfailingly. Most people took smaller inconvenient side-streets to avoid the Road wherever it might have popped up that day, and the patrolling Guards of Law such as herself. For no one wanted to crawl along at the speed of fifteen paces a minute. And no one wanted to pay the ridiculous Fine of all of one's life possessions.

Poor sleep-deprived idiot, thought Ierulann, and she jotted down the woman's name.

Beyond that, Ierulann felt no mercy.

Zuaren crawled silently along the edge of the roof of the tallest structure in the city. Vines of verdant hue sprang and wound like snakes on both sides of him. They had grown, clinging to one another all the way from the ground, hundreds of feet, like messengers of the earth straining to convey something vital to the sky.

From way up high as he was, perched dangerously on the edge of the abyss, on top of the world, he could see the whole accursed city illuminated by sunset like a terrible broken jigsaw puzzle, with rich buildings of rose granite intermingled in patches among the pale bleached limestone homes of the rabble poor. He could see chunks of roads and streets doubling upon themselves. He could see alleys ending in cliffs, and houses bursting from hillsides.

All of this would be different, he knew, the next time he closed his eyes in sleep, the next time the sun rose. All he had to do was stay awake long enough to accomplish the deed that he had come here to do.

Soon, he would rid this place of its malediction.

Having dealt with the sad business of the King's Road, Ierulann made her way toward her own austere residence. She walked confidently among the twisting clumps of uprooted and disjointed buildings—their foundations were oddly protruding in places, and patches of varicolored stone hinted at recent displacements—and meandering streets that often turned into dead ends. She had an odd true sense of the nature of the structures around her, and was never really lost in the impossible maze of the city.

That was one of the reasons she had been chosen to be a Guard of Law. Guards preternaturally knew the physical pattern of things in the city in all its fractured disarray. They alone could traverse the city daily and find any given destination with the ease of a hungry dog following the scent of roasted lamb.

Guards were also the elite warriors sworn to protect the very soul of this bizarre place. Ierulann's swordbelt held a fine long blade and a Serpent Whip. She had no fear when walking these streets, for she was possibly the best.

The sun began its golden leavetaking ritual of the night. And now there was another scent in the air of early evening.

Death. . . .

Ierulann absorbed it like a jackal. It plucked her senses, and suddenly a loud heartbeat was born in her temples.

Danger. . . .

She stilled. And then she turned about and rapidly began walking the way she came from, back to the center of the city. Alleys surfaced out of nowhere, and she took turns lightly, predicting their appearance seconds before openings came into view. She moved with her eyelids half-closed and her lips parted to the inrushing air that preceded her.

Something terrifying was about to happen. . . .

And she was the only one who was close enough to stop it. For she felt the pressing of many minds upon her, the entities of other Guards calling into her mind, directing her to move, faster, faster. . . .

Even now the immediate future was unrolling before her, before them all, like a map of this renewing city.

She must reach the Palace which stood higher than all other structures at the heart of this place, and which alone stayed in one place day after day. She must then gain entrance, and come within, and pass through innumerable corridors of marble and walkways trimmed with gold and sandalwood. She must race the final steps to the arched doors of the old king's bedchamber, where even now he was being readied for sleep—an esoteric ritual in itself.

There she must bare her sword and wait, hidden behind a drapery, or in the shadowed corner.

For, when the candles would be extinguished at last, their gentle aromas fading among the musk of precious wood and oils, the old one would sink into immediate slumber, releasing the nightly chaos of mirror-shard images inside.

And at that precise point, someone would come to kill him.

Zuaren dropped down softly, taking on the crouch of a panther, and stayed still beneath the marble overhang of an ornate balcony. Where he was exactly in this place of nightmares, he wasn't sure.

Ahead, several arched windows, opening upon dark chambers. Behind him, an indigo darkening sky.

And yet he needn't guess, for the scent of musk and myrrh was strong here, and all he had to do was follow it in the absolute darkness.

Which he did.

Zuaren moved slowly and silently, having withdrawn a short slim dagger from somewhere on his body. Its blade was dull hueless metal, and sharper than a razor. It would slice cleanly and effortlessly through decrepit flesh and bone. . . .

Moments later, he had passed through a corridor with extinguished torches on the walls, which terminated in a gaping maw of darkness. From beyond closed doors came the strong lingering aroma of incense.

Soon. . . .

Zuaren stilled his heartbeat to the level of a dead man, and his breathing became almost non-existent. Only assassins of the highest discipline could aspire to such living silence.

He placed his fingers on the cool metal and pulled the door handle toward him. Then he slipped within.

Inside, the curtains were drawn over the grand window, letting in minimal glimmers of the night.

Directly ahead sprawled the royal bed. Like a turtle the size of a world it squatted in the sea of shadows, taking up the center of the room.

In the middle of the bed, drowning in silk and pillows, lay a tiny shriveled form.

It was the old king himself.

His breathing came shallow and faint, and ragged upon occasion, as he moved restlessly in the very middle of his fractured Dream.

The feeling of illusory chaotic images of madness was so strong here, nearly overpowering. Zuaren felt them encroaching upon his own mind, clamoring with the great tumult. . . .

Soundlessly he moved closer—so close that he could see the outlines of the shrunken skull of the old king, and the sunken bones around his eyes—and began the measured strike with his dagger.

From behind him he felt another mind, one like his own.

Zuaren whirled around, beginning to leap into a defense-crouch, but it was too late.

A thin coil of agony struck his cheek, slicing him as cleanly as though he'd turned his own razor dagger on himself.

And only an instant later there came the hissing recoil of the Serpent Whip.

"Do not move . . ." came a woman's intense voice. "Drop your weapon by relaxing the grip of your fingers only. Else, you die now."

Zuaren was not a fool. He let go of the dagger so softly that it came down upon the floor like a feather. And he remained frozen, biding his time, recognizing this bitch out of the shadows to be one of the occult Guards of Law.

"Good," she continued. "Now take three steps slowly toward me, away from the King."

In the darkness, he grinned. He knew she would not sound an alarm, for that would take too much of her concentration. She was clever enough to recognize that any extra action on her part could cause the balance between them to topple. . . .

"Move!"

"Why don't you just kill me?" he said then, beginning to pace toward her while speaking for the first time, and his voice was like song. "You know I will not give up so easily, that I will be back to finish this job—"

"I know nothing," she interrupted. "And if you speak another word without being prompted, I will strike you down."

He laughed openly this time. "You will not. For that would be unwarranted, and you are a Guard of Law. Yes, I know your kind very well. . . ."

In answer, he felt lightning strike the other side of his face, as the Whip came cutting down out of nowhere.

Damn, but she moved fast! He had never seen anyone act with such a classic minimum of movement. Almost as good as himself. He stood pondering it while both of his cheeks now screamed with agony.

"You do not know me," she said, like ice.

And that was the moment he took to strike.

Zuaren drove forward like a maelstrom, and out of nowhere two short swordblades snapped open and extended from his hands like angry twins. He lunged forward with both simultaneously, and fully expected her body to crumple under the impossible onslaught. This move had worked with all other opponents over a dozen times.

And yet, she was not there.

As though she had predicted his move before it was even conceived in his mind. . . .

He swung, regaining his balance instantly, and this time saw her lunging shadow. This time his steel met hers with a clang, and they exchanged a lightning volley of hits and parries in the darkness, by preternatural sense alone, then disengaged.

To his wonder, they were perfectly matched.

"Why do you defend the mad one?" he hissed, stepping back, now trying to unbalance her with words. "Why not let me finish him off and rid you and this city of this excruciating curse of madness and mutability?"

"You are an idiot," she replied coldly, and then struck at him again. "You have no idea what you are about to do, and I promise you I will not let you do it."

"Don't you want to be free?" he exclaimed, this time angry in earnest. The execution he had been sent to perpetrate was an issue of perfect justice in his mind. He had been hired to rid the city of madness, and that was what he would do.

"No one is free," she replied then, unexpectedly. "Not even you. Indeed, there is no such thing as freedom. And if you believe there is, then you surround yourself by an illusion greater than this city."

"Why?" he mocked, lunging below her guard on the left. "Will you now tell me that we are all but pieces of the same great mad pattern, akin to this city? That we are all fated by the gods to bear another's madness? That it is our destiny?"

"No," she said, eluding his attack, like an eel. "I will tell you only that there is more to this than you think."

At that moment, there came a moan from the bed, where the old king turned on his side and continued to sleep restlessly. Nothing would wake him now until the dawn, not even the clamor of battle. The sensation of whirling madness came closer than ever to touch the edges of their minds.

Zuaren moved with impossible speed past the woman, and was again at the old one's bedside.

She gasped softly, revealing for the first and only time the true extent of her unease.

"What would happen if I woke him now, before I extinguish his life?" said Zuaren, sensing her sudden fear with his very mind, past the whirling sea of madness.

"Please don't! Harm him and you will regret it . . ." she whispered suddenly, moving in on him from another side, so that she was almost between him and the old king.

Almost, but not quite.

The king moaned again, like a sad old banshee. His form was skeletal in the semi-darkness. And for a moment it seemed to Zuaren that he could see the very Dream surrounding the king like a cloud, a vision of whirling city images, streets sliding apart and coming together like snakes, all striving to enter an almost coherent pattern, and above, a rose-gold sun. . . .

And in that moment a stab of pity entered Zuaren's heart.

But then the assassin slammed the feeling down inside him like a wall, the way he always did.

"No!" cried the woman, while at the same time he struck down with his right blade. . . .

Steel penetrated the ancient flesh, and passed deep inside.

In the cruel dark, the old one made no sound, only a single harshly expelled breath. Even in death, he never woke up.

What came next was chaos.

But, foremost, Zuaren felt terrible blinding agony. . . .

"No!" cried Ierulann, as she felt the weight of minds come slamming down upon her, the storm of madness breaking free at last, no longer contained by the poor husk of the ancient King.

Around her, the darkness howled. The assassin bent forward, the blade still imbedded in the dead one, as though suddenly stricken by a direct bond with his victim.

You must contain it! cried the familiar minds into her own consciousness, straining against passion, against the abandon that was all around them now, ready to swallow up the world.

The outlines of the bedchamber began to grow transparent, to fade in and out of this plane. Curtains blew open on the great window, letting in weak moonlight and a screaming wind.

And suddenly Ierulann saw ghosts of a million cities superimposed like crystals outside the window.

Transparent towers came into focus and were displaced by tall spires and walls of violet marble, obelisks sprang up into the marrow of heaven, only to collapse into sand, structures of pale sandstone and clay spilled and popped like mushrooms after a rain, ancient gilded domes stood up like bubbles of water, globules of dew from a distance.

The vision danced, and times and directions were mixing, and madness was upon her. . . .

Guard of Law! cried the voices of her fellow minds from afar. *Contain the destruction! You must do it, for you are the only one close enough to touch it!*

And Ierulann knew that, if she did not, then the city— indeed, the whole world—would collapse around her into a common Dream of insanity.

And thus she allowed herself to look forward into the future for just an instant longer, using the clairvoyance of her very being to piece together the fabric of things just behind and just ahead of her.

I am the moment. Nothing exists outside of the moment, and the past and the future line up to fall in tandem to precede and follow me.

I am the order and the law.

The madness howled around her tiny point of calm. For an instant, grotesque contorted faces out of hell threw themselves at her, and the walls around the room were gone, while the floor of what had once been the Palace sank and reformed below her feet.

The forms of the man who had killed and the ancient one who had died froze into stone of timelessness upon the Royal bed of firmament, which had once contained pillows and silk coverlets, but now was the surface of an ocean.

Contain the chaos, now, or never!

Even the voices of the minds had grown muffled, and were coming from such a great distance now, receding in the maelstrom.

"How can I?" cried Ierulann desperately in her mind. "How can I hold it and not be overwhelmed, and not myself go mad?"

I am the anchor point of the compass.

And suddenly she saw a second ahead, into the future, and she saw the assassin before her. She saw him from an odd tripled perspective—present, past, and future. His body was strong, his mind vital, and he was young. . . .

And seeing him in temporal chorus thus, Ierulann reached out with her mind, and she drew a part of her being that was cold calm order, and she forced it to come and wrap around the whole city like a great net.

Inward she pulled the madness, forcing it into her and then directly out into *him.*

She moved near him, and took hold of his stilled hand.

His name danced into her mind immediately, with a shock of contact.

Zuaren.

She saw and knew him inside-out, past and present and future.

She knew what he had been, what he was now, and what he could be.

And then Ierulann released the river of chaos, focusing it in a single fixed direction, letting it flow through her fingers into his ice-cold palm, into him. . . .

The one who had once been Zuaren shuddered, opening his intense eyes—pale as water—upon the world of moonlight and swirling homeless dreams, and in they rushed to populate him, their new strong vessel.

The night had grown still all around them. Transparent Palace walls thickened and began to solidify, and once again shut out the outside. But this time there was something solid and definite about their shape, something very new. . . .

Permanence.

Having dropped both his swords, Zuaren stood looking out, past Ierulann, past the walls, and past this reality into the dreams that were now forever anchored within him. And yet the insane spark was barely contained under his strong willful surface.

"What has come to pass?" he said softly. "What am I?"

"You are the new King of this city," said Ierulann, watching his glass-eyes. "It is your Lawful punishment. You who have come in ignorance and death now carry the burden of the Law, which is impassive order and can alone contain chaos. Now at long last we can trust the oblivion of sleep."

"**G**uard of Law!"

Ierulann turned. She was walking slowly along the King's Road, having gone automatically on her morning patrol through the fractured carcass of a city that had somehow stilled, frozen in time—for her senses no longer felt a doubling, a shifting. . . .

The woman from the night before stood a few steps away, dejectedly, holding onto a small sack of belongings.

"Here are all my earthly possessions!" she said. "I've come to deliver them myself, since no one came for them last night, and I want no more punishment. When I woke up, everything was the same as before! Is it not strange? My children are crying with hunger, but at least they are at my side!"

Ierulann watched impassively the joy in her eyes. "Keep your belongings," was all she said. "The new King cares not how fast you drive the Road."

At which point the woman started to weep in a joyful fit, and once again ended up on the ground watering Ierulann's boots. "Law is indeed merciful!" she repeated between her sobs. "Blessed Law!"

Ierulann said nothing, not wanting to spoil this one's last illusion—since there would be none tonight. Law is Law, she wanted to say. It is neither harsh nor merciful, merely new or old. But it is your position in relation to it that makes it deadly or gentle.

I too am like the Law, neither one nor the other.

Or at least I was once. . . .

And then Ierulann yawned deeply, watching the sun of morning ride up over the stilled city. It was time for her to sleep, and, possibly, to dream.

For, she also contained madness now, a tiny bit of it— would harbor it forever under her still surface, secretly helping to share the burden of the one who was now King.

No Law had required her to do that.

The city of No-Sleep is said to be old now, older than the world itself, ever since it stopped reshaping itself every night.

But the king is young here, and sane, and filled with peaceful reason. They say he has cool blue eyes and no memories of his past, sleeps soundly every night, and never dreams at all.

Miracles fill the city, for multitudes are now rebuilding their lives, and the greatest miracle of all, contentment, stands in a cloud above the rooftops.

If you visit, you will surely find something to your liking.

But you must promise to find one woman, once a Guard of Law, now a storyteller. Supposedly, she still owns a sword and a Serpent Whip, and is the only one who can tell you your dreams.

Dream Eight

The Garden, the Wind, and the Gong

The garden seemed to fill the whole world.

Nadir walked through air thick with the perfume of blooming flowers and the moisture of early morning. The dawn mist was fading, settling in the form of dew upon the mosses of earth and the trunks of trees, but visibility was still low. Shapes of green surfaced out of translucence, appearing to float over earth that had no surface, no bottom. And the great mountains in the distance had their tops rubbed off by the clouds, peaks dissolving into the silver darkness of heaven.

Nadir followed a narrow path toward the ornate structures of the ancient monastery that had been built upon the uneven ground. Parts of it were upraised on a hill—concave curving rooftops with shingles painted in deep jewel tones and encrusted with gold leaf, with sharp spires raised in the center—others lower down, and a great wide staircase lay winding up along the verdant slopes of the hill toward the pinnacle. At the pinnacle of the hill, at the foot of the ghost mountains that blended into heaven, was the Secret Temple of ancient wisdom that he sought.

And within that Temple was the world's truth.

Nadir was tall and strong, a young man with a straight back, carrying himself with the sureness of a warrior, and yet treading softly like a panther. His skin was dark as rich, newly watered earth, not because of exposure to the sun but because such was the color of his race.

There was a long sword in a scabbard at his side, with a blade that was heavy and curved and sharp. It was discreetly hidden by a travel cloak of simple bleached cotton. A cotton wrap covered his head, protecting him from the wind and sun, for he had come from afar—days and weeks and months away from here—from the scalding heart of the desert that filled with desolation the distant West and South of the Compass Rose.

Nadir had come here to the Kingdom in the Middle, the land of grace and harmony and the birthplace of the Princess Egiras, whom he was bound against his will to serve.

"Go and find the land of my birth, Nadir," proud and petulant Egiras had said to him many moons ago. "And when you get to the place of jade forests and jagged mountains and endless lilac heaven, take a deep breath in my stead and absorb everything so that you can remember it. Then, pluck for me any blossom that grows there and bring it here to me still living, together with a bit of my native soil, so that I may plant it in my garden and remember. . . ."

"But my Princess," Nadir replied. "How can I leave you without my protection, even for a day? I have been at your side all these years, never leaving you."

"I suppose I will have to manage somehow," the Princess said with her usual sarcasm. "Now go, for I order you to do this, else I pine away with homesickness, and it will all be your fault."

"I will be gone for a long time . . ." he whispered, bowing.

"Indeed," she said, turning her back to him, so that all he could see was the smooth waterfall of her ebony silk hair falling upon the lesser silk of her gold robes. And then, still with her back to him, she added, "I will expect you to be gone for so long that you will never come back."

He could not determine if her words were mockery or bitterness or disdain.

His breath was short, for he had climbed hundreds of steps to heaven. And now he stood before the gates of a building that was a monastery or a temple or a faceted jewel set in a mountain.

Nadir stood breathing harshly, gathering himself before going inside, and listened to the living silence.

Soon he could discern the sounds of the wind as it moved the metallic bell-chimes that hung in clusters at the entrance, and of the occasional bird call. Once earlier, as he had been climbing the endless stairs, he had heard the deep rumble of echo that was the great Temple Gong, but it sounded only on the hour.

And now there was nothing, and not a soul around. Only insects hung in the air.

Nadir took one last deep breath, and he put his hand on the mallet which he then used to strike the hanging copper plate. He waited.

And he continued waiting for long moments, for no one came to the doors.

There was a basin of water just at the entrance, and he watched its placid stillness. The water reflected the dove-gray morning sky, and the upside-down mountains without tops.

Eventually, Nadir put his hands on the wood of the door, and he pushed it gently.

The door swung inward with a soft creak of old ungreased joints. Twilight was revealed in the depths of the building.

Nadir stepped inside.

He blinked, and was met by the sight of a sterile chamber, completely empty of any furnishings. There were two wooden pillars that supported the roof on two sides, two small simple windows that let in daylight on the right and left walls. And on the wall directly before him there was another door, shut.

Before that door, blocking it, stood the motionless figure of a man in a robe of persimmon orange, that of a priest or monk.

Nadir inclined his head in a bow and put his hands palms together in the greeting of this land. Then he said in a stumbling accent, carefully pronouncing the sing-song syllables that he had learned in his travels through this land, "Are you well, sir? Be well. I seek to enter and to learn. For days I have followed the endless Yellow River and for many moons I have traveled through grass plains and forests past towns and great cities, all the way from the land of nothing but desert sand."

"Did you travel all this length just to come here?" asked the priest. He was indeterminate—neither young nor old—but his head was clean-shaven, as was monastic custom, except for his brows, which were thick and dark, and thus implied youth. His skin was smooth and pale like yellow parchment, in sharp contrast to the deep orange of his robe, and his eyes were nearly pupil-less, black and slanted.

"In truth," said Nadir, "I did not. I am here at the bidding of the one I serve, a stern Princess who now lives in a faraway desert but was born in this land. She has sent me here to the Kingdom in the Middle to bring her back memories not her own. However, in my travels through this land I have heard stories of your Secret Temple with its hidden Wisdom. And having learned of its existence, I am compelled to learn more."

"Then you are unworthy," said the priest. "Turn back. You may not enter."

Nadir blinked. "Sir, if I may ask, why do you say this? You do not know me at all, so how can you pass judgment on my worthiness?"

"You may not enter," said the priest in the same lifeless monotone.

"But I want to learn!" said Nadir, his eyes taking on a gleam of intensity as he took a step forward into the chamber.

In reciprocation, the priest glided with one fluid movement toward him, just one step, to match the movement of Nadir. And then he stopped again. His dark eyes did not leave those of Nadir.

"What must I do?" asked Nadir, watching the impassive face of the priest guard, seeing now that it was young and smooth and placid like the surface of the waters in a basin at the doors. And something about the sight of such impassiveness infuriated him.

"Do what you will," replied the one who guarded the door. "But you may not pass."

"Let me at least speak to your Master Xin An-Dwei, the one who is oldest and wisest in all of the Kingdom in the Middle. Let him make the determination and pronounce judgment upon me!" said Nadir.

"No," said the priest impassively. "You may not speak to Master Xin, and you may not pass."

"By gods, I will pass!" exclaimed Nadir. "What kind of logic is this, priest? Your words have no good reason and you are unfair in misjudging me! Why do you continue repeating this, and why do you refuse to give me a chance?"

In response there was silence. The priest guard remained motionless and continued to look at him, without blinking.

A sudden gust of anger came to overwhelm Nadir, a mindless elemental feeling. He frowned, pausing in consternation, while possibilities sped before his mind's eye. In reflex, the fingers of his hand tensed in a grip.

The priest watched his hand, saw the clamping of a fist in peculiar silence. And then he took a step back, bowing, with his own hands held palms together. Then he stepped back again, this time flexing his right, then left knee, and moving his hands in circular arcs in deceptively slow figures of combat. Finally he once again bowed, and stood still and relaxed, his hands at his sides.

"I don't want to fight you," said Nadir. "But if this is what it takes—"

In that instant the priest moved like lightning. A sword was drawn from out of the folds of his orange robes, and he spun it from one hand to the other in ornate dance-like warrior movements that Nadir had never seen in his life. So quick was the sword that it was invisible.

"Very well . . ." said Nadir through clenched teeth, and he quickly removed his own curved sword from its scabbard, holding it with both hands.

And it was not a second too soon. Because the next instant the priest struck in his direction, and Nadir had to parry impossibly quick multiple strikes, at the same as he was taking steps back from the onslaught.

Never had Nadir moved so fast. He had to use all of his concentration and balance just to parry the sword strikes, and still he had to retreat. Within seconds he found himself backing out the same door through which he had come in the first place. The moment he was outside, the priest quickly disengaged, and then moved backwards and inside, and shut the front doors in Nadir's face.

Nadir staggered to regain his footing, his heels catching against gravel, then growled in frustration.

And then with a yell of fury, Nadir ran forward brandishing his curved sword and was at the door, pushing it inward, and found himself back inside the empty chamber.

He stopped.

The priest was not there.

But the next instant he felt a breath, a wind, a *something* at the back of his neck, and he whirled around only to see the priest's sword crashing down on him, and he met the strike with impossible reflex, at the same time jumping wildly back, gulping air.

"Who are you?" Nadir panted inbetween words. "You are not mortal, for no human man can move like this!"

But the priest said nothing, and instead he continued to approach Nadir, whirling his sword so that it cut the air with a hiss.

Nadir watched him, no longer moving, stilled with amazement, anger, and a sense of fate. And then, just as the other was only a foot away, and within sword reach of him, Nadir straightened, and dropped his sword.

He stood frozen, unflinching, hands at his sides, and felt the hiss of air sliced by a downstroke of the priest's sword . . . which came down a hairsbreadth away from his neck and also stopped.

"Why do you drop your sword now?" asked the priest, continuing to hold his sword blade poised at Nadir's neck. The priest's voice was calm and placid, and his breath had not even quickened after the violence of their sword exchange.

"I am not sure . . ." whispered Nadir. "I am not sure why I dropped the sword. Maybe because in that last instant I felt that it was no use to fight you, who are my superior, and I resigned myself to your sense of justice."

And then Nadir exhaled in relief. "I see that I was right to trust your will. For you did not complete the strike when you could."

The priest suddenly smiled, and the shape of that smile transformed his face—no longer a placid empty basin of water, but bright and warm. He lowered the sword and with unexpected gentleness touched Nadir on the neck where the blade had rested only moments ago.

"I am glad it was your choice," he said. "If you had continued to resist, I would've had to kill you, and I do not want to kill yet another good man. Unfortunately we must maintain this test for all those who dare to seek the Secret Temple."

"Then what is the nature of this test, exactly?" asked Nadir.

"It is a test of pride and awareness of one's limits. Most who come here after all the travails—after having climbed up the stairs to the feet of the Sky Itself—most expect too much as the result of their extraordinary effort up to that point. Thus, they would fight me to their own deaths and never surrender, for they are blinded by their belief in their ability to win."

"I did not think I could win," said Nadir. "I thought nothing. I merely wanted desperately to enter the Secret Temple. But I admit, one more bizarre moment of this and I would have turned away."

The priest nodded. "Ah yes. There are such also, the ones who come and find me guarding the door, and who turn away simply because they are too much in awe. Very few find in themselves the right amount of balance to try hard enough, but also to know when to give up and be resigned to the truth. Do you know, kind stranger, that this kind of balance, this openness and flexibility in the face of reality, is one of the first steps toward understanding truth?"

And with those words the priest bowed deeply before Nadir, and he said, "Now you may enter beyond the door. Master Xin will speak with you and will take you to the Secret Temple."

Master Xin was tiny, ancient, and shrivelled, with skin that hung in limp folds over bony limbs, with a clean-shaven hairless skull and sparse white brows over narrow slits of eyes. The eyes were surrounded by an infinite number of wrinkles caused by laughter, and the Master's feathered lips quivered in a toothless smile even now.

As Nadir bowed before Master Xin, he had the impression that before him was a ball of orange robes draped over nothing but air, and topped by a dislocated wizened head.

"Welcome, my young son," said Master Xin in a high trembling voice. "So you made it past the guard at the door— good, good!"

They were speaking inside a tiny chamber lit only by a candle, which was just beyond the door that Nadir had had to struggle so much to pass. If this was the inner sanctum, the Secret Temple itself, it certainly didn't look much more than a closet. After Nadir had waited in this closet-room for several moments, Master Xin had appeared, and begun to talk immediately.

And now Master Xin asked Nadir more questions, all the while nodding.

"So you traveled from the desert lands?"

Once again Nadir admitted that his interest in the Secret Temple was incidental, and he confessed his true reasons for being in the Kingdom in the Middle.

"Ah, then you are here because you wish to learn how to better serve!" exclaimed Master Xin, interrupting him.

"Actually, if I could I would not serve any longer," responded Nadir, lowering his head. "I want to be free of the bonds caused by my childish promise."

"Is that so?" said Master Xin. "Well then, come along, and we will walk to the Secret Temple, and you can tell me your life story on the way. But be brief, son, for I am old and cannot listen to a life's worth of events in a life's span of retelling, for I have only one life of my own and it is near the end."

And then Master Xin giggled, and opened a small door in one of the walls that Nadir had not noticed.

Bright morning sun struck their eyes, for the door led to the outside. Nadir bent his tall form and followed Master Xin into the sunlight.

They were back in the garden, but this portion of it was on the other side of the monastery walls. The mists had cleared, and overhead the sky streamed blue and the peaks of the great mountains were revealed at last, white and crystalline and blazing in the sun, for they were covered with the powder that Nadir had learned in his journey through this land was called snow, and was the coldest thing he had ever known in his life.

"Is the Secret Temple much farther from here?" asked Nadir.

"It is very near, my son, come along," said Master Xin, beginning to walk in small quick steps along the terrace and toward a path that led away from this building, through the greenery. Nadir respectfully followed.

They moved along a clean gravel path, on both sides of which were tall verdant bushes and flowering trees with delicate white and rose-shaded blossoms of all shapes and sizes. Looking at them, Nadir was reminded of Egiras and her request. He must not forget to pluck an appropriate flower together with its roots and pack it in soil for the long journey back.

"Hurry now!" said Master Xin, interrupting his thoughts. "The sun is just rising over those distant peaks, and in another moment or so we will have the best view of the Eastern sky over this valley. The light itself will shatter into many colors, for there are still remainders of mist in the air, and you will see colors dance in the wind!"

And as Master Xin spoke thus, they had come to the end of the gravel path, and before them was the green expanse of a gently sloping hill. A small winding stream came down the hill like a serpent of mirror brightness in the sun, and it sounded like the mingling of rushing wind and bells as the waters ran over rocks and light spray scattered just at the edges of the shore. There were small islets and tiny ponds everywhere, some deep and opaque with growth, others clear and transparent against the rocks, and in those ponds moved bright forms of undulating great orange carp and their lesser hybrid golden koi, surfacing through the waters and then disappearing again.

"Ah!" said Master Xin. "Just in time."

And as if on cue, the sun came to shimmer past a certain outcropping of rock, so that its edge was a bare sliver against the silhouette of the mountain, and it struck the land at a diagonal.

Nadir stared and saw lines of sunrays drawn across the air. Where they passed through moist water spray, there were sudden splintered rainbows of light.

Rainbows rebounded and hung like cobwebs, and in their iridescence were tiny moths and dragonflies and other creatures that arose over the ponds and the greenery and swirled over the gardens like living dust motes.

"Well, now that you've seen it, how do you like it?" asked Master Xin, raising both hands to encompass the scene around them, spreading gnarled fingers and turning palms upward.

Nadir breathed in the air of the garden and he smiled. "It is beautiful," he said. "Perfect with peace. So beautiful that I admit with some shame that I would rather stay here, and not walk with you any farther toward the Secret Temple. Maybe we can pause here a while more?"

"Walk farther? Why, we are here already, my young son. Your heart senses it true," said Master Xin. "Behold, around you is the Secret Temple. Look around with wide receptive eyes, for this is it."

"But this is a garden!" exclaimed Nadir.

"What greater Temple is there?" said the Master, narrowing eyes in pleasure against the cool, water-drenched morning wind. "But deep inside you know this already. No Temple made by mortal human hands can ever compare to the Temple made by the gods themselves. That building of wood and stone that houses us and that many believe conceals the great Secret Temple from prying eyes, somewhere in its heart of hearts, is but a decoy for the masses who need this simple concrete *limited* thing in their lives. The real Temple is the whole world, and there is nothing as divinely blessed as a blooming growing garden."

Master Xin paused and looked at Nadir. "So now, Nadir, you know the secret. You can carry this Temple with you always, anywhere you go. And you can worship the gods anywhere where you hear the sound of the wind."

And in that moment a deep bass tone sounded from a distance behind them, issuing from the walls of the monastery. The echo of the sound resounded low and profound. And then it came again, twice.

"Listen!" said Master Xin. "The gong sends its sound all across the world to unite it in singleminded focus. For while the wind is the natural sound of the world, the gong is the voice of the wind intensified, a single unifying note that fills the Secret Temple and reverberates, building in strength. Notice how the sound is everywhere. . . ."

"Yes," said Nadir softly. "The sound seems to ring and vibrate in my bones."

"Good!" said the Master. "This is how you are bound to the Secret Temple. Each reverberation that echoes through you also echoes back upon the rest of the world, back and forth endlessly, until you become inseparable from the living fabric around you."

Nadir closed his eyes until he heard the echo behind his eyelids, and saw the sound, and then he took in a deep breath.

"Yes! Breathe it!" whispered Master Xin. "The scent of the blooming garden is also all-permeating, and it fills your lungs and then your heart and spirit with heady perfume, and it too is carried on the wind. Breathe deeply so that you will always remember this when you leave us. . . ."

Nadir's eyes flew open.

"I never want to leave," he said darkly. "I would rather stay here than return to serve her until she takes all my soul from me and drinks me dry. . . ."

"What is the meaning of servitude, Nadir? To serve is to be strong. By serving you render assistance to one who is weaker than you in one way or another. She needs you, Nadir; go back to her and serve."

There was a pause of silence as they both listened to the wind and the final dissipating echoes of the gong.

"But if serving means being stronger than the one you serve, and we serve the gods," said Nadir suddenly, "then is this not blasphemy? For would it not indicate that we are greater than gods?"

Master Xin smiled.

"Ah, but this is where things are turned upside-down. For in truth, the gods serve us. They are the ones who watch over us like children, allowing us to grow through our own means, and stepping in only to avert the worst kind of disaster. And the greatest evil is not always what we think it is. So often we mortals raise our voices in anger at the gods, at their perceived indifference or injustice, like a child who is denied a favorite toy, when in fact the child is preserved from true harm."

"How can that be?" said Nadir. "How can death and sorrow and pain and war not be true harm? For the gods never protect us from these horrors. And the gods allow us all to die. Where in that is divine justice?"

Master Xin thought for a moment, and then pointed once again to the panorama before them. "Look at the garden, Nadir. In the garden, some trees die and are uprooted, while others are planted. Some flowers are pruned and plucked, while others are propagated and grafted onto new branches to form new hybrids. Some of these trees and flowers are old, others young, and it makes no difference. But the garden continues, and it is all one thing, that of balance and justice, for every day it is different down to the tiniest leaf and blade of grass, and yet in its sum total it is always the same.

"And thus is the world. If you can sense that you are only one blade of grass, and that you are one part of the garden, then your fate and destiny and will and direction become amplified and at the same time dissolved, for you are all and nothing, the whole garden and a single blade of grass. And whatever happens to you happens to the whole garden, and whatever happens to the garden happens to you. You blend and you remain in eternal motion. It is only when you slow down to consider your separateness, your unique fate, that you fall away from the garden, for it continues to move and grow all around you."

"I need to think about this," said Nadir, looking at the jade-green hillside, carpeted with countless blades of grass.

"Think of this for as long as you live," replied Master Xin. "Indeed, the Secret Temple is maintained by means of thought."

"You are a great man, Master Xin," said Nadir with a sigh. "How I wish I had your wisdom and your immediate answers."

There came high-pitched old laughter.

"My answers are as old as this garden. And I am not what you think," said Master Xin.

"How so?" asked Nadir.

The old one paused to take in a deep lungful of the wind, then smiled blissfully, closing narrow eyes.

"I was born a girl child, and grew to be a woman," said Master Xin An-Dwei, as though only now remembering this detail. "I am old—an old woman, and few know it, even here in the monastery of the Secret Temple. And now it matters little and is all the same thing, because with time the distinctions between man and woman grow less and less."

Nadir stared at the ground in shame at his own blindness and oversight, feeling his dark cheeks grow hot.

"That is another thing you need to learn, that wisdom brings a mixing of the polar opposites, and if you have been born a woman, you become more like a man as you age, while if you have been born a man, you become like a woman. There is no shame in that, no weakness, rather the power of the divine comes to fill you more fully, for the divine is neither man nor woman but both, and the more of both you accept into yourself, the closer to godhood you move."

"I have so much to learn, Master Xin," said Nadir softly, his gaze still lingering on the ground in shame.

"Who doesn't?" Master Xin said smartly, and as Nadir looked up he saw a twinkle of hilarity in her eyes.

"But where to begin?"

"Good question, young son. When new acolytes come to learn from the Temple they are usually told to begin to learn what interests them most. It is a fallacy that there should be a specific order of discovery of truth, because your own natural urge for truth best dictates what you must learn next. Your curiosity and need to know guide you better than anything. So then, what do you want to know above all else? That is where you need to begin."

"Then I want to know how to move with the impossible swiftness of that priest who guarded the door!" exclaimed Nadir. "I still do not understand how he did it, and I would learn from him this art of combat."

"I see you like pain. Why is it always like this with all of you young ones? But do not fear, you will have your wish. Stay with us and learn this thing, this pain. And as you do, I will come often and watch you practice," said Master Xin and started to laugh, and would not stop.

W as it only a blink of an eye, or had many moons waxed and waned? Had the rains come and gone, and then the leaves of many colors of fire fallen in the garden, leaving bare branches to be covered with the white cold powder from heaven?

Nadir was not sure. He lived in a dream of fluidity, silence, balanced movement and ascetic control. Days flew by him like gangly cranes or like soft dun-gray sparrows, long and short. And through it all he was slowly changing.

The Secret Temple permeated him with the peace and silence, and had entered him through his pores all the way to his innards.

The garden of jade hues came to him even in dreams, and the gong resounded in the earth and in his bones, until the routine of the monks and priests had become his second heartbeat.

Nadir learned pain, and he learned release. And most of all he learned how to tread the fine line between either extreme.

And then all of a sudden one day he woke up.

For a memory of the Princess Egiras came to him, together with old soul-sick constriction and images of the scorching desert sun. There were so many women here in the Kingdom in the Middle who looked like her, beautiful and deathly-pale yellow, with black silk tresses and slanted hidden eyes. And yet, observing them, never was he prompted to remember her who had sent him here.

Instead, what touched him was the sight of a great pale flower with rose-streaked petals that grew alone among the thicket of dark leaves on a bush near the bench where he used to sit every day.

The flower—proud and pristine, a thing of variegated perfection of whiteness interlaced with rose, and yet with petals fine and fragile as rice paper—was surrounded in a bower of intimacy by dark protective foliage.

Simple appeared the deep green leaves, simple and dark and strong. They shielded the delicate splendid blossom from all sides, always nearby yet never touching, never encroaching upon its perfect solitude.

Without the embrace of the strong leaves, the flower would not persist. And this revealed to him in part the nature of his promise.

Nadir knew now that all peace and reverie was shattered, and he had to go back.

He had to return to her, and to serve her, and to keep his promise to her.

And, as though reinforcing the perfection of his that one thought, a wind swept through the garden around him, and he heard the distant strike of the Temple gong.

Dream Nine

The Compass Rose

The object floated in a water-filled pool in the exact middle of the world.

It had the shape of a four-point star, and its North-South rays were made of peculiar iron ore that aligned itself with the magnetic core of the world, and pointed North.

Its East-West rays were made of layers of buoyant cedar and sandalwood covered with resin to protect it from rot, for it floated in a water-filled pool and yet had to last forever, or at least until the gods deigned for the world to end.

The pool of water spanned a man's height in diameter, and was hewn from the heart of a rock formation sculpted in the semblance of a great rose.

The stone was marble, and the rose sculpture itself reposed in the middle of a grand hall that was in turn the center of the greatest palace the world had ever known.

The *taqavor* who ruled the palace was lord over emperors and kings, and had conquered all the lands around him, to the rim of the horizon.

His were the wide expanses that faced the rising sun; his were the boundless oceans at its back. His were the lands at the sun's cold right hand and its fiery left.

East, West, North, South.

The words had not existed before. They were newly brought into being by the force of the *taqavor's* desire to assign order to the horizon all around him, to anchor that which was uncharted.

Past, Present, Future, Alternate—the realm of other possibilities. Such were the additional ethereal directions superimposed in an infinite array of invisible layers upon the physical ones. And the words to describe them existed but had no life.

And then one day they were all bound together.

The *taqavor* who ruled the mortal world had assigned his artisans and craftsmen an immense task—to produce one object that would define the whole of his *empirastan.*

Before the artists could conceive the object's actual shape and function, and seduce it into physical existence, there had to be found a natural equivalent of this object—a shape or form or structure on which it could be modeled.

At first, the artists looked upon the sun itself, and wrought a flat golden shape with a multiplicity of rays extending all around it in a gleaming circle. Then the sculptors took over, and created a golden sphere studded with needles of rays, like a bristling pine-fruit.

But the *taqavor* took one look at the object and scornfully motioned it away with his hand.

"Take this away and create for me a thing not just of beauty but of inner power. For, this is an empty shell I see before me, and it does nothing to remind me of the power of my *empirastan.*"

The *taqavor* was no longer young, but he was strong, and luck and most of the gods were on his side. Thus he could still command instant terror in those who served him.

"But my Lord, this object is the Sun itself! Isn't its acute golden glory and uniform sharpness a fair representation of your realm?" asked one naive master of sculpture.

There came mocking laughter from the sovereign. "You call this a fair representation?" he said. "Look—as your golden pin-cushion rests upon the ground with its fine sharp needles, already the bottom-most points have broken off and have crumpled into gold razor dust, since they are unable to maintain the weight of this sphere. My *empirastan,* on the other hand, sits on the most solid firmament of the earth underneath it, and nothing can undermine its foundation."

"You are indeed wise, my Lord . . ." whispered the chastised artist, and bowed in shame.

"Maybe we can suspend the sphere from the ceiling," put in another artist, "and thus relieve the burden of its weight? Maybe we can set it on fire from within, just like the Sun itself, by creating a hollowed out replica and filling it with burning torches, so that the light would seep out through tiny holes—"

"Maybe I can have your tongue suspended from the ceiling and your anus set on fire from within, idiot?" said the *taqavor.*

The master artist blanched and retreated, and the prickly golden sphere was quickly taken away.

In the days following, the artisans watched the night heavens and considered replicating the full moon or its half-crescent shape, or even the tiny pin-points of stars.

But when the *taqavor* was told of this next scheme, he again voiced his displeasure.

"The Moon is round and dull and is surrounded by darkness. The Crescent is a weakling and its concave shape better resembles the blade of a farm implement than a royal treasure. The stars are puny spilled droplets of light. None of these are true Symbols of my realm. Go, and find me something that is!"

And the craftsmen and artists scattered forth from the palace, driven by terror and by the promise of immeasurable honors from the sovereign of the world.

The *taqavor* was left to walk his marble halls and the cultivated gardens, brooding in silence, and waiting. When no one was nearby, only then would he allow his gaze to lose its energy, and his eyes to grow dull with apathy and relentless depression. Not even the inferno of the brilliant sun overhead shining upon the luxurious greenery of his gardens and the rainbow of blossoms could lift his internal darkness.

For here, in the natural peace, above all places, old memories would start to surface—the ancient turmoil of wars that he had fought, the endless campaigns through the desert, and to the outer rim of the colder lands, to the island places beyond the great cerulean ocean, and the long days of nothing. . . .

He would stop and stare at delicate fountains circulating water and see instead the spray of sea foam upon the oars of boats filled with soldiers. He would blink and look away to rest his eyes upon a frieze of marble, and instead would see the blanched walls of cities before which he had sat in siege. . . .

Sometimes, the wind rustled jade-colored leaves in thick trees, and he would hear his name spoken, as though in a dream.

Cireive.

The speaker was a woman, and yet her voice was muted, most distant of all, and her shape was a blur. He remembered the woman looking down at him, knew the vital importance of her, and yet could not see her face, only vaguely remember an affiliation, or maybe even intimacy. She had looked at him, a small boy, holding him against her, warming him, humming a song that was not so much a lullaby as it was a keening cry of the ancients that had been sung for as long as he could remember.

My Cireive. . . .

And yet the wind would blow from another direction, or recede in silence, and her voice would recede also.

Then, in the remaining silence, something would catch him unaware, and he would suddenly hear screeching echoes of thunder, and a red bleeding sky in a cold land. In that instant a blazing form of *another,* no longer human, would speak through his very skull, and he would remember the words of a mortal woman whom he had destroyed, and thus re-made into a goddess.

The Skies heard you, Cireive, I am Damned.

And in that moment of inner rending the *taqavor* would close his eyes, squint tightly, with madness rapidly closing in, while shuddering pangs of terror slid down his spine. He would turn and walk back inside, sometimes moving at a run . . . just as he had run that time. . . .

The *taqavor's* son, the quiet studious Prince Lirheas, had long since noticed an oddity—it seemed there were never any women nearby. In fact, when his father walked the palace, the female servants were either absent altogether or retreated quickly and discreetly, lowering their eyes, and drawing the dark cotton shawls closer about their faces.

And in the *taqavor's* spacious House of Wives, it was rumored, the women had to put on face masks every time their Lord was due for a visit. But Lirheas, as the sovereign's son, was spared, and was never to hear even darker rumors about the details of his father's intimacies.

For, within the palace, the highest-ranked Servants of the Wives would whisper to each other and to occasional others that the *taqavor* refused to address by name the twelve beauties who had been designated his royal *taqoui,* and the remaining two hundred concubines. Instead, he would single out his evening's companion by saying, "You," and pointing at any given one of the women who stood lined up before him, their features completely masked and their voluptuous bodies nude.

And then the *taqavor* would walk ahead to his bedchamber in the House of Wives, and the chosen *taqoui* or concubine would follow, walking a designated number of steps behind him in resigned deathly silence.

What went on in the actual bedchamber was also unclear, but rumors would not fall quiet. It was thought that the women who serviced the *taqavor* were tormented and forced to endure unspeakable pain during the carnal acts; that he would rip out clumps of their hair, and draw gashes with a dagger in the skin of their breasts and buttocks; that he would strike, would draw blood from their throats with his teeth like a demon, in that same violent instant as he spilled his seed. . . .

The *taqoui* were thus pitied, and none would wish their fate upon any noble's young daughter. And yet the honors and riches bestowed upon the chosen women's families were great, and the *taqavor*'s House of Wives was continuously replenished with virginal newcomers from all the corners of his boundless *empirastan.*

Most recently, the *taqavor* had been so preoccupied with waiting for his artisans to present him with the symbol of his realm that his visits to the House of Wives—already infrequent and prompted only by occasional flareups of lust—seemed to cease altogether. Many days went past, flowing like slow molasses, several moons waned and grew full again, and the royal women started to forget the pain and humiliation that their Lord had caused them, for the old wounds and lacerations on their flesh had long since healed, and their spirits had rebounded. Abandoned, they had regained a joy of life, albeit limited by their perfumed prison.

It is said that human memory for pain is not strong and is easily replaced with complacency. Thus it was now, vague and ephemeral, and the old pain seemed not to belong to them, in retrospect.

Some of the *taqoui* were so relieved, and then so bored, that they stopped playing mindless games of chase and wargames of glitter-stones upon gameboards with one another. They stopped splashing in the bathing pools, and instead spent their solitary days learning the sciences and the arts, having bribed the servants to bring them appropriately learned teachers. Others turned to each other for physical intimacy, and spent their own unrelieved energy practicing truer acts of carnal love than they had ever experienced with their sadistic Lord.

Altogether, it was a time of respite and seething urgency for the House of Wives. And this time lasted until one day a new young woman was brought in.

She was brought in neither to be an exalted *taqoui* nor a lesser concubine. For she was plain, and she had no name—or at least she would not divulge it. In truth, the *taqavor* did not even know of her existence, nor would he have cared.

The young woman had ebony-dark hair, pale skin, and extraordinarily intelligent eyes. She was brought in to serve and cook meals for the chosen royal females, but ended up the one to entertain them with tales of the outside world, and of the colder lands whence she had come.

Since the *taqoui* had a sense of humor and some of them sharp sarcastic tongues, they soon took to her. And, since names were not to be used, she was referred to as "you with the knowing eyes."

The young woman would peel vegetables and tell them impossible stories of her native land. She would come in to brush a *taqoui's* hair, and would make her laugh all the while, until the royal wife would cry with the effort. In the evenings, just before bedtime, she would serve the women sweets and warmed wine, and would half-sing dreamlike stories. . . . And indeed, many of the *taqoui* would dream her tales that night, and would wake up flushed with wonder.

And that was not all. The young woman had an odd ability to draw. In her brief free moments, she sat down with sticks of eye-kohl and drew upon silk the faces of the royal women of the

House of Wives, drew them everywhere, in fact, and drew them from memory.

When she was in the kitchens, she would use ashes to trace patterns and outlines of faces upon bread-cloth. On the mosaic floors of the terraces that led into the gardens, she would be found on her knees sketching peculiar human shapes with charcoal, pictures that would be soon washed away by running overflow and spray from the nearby fountains, and the remainders swept by gardeners.

And one morning, as the Prince Lirheas took his walk upon the sandy beaten path of the Palace gardens, just near the House of Wives, he noticed on the ground at his feet a beautiful carved etching of a woman's face, traced deeply into the sand, sculpted almost like a shallow relief.

He stopped his foot just before it crushed the remarkable image. And then, as he stared, he saw a thin female shape in a dark shawl crouching another ten paces ahead of him on the path, and using a short dry stick to trace another image, this one in profile.

Seeing him approach, the creature in the shawl scrambled to her feet, and bowing quickly started to back away from him, allowing him to pass.

Lirheas walked past her, and then curiosity got the better of him. He turned around, but the woman was already moving quickly down the path, back to where he had come from.

"Wait!" he cried. "You, come back!"

The shawled one halted in her tracks.

Lirheas walked toward her, and said, pointing back at the drawn images, "Did you draw these, woman? Who are you?"

She nodded in silence, her face lowered, her eyes downcast, all obscured by the shawl.

"You draw very well," said Lirheas.

"Thank you, my Lord."

He was rather surprised to hear that her voice was steady, confident, and that there was a warmth coupled with humor, so that for a moment he thought she might have been actually holding back her speech not from fear but because she was laughing at him. And wanting to know that, to make certain, he said, "Look at me."

She looked up, and with a pang he knew he had guessed right. A thin pale face met his, and the corners of her lips were dancing with a suppressed smile.

And then he saw her eyes.

They struck him with a pang of intensity, something oddly familiar, something intimate—like coming home to ancient wisdom.

And Lirheas was made mute. He stood there, speaking nothing, unable to formulate a sentence, because in that instant a peculiar thought passed his mind, a thought that here was something momentous taking place.

A moment rich with fate.

And she was the one to speak first, to dispel it. "I serve the House of Wives," she said. "Forgive me, but I must get back, since my mistresses are expecting me."

And then she bowed again, curtly, almost as an afterthought, and did not wait for his dismissal, as she started back on the path.

Lirheas remained like a dumb thing, staring in her wake. He then glanced back to where, a few steps away on the ground, was the image of beauty that she had wrought out of nothing.

And before her, in his mind, the image paled.

After three moons had waxed and waned, the *taqavor* got tired of waiting. And he called his advisors and four of the bravest soldiers of his army, and he also called the most talented of his artisans to come before him.

They gathered before his lofty throne, in a hall of great gilded columns of mauve marble and carved stone blossoms.

"Have you found for me a true symbol of my *empirastan?*" he asked.

In response, trembling, they cast their gazes down.

"I see," said the *taqavor*. "You are all just as I thought, idiots with the imaginations of dumb beasts and the artistic craft of monkeys."

"My Lord," whispered one advisor. "The task you set before us is almost impossible, for how can we find something to fairly represent your *empirastan* when we have yet to span it?"

"True," muttered a soldier, a decorated hero of the old wars. "I have campaigned with you in all the directions of the horizon, and yet, my Lord, I have not seen an end to your *empirastan*, have not seen the true End of the World."

"Indeed," said another, "I have not either. Does the End even exist? The thought is so vast, it is beyond me."

"That would not be such a difficult feat, with your poor set of brains," quipped the *taqavor* once again in sarcasm, as he was wont to do with his advisors and those most near to him.

And then he added, "Of course the world has an End. Surely it must, for I have seen all of it in my conquest, and it rims the horizon."

"Then, my Lord," put in a courtier, "surely it would be a fair task to find out the nature of the Shape of the World that is your *empirastan*, before we can compress it into one Symbol. Is the world a round circle, or a square, or another odd shape?"

"But how can we find out?" said an artisan. "How many men would it take to line up around the rim of the world? An impossible feat!"

The *taqavor* laughed. "Your vision is even more narrow than his!" he exclaimed. "But I have anticipated all of you, and that is why I have brought my four bravest warriors here. It will take only four fearless men to find out. Four strong men, the four of you. You will each one of you go in the four opposite directions, taking whatever caravans, horses, and supplies you may need on your journey. You will take ships, if you must, to sail."

And then the *taqavor* pointed with his index finger at each of the four veteran soldiers in turn.

"You, Jimor, will travel facing the rising sun. You, Mareid, go in the opposite direction, facing the setting sun. You, Rihaad, take yourself to the right hand of the rising sun. And, finally, you, Vikenti, follow the rising sun's left hand."

"How far are we to go, my Lord?" asked one of the four.

The *taqavor* smiled. "You will go as far as it takes, unto eternity if needed. You will keep going, until you reach the End. And when you return, you will describe to me what the End is like. Does the world stop at the edge of a bottomless abyss? Do the oceans spill their waters into that same abyss? Or, maybe, it is an abyss of fire and the realm of the gods? I want to know if my *empirastan* borders upon the land of the gods, and in what manner."

"But my Lord," spoke the most venerable of the soldiers, Jimor, "how are we to know what the End of the World is like? How are we to know it when we see it? In our conquest travels we came to many places which had mountains the height of heaven, and had boundless oceans. We came to a stop before deserts ending over cliffs, and before other wonders, none of which we could surmount easily, and so we went around them."

"Well then, you've answered your own question," replied the sovereign. "For, in all such cases, you remember that we continued going, we found a way to move beyond or around these natural barriers. For none of these was the End. And thus I say now, you will know it when you come to it. Therefore, waste not another moment, and be on your way! I do not expect you back in many moons, even in many seasons. But if you fail, or perish on the way, your families and your honor will suffer greatly. So, do not fail me, and do not fail yourselves."

The men bowed before the *taqavor* and left his presence.

And he stood alone in the hall, all except for the self-effacing Prince Lirheas.

"Will they find it, father?" the young man asked unexpectedly, for he hardly ever spoke at all. "Or will they all perish needlessly on this impossible quest?"

The *taqavor* glanced briefly at him, with a measuring gaze which held in it mostly disdain. "Only the weak will perish. If they do not come back after five summers, then I will send others in their place."

And the Prince lowered his gaze before his Lord father.

Several moons passed, after the four expeditions had been sent off to find the End of the World.

The *taqavor* found himself walking one morning along the pale marble terrace of his sunlit gardens in the palace that was the middle of the mortal world. He paced, his mind in meditation, while from afar the parched desert wind came to wash over his pale hair—once the color of wheat, now all silvered like old steel. The wind reminded the *taqavor* that his Palace and his great city had been built around a great oasis, and only a little beyond the lush gardens stood empty desolation.

At this, his thoughts took a dark turn, and he felt a buildup of old fury, a decentralized hatred, and with it a surge of old lust.

The House of Wives was only a little away, at the other end of the gardens, and it had been a while since he had touched a woman's tender resilient flesh. And so he allowed himself the slow burning rise of anticipation as he walked toward the House, taking the quickest way possible, along a narrow sandy path.

As he approached the structure of exotic painted marble he could hear a strange din, and a noise of many female voices. There were also sounds of drums and the sweet wailing of *zourna,* and the strumming of strings, and, most surprising of all, the stomping of many feet.

The *taqavor* stopped, frozen in his tracks. In that instant his mind was inundated with a seething flood of thought-shards and all manner of images—all swirling in disorder, all wrought of doubt, fear, mistrust, and an underlying murk of jealousy.

His *taqoui* were engaging in a ritual that did not involve him, a moment of intimate freedom, of wild abandon?

And the *taqavor* resumed walking, this time with a dark determination, until he was at the doors of the House of Wives, and there was being met by obeisant servants. But he cast them aside, pushing the first of the men forward with such fierce strength that the poor servant fell and remained cowering on the stairs, and the rest drew back in terror of their Lord.

He continued through the entrance, and into the musk-filled soft luxury and darkness of the House. Then, as he picked up the pace and was beginning to race forward, frightened men and women servants scattered from him in all directions as he encountered them in the hallways.

At last, he emerged in the internal courtyard and the inner private gardens, and was met by the rich clamor of celebration, of dance music and wild drums. It resounded on the wind like aerial perfume, and yet to his senses it was poison.

Seeing the *taqavor,* the musicians stopped playing their instruments, their tunes flattening out in dull final notes, and the drums quieted into nothing but echoes on the wind.

The *taqoui* froze in place like glittering temple statues, and then all swiftly came down kneeling, and placed their foreheads to the earth. Strings of pearls swept the ground, and fine gauze veils were gently fluttering in the breeze.

Silence.

The *taqavor* walked to the center of the courtyard, his footsteps ringing against smooth marble tile warmed by the midday sun. He then stopped, feet planted apart, and glanced around him at the prostrate female figures.

Then he approached one young *taqoui* kneeling in silence, her form moving only with breath, and he stepped on her strewn auburn hair with his sandals.

"You," he said very softly. "Tell me what has come to pass just now."

The young woman gasped and then went so still that her breath ceased. She barely whispered, her face still to the ground, "It is nothing, my Lord. . . ."

The silence all around was profound and thick with fate.

"Is that so?" said the *taqavor*. And then his foot moved in closer, and he rested the toe of his sandal very lightly against the trembling woman's bare neck.

"If I put my full weight on this foot," he said softly, "it will break your neck. So, tell me again, woman. What has come to pass?"

Before the half-faint *taqoui* had a chance to formulate a reply, another female voice came from behind him, from the doorway returning to the House.

"My Lord! Why, you have spoiled your own surprise!"

The *taqavor* removed his foot from the unfortunate on the ground before him, stepped back, and turned to stare at the speaker.

A thin female covered with the poor shawl of a servant stood at the door, holding a large bowl of stacked honey-pastries and sweetmeats. She walked forward with determination and bowed deeply before the *taqavor,* casting her gaze swiftly to the ground before he could see her face.

"Forgive me for speaking out, my Lord," she said gently, in a steady soothing voice, "but we were not expecting you today. The whole House is in turmoil, preparing a marvelous event in your honor—a feast for your delectation, with dancing and musical entertainment. As you can see—" and she motioned with one hand generally, while she continued to balance the heavy overfilled bowl with the other—"the *taqoui* and your concubines are working hard to make your surprise the most dazzling spectacle. It will please you very much, indeed, it—"

The *taqavor* stared at this lowly creature speaking, nay, babbling, calmly in his presence, with amazement. The amazement was such that it had made him forget anger, and inflamed him with a need to find out more. . . .

"Who are you? What is this that you speak?"

The creature bowed again. "I am nothing but your humble servant, my Lord. I serve you and the House of Wives. . . ."

"And who will be eating this, since I have not been yet invited, and arrived unexpectedly?" said the *taqavor,* pointing to the bowl of delicacies, and expecting to catch her in confusion.

But the creature was incredible.

"This? Oh, no one will be eating this, my Lord, for it is not food, but the raw materials of my artistic craft. I will be using pastry to create a voluptuous statue of your First *Taqoui.* For practice, of course, since the real statue will be made on the day of your feast, and presented for you to . . . eat."

The *taqavor* stared in disbelief, his brows narrowing.

She noted the beginning of that terrible frown, the encroaching doubt.

"My Lord, let me demonstrate for you!" said the woman suddenly. And as he watched this insane thing taking place before him, she put down the bowl on the ground, and then crouched, and grabbed a handful of sugared gooey pastry in one hand, and with unusually adroit movements started to roll it into a sticky ball.

And then, before his unbelieving eyes, the woman rolled more honey dough—some pieces long and cylindrical, others spherical—and then started to put them together and shape them into refinement with thin strong fingers.

The *taqavor* watched her work in silence, in a sunlit courtyard of kneeling shapes of the Wives and the frozen musicians. He ignored the wind singing against the stone and the whisper of leaves, the rustling veils. He saw only skinny pale hands moving rapidly, and before him an impossible thing taking place.

The statue stood upright. It reached only to his waist, since there was not enough pastry to do something on a larger scale. And it was growing in intricacy every second. In a matter of breaths, a formless lump of honey and sweetmeats was now the figure of a woman with soft hips and full breasts, with every contour defined.

The artist continued to shape her, running fingertips through the head-lump to form locks of hair, then squeezing the holes for the eyes, the slender nose, the fine nostrils, the shape of the chin. She pulled longer thin rolls of dough to create more curving locks and wreathed the smooth forehead of the honeyed mass in spider-thin etchings mimicking the filaments of human hair, done merely with the raking of nails. . . .

At last, she put the finishing touches on the statue, so that the tiny sharp nipples on the breasts stood out sensuously, and the thighs curved and streamed into slender legs, tapering to feet with tiny shaped toes. From the shoulders of the statue grew upraised arms, and the hands curved, flowing into palms and dainty fingers like lotus-blossoms.

The statue balanced impossibly on its slender feet upon the marble floor, without the assistance of the artist. How could this be, without some invisible assistance of the gods?

"It is complete, my Lord," announced the woman suddenly. She got up from her crouch, but her head remained lowered, and she wiped her sticky hands upon her old tunic and long cotton pants. "How do you like your little *taqoui?* Though tiny, she is edible in all senses of the word. But I promise you, when I make the real one for your actual feast, she will be life-size. . . ."

For a moment, the *taqavor* was speechless. And then a smile came to his lips, an unusual smile in its innocence. He stared at the small statue, and then approached it, to look at it from all sides.

"It is indeed perfect . . ." he admitted.

In reply, she once again bowed.

"She is so perfect," continued the *taqavor,* "that from this moment I forgive all of you. And you, woman, I forgive you also, for speaking in insolence. Indeed, you lie so well for the others—for I know that you all deceive me even now, do not for a moment think otherwise—and yet you justify your colorful words with such impossible proof that it is the only thing I can do. Furthermore, if you can create an intricate form of wonder out of pastry, what other thing can you do, given proper materials of the artist's craft?"

And while the multitude of wives let out a great breath of relief, and there were animated rustlings on the ground from all directions, the woman continued to bow, and she replied to the *taqavor,* "I can create anything for you, my Lord. Anything that you desire."

"Then you and none other shall be the one to create for me," he said, "the true symbol of my *empirastan.*"

In his favorite hall of violet-veined marble, the *taqavor* sat in a high seat and conversed with the lowly woman who had no other name than "you with the knowing eyes." A few steps away stood the quiet Prince Lirheas, with his back to them, looking out with an absent gaze through an arched window into a sun-filled garden. And yet he was aware of their every nuance of conversation.

"My finest soldiers have gone in all directions to find the End of the World," the *taqavor* was saying. "When they return, they will describe to us what is the nature of the End, and from their description I want you to create the one symbol."

The woman stood before the high seat, which was elevated five steps above ground, so that the feet of the seated *taqavor* were at the level of her eyes. She still wore simple servant clothing, and her eyes were downcast. But now, her back remained straight.

"There is no need to wait for their return," she said, "for the symbol is as simple as the directions of the wind. It is the wind rose. A shape of four rays to represent the four greater winds, and, between them, four lesser winds. Then behind these eight, like petals of a rose, a layer of eight half-winds, and behind those in turn, the rest of the quarter-winds, in sixteenths—if you choose to make it into a true blossom."

The *taqavor* listened in interest. "Go on, woman. . . . Tell me more of this wind rose. How do you know of it?"

"All those who sail know of it, my Lord," she replied, "for to navigate the expanses of the seas one has only the sky and the wind. And one learns to give the wind many names and fathom its true nature."

"Why is it that I don't know this?" said the *taqavor*, his brow furrowing. "I have been on many ships that crossed oceans, and yet no one has ever told me of this wind rose. And why should you—?" and then the *taqavor* laughed. "I see," he said. "That is why your name is 'you with the knowing eyes.'"

In reply, she laughed also. It was a startling sound, to hear a woman laugh in the *taqavor's* presence. The timbre of her laugh was rich and comforting, like energy in the air.

"The wind rose is a simple seafarers' thing, not for those higher up to be concerned about. People have not told you of it, because they cannot speak freely to one as lofty as you. You are as distant from them as the sun is from the sand, observing the world from remote great heights. And they do not dare tell you things unless you directly ask," she said. "As for me—since my position is on the very bottom, many things fall my way. My eyes have learned to take in much of the world, my Lord. And, having observed much, I can tell you in truth that only the wind sees all of the world at once, from all directions. Only the wind can fathom its true End."

"Yes. . . . The wind is everywhere," suddenly spoke up the Prince Lirheas. "The wind is what can span the world, and thus all of your *empirastan,* father!"

The *taqavor* stared ahead of him with inflamed living eyes. For the first time, the flame was not anger but exultation.

"It is true, yes!" he whispered passionately. "The wind will be my symbol."

And then he turned to the woman standing straight before him. "Your wisdom is great, 'you with the knowing eyes.' For that, I will reward you greatly. Create for me the physical shape of this wind rose, capture the wind and give it solid shape, and animate it so that it serves a true function. And, after you are done, you can have your desire. Thus there is no need to wait for my men to return, for the world's shape is surely the wind rose!"

The woman bowed before him, saying, "My Lord, it will be as you say. I will proceed immediately. But I must inform you, it will not be a quick task. For to compress the essence of the wind into one lesser shape may be as easy as creating a rose blossom, but to create a shape that actually performs a function may be as arduous as finding the End of the World."

And the *taqavor* nodded. "Then do what must be done, for as long as it takes. This symbol must be made true."

The woman with the knowing eyes was removed from her daily servitude and given her own living quarters, not in the House of Wives but in the Palace itself.

Prince Lirheas would observe from a distance as she walked the halls and the garden galleries, conversing with the best artisans of the *taqavor*.

It was odd to observe that they did not resent her presence or think of her as infringing upon their duties. Rather, they embraced her like a peculiar living and breathing gift of the gods, sent out of the blue sky and the thin air to assist them in an impossible task.

The woman consulted with sculptors, painters, and carvers of fine wood reliefs. She even spent time with the arrangers of flowers, and Lirheas watched her bending over great royal vases and counting the number of petals in flowers of different species that had been collected from the *taqavor's* own gardens.

Then for days she would draw. Again, the Prince would come upon her everywhere, this time seated on garden benches, with rolls of parchment spread about on the marble tiles, sketching with sticks of charcoal and dried rolls of thick cotton soaked in ink.

She drew shapes of flowers and stars with many rays. She drew roses and lilies and the blossoms of lotus. She formed repeating patterns of flowers, and covered sheet upon sheet with impossible lines of intricacy.

Once, Lirheas made himself pause before her as she drew a symmetrical star with eight rays, and he asked her, although his heart was beating much too fast in his chest and his temples rang with the coursing of internal waters, "What manner of star flower is this, woman? I have never seen such before."

And for the first time she looked up at him, meeting his gaze.

She replied, telling him something, but all he could see was the gentle color of her eyes, violet as amethysts and warm as the soothing wind currents of night—the kind of night that comes once in a million in the desert, when the air itself is strong with the sun, and pungent sweet richness lingers for hours in the darkness. . . .

The moment was past, and Lirheas nodded, then was on his way again. Only this time a smile came secretly to him, a smile that no one would see.

The seasons passed, and two winters swept the world, putting the desert into starkness, and the palace and the world around it weathered the cold as it usually did.

The *taqavor* brooded, but seemed to do so less than usual, and often came to observe the workshops of his artisans, where he would see the woman without a name and his master artists hunched over pieces of precious metal and stone, over wood and over silken fabric, forming delicate shapes of flowers and stars. . . .

And then, one day, everything changed. For the first of the four expeditions sent to find the End of the Word returned.

They had returned from the direction *opposite* that in which they had been sent.

And the *taqavor* was given unbelievable news.

"**M**y Lord," spoke Jimor, a wizened soldier with a face turned into leather hide by the sun and wind and exhaustion, "I followed the face of the rising sun, just as you had instructed me. Every dawn, I would wait for it, and would find the precise place where it rose, and would mark the land around it, the very shape of the horizon, indelibly into my memory. Then we would follow it until the sun set at our backs. This went on for an endless cycle of days as we crossed the deserts, then came to a place of sparse forests and, eventually, thick green growth, where we hacked our way with swords and long knives.

"We traveled forever, it seemed, and the days turned cold, then warmed again. At last, we came out of the rich wilderness into an open place, and before us lay a great ocean. Here we paused for a number of days as my men built a vessel of the sea out of the wood of the great forest at our backs. We tested the wood for buoyancy, rigged sails from caravan tents, and carved long oars, at the same time gathering a good store of food supplies and sweet water. And, when the vessel floated properly, we cast off.

"We sailed for so many days without seeing land that many of us began to think we would reach our deaths before we reached the End of the World—for our supplies were nearly entirely depleted. I, meanwhile, cast my gaze upon the horizon, where the sun rose every dawn, and adjusted our course accordingly. Once or twice we saw sea birds flying overhead, and this was a good sign, for it indicated a shore was not so far away. And yet we never found it, for I could not deviate from our single-minded course toward the rising sun."

"Go on," said the *taqavor*. "What happened then?"

"Well, my Lord," said the old soldier, "to tell you the truth, there was so much of the same thing, such a long expanse of terrible monotonous ocean, that some of us nearly went mad. I had to hold off a mutiny more than once, when my poor crazed men wanted me to turn off course to reach the nearest shore.

"But luck was on our side. The weather was incredibly fair, and the wind blowing in the direction we followed never let up or turned into an uncontrollable gale. In some ways, we could have been sped along by benevolent gods.

"Eventually, as we reached the last of our strength, we saw shapes of land on the horizon, silhouetted against the rising sun, and we knew we were saved. Within a day we reached a shoreline covered by odd black sand, like ashes or coal. Beyond it was another forested expanse, this one cooler, and the wind here blew sharply among peculiar trees that had rich sharp needles instead of leaves. We did not spend long marveling at them, however, because we desperately needed water and food.

"After unloading what few things we had with us on the vessel and beaching it properly, we ventured deep into the forest of needle-trees. Again, to our luck, we found a small fast brook and, yes, we found game.

"After regaining our trust of land, and resting for a few days, we continued ahead, hunting the game meanwhile, eating the flesh and collecting the skins of the various creatures for various uses. There seemed no end to this forest, and the weather started to get colder again, and there was less game, and fewer running streams on our way. Many of us put on the animal skins for warmth, and used some of the fur to wrap ourselves in at nights.

"After some time our breath became visible in the air. And the land itself seemed to rise, so that we saw mountains in the distance. The mountains were great pale shapes, covered with a whiteness that only some of us recognized properly to be a thing called snow. Surely, we had reached the End of the World."

"And was it? Was it the End?" said the *taqavor,* his eyes glittering with excitement.

"I am afraid not, my Lord. We gathered supplies, and made our way slowly into the cold rising lands, where there was almost nothing growing in the earth, and only bare freezing rock—a horrible dying place. At several times, terrifying white storms caught us, and we hid in caves or behind outcroppings of stone. The whiteness called snow is frozen cold water. We learned this eventually, and we learned to drink this snow when there was no other liquid.

"At this point, some of us died. This was truly the dark time. And there were many mornings that resembled night—the world was so opaque and obscured with snow that I could not see the place where the sun rose, so we had to wait out days.

"I don't know how long it was, the ice agony, but eventually the land started to descend again, and somehow we had come out of the mountains into sparse flatland, and, yes, there was once again a source of food."

The soldier sighed, then continued, "And thus, my Lord, we went on and on, and there was no End. Nothing that would resemble an endless abyss or a burning uncrossable inferno. Eventually, we came into warmer lands again, and then, suddenly, after many moons waxed and waned, we were before another desert. And here we found some human towns and settlements. The people here had paler yellowish skin and oddly slanted narrow eyes. At one of the settlements, although we could not speak their tongue, and I do not particularly remember conquering them in your campaigns—there have been too many peoples who have fallen before your armies to recall their distinctions—we managed to obtain pack beasts in exchange for our animal skins, and then embarked upon a trip through the sands.

"As we moved, this time burning under the fire of the sun, I continued to watch its pattern, to make sure that we always followed the direction of its rising. We found a number of places that were oases, and then suddenly we encountered one familiar city, the one they call 'No-Sleep.' For, surely, there could be only one place where the puny kings are madmen, and magic changes the fabric of the city every night."

"I remember passing it in our campaign," said the *taqavor*. "Indeed, I did not choose to stop within its insane walls, for I wanted nothing to do with such madness, and so I let the city be. This is possibly the only place in my *empirastan* which I do not care to claim. I let it be, an island. But—go on."

"Well, my Lord, we passed this place and kept going, onward and onward. The desert seemed to become more familiar with each breath, even the wind was that of home. I knew something was not quite right. And then, my Lord . . . we came upon your great city."

"What?" said the *taqavor*. "That cannot be! Surely you had strayed off course and were lost, and wandered back the way you came!"

The old soldier Jimor lowered his gaze. "I know not, my Lord . . ." he whispered. "But we came from the road that leads in the other direction, on the opposite side of your city from the one along which we started our journey. I know not. I did what you told me, and followed the rising sun. . . ."

The *taqavor* got up from his high seat, and came down the steps to stand before the old soldier. There was cold fury in his expression, and he took the old man by the shoulders, his fingers biting in like claws. "Then where is the End of the World, Jimor?" he said. "If you did like I told you, you would be there now. Tell me! Either you lie, coward, or you have gone mad from the journey! Tell me!"

But the soldier remained standing like a weather-beaten cliff, immobile, and his gaze was lowered before his sovereign.

"I don't know, my Lord . . ." he continued to say quietly. And then, like a proud felled tree, he came down on his knees before the *taqavor,* and put his forehead to the cold marble floor, and whispered hoarsely, "I have failed, somehow, I do not know how."

"Yes . . . you have failed me indeed, old soldier," said the *taqavor,* staring down at the man on the ground before him. "With your failure, you are no longer one of my favored. I take away your honors and your family lands, and I strip you of the memories of our campaigns together. From now on, you are no one to me—go! And may I never see you again, else my reaction will be your death!"

And then the *taqavor* turned his back on the unfortunate.

Jimor, now a man without old honor and thus without anything, continued to lie on the floor in silence, for several long moments. And then slowly he got up and walked out of the hall, past frozen courtiers and into eternal silence.

Prince Lirheas turned to his father, and parted his lips to speak, but remained wordless.

The *taqavor* stood like a being of stone himself, looking out before him. Then he gathered himself and said, "I will now have my refreshment brought to me."

L irheas stood in the garden before a small shallow pool carved in a rectangular shape out of pale stone. He watched the woman with the knowing eyes stand at the other side and float lily blossoms upon the clear mirror surface of the waters.

"See what natural balance resides in these petals." She pointed with the long fingers of one strong, work-roughened hand.

She took pieces of several varieties of carved wood, all of different star-shapes, and set them too afloat on the water's surface. "And now, watch how the wood also balances, although it is much heavier than the delicate flowers."

"What makes the wood float, but not a stone?" he asked, watching instead her face, its features relaxed and yet focused at the same time in an intellectual contemplation of the items upon the water. "How does a ship made of wooden timbers, carrying on it such immense weight, manage to stay afloat?"

"Air, for one thing," she said, with a light smile.

"What?"

"My Lord Prince, things that have pores, or tiny little pockets to contain air, can float. For air is lighter than water, and it makes things that try to contain its freedom light as well, as it hides within. Air transfers its light nature even to the walls of its natural prison."

"So the more porous wood will float better?" he asked.

"Yes," she replied. "And yet you did not ask the complete question. For what is it that makes all things float, not just on water but on other substances of different thickness? It is the nature of the two things—that which is the liquid that supports, and that which attempts to float. The overall amount of matter of the thing that floats on top must be less than the liquid underlying it. Otherwise, that which is on top, sinks."

"I am not sure I understand . . ." said Lirheas. "I thought it was the will of the gods that had decided for us that some things will float and others will not?"

"The will of the gods," she said, "is exemplified by the natural laws of the world. For the gods set the original universal pattern, while the specific things in the universe comply with the design. Thus most varieties of wood happen to be the kind of thing that, according to the original design, is less dense in its physical nature than water. Of course the gods intended it thus. The only difference here is in the way you explain it, and the way I explain it—that is all. Both of us express the same seed of truth."

Before Lirheas could retort—for he was getting inflamed with curiosity of thought, and had actually forgotten to look at her in the usual way but was paying heed only to the actual meaning of her words—a servant messenger came running from the Palace.

Apparently another of the three remaining expeditions had returned, and there was genuine news of the End of the World.

Inside the Palace, the *taqavor* was hearing out Rihaad, one of the four men who had taken the journey to the right hand of the rising sun, toward the depth of the desert.

"The first thing I ask, before you waste my time with a rambling tale of delirious nonsense, is whether you found what you were sent to find," said the *taqavor*. "Well, what do you answer, soldier?"

Rihaad bowed deeply, his face and skin as weathered as had been the complexion of Jimor, and said calmly, "Yes, my Lord, we have found the End of the World. It was the most wondrous sight, and let me describe to you how it came to pass."

"Good, then proceed."

Rihaad went on to tell his tale. In the initial telling, his travels resembled very much those of the first expedition. However, after this expedition had come to the end of the desert, and was faced with the greatest mountains the world had ever seen, his story took on a different flavor.

"We paused at the foundation of the mountain range, my Lord," spoke the soldier. "And then, after readying our stores of food supplies for the most deadly part of the journey that lay ahead, and after equipping our pack animals with hooves of iron, we ventured forward. Ahead of us was an interminable climb. The mountains themselves seemed to lead to heaven, for when we looked up we could see only clouds and no sky, only the whiteness of craggy peaks, eternally far away.

"By day, with the sun riding our left shoulders, we continued in the direction you sent us, and by nights we rested, trying to conserve our diminishing strength. Winds struck at us, winds of such force that we could hardly keep upright, and our pack beasts struggled to move a step at a time. And higher and higher we climbed.

"At some point, my Lord, it became oddly difficult to breathe—as though the air itself had grown thin—and we began to gasp at every step, and had to abandon our pack-beasts due to the steepness of the climb.

"We continued forward. Upon reaching the highest pinnacle we were indeed above the clouds, which floated in stately, divine flocks at our feet. And at that point the man walking in the front stopped dead in his climb, and shuddered in awe at the sight that lay before him."

"Was it the End of the World?" whispered the *taqavor.* "Tell me!"

Rihaad smiled, then nodded tiredly. "Indeed, it was, my Lord. For ahead of us lay a precipice. And, as we looked down into it, there was . . . *nothing.* Not even clouds. . . . Only pallor as white as milk, for surely here was the End of the World, and things were blurring into whiteness, losing their mortal shape at last."

"Ah, go on! What did you do next?"

"Well, we waited, my Lord. We wanted to make perfectly certain that this abyss of *nothing* before us was indeed what we thought it to be.

"And thus we sat on the edge of the precipice, and we squinted with our eyes and stared for three long days into the whiteness. The wind continued to blow at our backs, and froze us into solid stone, and yet we would not move from our honorable posts."

"Did you attempt to cast stones into this abyss, to see what would befall them?" said the *taqavor,* his gaze dancing with excitement.

"I was the first man to throw a rock as far as my arm could manage," said Rihaad, nodding. "The rock disappeared into the whiteness in perfect silence, and there were not even echoes of it striking bottom. Thus, after the three days of waiting, we were sure. Not even a spot of cloud ever marred the monotony of that deathly white, neither a bird flew, nor a beast made sounds in the abyss. We heard nothing over the hiss of the ice wind."

The more Rihaad spoke, the more the *taqavor* was beginning to smile. Finally, he got up from his seat with barely repressed manic energy, saying, "Enough! I believe you have indeed found it, my faithful soldier! The End of the World is a pale abyss of gods' milk!"

"And yet I am afraid your faithful man has made a mistake," suddenly interjected a strong female voice.

Everyone turned to look at the woman with the knowing eyes as she moved away from the edge of the hall and walked forward to stand before the *taqavor*.

"What? Why do you say this, woman?"

"I am very sorry to dispel this fair notion, but it is a rather simple thing. If you recall, my Lord, our conversation on the nature of the wind rose. The wind is everywhere. It blows to all the ends of your *empirastan*. Consequently, since according to your man the winds continued to blow into the white abyss, to blow strongly at their backs even as they held their vigil, there was something else beyond this abyss, on the other side."

"But surely," exclaimed Rihaad, "the winds were simply being swallowed up just a few steps ahead of us, where the whiteness began!"

The woman turned to him and shook her head. "You cannot be sure in saying this. For how can you claim it unless you yourself had been there, riding those gale winds unto their final moment before oblivion?"

"But I stood at the edge of the precipice!"

"And yet you never ventured beyond it. Thus you can never say that you have final proof."

"What? Do you expect us to have cast ourselves into the abyss to test its nature?" Rihaad threw angry, frightened glances from the woman to the *taqavor,* and tried again. "Whoever you are, insolent woman," he sputtered, "you have no reason to dispute my truthful story!"

"There was no need to cast yourself into sure death. But there is always the need for ultimate proof before you make your final great claim."

"She is right," said the *taqavor* grimly. "And you, Rihaad, are a pompous fool. I see now what has come to pass. You allowed a mountain to stop you, superficialities to obscure your judgment. You did not do as I directed you, for I told you to try to overcome all obstacles in your way. And because you did not try, you failed. Even now, I see you do not lie in your tale, but merely assume the easy answer. And for that I banish you and yours eternally from my side! I have enough narrow-minded idiots around me as it is."

And saying that the *taqavor* turned his back on the expedition that had followed the right hand of the rising sun.

"What is this? What are you doing?" said Prince Lirheas to the woman whose every daily task he now came to faithfully observe.

They were standing in the small workshop of a blacksmith craftsman who worked with various metals and who had given the woman access to the tools of his trade.

On the flat table surface before them were several natural iron ores, samples mined from the depths of the earth. She was leaning forward, studying them attentively. She picked out one, with an exclamation. "This is the one!" she said. "This is called a lodestone."

"And what is a lodestone?" he asked, looking at the chunk of very dark rock. It had a faint reddish and ocherous tint.

The woman smiled lightly, saying, "This particular type of iron ore that is quarried in some places has in it the very forces of the earth. The gods have locked within it the strange ability to locate always the one direction which lies somewhere to the left hand of the rising sun. The people of my land have relied on it for as long as we can remember. For we also come from the left hand of the rising sun—the colder land, as you call it."

Lirheas listened with great interest, for this was the first time he had heard her talking about a personal thing, something that was not related to the work before her.

"How did you come to be here, serving my father?" he asked quietly, suddenly unable to look at her and instead watching the piece of rock before him. "Who are you, that you know so much wisdom and the truth of the world?"

"How did any of us come here?" she countered. "The whole world is now the *taqavor's* boundless *empirastan*. To serve him well, one must indeed learn as much of truth as it is possible for us mortals."

"Why?" said the prince.

"Because in the end only truth will save us," she said softly, with a strange intonation, a mood that he could not quite pinpoint. And then she returned to examining the iron rock before them, talking of its properties.

But Lirheas no longer listened. She frightened him, suddenly. Or maybe it was not so much she as what her words implied. For there were suddenly half-formed things, new, remote and dark, on the edges of his consciousness, things of mystery, of an abyssal unknown, just waiting for him, for them, for everyone, at the next turn of awareness. . . .

And thus his mind—as it had done so often before with others before this one woman came into their life—his mind drifted away gently, into its own remote place, so that he was removed from this reality, removed to a safe, gentle condition, and he did not have to think, or consider, or fear, or wonder.

Another span of several moons, a subtle change in the nature of the warmth of the days, and the third expedition of the four returned to the great city of the *taqavor*.

Mareid was the one who had been told to follow the face of the setting sun, and so he and his men had gone in the direction opposite that of the first expedition.

"To measure the exact direction of our daily movement, my Lord," spoke Mareid—a thin tall soldier, weathered and already dark before he had set out, for his was a race with skin the color of dates, soft rounded features and wiry night-black hair—"one of us would be watching for the first glimmer of the rising sun at dawn, and would thus stand facing it directly. Meanwhile, a second man would stand lined up exactly against his back. Back-to-back we stood, and the one who was facing away from the rising sun would point with his hand. That was the direction we took."

The *taqavor* reclined in his high seat and watched the tall soldier with a merciless cold gaze. "And have you found the End of the World, man? Or have you found only illusion? By all the sacred gods, do not even begin to lie to me, nor try to excuse yourself. I must have the truth."

"I do not know what to call it, my Lord," replied Mareid. "But we found a strange thing—the End of the World recedes as we approach it, for what is on the horizon is always different from what it is when we arrive there."

"Is that so? And does the horizon run from you in particular, or just from your luckless expedition?"

Mareid bowed deeply, placing his right hand over his heart. "My Lord, I beg you to forgive me for not having the right words to describe this, and hear me out, even if it appears laughable. There is one other interesting thing we have noticed, particularly on our travels over two great oceans—for indeed, if one follows the setting sun there is mostly water, and very little dry land past this desert. We noticed that when there is a deadly calm, without winds over the ocean, and our ship sits for days without sails while we row with as much strength as we can, there are creatures swimming alongside us in the ocean that have a purpose and a destination.

"What creatures?" said the *taqavor,* stopping himself halfway in a yawn. "Go on, for today I feel magnanimous and I am willing to listen to your imbecile tale—but not exceedingly long. So make it good, soldier."

"Yes, my Lord. As I was saying, there are peculiar creatures that have the bodies and fins of great fishes and yet breathe mortal air. The greatest of them have thick water-repellent hides, and they are known to grow to be the size of a ship, and blow tall fountains of water from the nostril holes. The lesser ones can grow to be the size of a man and have smooth rounded heads with long narrow snouts.

"The lesser of these creatures with long snouts accompanied our ship for many days, sailing alongside us in the calm waters while we rowed, and then would disappear for days. Then they would return. It was as though they knew how to find us, and knew their way around the endless waters. Maybe the gods had given them the knowledge of directions. But no matter—the reason I speak of this is because, upon more than one occasion, these creatures saved us by showing us the true direction when the sun was not to be seen in the sky, and the sea mists had grown so thick that the land and sky mixed into one. At such terrifying times, afloat on the great water, all alone, we were oddly reassured to hear the creatures' wild cries, and we followed them, having no other choice.

"When finally the sun came out, and the days changed to clear skies and sailing wind, the creatures left us. Surely they knew we would now be safe and could be trusted to find our way."

"Marvelous, these sea creatures of yours," said the *taqavor.* "Too bad I could not send them on an expedition in your stead."

"My Lord. . . ." Mareid's face was drawn and he was stiff as a column from the growing fear. For he had known the *taqavor* to laugh and mock cruelly before he doled out the most severe punishment.

"All right," spoke the *taqavor.* "After you made your way over this interminable ocean, what then? Did you reach land and proceed to chase the horizon, or did you simply turn back after a good rest and come home the way you left?"

"Both, my Lord . . ." whispered the poor man. "Let me explain! For we did not at any point turn back, and yes, we continued to move in the direction of the setting sun, and when we reached land, as you correctly surmise, we continued our journey on solid ground."

"And?"

Mareid's gaunt form trembled as he bowed once again, and this time he remained thus bent. His speech meanwhile became more hurried. "And then, as we moved through wide expanses of sparse lands covered not with sand but with sharp pale grass, terrain turned into forest and marshes, for water was in the ground, making it rich like mud. As we waded our way out of the swamps, there were many rivers with waters gold and blue and opaque with mud—first small gentle rivulets running though grassland, then wider streams, then rivers which we had to swim, building rafts for our belongings. And then, my Lord, the lands again grew warmer, and there came an end to the river country.

"For several long moons we moved through drier forest, then open land, passing some human settlements where the people could not speak our tongue, nor we theirs. And then, at last, the earth grew rich with sand, and we were in a desert . . ."

"And did this desert, by any chance, look particularly familiar?" said the *taqavor*.

"Why yes it did, my Lord!" exclaimed Mareid, straightening. "You may find it unbelievable, but we were soon at the gates of your glorious city! What I am about to say, my Lord, may sound insane, but it appeared we had come in a great circle around the sun!"

"Either that, or you had lost your minds from the sun's heat, since it shone on you for so many days," said the *taqavor*.

"I am so sorry, my Lord . . . I know it sounds mad, but one thing I am sure of is that we kept going in the right direction!"

"All right, I allow this much—maybe at one point you ended up at the End of the World and you did not even know it . . ." mused the *taqavor*. "For what if the World ends suddenly, and then flips over, and you continue walking on the underside, upside-down in relation to the rest of us?"

"Why, yes, it is possible, my Lord!" said Mareid with excitement, picking up on the scenario. "It could be that the world has its exact opposite on the bottom, including land and mountains and oceans, and even a sky! Maybe other peoples and nations fill its nether regions, and they walk upside-down and underneath us even now, and neither we nor they know it?"

"This would imply that there are in fact *two* worlds of mortal men . . ." whispered the *taqavor*. A darkness once again obscured him and took away all traces of levity. "No, I do not like this thought at all. . . . For then my *empirastan* might be comprised only of the world on this side, and not that of the under side. And in that case. . . ."

As the thought completed itself at last, the *taqavor* screamed in rage, so that everyone in the hall trembled at the terror of his voice. And, screaming, he arose from his high seat and struck down the poor soldier before him with a powerful blow, so that Mareid lay flat on the cold marble, his face bleeding from the force of the anger. His lifeblood fell in a random splatter pattern of red upon the marble.

"No!" screamed the *taqavor* in fury. "For I am the ruler of the whole world! It is all mine, my *empirastan!* There is no one and nothing underneath, and the earth has no opposite side! I say it and thus it is, before all gods!"

After that, it seemed the *taqavor* had become a changed man. If it were possible, he was even more feral. As the days flowed, he spent more time in seclusion, more days walking lone galleries in his gardens or else locked in his private chambers, where he was heard pacing endlessly, muttering to himself, his footsteps making echoes upon the stone floor.

"One more!" he was often heard to say. "One more left! When the last one comes back I will have the true news of the World and its End, at last! One more!"

In the meantime the woman with the knowing eyes continued with her immense task of creating the one object that would capture in it the essence of the wind rose and thus the world.

Under her directions, a hall was selected—one which stood in the very center of the palace structure—and within it were placed great blocks of fine polished marble stone. Once arranged, these blocks were carved by the *taqavor's* own sculptors into a statue of a great flower blossom, a many-petaled rose. From the distance of the hall entrance, from all sides it looked like nothing but delicate lifelike petals, but, if observed from the top, in its middle could be seen a great round carved hollow filled with water, forming a shallow pool.

Once, the *taqavor* himself passed by as the sculptors and artisans were working in the hall, and he noticed the woman standing there, directing their work, and almost did not recognize her. For a moment a frown filled his features, a frown to see a female creature whose face was unobscured—and then he remembered who she was.

"You," he said. "When will I have the living symbol of my *empirastan?* Is it ready yet?"

And the woman, dressed plainly like a servant and wearing the same demure shawl as always bowed before him and said in a familiar, strong, calming voice, "Behold, my Lord, this is its cradle being built. When it is done, the symbol of the wind rose will lie within the heart of the rose of stone, floating upon calm waters."

"Then I await its completion." The *taqavor* nodded.

The Prince Lirheas, standing as always to the side, noticed as he observed the *taqavor* discreetly that his father's eyes were fevered. And his father's gaze was unfocused and dim.

Then the *taqavor* was again on his way, forgetting the whole thing, it seemed, like an old man.

Indeed, it was a tangible relief to have his heavy presence out of the hall. Lirheas once again turned his unyielding gaze to watch the woman as she moved in her artistic energy and fluidity. For, more and more, she was the only thing he saw.

The *taqavor* was preoccupied in the House of Wives when he was delivered the news that the fourth and last expedition to the End of the World had returned.

The news was relayed from the other side of a gauze curtain in a luxurious bedchamber that hid the *taqavor* and one of his *taqoui* moving in the carnal act. The information had such an effect on the sovereign that he grunted in triumph and immediately spilled his seed. He then removed himself prematurely from within the woman underneath him, while she moaned and continued to grind her loins in unrelieved lust.

Back in the palace, a tired and gray-haired man awaited the *taqavor,* the soldier called Vikenti who had been directed to follow the rising sun's left hand.

"We have returned at long last, my Lord," said Vikenti, his voice hoarse and dry as though he had not spoken for all these seasons since he had last been here.

"Tell me, have you seen the End of the World, of my *empirastan?*" asked the *taqavor.* "For I must know it at last, and you are the only one left of the four who might give me a proper answer. . . ."

Vikenti was indeed an old soldier, and far from a fool. "What happened to the others?" he asked carefully. "What news did they bring, Jimor and Rihaad and Mareid, my old comrades in arms?"

In response the *taqavor* laughed. He sat in his high seat and shook with paroxysms that resembled dark fury and pain and madness.

"They brought back nothing," he said at last, quieting into a dark sobriety. "One by one they came back. And their tales were filled with lies and delusion. For they had been lost, all of them, deviating from their true purpose in one way or another. And now there is only you. All hope rests on you. What news have you to tell me?"

And the old soldier Vikenti sighed, for at that point he suddenly knew the exact nature of the fate unfolding before him like a carpet of twilight.

"My Lord, what I have to tell you is a thing of wonder. And yet I am afraid this thing will not please you to hear it. You may also consider me mad and lost and full of delusion. For I am now convinced that the World, the great boundless *empirastan* of yours, has no End."

"What?" whispered the *taqavor.* "Not you, too. . . ."

"Father . . ." Prince Lirheas suddenly spoke out. "Maybe this man does indeed say only what he has been given to see by the will of the gods? For I am beginning to suspect either that the gods do not want mortal men to know what the End of the World is or the answer may be beyond our meager understanding."

"The reason why I say the World has no End, my Lord," said Vikenti, "is because I traversed the world in a straight line, heading to the left of the rising sun, while the sun remained on my right, and yet I arrived back in the same place I had started from. This is a miracle! How else to explain this?"

"Your mind has gone mad, just like the others," hissed the *taqavor*. "That's how I explain it."

"And yet the same thing, the same exact madness, seemed to have taken over the minds of three of your men, my Lord," said the woman with the knowing eyes, and everyone turned to stare at the source of her calm voice. "The fourth man, Rihaad, merely did not finish his journey after being deceived by the great mountain. For, if he and his men had ventured past the eternal whiteness of the abyss before him, it is possible he too would have eventually come back to the origin of his journey, this very city."

The *taqavor* stared at her with dilated eyes. "What are you saying now, woman? What do you mean? What—"

"Let me show you a miraculous thing, my Lord, and in the showing I will illustrate the mystery of the World and its End."

Saying this, the woman turned to a servant and said in a voice of authority, "Go and fetch me four long hair ribbons."

Everyone looked extremely confused while the servant ran to do as bidden. Soon he returned carrying four brightly colored ribbons of silk.

"I am going to show you four journeys," said the woman, taking the ribbons. She placed the first ribbon flat on the marble floor, and pointed at the end nearest to her. "This is the journey's beginning, and this is your city."

Next she pointed to the other end of the ribbon, saying, "This is the journey's end, also in your city."

"Impossible," said the *taqavor.* "Obviously, if the four expeditions had kept moving in a straight line they could not have come back here to the city!"

The courtiers made noises of acquiescence. Lirheas, standing a few steps to the side, looked on with growing intensity.

And then the woman with the knowing eyes smiled. She leaned forward and picked up the ribbon from the ground. She took both the ends of the ribbon in her fingers and placed them on top of each other, so that the ribbon formed a hanging loop.

"Now look," she said. "The journey's beginning and end are in the same place. And look at the shape of journey itself. The line that you had thought all along to be on flat ground is in fact the surface of a great arc, a complete perfect circle."

"What does this mean?" said the *taqavor.*

"It means," she replied, "that the earth, the very world is not what we think it is. But—before I name its nature, let me show you the rest of the journeys."

She took out the three remaining ribbons, and also folded them in on themselves, so that all ends were held by her forefinger and thumb. At the same time, she also moved two of the ribbons to positions perpendicular to each other and two directly on top of each other, just like the four directions the expeditions had taken. And then, still holding the ribbons with one hand, she straightened out the hanging loops and raised them so that all of them approximated circles.

"Look now, my Lord, and all the rest of you," she said loudly. "This shape that is made by the four journeys. What do you see in its outline?"

It was Prince Lirheas alone who answered. "I see a sphere . . ." he whispered.

"Yes!" said the woman. "For indeed it is thus. The journeys that traverse the world outline the true shape of the world, and we see it is round—a great ball suspended by the gods in the air, bathed by the winds which are indeed everywhere along the ball's perfect surface. Being a sphere, the World has no End and no Beginning."

"That is impossible!" said the *taqavor*. "How can we walk upon the round surface of your sphere world?"

"That I do not know," said the woman softly. "Something, some divine force holds us in place. And yet, because the sphere is so vast, we cannot see the full curvature, only the nearest edges, which are the horizon, and which to us appear flat."

"There is no such force! What nonsense!" said the *taqavor*. He got up from his seat and began to pace the floor before the court.

"This whole madness is giving me a headache," he said eventually. "Begone from my sight, all of you, and I will not hear any more of this. And you, woman, finish the symbol for me, finish your wind rose. And speak not another word. Because of your previous wisdom, I forgive you. But not any more. Thus you will speak not a word, ever, to me or to anyone. Be silent, forever. Now, go!"

Those who yet remained watched in terror. But the woman smiled softly, and then she cast her gaze downward and bowed deeply. And in silence she left the *taqavor's* hall.

The finished Rose was a great wooden four-pointed star of the lightest sandalwood and cedar. One of the four rays contained a slim rod of lodestone, and was counter-balanced on the three remaining rays by their thicker layers of wood.

Delicate resin was applied to seal in the wood and to protect it from rot, and then the object was placed carefully in the pool at the heart of the stone rose. And to everyone's amazement, the four-pointed star turned a certain direction, and remained permanently aligned that way. No matter how many times it was rotated in the water, it would return to its original position—the lodestone ray would point to the left of the rising sun.

The *taqavor* was shown this oddity, and surprisingly it amused him, for he spent long hours entertaining himself by spinning the wooden Rose, and watching it return to its original orientation.

It was indeed a living symbol.

And yet it was a disturbing symbol, for in its functional silence it spoke and hinted of things that were just at the edges of the consciousness, things that warped the reason and forced it to start thinking along a dangerous line. . . .

Eventually it came to pass that the *taqavor* spent days staring at the Rose while he thought of things ordinary and familiar, thought of the winds and his *empirastan.*

But he never dared think of edges. . . . Not in the beginning. Not of edges of things. But then edges began to obsess him, as always happens with little details in the beginnings of such madness.

The *taqavor* observed edges everywhere, fine lines or blurred lines, or even implied lines of visual illusory meaning. Edges that signified ends. . . .

Soon the *taqavor* wanted the edges marked and labeled clearly, even in places that had none. He called upon his artists and had them paint four distinct opposite edges in the stone of the pool that contained the floating Rose. Then, he decided to name the edges, in order to assign them even greater permanence.

Mumbling nonsense words for hours to himself, he finally decided to call the edge where the lodestone always returned "North" and its opposite ray "South." The end that faced the rising sun he called "East" and its opposite "West."

And he would ask everyone what they saw. Only—no one's answer would satisfy him. Because the madness had grown deeper, riding in the back of his mind now in all things.

Eventually he knew he had to call *her* back. For she was the one who had planted this seed of insanity in him, who had expanded his thoughts past their mortal bounds and edges into a world of divine terror without a limit. . . .

The woman with the knowing eyes came wordlessly to him when called. In silence she stood and listened to his rantings about edges and lines and meaning—while he leaned over the stone petal pool and spun the Rose in the water, and his hands shook.

"Speak, damn you!" the *taqavor* finally exclaimed, "I revoke my earlier command. Tell me what is the truth of all of this."

"My Lord . . ." said the woman, her unused voice cracking at the first note. "The truth is here before you, in part. You see it working in the nature of the Compass Rose. For the compass is an object that my people use to find directions, a thing of lodestone and wood floating on water in a simple bowl. That is all this is. A humble instrument of navigation that works according to the laws of the world."

"And what are the laws of the world?" whispered the *taqavor.*

"The laws are too many to mention. We see them all around us, simply with our eyes. Look!" And smiling she spread her hands wide to indicate everything.

"Your eyes . . ." said the *taqavor,* looking at her. "They are not . . . like my eyes. You see differently from anyone."

"Not so, my Lord," she retorted. "I only appear to see more because I choose to completely face what lies in all directions before me."

"No . . ." said the *taqavor.* "No, woman, you do not, and you may not. Indeed, now that I look upon you I see no difference in your eyes and mine. Or maybe, yes, there is a difference. I see in your face no eyes at all."

And then the *taqavor* called his guards in the loud voice of a mad screeching carrion bird. "Her eyes!" he said over and over. "You must make sure that we see no eyes in her face. So that she will not see our eyes either, nor other things in the world."

The woman made no sound at first, then only a muffled gasp escaped her as she was taken by rough hands, and a guard's knife was plunged in her eye-sockets, one after the other, gouging out her eyes.

Prince Lirheas heard it in his mind, that soft gasp, a mere sigh, as he came running into the hall, a terrible premonition of sudden falling night upon him, upon her—for in that moment the distinctions of their entities blurred.

"The world is a sphere," she whispered, blood running down her face out of the empty sockets. "And I have seen it. It is too late for you to take that away—even from yourself."

"Ah, for that I forgive you, woman," cackled the *taqavor* as he spun the Rose in the water. "I forgive you and grant you a life, only without your eyes. A life for a Rose!"

And then he added, "Who will take you now, 'you *without* the knowing eyes'? What will you do, in order to see, in order to know?"

"I will take her!" exclaimed Lirheas, his own eyes roiling with tears, clouded. In his vision swirled the form of the beast before him—the hateful monster who had fathered him—and of the woman who was more precious to him than his own vision or his own life. "She will be my queen, and she will see through my eyes. . . ."

But the *taqavor* did not hear him. He spun the Rose and stared at some distinct, precisely delineated point before him with his own eyes which had never seen truth, only its edges, and thus were vacant and blind.

And so it came to pass that, for a moment, truth was glimpsed up close, and then once again obscured.

Truth is like the wind. Not even eyes can reliably serve you.

The only corporeal evidence that remains is the Compass Rose.

Dream Ten

Gods and Fleas

"Once upon a time," said Annaelit, the Teller of Tales, "a wicked minor god—nay, a sarcastic puny god—decided that humankind in and of itself contained very little to amuse the divine Pantheon. And so, one godlike morning, this deity gathered a fistful of his beard shavings, and shook it out profusely over the universe."

"Aieee!"

The children gathered at the storyteller's feet clapped and giggled and squealed in wicked delight.

"You all know what happens next, don't you?" said the young woman, feigning disgust. "How is one supposed to tell you anything when you already know all the best stories?"

"Tell it anyway! Tell us the rest!" they cried while rolling around on their backs and flailing their limbs. There was much stomping of feet against the beaten floor of the hovel.

"All right then, but I will make it short, since it is getting late, little goslings. Where was I? Oh yes, the divine beard shavings.

"And so the god shook them over the universe, to all the four corners of the Compass Rose. And, wherever his stubble fell, little annoying creatures called fleas appeared. You all know fleas, right?"

"I know fleas!" cried a boy near the front. "My sister Ikke has them!" And he screamed in hilarity as his older sister walloped him on the head with an old towel.

"I do not, pig!" cried Ikke. "You are a filthy liar to say that, Joar! Pig!"

In reply, Joar made oinking noises, while the other children giggled.

"All right, enough," said Annaelit. "Now then, the fleas were put on this earth for a very good reason. Does anyone know what it is?"

"For punishment!" piped up another child, a little grimy girl in the very back.

"Why do you say that, Milae?" asked Annaelit.

"Because fleas are nasty!"

"Are you very sure? Not that they aren't nasty, but—are you sure that is the only reason?"

"Yes. No . . ." said little Milae, rubbing her sooty nose vigorously.

Annaelit smiled. And then, maybe because she was contemplating some inner joke, she snorted and chuckled.

"I'll tell you the true purpose of fleas. But only if you promise to keep it a great secret, and tell no one else. Fleas are a mixed blessing, little goslings. They were given to us so that we could scratch ourselves like monkeys, and amuse the gods, as we pick these little monsters off each other. And in the process, as we make the gods laugh, we also grow closer to one another in friendship. That is the one thing the wicked puny god never had in mind when he created fleas."

"But why is this such a great secret?" asked another child. "Why can't I tell this to Grandmother?"

"Well, you could. But you might not want to, at least not until you'd thought about it long enough," said Annaelit. "All stories have a curious and even dangerous power. They are manifestations of truth—yours and mine. And truth is all at once the most wonderful yet terrifying thing in the world, which makes it nearly impossible to handle. It is such a great responsibility that it's best not to tell a story at all unless you know you can do it right. You must be very careful, or without knowing it you can change the world."

"Then why do you tell stories, Annaelit? Aren't you afraid?"

Annaelit smiled. "Of course I am afraid, little one. Each story I tell runs in through my heart and out through my mouth, and plucks a bit of myself with it. And, yes, it hurts. But the gods decided to make me a storyteller, and there is nothing I can do to alter it."

As the children thought about it, the room grew quiet.

"Oh, and another thing about that changing the world business," said Annaelit. "I tell the story to you now, but in each telling the story itself changes a little, changes direction, and that in turn changes you and me. So be very careful not only in how you repeat it but in how you remember it, goslings. More often than you realize it, the world is shaped by two things—stories told and the memories they leave behind."

When Annaelit was done, and had sent the children scampering to bed in their neighborhood hovels and caravanserai on the fringes of the city, it was more than an hour after sundown. But she was far from done for the evening. The storyteller had another appointment that night, one that was not to be postponed or denied.

Tonight, in the heart of the great city, Lord Ostavi was holding a feast in honor of his esteemed visitor, Lord Dava, who had come here from another, even greater city, and was negotiating new and profitable contracts of trade. If all went well, dozens of rich caravans would embark on regular journeys between here and there. Salt and spices and oil and silk, fruits of the vine and fruits of the quarry—all would be carried from East to West and back again.

From this arrangement everyone would profit, especially the fathers of those poor children to whom Annaelit told tales without ever charging a single coin. These men would drive the caravans and earn bread for their families. Thin children would grow round and glowing with health. Smiles would grow, without any need for stories to take their minds off the lack of food.

Annaelit lit a pair of candles, and in the growing dusk she pried the lid off her old clothing chest and rummaged through it, illuminated by the flickering golden light. At the very bottom, concealed by plain cotton dresses and shawls, she found a heavy caftan of deep jade silk, embroidered with rosy pearls and fine delicate mosaic patterns, and trimmed with gold thread at the sleeves and around the collar.

The caftan was long, nearly down to her ankles, and she put on underneath it a fine silk shirt of pale amber yellow, with a collar tied demurely high at her throat, and matching pants. Rummaging further in the clothes chest, she found a pair of similar heavy jade slippers, also trimmed with fine gold thread.

These and none other could support her properly as she would stand later tonight and speak the truth of the world.

Next, Annaelit took out a wooden comb and unpinned her dark auburn hair from a bun at the nape of her neck. She brushed it with a hundred strokes until sparks of electricity came dancing from the tips and her hair nearly stood on end in a halo of gossamer. It would add a strange shine to any tale told.

From a basket underneath her poor bed she took out a box in which were a small hand mirror, tiny fluted glass jars of perfumed oils, paints, and sticks of kohl. Sitting on a squat footstool, she applied the kohl with sure hands in an outline around her eyes, watching their lapis color dance in sudden pallor against the dark paint and reflect back at her from the mirror. Her eyes were filled with stories, and this was the only time that they could be seen properly, since at other times she walked with her face downcast, as was appropriate for simple serving women.

To complete the transformation of her face, she dabbed a bit of rose powder on her cheeks and took out a deep agate-red oil which she applied in a gloss over her lips. This last detail was particularly important, because truth would now have an easier time as it ventured forth between her lips and out of her mouth.

Finally, from a pouch of white silk she took out her greatest treasure, a net of gold chain and pearls that she placed over her forehead and her hair, letting a jeweled fringe dangle over her temples and a single long cascade of pearl emerge from the center of her forehead to rest between her eyes.

Her words would also cascade gracefully and be well framed tonight.

She straightened, looking at herself in the hand mirror, and a smile like a new story tested the slippery smoothness of her lips. Then Annaelit took a plain floor-length shawl and drew it around her, over her glittering hair and close over her face, which was now charged with the ability to change worlds. The shawl obscured her form and would serve to protect her in the uncertain streets of the city.

At last, with a puff she blew out the candles and the room of the hovel was submerged in bluish darkness.

The door creaked, and like a shadow in the dusk the storyteller was gone.

Lord Ostavi's Palace stood on a rise, a natural cliffside, and overlooked most of the city. The walls of the Palace were of heavy rose granite, brought here from a distant quarry by caravan. Within the outer walls, the Palace structure itself was a work of carved frieze and slender colonnades, and everywhere rhythmic beating fountains of clear cool water.

It was night, and the fountains were illuminated by rows of oil lamps and the brightly lit windows of the Palace. From within came the sounds of music, and in the grand central hall was an extravagant feast.

Handsome young Lord Dava, dressed like a savage in a garish finery of persimmon, crimson and violet silk, with a circlet of gold around his dark hair, sat in a place of honor upon a mountain of soft cushions—exactly across the room from his host, the opulent Lord Ostavi.

The latter reposed like a tastefully attired wine barrel upon an equally grand mountain of cushions and fine throw rugs. A long crimson carpet was strewn on the marble floor between them, stretching from one cushion mountain to the other, and armies of servants ran back and forth between them, offering delicacy after delicacy, piled on gold platters, and endless jugs of fine wine.

At the same time, a number of female dancers, clad in fine gauze veils and twined ropes of gold, twirled and pranced between the two Lords. They swayed to the beat of the drums, narrowly missing the rushing servants with their trays, and their gymnastic feats of avoidance would have amazed any a properly attentive and aware audience.

"Hello there, Lord Dava!" cried out Lord Ostavi over the great din and the music and the dancing beauties, all the way across the grand hall. "How are you enjoying the feast, my dearest friend?"

"What?" yelled back Lord Dava. "What did you say?"

"I said, how is the feast? Are the food and the drink and the entertainment to your liking?"

"Yes, she is!" replied Lord Dava. "I particularly like her buttocks!"

As Lord Ostavi sat back to better consider this reply, a high-ranked servant crawled up the mountain of cushions to whisper in his ear, "The Teller of Tales is here, my Lord, as you requested. Shall I bring her in?"

"Huh?" said the noble host, still visualizing someone's buttocks, and then the meaning reached him. "Ah, yes! Bring her in immediately!"

He clapped his hands together loudly. Tambourine players at all ends of the hall made an even louder racket to signify that the Lord was calling for attention, and after some moments the cacophony came to a halt. The dancers retreated to the edges of the hall, delicately pulling their veils over their faces, and the servants with platters grew still and then wilted into obeisant kneeling positions on the floor.

"Now then," said Lord Ostavi in the sudden silence, clearing his throat dramatically, "we have a special treat prepared for my dear guest Lord Dava. A storyteller of great talent and wisdom is at our disposal tonight. She will pour forth stories like honey song, and you will be enthralled, I promise you."

In reply, on the other end of the hall, atop his pillow mountain, Lord Dava yawned. "Does she tell tales of sorrowful romance, Lord Ostavi? Or is it silly comedies we are to endure?"

"Endure? Come now, you have not heard the fruits of the wondrous sweet tongue of Annaelit. Listen to her this once and, I promise, you will be in love!"

"I am in love already," Lord Dava retorted petulantly from across the hall, and echoes rang all around him for emphasis. "I am hopelessly in love with a goddess of this city's High Court, whose lovely form I saw yesterday morning in the marketplace when I was on my way here to you, my Lord. They tell me her name is Makeia, and she is the third daughter of some Lord or another. What does it matter? She is the one I must have, else my heart pines away into oblivion, and my reason darkens. . . ."

"That would be the effect of the plum wine, my Lord," came a sudden bright voice. "True love has quite a different influence upon the reason and the heart."

Annaelit, the Teller of Tales stood between the two cushion mountains, in the center of the red carpet that ran from one Lord to the other.

"Oh, is that so?" Lord Dava sat up on his elbows, and took in the rather curiously pleasant female form before him.

"Ah, Annaelit, there you are," said Lord Ostavi in the meantime. "Your appearance is fortunate as always, clever girl, I say—"

But Annaelit bowed very curtly before the host, and then immediately returned her attention to the guest. "Yes, it is so," she replied in a firm voice, as though reassuring a child, and surprisingly her tones acted soothingly upon Lord Dava, so that he settled back down on the cushions, taking a swig of wine from his carved goblet.

"Now," said Annaelit. "Since you, my Lord, are so curious about the nature of love, let me tell you a true story. It is the same story I told Princess Makeia when I was at her feast two days ago, and I think you too will find it enlightening. And after I am done—"

"Wait!" exclaimed Lord Dava. "Did you say you were actually in the presence of my divine beauty two days ago?"

"Well," said Annaelit, "you do look ravishing in that silk, Lord Dava, but I wouldn't use those words to describe your particular looks. And no, regretfully, I was not in your company at that point."

"Not me, woman! I mean Makeia—she is the divine beauty of whom I speak!" said Lord Dava.

Lord Ostavi cleared his throat, and motioned for a servant to refill his goblet of wine.

Interesting, Annaelit thought. *Too many verbal asides tonight. I cannot seem to get started with the story. Is it me or them?*

Indeed, there was something a little different about this evening—an inexplicable sense of mischief and suspense in the air. Annaelit could almost feel a cloud of randomness over their heads, a shifting of control by minuscule degrees. But she could not quite identify it, could not pinpoint what it was exactly that was causing everyone's words, including her own, to get subtly off track. . . .

"I see," she said. "In that case, my answer would be yes. And now, my Lord will be made very happy to know that I will be attending a gathering which includes Princess Makeia, once again tomorrow evening."

"What? Your Lord?" said Lord Dava, wrinkling his brows. "And who would that be?"

"Why that would be you, Lord Dava. It is but a figure of speech. In a form similar to divine beauty. But—allow me to return back to the Tale I am about to tell."

"Very well," said Lord Dava, beginning to take another deep swallow of the wine that swirled in his goblet but instead managing to release a pungent burp into the aforementioned container. "But first you must describe to me the Princess Makeia in close detail, for I can listen to nothing else without first reaffirming my ailing spirit with the vision of her loveliness. . . ."

In reply, Annaelit lifted her right hand dramatically and began to pace like a dancer in the center of the great hall. She was about to take control and imbue this evening with storytelling enchantment. Only why was it that her normally lightning-quick mind was drawing a blank?

She paced thus, saying nothing, gathering her panicking thoughts, for the duration of several long breaths. And then, just as suddenly, she stopped.

"Behold!" she exclaimed, her hand still upraised, so that both the lords stared at it in expectation.

But Annaelit lowered her hand, and was pacing once again, her jewelry tinkling softly, and her veils fluttering.

What in the world is happening to me?

Lord Dava was by then feeling quite fermented himself, and the moving form of the storyteller tripled in his vision. Lord

Ostavi was not too far behind, and was seeing at least two quickly pacing Annaelits dressed in caftans of jade silk.

"Behold a form more radiant than the desert sun at high noon!" said Annaelit at last.

Lord Ostavi blinked, then squinted, saying, "I see it. . . ."

"Yes!" exclaimed Lord Dava. "Go on. . . ."

"Behold gleaming satin hair like a waterfall, a deep sienna color that pours like liquid bronze and yet is wafted by the perfumed wind of your gardens!"

"Oh, yes!"

"Behold skin soft to the touch and delicate as the ripest peach, and great slobbering lips tender like the succulent cherry fruit, dripping liquid juices . . ."

"Ah!" moaned Lord Dava. "Yes, go on, for that is she!"

"Actually," said Annaelit, bringing her voice down to a normal volume and smoothly covering the fact that only moments ago she had had no idea what she was saying and why she was saying it, "I am describing her mare—definitely slobbering after it had been watered from a pail. I must add, the poor thing was tired and its beauty somewhat marred by a ride through the markets—I haven't even begun to describe its mistress yet."

Lord Ostavi's eyes bulged a little, and then he let go a loud belch. "The mare . . ." he said. "I must see this marvel of a mare sometime. Really, I say—"

"Really, you must," said Annaelit, feeling oddly lightheaded herself and aware that she was babbling. "Now then, as I was saying—"

"No, no, no, wait!" said Lord Dava. He clumsily shifted his weight on the pillows in an attempt to rise, but instead ended up toppling down even lower in the soft mountain. Two of the smallest pillows propping up his elbow slipped out from underneath him and went flying like projectile weapons to hit two nearby servants smack in the face and on the chin respectively. "What exactly did you mean, Lord Ostavi, by referring to the lovely Makeia as a mare? I do not like that at all, you know."

"What?" said Lord Ostavi. "What was that again?"

"My lords," began Annaelit, feeling the subtle flavor of confusion grow stronger, and herself losing the last bits of cohesion, "I think at this point a small period of rest for both of you may be the best thing, while I continue this storytelling session another time—"

"No!" Lord Dava let out a drunken roar. "I want an explanation! That is, I want to hear what this lord here who has been my dearest host, up to this moment, this lord—lord—"

"Lord Ostavi . . ." said Annaelit.

"Yes, Lord Ostavi—I want him to tell me what he meant to imply about Makeia's mare-like condition? Or was it her appearance?"

As Lord Dava spoke, Lord Ostavi's own wine-flushed face began to turn an even deeper shade of purple.

"My *dearest* Lord Dava!" he roared back. "If you were not my guest, I would tell you without wasting another moment that I have no idea what you're talking about since you are absolutely as drunk as a goat! But, since you are my guest, I must control my tongue. And thus I inform you with loving gentleness that suddenly the hour grows late, and it is time for us to retire to our sleeping chambers, and continue this feast in the morning!"

"A very wise decision, my Lord," whispered Annaelit. "And I promise to continue my story another day."

Lord Dava's jaw dropped. "Drunk?" he said, staring like a madman at his host. *"Drunk?* Did you just call me a drunken goat, my dearest Lord Ostavi? Because, if you did, I am afraid I am going to take great offense right now. Yes! By gods, I am offended to the point of wanting to take you outside and give you a lesson in hospitality myself, upon your donkey, I mean upon your—"

The roar that came from Lord Ostavi was truly terrifying. "Out!" he screamed, while the food servants and dancing girls in the hall began to scatter in panic. "Take this son of a braying ass out! Now, before I kill him with my own three—I mean two—hands! Gods hear me, I will not commit guesticide!"

Annaelit stood in the middle, her hands shaking, memories of former storytelling sessions passing before her eyes. She watched as Lord Dava, struggling only slightly, and mostly grabbing everyone around him—both male and female—in inappropriate places, was carried out of the hall by three of Lord Ostavi's guards, and two of his own bodyguards. "I am going to kill you, Ostavi!" he bellowed from the doorway. "After I move out of your house tomorrow, and you are no longer my host, you immediately become a dead son of a whoring sheep! And there is no such word as 'guesticide'!"

When the feast hall was cleared of Lord Dava and most of the servants, Lord Ostavi collapsed. He lay back upon his tousled mountain of pillows and groaned, holding his head and muttering to himself, oblivious of everything. "It's too bright in here!" he moaned. "Someone close the curtains. Or remove the sun. Yes, right there, please. Yes. . . ."

Annaelit bit her lips and, breathing as lightly as she hoped would make her invisible, started to tiptoe out of the great hall. She moved past one or two nonchalant servants who were picking up dropped platters and mopping up spilled wine with washcloths, while others went around extinguishing oil lamps. Just as she reached the exit she heard a snore coming from the venerable host's direction.

Outside the Palace, the darkness was chill and oil lamps burned brightly within delicate spheres of colored glass to illuminate the mirror waters of the fountain reservoirs, the fountains themselves having been stilled for the night.

Annaelit stood with her shawl once again wrapped around her, her mind in turmoil.

What in the name of all the gods had happened? She had come here to tell a story, but instead her words had inadvertently caused an idiot drunken fight between two powerful lords about to seal a trade agreement. Indeed, this was an insult to her fine skill! For Annaelit was known to soothe with her words, to create harmonious wonder, to smooth out bitterness from the brows of angry men.

What had come to pass?

She hurriedly began to walk past the gardens toward the outside walls. Their priceless rose granite appeared gray, as do all things in the night. In angry silence she berated herself and examined her behavior and words from all sides.

And then one of her sides began literally to itch, and she scratched herself angrily and continued walking. A couple of steps later, something definitely bit her on her neck, then her lower back, and she scratched herself again, thinking that the Palace might have looked magnificent but must have been filthy with fleas.

And, as soon as she'd thought that she felt two more bites, on her arm and on her lower calf. And then a third one happened smack in the middle of her behind.

She heard a distinct sound of soft laughter.

In the darkness, Annaelit stopped.

Keep walking, mortal, said a voice in the night, in her head. *Just a little more, and you will be outside the walls.*

Annaelit felt the fine hairs on her arms beginning to stand up, and her eyes were open so wide that they hurt.

Nevertheless, she resumed walking.

As she passed the sleepy guards at the gate, who gave her bored glances, she felt another bite behind her ear, and the voice again spoke, *Now turn to your right, woman, just as you leave the gate.*

"I don't know who or what you are," muttered Annaelit under her breath as she turned the corner. "But I am not what you think, I promise you that . . . ."

"And what are you?" said a man-shape in a dark cloak of night, catching her as she ran directly into his chest.

He smelled of the final blooming lilac and night dew and the raw wind.

"Aieee!" screamed Annaelit lightly, then put her hands forward against his chest and felt something give way before her, a resilient energy in the air made into solid matter.

He was warm to the touch, like an ordinary man, and yet Annaelit felt that she was in physical contact with someone or something more.

"What am I? I am a simple storyteller, poor and useless despite my fake jewels, and without a single coin on me. And who are you?" she babbled, continuing the pretense of relative normalcy more for her own sake and taking a step back from this odd embrace with electricity.

"Who do you think?" he replied, his mortal voice low and soothing and, surprisingly, very much like her own when she was telling a mesmerizing story. The night was moonless and dark, and she could not see his face, only a silhouette against distant lamplight.

"I am not afraid," she said. "Really, I am not. Which of the gods are you?"

She sensed him smile, like a warm fluctuation in the air, in her very mind.

Think, he spoke to her awareness, *Think, storyteller. I am the one you most often mock.*

And then, in the ordinary voice of a man, he said, "You know me as the god of Things Left Over, because you choose to think that there are things in this world that are superfluous. And thus you delegate them all to me, like your trash."

And again he laughed. Currents of subliminal power moved in the darkness about him, and once again her hair stood on end.

"Pokreh . . ." she whispered. "You are Pokreh! Otherwise known as—"

"Otherwise known as the puny god of something or other, and in your own words a wicked, puny, sarcastic minor god."

"Oh!" said Annaelit. "My own words? How did you know?"

"Come along, walk with me," said he, taking her trembling hand, and once again she felt the touch of something warm, strong, and yet electric.

They moved past the Palace walls, and down toward the thicket of the city. Annaelit did not dare turn her face to look at the tall being gliding like a shadow at her side.

"Where are we going?" she whispered, staring ahead of her.

"Where would we be going at this hour? Home, of course. You need to get some sleep before tomorrow. Because tomorrow things will really begin to happen."

"What?" said Annaelit. "What things? What have I done, Pokreh? And I am sorry with all my heart for telling the stories about you. I promise I will never tell them again—"

"Nonsense," he said. "Those are your favorite stories, and you cannot help telling them over and over. But you do not tell them the right way. Particularly the story about fleas."

"'The right way'? What do you mean? I regret sincerely that my words have offended you, but these are the stories as I know and understand them, the same stories that were told to me long ago. . . ."

"And that's the problem," he replied. "For the one who told them to you long ago did not understand them either. And now you do not properly understand them, at least not quite, and yet you continue to repeat them like a dumb thoughtless thing, and aggravate the falsehood."

"My Lord Pokreh . . ." said Annaelit. "I am only a poor storyteller—"

In that instant she felt three simultaneous bites in three different places on her body, and she could not help but cry out.

If you were only a poor storyteller, spoke the god in her mind, *do you think I would bother with you?*

"You are simply the best teller of tales that has ever lived upon this mortal earth," he replied in the same low measured voice, as though nothing had happened. "And for that reason the great responsibility to tell things as they are lies the strongest upon you. Your words have power. Look what happened earlier tonight, at the feast."

"Do you mean to tell me," she whispered, "that it was my fault I started to tell my lords that moronic rambling nonsense about the Princess Makeia's mare? Whatever possessed me to do that? Not you?"

"Of course it was your fault," he said. "I merely watched you lose control. Even now, it was you who called me here, because deep inside you firmly believe that, as the god of Things Left Over, I am the one to pick up the useless pieces, such as yourself."

"What will happen tomorrow, my Lord?" she asked as they continued to walk along the winding silent streets of the city, past sleeping beggars and lurching silhouettes of strangers with obscured visages. In the faint illumination of the night, faces lost their three-dimensional humanity and dissolved into flat shapes of darkness broken only by eyes like spots of liquid. The eerie sight of them would normally have made Annaelit speed up her pace with barely suppressed panic. But tonight there was a god at her side, and she couldn't care less about stepping on a cutthroat in the dark.

"For one thing," spoke the god, "you will no longer be able to tell certain types of tales. Nothing funny or sarcastic that requires complex interpretations of truth—try telling them and you will court disaster. Only the sad stories are left to you. The ones that are most simple and straightforward, and illustrate truth in a clear light."

"Oh! What then will I do? I have another storytelling session tomorrow night! The Princess Egiras herself is not easily moved one way or another, but hates to hear her guests weep, and will require only lighthearted stories! Oh, what shall I do?"

Time seemed to fly by more quickly because her mind was embroiled in contemplating such terror, and Annaelit did not even notice that they had arrived at the doors of her hovel.

"What shall I do, Pokreh?" she repeated, releasing his divine hand to open the old rusty lock of her door with both of hers, rattling and pulling on it with great effort. Finally the door gave way, and she turned around to bemoan her condition one more time, and to invite him in.

But there was no one there. Pokreh, the god of Things Left Over, was gone. . . .

Only the night was left, pitch black as chaos.

T he feasts at the House of the Princess Egiras were known for their extravagance and for things most unusual.

Egiras was exotic, beautiful as a panther, and had a particularly sharp tendency toward sarcasm. When she had first come to the city she had been received with disdain by the High Court. After all, she was an unknown, and her foreign homeland's very existence was suspect, the stuff of vague legend. Besides, she had come with nothing but a small caravan and a retinue of servants, a box of priceless jewels, and the relentless escort of a single warrior bodyguard—he was a silent black man of imposingly noble stature, always seen at her side.

But within a matter of days Egiras had bought some of the choicest land in the best part of the city, and with it a great villa.

And then she became their unspoken queen. For her demeanor was capricious divinity and her appearance a cold disdainful elegance, and her natural manner of snubbing the highest nobility caused them to be piqued by her out of perverse curiosity. Indeed, within a moon's waning, she had the city nobles fighting for her attention and courting her favors. It was now considered a distinction to be invited to one of her exclusive feasts.

Annaelit had been fortunate to have pleased Egiras often with her storytelling, and thus she was a frequent contributor to an evening's entertainment.

Tonight was one such evening. Annaelit dressed particularly carefully, and applied her kohl and makeup with slightly trembling hands, all the while thinking of an appropriate story to tell the noble guests of Egiras.

She also thought of a certain minor, puny, sarcastic god.

A nnaelit was admitted into the great House of the Princess soon after sunset, while the dusk was still ringing with the clamor of departing sun. Final dust motes of the sunset's energy were spinning through the bluish translucent fabric of air. Indigo night intermingled and yet never blended with light particles of burnished gold.

The guests were gathered on a balcony to experience the final vestiges of this glorious sunset, the dancing energy all around them, and to drink warm summer wine. The villa balcony overlooked splendid gardens that in the evening appeared a sea of green moving limbs quickly turning to jet black.

"Look! I see the first star of the evening!" cried one of the guests, a young woman, pointing at the horizon. She was dressed in silk the color of lapis and wore her long ruddy hair unbound, so that it cascaded unadorned down her back. In her choice of coloration for the feast, the woman was like swatches of this very sunset and encroaching night.

"I see only a distant lamp being moved through the windows of a house," retorted a low sarcastic female voice, with just a hint of amusement. "My dear Lady Makeia, it is far too early for proper stars to show themselves at the Western horizon. Indeed, it has just recovered from the day's inferno, barely dispatched with the sun, and now lies simmering in cool soothing blueness. But—watch the opposite rim that is the East, if you would see stars."

"Ah, Egiras, love, must you be so pragmatic?" Makeia laughed. "The stars come out everywhere, and I still insist that I saw the first one tonight."

"Then I let you have the star of your choice, my dear," retorted Egiras. "What do you say, Nadir?"

A little behind her, a tall man-shape stirred in the shadows of the balcony, and then a soft voice said, "It is as you wish, my Lady Egiras." The tone of his voice was like deep balm.

Egiras laughed, shaking it off, that eternal feel of comfort at her side, that eternal sense of his presence, as though it irritated her at some level. "Apparently it is always as I wish, for Nadir always agrees with me." She added, "I need not even bother to ask. Don't you, Nadir? See, there—do not even reply, for I know what you will say."

"How did you manage to get such a handsome warrior to serve you with such loyalty?" said Makeia, glancing coyly toward the man in the shadows. In the rich twilight she could not see him, and yet she knew there were muscles like iron and satin and a well formed face of surprising gentleness hidden somewhere in there, in the dark.

"Ah, that is a story I shall tell you properly some other day," said the hostess. "But speaking of stories, where is my favorite Teller of Tales? Someone go fetch Annaelit, for it is time!"

"I am here, my Lady," said Annaelit, waiting just a few steps away from the noble crowd.

Egiras turned, seeing the storyteller's familiar outfit and form. And the slanting almond eyes of the Princess widened with excitement, reflecting distant persimmon-gold fire. For even now oil lamps were being lit all around them in the gardens and all over the villa.

She clapped her hands to attract everyone's attention, and announced that it was time to return inside for the evening's entertainment.

The noble guests followed her, and soon the party had spilled back from the balcony into a cozy chamber filled with warm golden glow and furnished with divans and soft pillowed lounge chairs.

"Make us laugh tonight, Annaelit!" exclaimed the Princess Egiras, settling into one of the seats. Here in the bright interior light, one could see her sleek beauty, her hair like a river of smooth jet waters, pouring in long waves to her ankles.

A few seats away, the tall dark-skinned man called Nadir sat back silently, watching her. His form was rich with contradictions. There was a sense of quiet contained power—merely in the capable way he folded his hands and the confident but gentle curl of his fingers which seemed relaxed yet were primed for movement in a split second. And in that same gentle silence he appeared self-effacing, and his clothing was so simple that it stood out from the rest of those present.

And yet the acute presence that was in his eyes gave him the demeanor of a lord.

"Before you begin your tales, I want to know the latest gossip," said Egiras, taking a delicately fluted wine goblet from a servant. "So tell us, girl, what is it that I hear has happened this past night at the Palace of Lord Ostavi? Were you not there when he entertained the illustrious stranger Lord Dava? It is spoken all over the city that there was an imbecile drunken display on the part of both, and now they are the greatest of enemies—the dear fools. Well? Have you any news?"

Annaelit bowed to the hostess and the rest of the fine gathered company. "I was there indeed, my Lady, and had the misfortune to observe some of it."

"Hah!" exclaimed Egiras. "Tell us, what caused this fight?"

Annaelit smiled ruefully. "Words," she said. "Words caused it."

"Words always do. But what was the actual catalyst, the thing that made Lord Dava so utterly mad, as the rumors go?"

"Hard to say, my Lady. . . ."

Egiras raised one fine dark brow. "Don't be silly. Tell us now, girl. No one will fault you for divulging only a bit more of what is mostly already known."

"Very well," said Annaelit, glancing at the red-headed Lady Makeia. "If you must know, the cause of it all is that Lord Dava fancies himself fatally in love with the Princess Makeia."

"What?" It was Makeia's turn to raise her brows. She laughed.

"Why, I do believe the tale grows more flavorful by the instant . . ." said Egiras in a purring tone, settling deeper in her chair. "Go on, girl, tell us the details of this infatuation."

"But—" exclaimed Princess Makeia. "I don't even know this Lord Dava!"

"Obviously he thinks he knows you, my sweet," retorted Egiras.

"He also seemed to be extremely confused and the wine had gone to his head. I think he had seen a glimpse of the Lady Makeia somewhere."

"How ridiculous," whispered Makeia. And then she added, "Incidentally, would you say the Lord Dava is handsome?"

"Handsome enough," whispered Annaelit. "But now, my Lady Egiras and the rest of my Lords and Ladies, would you like to hear me tell a tale?"

"I would rather like to know how handsome this Lord Dava is," interrupted Makeia. "Do tell me more. Is he tall with great shoulders, and dark smooth skin, like Nadir here? Or is he fair-haired with pale eyes—?"

Annaelit was suddenly beginning to feel very light-headed once again. It was as though the events of the previous night were happening all over again and she was once again edging out of control. . . .

The truth, she thought to herself. *Speak only the stark truth that is without embellishment and hence imbued with life's sorrow. Think, idiot girl!*

And she replied, "My Lady Makeia, if you must know, Lord Dava is fair-haired with pale, striking eyes. In fact, he is the very epitome of another man—a great ancient lord, the one who lived when the world was young and the wind blew in unnamed directions—the same lord who conquered a great *empirastan* that spanned most of the mortal world, and whose given name was Cireive. For, they say, he was fair as the sun."

"Oh," said Makeia. "Do go on."

And, as Annaelit launched with regained smoothness into her Tale, it seemed a great weight of discomfiture, of tense self-doubt left her chest and shoulders. With every word she spoke her voice gained confidence, while there came a gathering of something electric in the air.

The Princesses Egiras and Makeia and the others sat still and expectant, mesmerized by the curious music of the suddenly unfurling Tale. For Annaelit had caught them by surprise, and now held them by wonder.

"Before the Lord Cireive, handsome and fair-haired like a god of the sun, had become the great ruthless *taqavor* of all the mortal world," spoke Annaelit, "he was first a young man and, before that, a small boy of great yearning.

"The boy called Cireive was born in the last embers of spring to a woman of ancient noble blood. Or maybe not—one legend says he was the son of a poor farmer's wife who tilled the fields. In any case the woman never told anyone who the child's father was, and thus incurred the rage and shame of her family. She bore the child alone and remained oddly silent all through the first seasons of his life, only singing to him softly as he suckled at her breast.

"It is said the woman's songs were so haunting that she made the birds themselves grow silent in the gardens as they listened to her. And, as the child lay in her arms and listened too, he was imbued first with wonder and then with a longing to know the origins of things, of that sound that issued forth out of the woman who was his mother, and of the source of herself and himself.

"'Why do you sing? Who am I, Mother?' he asked, and legend says it was one of the first things he uttered. In reply, the woman held him tight to her, and said nothing at first, only smiled. And finally, after long moments of sun-warmed wind and silence, she said, 'You are Cireive, my son. And I sing . . . you.'

"At first that answer was enough. For this woman, his mother, looked at him like the sun itself, warming him with the balm of her presence, and through her voice he felt connected to the whole canopy of day and night and sun and stars and earth and water and sky. Truly, she formed him with the sound issuing forth from her lips and her chest and her lungs, and in the forming made him a part of the universal fabric.

"But, as the boy grew and learned his place in the world, he learned that the song of his mother was but one small sound in the greater clamor all around him. And he also learned that he was made up of two things—pride and shame. He was a blending, half everything and half nothing. He was the son of a woman and the unknown. For he had one given name and yet no name at all, and his father was a ghost.

"As time flowed onward, the condition of having no real name became a complex thing of peculiar agony for the boy, even though he had a given name. A true full name could be bestowed only by the father—or at least that was the ancient tradition of their people. And one without a full name, thought Cireive, was no one at all.

"The boy Cireive yearned for the cloak of tradition to envelop him, yearned to be like all, like the ancients. And he grew accustomed to bearing the shame and the barbed words of others which reminded him of who he was, and who he was not. Eventually the barbs fell upon an impervious core that had become his inner self, for time had become a solid thing of many protective layers, encircling his spirit.

"No one knows what one thing was the catalyst, what brought him to the edge of bitterness and beyond it, but his spirit, being thus wrapped away securely, could no longer hear the words that caused pain, and at the same time could not hear the distant perfect song that his mother sang and that was a silver thread between him and the all.

"By the time Cireive was a young man, he was veiled in layers of only himself. And such solitude, such separation from the world, made him first bitter, then panicked and frightened like a fluttering caged bird, and then a thing somewhat mad. For he no longer heard the world around him, no longer heard pain or joy, and only the ringing inner silence. And, being thus deaf, he was more than anything vulnerable to illusion.

"They say the Lord of Illusion took hold of him earlier than most. The Lord of Illusion spun a web of gentle comforting softness to fill in the emptiness and the fading memories, and to buffer him against the noise of silence. Then, from the embers of Cireive's own memories, Illusion spun a new thread of brightly shining silver in place of the one that had been his mother's song. And this thread connected Cireive not to the world but to things beyond and outside the universe, to the primeval dark that lies beyond the false wonder and veneer of Illusion—"

"What an odd story . . ." Egiras interrupted suddenly.

Her words came low and jarring, and everyone surfaced out of the spell of the Tale. Annaelit paused mid-sentence, also thrown out of the rhythm she had created, and said, "It is actually a true story, my Lady. It happened to a real man, a very long time ago."

"That's what you storytellers always say," said Egiras. "All your stories are invariably true and all your heroes sympathetic and fallible—for, no matter how powerful they are, they are always weak in some sense, vulnerable to one thing or another, and fall into temptation, even though in the end they may redeem themselves and save the world. How mortally dull! I am in the mood to hear a different tale. I want no weakness. No human weakness, do you understand, girl? I am tired of such."

"But," muttered Princess Makeia under her breath, "I would rather hear the end of this one."

Annaelit bowed, and said, "What would you like to hear then, my Lady Egiras? I am afraid that most human tales deal with mortal weakness. Would you rather hear stories of gods?"

"I would like," said Egiras, staring away into the distance at a lamp casting a golden sphere of glow, "tales that spin bright visions not of things that have been but of things that might come to pass. And no, gods are dull also, in their omnipotence. Tell us instead a tale never heard before, not of human pain but of impossible wonder."

"And what is wonder, my Lady? And in what way does it differ from Illusion?" whispered Annaelit.

"If you need ask, then you do not know it. What kind of a Teller of Tales are you? I'd thought better of you, girl."

Annaelit smiled. "I ask you because wonder is a personal thing that is different for each of us. I would know *your* wonder, for this is your House, and it is to you that I will tell this tale."

"Ah, then you are a wise reader of souls after all, Teller of Tales. Very well. To me, wonder is that which I do not know and cannot know. Do you understand? It is something I can only just sense at the edge of my vision, something that pulls at me and gives me the urge to live, and which lies in the future ahead of us. And, unlike Illusion, wonder is a thing true."

"Wonder is your next breath, Egiras . . ." Nadir said unexpectedly. "And Illusion is this very breath that you take now."

"And what is that supposed to mean?" said the Princess, turning around to glance at the dark man with sudden intensity.

From Nadir came soft laughter. "Nothing," he said. "It can mean nothing at all, my Lady. Take it however you will."

But Egiras stared at him, without blinking, and said, "Maybe I should be the one to tell a tale. I will tell the story of you, Nadir, of how you came to be what you are now."

"Then it would be a very boring tale indeed," he retorted. "For I have spent most of my time serving you, and the rest of it studying the mystical art of war and the mundane soldier's trade."

"Yes," said Egiras, "your tale is mostly dull and pathetic. And yet—may all the rest of this noble company listen closely now—I sent you away from me to learn from the masters in my own distant homeland. You have been to the Kingdom that lies in the Middle, and have seen the sun dissolve in exquisite gossamer mists of lilac and gold over the land of my ancestors— a land which I myself have never seen, since I was a tiny horrid child. Why do you think that would bore my guests, to hear of my homeland, an exotic place they will never know?"

"Maybe because it would only satisfy *your* wonder, and not theirs," replied Nadir, a deepening remoteness in his voice.

"The Kingdom in the Middle—is that where you learned your impossible techniques of hand combat, Lord Nadir?" asked one of the guests.

"I learned there the art of defense," Nadir said gently. "It is quite different from the art of aggression, with which I was already familiar in my soldiering. I came to the Kingdom in the Middle as a warrior and left it as a priest."

"A priest? You never told me this," Egiras said abrasively.

"You never asked. But do not fear, my Lady, it is irrelevant. For the god I serve has no name, and the god's Secret Temple has no place. Besides, it is enough, this talk of times past. Let us instead allow the Teller of Tales to continue with the practice of her craft. Did you not want to hear a tale of the future?"

"Unfortunately," said Annaelit, once again speaking, "I can only tell a certain type of tale today, one which is of the past and the present only. A tale of things that are real."

"And why is that?" Egiras regarded her without blinking.

"Because, my Lady, that is the will of the gods. Tonight is the Night of Truth," said Annaelit, with a look in her eyes that made even Egiras finally glance away. "And on this night I can speak only of things that have come to pass, or things that are happening even as we speak. I can tell you many wondrous tales of mortal lives. Some of these lives you have heard of previously. And yet tonight you will hear their stories told differently, unembellished and real, as they really came to pass.

"If you crave wonder, there is the true tale told to me by one called Ierulann, once a Guard of Law and now a storyteller, who related to me the details of the final changing of the City of No-Sleep from a state of oscillating madness to one of serene permanence. And, if that is not to your taste, there is the even more peculiar tale of a woman captain, called Lero and reputed to be insane, who commands an unsinkable ship."

"Lero . . ." Egiras repeated. "Why do I know this name?"

"Because we have once been on her ship," said Nadir. "Long before we came to this city, we sailed the *Eye of Sun* to cross the endless ocean that you hated so. . . ."

"The *Eye of Sun!* Yes, I remember now, the ship, the endlessness," mused Egiras. "The sun itself was different, not like it is in the desert, but sharper than daggers striking my eyes, as it reflected off the green then gray then blue expanse of cruel water, everywhere, as far as the edges of the world. I remember being onboard, and the balmy wind and the sour rotting stink of salt, all permeated with nausea. . . .

"I would watch the huge canvas sails unfurl and fill with ravenous wind. The main sail had the image of a great almond-shaped eye on it, within a golden sun—an intensely peculiar symbol painted in garish shades of blue. Then, having tired of sails and with nothing else to observe but your shadow at my side, Nadir, I would watch for days and nights on end how the tall strange captain stood staring at the heavens, noting the position of the noonday sun at the zenith, and the stars attached to the celestial dome, and comparing them to old charts and objects in the seascape unnoticed by the rest of us.

"There was a strange object on deck, to which the captain often referred—a marvelous thing floating in a bowl of water, with sixteen points, like a star. They called it the wind rose, and also a compass, for it pointed North always, and one could tell the rest of the directions from it.

"I never knew the captain's name, never cared to notice she was a woman. And yet I remember somehow, despite myself: Lero. How odd. They all seemed to obey her as though she could sink that ship with one word. What perfect terror she invoked."

"Not terror," whispered Nadir. "There are other reasons why one would serve."

At that, Egiras laughed. Her beautiful face contorted, marring the smoothness of her ocher porcelain skin, and then she spoke in sarcasm. "If one serves for any other reason then one is a fool, and deserves the fate of servitude."

"There is another tale I can relate," said Annaelit, sensing the pressure of unspoken things resonating between the Princess and the man, "a tale of a woman we all know, Belta Digh, who owns a popular tavern in this very city. It is rumored, and surely it is true, that Belta Digh's tavern serves a drink that takes your pain away. They say she once made a deal with death itself, and in the doing she redeemed a mortal life, and redeemed death also from the old curse of a goddess. Oddly enough, this is the very same goddess, Risei-Ailsan, that came into being through the will of the man called Cireive, the one whose tale I began to tell you."

"Strange indeed," Egiras said, "that these tales of yours seem to be connected, almost in a circle. Or did you intend for this to happen, sly Teller of Tales, so that you could return to the original story?"

"Oh, good!" put in Princess Makeia. "I care not what is connected, but I do want to hear of this ancient *taqavor* with his sun-hair and his mysterious bargain with the Lord of Illusion."

"Not intentional at all," said Annaelit. "Rather, these tales have one thing in common, and that is the share of truth they convey. And there is one more tale I have not mentioned yet, one of such immediate truth that I do not dare to even speak of it, for it will bring fear to all of your guests, my Lady. And to you."

Saying that, Annaelit lowered her eyes.

Egiras's attention was caught. She watched the storyteller in silence, pondering. And then she said, "You make me curious. What kind of tale would make me afraid? And why? I would hear it."

"Yes!" came the voices of the guests, as many in the room began to shiver with delicious anticipation and others came alive from their torpid complacency. The warm lamplight cast a persimmon radiance upon their glittering forms, the smooth jewels winking in the women's hair and the great chains of expensive metal in the robes of the men, earlobes hung with fine rings.

Annaelit took several steps away, and stood in the center of the room, looking from one face to another, finally meeting the haughty, slanted gaze of the Princess Egiras.

"This is a tale, my Lady, that unfolds even now, and has no ending," she said gently, folding her hands at her waist. "It is a tale of *you*. For here you sit, Princess Egiras, in your finery, in a beautiful hall that stands within a fine House, in a city that has been built in the heart of the desert. Around you unfolds the rest of the world. Behind you is the past of your life. And before you your next breath indeed lies. And with each breath, yes, even now as you draw it in, lies beckoning wonder. Or Illusion."

"What . . . ?" whispered Egiras, her pupils dilating like those of a serpent in the primeval night.

But Annaelit continued speaking, ignoring her. "I tell your tale," she said, "and you live it. Whether you choose wonder or Illusion is for you decide. And for that reason I cannot end your tale. For, the tale has not yet played itself out. . . ."

"This is complete nonsense!" Egiras interrupted suddenly.

"What in the world are you saying, girl? What—?"

"It is a strange night," said Nadir, interrupting her in turn. He arose from his seat, his shape of awe-inspiring stature.

"I've had enough of tales," he said gently, and then walked across the chamber, past the seated guests, and stepped out onto the balcony. Lamplight faintly illuminated the simple cotton of the robe clothing his back and drowned in the tight curls of his jet-black hair. The curls grew so close to his scalp as to define the shape of his skull.

The man stood with his back to them all, watching the night.

"Nadir has the right of it," said Egiras with a blank expression, also rising from her soft chair. "I too grow restless with your strange stories tonight, Annaelit. You no longer please me. . . . Go and collect the payment at the doors for your dubious services. I will not be calling you back again."

Annaelit cast down her gaze politely and then bowed. "As you wish, my Lady. I humbly beg pardon for your displeasure. I did not mean to frighten you or your guests. . . ."

"Frighten?" The voice of Egiras rose like a sudden gust of scalding wind. "You do not frighten with your idiot blathering. You merely bore! How dare you suggest that your foolish nonsense stories would have an effect on me? Out!"

And the Princess lifted a slim pale hand encased in bands of spun gold and encrusted with pearls, delicate and deadly as the neck of a swan that culminates in a sharp beak. With one finger she pointed to the door.

Annaelit, knowing that the best recourse was silence, wordlessly complied. As she humbly left the hall she could feel a gaze of sympathy upon her back. Its power was almost physical.

She knew it could be none other than Lord Nadir.

I am ruined, thought Annaelit, holding a meager purse of coins in a very cold hand as she walked back to her poor hovel in the dark silence of the night city. *With the dismissal from the House of Egiras, no Lord or Lady will ever invite me to a noble gathering to tell a tale. Reputation is a precarious thing, hinging not so much on what is real but on what is perceived to be in style. I am now known as a bore, and my stories are likened to nonsense. All because I chose to listen to the advice of a puny, wicked god and speak unadorned truth.*

There was a lump in her throat. And as she walked, stumbling with her fine embroidered slippers upon decidedly wicked cobblestones, Annaelit's vision blurred suddenly. Salty water gathered in the corners of her eyes, and lamplight and torches became smears of dislocated light.

In that very moment, a flea bit Annaelit on her rear end.

But she ignored it, furiously allowing the itch to sear her with unrelieved irritation. Her steps grew more and more hurried, so that she practically flew along the city streets like a bird of night, ignoring the ground before her.

You cannot run away from yourself, mortal, spoke a familiar voice in her head.

"Maybe not," replied Annaelit, gasping for breath. "But maybe I can just run. . . ."

Do that, and you ruin your only good pair of shoes. And then what will you wear to Princess Makeia's intimate gathering tomorrow night?

Annaelit came to a complete sudden stop.

"What?" she whispered. "Stop tormenting me, Pokreh!"

"You give me too much credit," said a tall man, stepping out of the shadows of the street that abruptly curved before her. "Mostly, you torment yourself."

Thus it was that once again Annaelit ran head-first into the chest of the god.

"Aieee!"

Electricity stood in the air.

"You!" Annaelit gasped. "What more do you want of me, now that you've caused me to make a muddle of my profession before the most important aristocrats of this city?"

The god took her hand and laughed. "Was it not a good feeling to speak the truth? You've made Egiras secretly shiver with the words you laid before her."

It was Annaelit who shivered now at the touch of the divine against her cold fingers.

But the young woman was wise even then—for, even in their lightest moments, all storytellers ultimately are. And she met the gaze of the god from within the concealment of night.

"Enough! What is the lesson you would have me learn, Pokreh?" she said suddenly, and her direct words reached out like a keening cry for mercy. "Tell me once and for all, for even now I am living out *my own story,* and whoever observes my story from the outside, is, right this instant, curious to know—is in fact exasperated in waiting to see what unfolding of events my own next breath holds. . . ."

The darkness resounded with joyous laughter.

Ah, Annaelit, at last. Only you would be aware enough to ask the truest question of all. And, thus, I grant you the answer.

"The lesson I would have you learn, and carve indelibly into your soul, is this," spoke the semblance of a man before her. "In all stories there are those who appear to be the principal players, and those who seem like the chorus of background voices, insignificant and self-effacing. The truth, however, is that all of these distinctions are relative. One observer looking upon the living story would see one set of main characters, while another observer—a god if you must—will look upon the same set of players and see the merits of others as primary. And yet take enough observers or take no observers at all and it becomes clear as sunlight that the story of life is played out by a cast of mortals who are all equal in importance and stature. None are secondary, none are useless, and *none are ever left over.*"

"How can that be?" whispered Annaelit.

"For one thing," replied the *one* before her, "at the time of final reckoning, death comes to all of you equally, and takes you into her loving embrace. Death has no favorite players. Death, the Hag that you mortals so fear, loves all of you best."

The god put his hand on the woman's forehead, sensing her begin to tremble greatly. His touch was electric, and it convulsed her—but only for an instant.

And another one is time, whispered the god in her mind. *Time treats you all as it treats grains of sand. In truth, it treats all of us equally, whether we are gods or fleas. Time leaves nothing behind as it sweeps us along in its relentless river.*

"Then why are some of us born to privilege, power, joy, while others languish all their sorry lives in poverty, darkness and silence?" said Annaelit.

"Because," said the god, "like the opposite directions of the Compass Rose, all things have two sides. You, being mortal and anchored to a specific point of life's continuum, can see only one side at a time, while its opposite side seems to stretch beyond the farthest horizon, and thus be out of reach. But I tell you now—as I, an outside observer, look at your world from all sides at once with my divine eyes—that very same privilege hides limitations, power hides vulnerability, joy obscures suffering, while poverty disguises fulfillment, darkness is but a shadow of light, and silence is the loudest voice of all."

"You speak deliberate words of paradox, my Lord," said Annaelit.

"I merely juxtapose the opposite sides in order to show you that they come from a single source. You know this already, deep within the fundamental core of you, yet often you refuse to face it, choosing easy Illusion over intricate wonder. All things are equal for the very reason that all things are relative, and your world is a wondrous moving puzzle that you mortals will one day grasp in its entirety. Remember this when you are tempted by the intense cravings of Illusion.

"For Illusion *pretends* to be wonder. It insinuates itself, then fixes you by the very force of your obsession into a single narrow perspective, and stunts your spirit's natural flexibility. Let me tell you now a secret truth: flexibility of perspective is necessary for the divine movement along the continuum of life, encompassing time and space. Being stationary in a moving universe results in a peculiar blindness of spirit—since all the glorious universe hurtles past you unobserved while you concentrate on the one false thing that seems to you of greater importance than all others, and the final stage is a spiraling downfall into the unknown.

"Wonder, on the other hand, enhances mutability. Wonder is the natural urge of mortals toward that which is greater than themselves, that which is divine. And, in the process of striving to observe true wonder, your spirit's movement is reaffirmed. Then at last you learn the other great secret—there is no better place to be, nor is there a better time to exist, than the time and place that defines *you*."

And saying that the god in the shape of a man disappeared in front of her, dissolved into the recesses of night.

Annaelit blinked, and felt prickling and ridiculous fleabite on her elbow, and another on her side.

Even the flea knows and enjoys its place, mortal . . . sounded a faint echo, and then there was nothing but the hiss of the wind.

"Annaelit! Annaelit, Teller of Tales! Are you within?" The well-dressed servant of a noble house knocked relentlessly at the door of her hovel. "You are required to attend the Princess Makeia this evening, and to complete a tale that you started."

"Is that so? Do you mind pounding on this wood with a bit more force so that my dead ancestors can hear you also?"

Annaelit held the old door barely ajar to let in the bright daylight and the overwhelming sight of the messenger. After the soothing twilight inside, it was agony to her squinting eyes.

It was late morning and her temples rang. Not to mention there was a sense that phantom fleas had been biting her for hours on end. Indeed, this sleepless torment had prevailed all through the night.

"The Princess expects you promptly," said the servant pompously, ignoring her words. He offered her a very clean and uncalloused hand which held a satin purse. And, as Annaelit's fingers came in brief contact with his, quite unintentionally, he seemed to pull them away in a hurry, as though a flea had bitten him in that instant also.

Surely I am growing mad from all this—this—whatever it is, she thought tiredly.

Annaelit took the purse through the slit in the doorway, and asked, "Who else will be there of the noble lords? Tell me now so that I can prepare my Tale accordingly."

"Such information is not at my disposal," he replied, starting to turn away from her and her poor dwelling in distaste.

Annaelit thought for a moment. The purse of gold coins weighed sizably in her palm. Its contents would surely be more than enough to drive away that distaste, and also to imbue the servant with sudden extreme affability and willingness to accommodate her.

"Wait! If I were of a mind to give this purse to you, friend," she said in his wake, "would you be willing to do a tiny little thing for me?"

And as the haughty servant immediately reversed his motion and directed himself back to the door of the hovel the storyteller said, "I want you to make sure that a certain pair of noble lords are invited and will show up at Princess Makeia's gathering tonight."

Princess Makeia's villa was as fine as that of Egiras, and suffocated in a lush excess of gardens. Red-headed Makeia herself received the noble guests one by one with an eager childish smile which belied her formal outfit.

"Oh, Annaelit, you're here!" she exclaimed, nearly jumping up from the perfect seat where she had been so skillfully arranged and draped by her handmaidens. And then, remembering herself, Makeia sat back once again, and whispered to the storyteller in a conspiratorial tone, "Sit there until I call you! And be sure to try those grapes, they are utterly sweet."

In that instant the servant at the doors announced the arrival of Lord Ostavi.

The voices of the guests in the room faded, and everyone turned to stare.

Princess Makeia's eyes grew very bright and sparkly, for Lord Ostavi was hardly the sort to attend random evening entertainments, especially not the kind that would be arranged by a silly young Princess. "Oh my, do show my Lord in, please! I am impossibly honored!"

Lord Ostavi was a large heavyset man of middle age and imposing stature, with expensive jewels gleaming along the rim of his satin headdress and scattered like stars in his groomed dark beard. Many chains of precious metals adorned his intricate robe and caftan, for he was obviously dressed for negotiations.

"Peace and prosperity to this house, my dear Princess Makeia," he said in a warm baritone, coming right down to business. "I am here just as you requested, having come to receive the apology owed me. Where is he?"

"Apology?" Makeia breathed. "Where is who?"

In that very instant the servant at the door cleared his throat loudly and announced the arrival of Lord Dava.

"Oh!" Makeia said, while her cheeks and forehead flushed delicate pink.

Lord Dava came into the room wearing brilliant orange and purple, his fair hair swept back with a circlet of braided silver and gold, and his handsome face brimming with intensity. Like a ship navigating the night toward a beacon of light, he turned directly to Makeia's beautifully arranged high seat.

And then, seeing her, his eyes widened, and he quickly looked to the floor in childish confusion. Sinking almost in a faint, he knelt before her, saying in a barely audible whisper—mumbling, in fact—"Oh most beautiful one. . . . I never dreamed it possible, that you would call me to your side. . . ."

"Lord Dava . . ." Makeia said breathlessly, also mumbling. "I am graced by your presence in my house. . . ."

At that point Lord Ostavi loudly cleared his throat.

Lord Dava, still on his knees, turned around at the sound. "You!" he said, and immediately scrambled to get up, his hand going to his belt, where there would normally have been a sword.

Annaelit chose that moment to get up also, even faster than Lord Dava, and then moved to the center of the room, where everyone could see her.

"My Lords!" she said loudly. And her storyteller's voice, trained to project forward and ring, seemed in that instant to have a particularly unusual resonance, so that it filled the walls with a living energy, like electricity.

"There is a short, but very special Tale that all of you must hear," she said, "and for that reason you must contain your natural impulses for just a little bit."

"Wait," Lord Ostavi said. "What are you saying, girl? What Tale? I am here on a serious matter of honor—"

"And I am here because the Princess Makeia asked me to be here!" exclaimed Lord Dava.

"I did? Oh!" muttered the Princess, frozen in anxious and decorous beauty in her skillfully arranged seat, and really *really* wanting to be able to fidget in her place without upsetting the dramatic picture she presented.

"You are?" exclaimed Lord Ostavi, staring at Lord Dava, and beginning to roar like a bear. "Then you are not here to apologize to me?"

"May this whole city be stricken before I apologize to an old baboon like you! I would rather—"

"Once upon a time," Annaelit said in a hypnotic voice, "a wicked minor god—nay, a benevolent god with a wicked sense of humor and a tendency to disguise the extent of his love in the form of sarcastic laughter—decided that humankind in and of itself contained very little to amuse the divine Pantheon."

"Oh!" Princess Makeia said again, this time suddenly twitching her cheek. She pretended to move an impeccably coiffed lock of hair behind her ear, which unfortunately threw her carefully draped veils into disarray.

"And so," continued Annaelit, "one godlike morning, this deity gathered a fistful of his beard shavings, and shook it out profusely over the universe."

Lord Ostavi attained a very intense look on his face, somewhat between a frown and a sneeze, and then he vigorously scratched behind his right ear, and then the side of his nose.

"The god shook the beard shavings over the universe, to all the four corners of the Compass Rose. And wherever his stubble fell, little annoying creatures called fleas appeared."

"What? Argh!" exclaimed Lord Dava and clenched his fists, at the same time clenching other parts of himself unknown to all in order not to scratch himself in unseemly places.

And in that moment all around the hall guests began to shift in place. Suddenly everyone's hands moved involuntarily to scratch—some overtly, others in stealth—and then rearrange clothing as politely as possible.

"What in the world is going on?" someone asked, slapping himself in reflex, and no longer bothering to hide it.

"Fleas!" Annaelit said loudly and cheerfully. "Now then, the fleas were put on this earth for a very good reason. Does anyone know what it is?"

"This is an abomination!" growled Lord Ostavi, scratching himself with both hands now, and rotating his shoulder blades because there was a place at the small of his back that he just couldn't reach.

"Sorcery!" cried out Lord Dava. He ran a couple of steps and sat down on the closest divan, and began to rub his back against the nearby marble pillar.

"I always knew you were a monkey," panted Lord Ostavi between bouts of itching, while he rubbed at his belt and his armpits. "Just look at you, a young good-for-nothing, making a fool of himself."

"Really? And you are such an example of noble restraint," responded Lord Dava with a sneer of handsome white teeth, as he violently rubbed the backside of his knees, then his stomach.

"Oh stop it, both of you!" exclaimed the Princess Makeia, as she scratched her sides and then her waist, moving against the high back of her chair. "And you, Annaelit, in the name of all the gods, stop this—this—whatever it is! I cannot stand this terrible itching!"

The guests began to hurriedly vacate the hall. There were moans and groans and growls as they left the room, some racing outside, others beginning to jump up and down in a frenzy.

"Now look! My evening is ruined!" Makeia wailed, ripping off her veils and using them to rub her back like a towel strung out taut in both hands, while her abundant hair came out of its lovely arrangement.

In the mayhem Annaelit alone stood still as an island.

"My Princess," she said. "This is not my doing. For I am only the vessel, the voice that tells the story that has to be told."

"It must be that idiot Dava, then!" cried Lord Ostavi, stomping his feet and jumping up and down in place. "Didn't he just say that he'd rather this whole place be stricken with something or other than apologize to me? Obviously some gods must've heard him!"

"Argh!" cried Lord Dava, sliding back and forth against the seat of the divan with his behind. "I have nothing to do with this, I swear before all!"

"As I was saying," continued Annaelit. "Does anyone know the purpose of fleas?"

"I do!" roared Lord Ostavi. "They are an abomination of the gods, sent upon us as a punishment for our transgressions! Let me know what must be done, and I will do whatever it is I have to do, and sacrifice gold in whatever temple—"

"I am very sorry, my Lord, but that is incorrect," Annaelit said. "Anyone else care to respond?"

"No!" cried Lord Dava. And then he amended, "Yes! Fleas are a trial of our patience, and we must endure them in silence and nobility—"

"Once again, not so."

"Argh! For the sake of mercy, woman, tell us!"

Princess Makeia had gotten up and was prancing up and down in a frenzy. She lost one of her slippers and it went flying under the divan across the room. "Fleas . . ." she said between gulped breaths, "are obviously here to . . . to make a laughingstock of us for the gods! I mean, look at us!"

And immediately Princess Makeia grew still as the itching left her. She stood reeling, then cleared her throat as though nothing had happened and ran her fingers through her tousled hair. She looked absolutely charming.

"Very good, my Lady," Annaelit said. "You have stumbled upon one of the reasons, and you are thus freed."

Makeia looked around in relief and confusion, seeing that there was no one else left in the chamber besides Annaelit, herself, and the two lords.

Lord Dava had gotten up from his seat by this point, and he and Lord Ostavi were dancing like desert nomad madmen, their hands flailing every which way and sweat running down their faces.

"All right, all right!" Lord Dava began to scream finally, "I will apologize!" And, turning toward Lord Ostavi while continuing to scratch himself everywhere, heedless of how it appeared, he gasped, "I am sorry, Lord Ostavi! I beg your—argh—your humble forgiveness—owh!—for saying certain disrespectful things to you when a guest in your house!"

"I accept your—argh—apology!" retorted Lord Ostavi, as he leaped around with unexpected lightness for someone of such a bulky frame.

"There!" cried Lord Dava, "I've apologized! Let this hell be done with!"

But oddly enough there seemed to be no relief for the two lords, and they continued their macabre jumping spree.

"Hmm . . ." mused Annaelit, putting a finger to her lips, which normally seemed to help her concentrate. "This is a bit unexpected, my Lords. I was so very sure that an apology and your congenial peacemaking on both sides would result in an end to your ordeal. After all, the moral of the story was to have you picking fleas off each other and thus amusing the gods."

"Lord Dava, could you get me right there, please?" said Lord Ostavi, turning with his back to the other. "Yes, there, just a little higher, yes!"

"No problem, Lord Ostavi," replied Lord Dava, scratching the other vigorously between the shoulder blades. "Now, would you mind getting me, please, my good friend? Right here, yes! Oh yes!"

And as Lord Ostavi in turn rubbed his former enemy's back, both of them moaning in agony, Annaelit and the Princess Makeia watching them in blank puzzlement, Annaelit mused out loud: "Maybe we need to present them with a Trade Agreement to sign, before the gods choose to set them free?"

"You know, that's not a bad idea," retorted the Princess, and then immediately called over some vigorously scratching servants to fetch city scribes and lawyers.

As the servants went on their errands, dancing in an itch-frenzy, Princess Makeia took her turn to muse aloud. "I wonder if this divine flea infestation is all over the city, or if it has only honored my house?"

Her question was answered within the hour as two lawyers and three scribes dressed in fine clothing came jumping into the hall, scratching themselves with a fury that comes only with their honorable professions, and carrying a hastily written-up Trade Agreement.

"I'll sign it, whatever it is!" screamed Lord Dava as he lay on the marble floor, flailing his feet in the air, while Lord Ostavi continued to spring up and down and shake himself like a newly hatched and yet somewhat portly chicken.

"What's this?" Lord Ostavi moaned, squinting, holding the parchment with one hand as with the other he rubbed his ankles. After one of the scribes had read it to him, he went on, "All it says here is that we agree to trade! Where are the details? The caravans? The bales of silk? Boxes of spices?"

"My Lord, have you any idea how many attempts it took for me to write this one unsullied sentence without scratching myself?" muttered the scribe, twitching in place. "Why, it's the best I could do, and I am the best! Behold how shaky my penmanship is—an absolute disgrace, yes I know! Well, I was the only one able to even hold the quill in my trembling fingers! Indeed, it is late in the evening, and the whole city is scratching itself as we speak! All work and trade have stopped, all pleasures, for we are dying from this plague of fleas, my Lord!"

"Enough! Just let me sign the damn thing, Ostavi!" wailed Lord Dava. "Give it to me! Argh!"

Seizing the parchment from the other's hands and grabbing a writing implement from the scribe, Lord Dava proceeded to scribble a very shaky X in lieu of his signature. He then passed it to Lord Ostavi, who scribbled another X right below.

"It is witnessed!" Lord Dava cried. "Now, seal it! Quickly, you idiots, before we expire!"

A leaping and scratching lawyer approached. First he tripped on one end of his long cotton robe then straightened himself and started to tip the jar of wax with a wobbly hand over the parchment that lay on the marble floor.

Time seemed to slow into eternity when an uncontrollable bodily twitch caused an unexpectedly large and thick dollop of wax to come snaking down and land in hot droplets on his bare toes and his sandals. The lawyer opened his mouth to let out a howl, but, masterfully, suppressed it into a grimace of silently bared teeth and crossed eyes, an admirable display of official dignity. At last, with luck and one quick movement, he managed to pour a proper-sized dab of wax in the appropriate location on the parchment.

Not wasting an instant, a second lawyer danced up to him carrying a prominent city seal, and he slapped the seal onto the wax, at the same time rubbing his backside.

After several long itching seconds, the seal was pulled away, and the Agreement was complete.

And yet nothing happened. There was no relief to the itching. In fact, it seemed to have intensified, judging by the beet-red complexions of the two lords, the lawyers, the scribes, and all the rest of the affected.

"Oh, my . . ." said Annaelit, biting her knuckle in anxiety. "I just don't know what to do. I was so sure the Trade Agreement would be the key factor here. . . ."

"No!" roared Lord Ostavi. "Oh, make it stop, please make it stop! You are a clever girl, Annaelit! Do something!"

"My Lord . . ." she said. "I am sorry but I just don't know what to do."

"Think!" howled Lord Dava. "You are the one who told the Tale that started all this! And now you have to tell a Tale that ends it!"

"Yes, because this is the lousiest story I have ever heard!"

"End it *now,* Teller of Tales!"

And, as they all stared at her, between their spasms of itching, Annaelit cleared her throat and tremulously began to tell the end of a very odd Tale. "Thus it came to pass that the fleas were tormenting the two great lords and—and—oh, I can't!"

"What?" roared Lord Ostavi.

"I cannot tell this Tale . . ." whispered Annaelit, shaking. "Don't you see, *I* am in it. I cannot tell my own tale! No storyteller can!"

In that moment there was a crackling in the air, as though a thundercloud had broken open in the chamber, and the residual electricity licked the walls with a bluish shadow that stood in contrast with the warm, golden lamplight.

And in the next heartbeat, a *man* stood in the room before them.

He was tall and well built, and yet his face managed to remain shadowed—an unreadable spot.

"Pokreh! God of Things Left Over!" Annaelit cried.

Yes, it is I. For something is very much left over in this moment of moments, Teller of Tales, spoke a voice in her mind.

"What must I do, my Lord? Tell me what I must do to free these people from the agony of the ludicrousness? For it is my fault, and my story! And yet I cannot end it, surely, for I am a player in it. I am in this Tale!"

In that moment, the god laughed. His voice rumbled amid the crackling electricity. "Look at you all," he said. "Scratching silly flea-ridden mortals, who have brought this upon yourselves, and continue to do so."

He pointed a finger at Annaelit, saying, "You. Why do you think you cannot end this Tale?"

"Because I am in it!" she said. "How can I?"

"How can you not? Who else has the ability to guide and conclude your own Tale but you?" said the god. "And I do not speak merely of any Tale you tell, but of a greater Tale, the one which unfolds around you and engulfs you in the river of time."

"I thought—" said Annaelit, "I thought that it was written and navigated by the will of the gods such as yourself."

Nonsense. The navigator in the living story is a player as much as the others. The gods merely draw the symbol lights upon the sky, to be read. The navigator is the one who makes use of them. The navigator follows the road formed by celestial symbols toward a destination at the other end of the Compass Rose, always moving toward the distant horizon which comprises the wondrous opposite side.

The navigator fathoms and then forms the road always from the elements of the world . . . The navigator, and the captain, and the ship, and the ocean, and the journey, and the destination—all of them are you.

Behind you, before you, and beyond you. Such is the living story.

And then the man spoke out loud. "End the Tale now, Annaelit. For if you cannot, no one can. Neither death, nor time, not even all the gods combined."

For none of us are you.

"And so it was," replied Annaelit, "that Pokreh, god of Things Left Over, came to bring wisdom to a foolish woman whose name was Annaelit, Teller of Tales. And in that moment of wisdom, the divine plague left the others around her, and the Illusion of fleas was now in the past, in back of them all, while ahead lay something else—the rest of their living journey."

And as the last word fell from her lips, like a blossom of light, peace indeed settled upon all those present and the agony left them.

Lord Dava and Lord Ostavi stood still, breathing heavily from their ordeal.

"Your lesson, but not this Tale, is now concluded," said the god with the obscured face. And, as he faded from their sight, there came soft laughter, to echo and dance between the walls, like a million tiny insects receding. . . .

"Once upon a time," spoke Annaelit, the Teller of Tales, in a hovel filled with children, "there were young clever children listening to the words of a certain Teller of Tales."

"That's you, Annaelit!" A little girl giggled.

"Why yes, and so it was." Annaelit smiled. "Now then, the children's homes were comfortable, and there was always food on the table, for their city had prospered from a healthy trade between two lands. And yet something made them come repeatedly to a poor little old hovel where she lived, that Teller of Tales whose name was Annaelit. Do you know what it was?"

"What?" cried a little boy. And then he scratched himself, for a tiny little thing had just bitten him behind the ear.

"Why, surely you know, children!" retorted the storyteller, smiling. "Just think what it could be that caused the children to return to a poor hovel! Surely not the fleas?"

"The stories!" cried a very tiny girl. "The children liked the stories!"

"Very good, Leti!" said Annaelit. "Now, can any of you tell me what it is about the stories that made them come back?"

"Is it the words?" said Leti, staring back at Annaelit with intense eyes.

"Sometimes," replied Annaelit. "Sometimes it is the words. And at other times it is the people and the things and the places that come alive in the stories. But most often it is that thing that neither the people nor the places, nor the stories themselves, could describe to you, but can only hint at from a great distance on the opposite side of the horizon."

"What is it? What's on the horizon?" whispered another child.

And Annaelit smiled again.

"Oh, it is a delicate precious thing," she said. "Some of the storytellers call it wonder. And I promise to tell you more of this extraordinary marvelous thing another day. But for now, my children, at last, this particular Tale is concluded."

Dream Eleven

Night of a Thousand Moons

Legend has it that once in a thousand years comes a night in the deepest Midsummer when a thousand moons fill the sky. In that moment, terrible wonders take place. Also, strange trickeries are wrought, as the Lord of Illusion takes advantage of mortals.

Whether you go South, North, West, or East of the Compass Rose, you will find everywhere, from the lowest town to the greatest city, there is Carnival held every year on that night. All work ceases from sundown till the next dawn, and the whole world is mad with revelry, superstition and Illusions of light.

On such a Carnival night, you may dance and drink and lose all sense in the pleasures of the moment. . . . But above all else you must don a mask to cover your face from things unspoken. For it is said that if you do not, and the moons come, you will be lost forever. . . .

"Masks for sale!" cried the street peddler, pushing forward a gaudy cart on three wheels. It was a contraption piled high with masterpieces and travesties of porcelain and clay, feathers and ribbons, golden braid and purple sequins, and other bits and pieces of stuff like the rainbow.

Yaro stood with the heavy basket of potatoes balanced on her bony hip, and watched the peddler roll by with his merchandise. She was returning from the market with goods for the table of her mistress and had little time for idle gawking. But the shiny colorful mass caught her nearsighted eyes with its undulating sprinkles of reflected rhinestone mini-lights from the sun-glare, the smooth blots of bright colors.

Yaro blinked, then turned, rearranging the basket and her faded shawl, and was once again on her way through the narrow twisting city streets. Her head was kept perpetually lowered, and her gaze directed to the ground, as was proper for a lowly servant and as irked her considerably, since Yaro had a willful streak. Somehow she managed to avoid running into the increasingly raucous passersby and keep the contents of her basket intact. Soon she would reach the higher ground where the gardens began, and where the finer houses stood, including that of the Princess Egiras, whom she served.

Tonight was Carnival night. Early afternoon, and already stores were closing for the revelries ahead, while joy-establishments were getting ready for the crowds and mask sellers were everywhere, flaunting the most extravagant of their wares.

Masks must be worn on the Night of a Thousand Moons. From the lowliest beggar to the richest lord, all would put on the shield of safety over their faces, with the eyeholes covered by lenses of amber crystal. It was the only thing that could offer protection from the occult terror that would come if this Carnival night were to be the fateful one in a thousand.

In her pocket Yaro had a simple mask sewn of goatskin, with tiny thin amber lenses, the cheapest thing she could buy off a higher servant who had used this mask last year. It was customary to have a new mask for every Carnival, but Yaro was too poor to worry about hand-me-downs.

At the great house of the Princess Egiras, Yaro came through the back servant entrance, stumbling under the weight of the basket, and nearly ran into the wide chest of a tall silent man, with skin dark as the desert night, who stood lounging at the doors.

"Oh! Sorry, my Lord Nadir!" she mumbled, and felt warmth come rushing invisibly to her dark cheeks.

He had reached out a hand in reflex, and gently straightened her basket which had been threatening to spill over.

"You carry a heavy load," he said softly. His eyes were darker than black, pupil-less, and somewhere deep was a richness of wisdom, like the earth.

"Thank, you, m'Lord," she said, and then moved past him into the hallway and then into the kitchens. As she disappeared from his sight she experienced vertigo at the sense of a trail of his gaze upon her back.

Nadir was a mysterious warrior from a strange faraway land, the personal bodyguard of Egiras. He stood higher-ranking than any servant, and yet was always kind to her. It always puzzled Yaro why his name meant "the lowest of the low."

Yaro hurried through her chores, through the bustle of other servants all preparing the Princess's feast. When the afternoon sun started to incline to the West, she took a small moment of rest, filled her old wooden bowl with soup, and carried it to the tiny room in the servants' quarters where her old mother lay in their shared pallet-bed.

"Yaro, child of dust," chided her mother, frail as a stick, as she turned her sunken face to the slit of light that came through the doorway.

"Here, I have brought you dinner," said Yaro, and she propped her mother up with a second pillow and proceeded to spoon-feed the old woman.

"Will you go to the Carnival tonight?" said her mother between swallows.

"I might," replied Yaro. "If the mistress wants me to be at her side, I might. But if there are more chores. . . ."

"Do not go!" said the old woman. "The Lord of Illusion stirs the air. I have a bad feeling about this night. The moons might come."

"Ah, the moons never come, mother," said Yaro.

"And so they say. . . ."

Yaro laughed. She then wiped her mother's lips with a bit of rag, wiped her own tired brow, picked up the empty old wooden bowl, and headed back to the kitchens.

"If you go, be sure to wear the mask, you hear?" came her mother's faint cry in her wake.

"What is this ridiculous thing?" said Princess Egiras, a beauty with delicate yellow porcelain skin, slanted eyes, and floor-length raven hair. With hands like swan-necks bound in collar-bracelets of gold, she picked up an ornate mask from a silver tray offered to her. "The sun is setting, the Carnival lights are being ignited, and I have nothing to wear outside. Do you expect me to put on this monstrosity?"

"Your Brightness," said the blanching servant, "this was the best mask that the merchant Riho had to offer. . . . Behold, it has three layers of braided pearls on a rim of lapis, and the gold surface is polished to shine brighter than the Thousand Moons! The eyepieces are the finest amber stones—"

"No need to describe to me what is obvious," said Egiras. "It is nevertheless ugly in all its glory, and I will not have it. Take it back. And then bring me another mask. Something to match this lavender silk."

"But Your Brightness! The stores are closing! Where are we to find this other mask for you, when the best mask seller's most expensive work does not please you?"

In reply, Egiras turned her back on him, and moved coldly to stand by the window and watch the sunset.

The servant fled in terror, knowing without being told, her answer.

"**Y**aro! Yaro, you are quick, you can run faster than anyone," commanded the head servant breathlessly, wiping a sweating brow. "The Princess must have another mask for the festivities, and you must run to Riho's or to the jeweler Vael and see if they can make you something fast! Tell them the price is not an issue, the Princess will pay them handsomely—"

"This is madness," said Yaro tartly, unable to hold back. "Surely, *time* is an issue. Who can make a mask worthy of Egiras in half an hour?"

"Don't be smart, girl," said the head servant. "Do what you are told, or I will personally throw your sickly hag of a mother out onto the street. Go and do this thing now, and be quick about it! Remember, you will not be allowed back into the house without the mask!"

Yaro bit her lips, and then bowed her head.

"Hurry now! There is no time!"

In reply, Yaro fled.

A thousand moons will come tonight
Their radiance will be cold and bright
They say it is a frightful sight
Come, silver fire!

The evening sky was rich ebony with a fringe of fading rust at the horizon, and the Night of a Thousand Moons stood over the bowl of the city. A million fiery eyes opened that were Carnival lights, and they winked endlessly.

Yaro snaked her way through the crowds of faceless revelers, though streets hung in gaudy paper lanterns showing all phases of the crescent, and moon-orbs like bunches of grapes. She was returning from the stores of Vael the jeweler and other establishments famous for extravagant masks. At last, she carried a mask wrapped in silk.

A foreign craftsman had provided her with this mask for a great sum that the Princess would have to pay the next day. He had been gone in the back room for some time, so that Yaro was breathless with fear of being late, but finally he had come forward and laid a thing of utter whiteness upon the silken countertop.

It was a block of candle wax. As white and luminous it was as Yaro's skin was black and dull.

Yaro stared at it, then back at the man.

"I can make your Princess Egiras a mask that has no rival, a mask that she will fall in love with." he said in his foreign accent. "However, I will need your face for the mold."

"But—" said Yaro.

But he had already brought out the tools of his trade and begun a fire in the work-bowl.

Yaro stared in superstitious awe, seeing the man's hands move like magic over the flames, and possibly seeing the surface of his palms grow luminescent.

"You are a sorcerer . . ." she whispered.

He did not reply, but took the block of wax and now held it over the flames and began molding it with his fingers. In seconds the wax became a formless white lump, and then started to glow.

He turned to her then, and said, "This will hurt. Are you willing to endure pain for your Mistress? Your skin may burn, and your eyes will water endlessly, blurring your vision from the pain. It will be so bad that when you look up at the sky you will see several moons where there is only one."

My vision is already blurred, and I see a trio of moons every night, smirked Yaro in her thoughts, while inside her a cold resolve built. "Since I must come back with a mask, or not at all, none of this will matter. Therefore proceed, sorcerer."

"Well then. Close your eyes, and do not move, no matter what."

Yaro obeyed, drawing a single breath and holding it, while the incandescent lump was placed against her face.

Searing white agony.

Lightning.

The world was falling from under her, and her skin was lifted and replaced with liquid fire. . . .

It was no more than ten seconds of pressure against her face, but when the wax was lifted Yaro had aged ten years on the inside. It would not matter how she looked now, she could feel herself an old woman, drained.

"Do not open your eyes yet. Here, wash your face to soothe the pain," said the man, putting her hands upon another bowl containing cool liquid.

Yaro obeyed blindly, reeling. She placed her hands in the bowl, and cupping her palms washed her burning skinless flesh with something that must have been a salve—cool like the illusion of wind, and soothing—because her pain eased, and soon her dripping eyelids lifted of their own accord, miraculously free of any injury.

Outside the store she could hear singers on the street howling familiar verses and crescent drums beginning to pound for the processions that would last all night.

> *A thousand moons engulf the night,*
> *All things of darkness come to light*
> *Illusion falters from things bright,*
> *Come, silver fire!*

And then Yaro looked before her, blinking, and through her teary vision she saw the man holding a white wax mask.

It was like a lump of the moon. Plain, unadorned by any pattern, and with a surface dull and matte as sugar powder or ground chalk.

It was perfectly beautiful.

And, in the place where the two eyepieces were, it had two great convex agates.

Pupil-less eyes of the blind.

Yaro sucked in her breath, whether from the beauty or from terror. . . .

"It is done," said the man. "Take this to your mistress, and send me payment tomorrow. Only—be sure to give this to her yourself. Let no other hands touch this mask, for then its charm will be dispelled and I can no longer guarantee her pleasure."

Yaro nodded wordlessly, and took the waxen thing wrapped in silk, and bore it close to her shallow breast. Without looking back at him who had made the mask she came running out into the fire-swept night.

Princess Egiras stood at the balcony of her house, watching the tumultuous street below. Moon-jewels of the Carnival lights tumbled in the darkness, and songs of abandon pounded through the roar of the crowds.

The sky was ebony, lit with stars only, and the moon had not yet crested the horizon.

She stared, and for a moment saw the dislocated shadow of a man fill the sky. They said the Lord of Illusion made this night his own. She blinked in indifference, knowing him intimately, having seen him many times during other nights, and the shadow was no longer.

Egiras wore no mask. Behind her, like a leopard ready to pounce at the smallest danger, stood a silent tall man wearing a simple black wrap over his face. And farther back cringed variously masked servants.

"Where is my mask?" said Egiras, her back to them. "I will start counting. If I count to three and still there is no mask, then three of you will be blinded in one eye tomorrow at dawn. And, if I continue counting, every third of you will lose one eye until there is none left in this room with more than a single eye. I will hire new servants tomorrow. The rest of the house will be beaten."

The man standing behind her shifted his weight, then spoke softly, "My Lady ... Why not merely take away their masks? Leave their eyes, and let them face the moons naked. On the morrow, their fear will have punished them plenty, if they survive this night."

Egiras turned, and a smirk marred her perfect face, painted by the shadows and lights from below.

"Ah, Nadir," she said. "You are wise as always. I believe I will do just that. One!"

The servants drew in a collective gasp.

"Two!"

"Stop, my lady!"

From the back came a commotion as a thin black-skinned girl came running—girl or woman, Egiras could not tell. She carried in her hands a thing wrapped in silk.

"Your mask, Your Brightness!" the girl panted, wiping her brow, and Egiras noted the strange seared sheen of her face, as though her skin were appended to her flesh by means of nothing more than a good word.

Everywhere, gasps of relief.

"Finally," said the Princess. "Bring it to me. What is your name, girl?"

"Yaro ..." replied the skinny thing, and proffered the silken bundle.

Egiras took the silk, and unwrapped ... a piece of the moon.

Within the span of an indrawn breath, she was enchanted. The smooth moon-pallor was reflected into her eyes, and her vision convulsed with a pang of involuntary heart-rending agony.

But—only for a moment.

"This is ... perfection," breathed Princess Egiras. She stared, then put on the pale mask over her eyes, and tied it at the back with a hastily provided ribbon of gold. And with that the room let out another sigh of relief.

"Now," said Egiras, "I go to celebrate the Night of a Thousand Moons."

A thousand moons spill fiery light
A thousand hearts convulse in fright,
As judgment rains from heaven's might
Come, silver fire!

The first singer finished on a rising note and rolled his crescent drum while crowds of faceless ones roared approval. The second singer was a young woman, and she danced ahead of the procession, wearing nothing but ropes of spun-gold—or surely an illusion of such, thought Yaro.

Yaro trudged tiredly behind the chair of her mistress that was being carried in the parade. Princess Egiras rode high, like the moon herself, covered by a pale luminous simple mask that momentarily seemed to shimmer like mother of pearl and at other times seemed merely dull, like a wax candle.

"Look!" suddenly came cries from everywhere. "The moon! It rises!"

For a moment the harsh sounds of the Carnival came to a lull as all eyes turned to the horizon in momentary terror.

But the moon was only one. She sailed slowly, like Princess Egiras's mask, rising gently in the heavens.

Relief was universal.

This was not to be the fateful night in a thousand. For, even in the wildest pleasures of their revelry, none would forget the real reason for marking this night. All would tighten the laces of their masks, rearrange silk, wood, leather or metal closer against their skin.

Yaro had her own simple mask on, and its friction caused searing pain against the raw surface of her face. She had a great urge to remove it, moons or not. But to do that could mean inviting occult dangers. Even if the moons did not come that night, traditional superstition was strong. Thus one must cover the face till the new sunrise.

The procession moved through the crowds, twisting like a snake along convoluted streets, pausing at various city landmarks. At one point, near Tsaveh Dahnem, the popular tavern belonging to Belta Digh, a beggar child ran forward and slipped and fell at the feet of the chair-bearers of Princess Egiras.

As the small boy stumbled, his poor excuse for a mask, made of bits of rags, slipped off his face. It was immediately pounded into the ground by the feet of the dancers and the rest of those who walked before Egiras.

The boy rolled away like an eel, barely escaping the feet of the mob himself. After they passed, Yaro watched him run forward onto the street, and crawl around in the dirt, touching the bits of his mask. With her nearsighted eyes she barely saw him begin to cry, skinny shoulders trembling, tiny silent sobs lost in the clamor of the crowd.

Yaro dropped back from the procession and made her way to the child's side. Without thinking, she took off her own simple goatskin contraption, and said, "Here, you take this."

She placed the mask into the little grubby hands of the child, who stared at her with round terrified eyes, black and pupil-less in the darkness, and then took the mask from her in awe.

"Put it on now, child," said Yaro sternly. "The night is not over yet, and, who knows, the moons might still come."

"Oh, thank you! Thank you, great lady!" cried the beggar boy, using the slightly insincere tone of someone whose daily litany is to thank for alms.

But Yaro didn't mind his half-duplicity. She turned to go, feeling her bare face burn with the night wind, free of any protective covering but also free of pain.

She was unmasked and unprotected under the ebony sky of this Night of a Thousand Moons.

Through amber-filtered wondrous light,
An ancient magic you invite
To fill you with the moon's delight.
Come, silver fire!

"**W**here is your mask, Yaro?"
        Yaro had come up slowly behind the entourage of her mistress, and surprisingly here was Nadir at her side, like a dark looming ghost in the crowd of the Princess's retinue.

And, though she was too nearsighted to see his expression, she heard a note of concern in his quiet voice.

The next instant he was removing his own mask and thrusting it into her hands.

"Oh, no!" she retorted. "Please, my Lord, it is not necessary. I need none—"

"Then I don't need one either," said he calmly. "As you wish, but I will not wear mine. Either you take it or I toss it aside."

For once Yaro really wished she could see his eyes, to see if he was laughing at her or if this was real.

"Why, my Lord Nadir?"

His voice smiled. Really, it did.

"It wouldn't be fair otherwise." And with that he was gone back to their mistress's side. His mask remained in Yaro's fingers.

In moments there was a commotion. Yaro heard the voice of Princess Egiras raised in petulant anger, saying, "What is the meaning of this?" And then she heard Nadir's low protesting reply.

"Wouldn't be fair, my foot!" mumbled Yaro to herself, then moved forward in determination, and paused before her mistress's chair.

"Here is your mask, Lord Nadir I believe you dropped it," she said smartly, and offered his own mask back to him.

In her high chair, the Princess turned. The moon-wax eyeless face of Egiras greeted Yaro. All around, feathered masks of beasts and demons and gods stared at her, blurring into a kaleidoscope in her poor vision, as the whole household of the Princess witnessed this incident.

"You are indeed the mask-bearer for us all tonight, girl," said Egiras then, and motioned to Nadir. "Take what is yours."

"I am afraid I cannot do that," said the dark man. "This girl, this mask-bearer for us all, has no mask of her own. I did not drop the mask. I gave it to her."

"You are insolent!" said Egiras to Nadir. "And you, girl, why is it that you have no mask? Do you disdain this festival?"

"I have no mask," said Yaro, "because I want none."

"Have you no fear of the moons?"

"Not in particular, Your Brightness."

"What?"

A pause of silence.

Egiras raised her hand and the chair-bearers stopped. The dancers and the singers paused, and the drummers grew silent. The street crowd hushed.

"Then do you imply that I am afraid? That I might need a mask? How dare you?" said the voice of the Princess from beyond a waxen white thing of chalk.

Yaro's mouth parted in surprise. "Your Brightness," she said as humbly as she could, "I beg your forgiveness, for I truly mean no such thing! I merely gave my mask to a poor child, and now I hardly miss it at all. . . ."

"Foolish girl! If you had not given me this perfect mask I would have thrown you out of my house and service this instant. Get you a mask like all the others, and walk in the back of the line!"

Yaro stared, and the pale lump of wax stared back.

Overhead, the solitary moon rode high.

Urge of madness. . . .

"I will not," she said then, suddenly. "I will not walk in the back of the line. And I will not wear a mask, because my face is already a mask. My skin is singed and the flesh underneath is wailing out in pain because of that very thing you now wear! I have given my skin up for you, Mistress, but I will not give up my free choice. Be it as you will—I leave your house and your service, and take my old mother onto the streets, and may the gods watch over all of us!"

"Get out of my sight!" cried Egiras. "But first, guards, have her flogged for her insolence!"

Urge of madness. . . .

Yaro felt a burning sensation.

It began like a tingling over the surface of her face, replacing momentarily the dull pain. It spread and radiated suddenly, so that the guards who began to move toward her paused, and she could almost feel their stares through the macabre faceless masks. . . .

Yaro brought her hands up to her cheeks, and saw whiteness on her palms. Whiteness of reflected light. Truth or Illusion?

Am I doing this? It cannot be!

Yaro's face was glowing.

And then there was an inhuman scream. Several feet away, in her high chair, Princess Egiras felt a burning terrible sensation along her skin, like fire, and when she touched her pale beautiful mask in reflex her fingers were scalded, and she had to let go in agony.

The wax of the mask was suddenly incandescent, radiant, burning moon-white. The mask itself was burning.

No, I am not doing this! Yaro's thoughts raced.

Egiras continued screaming, and then, feeling her skin burn in flames, she ripped off the mask, wailing, tossing it down and putting her hands over her face, while her retainers and servants surrounded her.

But the mask did not fall.

Instead, while the crowd hushed, staring in terror, the mask began to *rise* in the air.

Like a piece of the moon.

The sky above was a coverlet of dark velvet, and stars were scattered like servants around their queen luminary. The mask rose quickly, like a bird in flight. And the higher it climbed the more it resembled the moon in shape and demeanor, until finally it had grown tiny and distant. When it reached the real moon, there was one bright explosive flash of silver light.

The whole city held its breath, and then the whole city screamed.

Yaro alone stood silently, calmly, her glowing face turned to the heavens, while overhead a miracle took place.

The moon split asunder. And in its place there were two moons, like twins.

The next second, in the blink of an eye, the two moons also split in half, rounded, and each one in turn gave birth to a twin. Then the four moons multiplied into eight. And the eight into sixteen. . . .

With each progression, the night grew visibly brighter, as the amount of light increased madly.

There was panic. Screaming masked humans ran madly for cover, and the chair-bearers dropped their mistress smack in the middle of the street. Others fell down on the ground and covered their faces, despite the protection of the masks against the supernatural light.

Egiras fell moaning, covering herself, covering her face. Even when turned earthward, her now blinded eyes continued to see moons imprinted upon her retina. . . .

At her side knelt the gentle great figure of a man. He was an island, poised, oddly unaffected by the glare of impossible light. Nadir reached forward, calling her name in his steady voice, taking her with his strong unyielding hands. . . .

The moons continued multiplying. It was now as bright as day. Yaro had lost count of them, seeing a whirling mass of orbs floating like lily-white grapes in a pale silver day-sky.

And then, in seconds, there was no more sky left.

There were only the moons.

There was so much light now that it was impossible to look and see anything. Yaro closed her eyes, but she could see the moons through her eyelids.

And then all the sounds of the world receded, and she heard a voice.

Yaro. Yaro, child of dust. Open your eyes and see what you have done.

Compelled, she opened her eyes, and stared at the alien lightscape that was now the world. And for some reason her eyes could endure the brightness.

Before her stood a fluctuating dark silhouette, a dislocated night shadow against the mad light. For a moment he seemed to be a man, mysterious like the craftsman who had made her the mask. And the next he shrank into the little boy child for whom she had given up her own mask.

Yaro, he said, *you must stop this now. You are doing all this, you know. I have given you the ability to make your own free choices, and now you have taken the Night and made it into its opposite. Return the Night to me, Yaro.*

"I?" she whispered. "I have done this? Who are you?"

I am the one who rules it.

"How can that be? How have I done this? I am nobody. And you are Lord of the Night!"

You have done this, and none other. The Night of a Thousand Moons is a Night of Illusion. Look again, look closely. And tell me what you really see.

Yaro closed her eyes, and when next she opened them there was only soothing darkness. High above, in a bed of the heavens, in velvet darkness, rode one single white moon.

She stared, and suddenly realized that no longer did the moon seem blurred around the edges, nor tripled in her poor vision. For the first time in her life it was crisp and perfect and round.

And it was perfectly alone.

All the other moons had gone. But the shadow form before Yaro was still there, still real.

Stop your Illusion, he said. *You willed the moons to be. It is over now, it is enough. The real world is dark.*

And there was a feeling of completion within Yaro. A soothing calm. And yet something continued to burn, just at the edges of her consciousness.

"Lord of the Night, or whoever you are. I don't believe you," she said. "If this is indeed an Illusion, then I have no power over it. However, it is obvious that you need something of me, and thus you attempt to deceive me. In truth, the Illusion is this darkness. You want me to believe in my own self-importance, to believe that I, a nobody, might have power over the world, out of nothing.

"I am not sure why you want this from me. Maybe because each new soul that forgets its place in the great scheme of the world forgets also humility, becomes misguided, and thus falls under your rule?"

Yaro laughed to herself then. "Yes! You test me now because my soul has come to a new boundary of experience—I am weak, a nothing, and yet I *aspire* to something more. I am thus most vulnerable to Illusion! One such as Nadir you can never have because his humility is his strength. And one such as the Princess Egiras is already yours, and so you do not tempt her with choices, only mollify her emptiness with delusion."

And suddenly the bright impossible light of a thousand moons struck Yaro once again with all its fierceness.

And the shadow man screamed, howled in anger, and he began to fade then, under the thousand sources of killing light.

"Good riddance, you flea-ridden monkey of a god! I knew you were the Lord of Illusion, I knew it!" gasped Yaro as she fell down on the stone of the street, shielding her eyes from the very real, very terrible light. "You planned this elaborate setup just to lure me, another mortal, to your power—taking advantage of my natural willfulness and of the coincidental wonders that you knew would come to pass. How many others like me have you conspired to deceive tonight?"

And then, lying on the ground, she chuckled softly, mumbling to herself, "Well, not this Yaro, child of dust! I knew, because you could not have given me free choice. It has been mine all along. But, most of all, I knew because for that one moment you let me, a blind woman, see the moon with perfect eyesight! Do you think I am an idiot?"

Thus Yaro laughed, shoulders quaking, at the Lord of Illusion, until she thought suddenly of free choices and of what had been done, of her old mother who would now be thrown out on the streets.

And, mid-laughter, she began to weep.

The Night of a Thousand Moons fades from memory with the new dawn. Wonders cease, and the world returns to its normal routine. Once in a millennium it happens, and every time afterward it is forgotten that there is no danger at all, only wonder. No judgment, only glory. No destruction, only light.

The only thing that must be feared is the Lord of Illusion.

He is forgotten also. And yet he is the only reason to take care, for he harvests us mortals like the wind of night. On that night, only wisdom will prevail against him.

And it will not matter if you wear a mask.

Dream Twelve

The Cup

It is not an easy thing, serving a self-imposed blind woman who has eyes and yet refuses to use them. It is three times as difficult to serve one who is also a Princess, a shrew, and very possibly a madwoman.

And when that creature happens to be the Princess Egiras, the one who has gone mad after seeing a Thousand Moons in the night sky, the task is nearly superhuman.

I am Nadir, and I took that task of servitude upon myself a long time ago. For I had committed a single act of dishonor against her kin. And to atone for it I, a foolish child, had made a single promise.

The gods heard me, and from that moment on my life became intertwined with the life of this woman—a mortal, yet on some other level an occult being bound to Illusion.

As a result, I too was indirectly bound to the Lord of Illusion against my very nature and my ardent heart.

Thus I am a self-imposed fool.

When the desert gale winds ceased to blow after the storm season and the grains of sand settled down in uniform whiteness upon the dunes, a small caravan left the city, traveling East.

The caravan bore no merchant but a wealthy Princess of foreign extraction who was returning home to her distant land of birth.

Her homeland lay somewhere toward the rising sun, beyond the mirage-rim of the horizon. And the caravan moved forward guided only by the great light in the sky as it traversed the upturned celestial bowl.

For the Princess whom it carried was blind to the world. She was unable to describe their destination, despite having two beautiful unblemished eyes slanted like almonds, with pupils that were darkness itself, without movement or bottom, and with a thick short fringe of lashes over unusual twin folds of her eyelids. Only the tall dark-skinned man with coarse hair and large pliant features, who was ever at the side of the Princess was rumored to know the way, having been once to the distant land.

Even in secret, the servants who accompanied the silent blind woman called her only by her true name, Egiras, and had no other nickname to give their mistress behind her back. And they feared her, as one would fear the night.

Three handmaidens came with her on this journey. There were also menservants, all of whom were skilled men-at-arms in addition to being members of the household. Finally there were the hired guards.

The black-skinned man who was always near the Princess Egiras—her henchman or bodyguard—was called Nadir. It was whispered among the servants that he could single-handedly defend their Princess from harm, if such a need arose. They said he was like a great ebony panther that was the minion of the deity of night—a beast which, when unleashed in anger, could wreak extraordinary destruction.

Supposedly he had absorbed the mysterious powers of night from having spent time with savage wise men in the hidden holy places of the Princess's distant homeland. He had come forth out of that land a priest of the most occult terror. And to cross him in any manner meant being exposed to this terrifying unknown.

They spoke many other absurd things about him, tongues wagging eagerly.

Ironically, the meaning of his name was rarely discussed or questioned. It meant "the bottom," the "lowest of the low."

Nadir, the lowest one.

Despite all the fearsome rumors, no one could remember the last time when Nadir had lost his temper. No one observed him lashing out in violence or imposing his will unreasonably upon any of the household. On the contrary, he was like the wind moving grains of sand, a constant shadow sound that one stops hearing after a while in the desert.

Such was Nadir's presence, a safe constant. Even before the Princess had become as helpless as she was now, he would walk behind her unobtrusively, remaining in her vicinity. He protected her with his being like a wall of stone. Wherever she would go, he came after, more intimate than a shadow. For unlike a shadow he was there both in darkness and in light.

All the while Egiras abused him with unreasonable commands and a harsh tone. Even his name was pronounced with derision, as she constantly provoked him to react with anger—the one thing he never did.

Instead, the anger rebounded back upon her, and she burned with unresolved futility, tormenting him even more cruelly than before. And he endured it all.

He remained her loyal minion, even as she mocked his every act and breath. And it was not precisely understood how or why this Nadir, this terrifying and yet humble one, came to serve the petulant Princess, or what secret power she held over him.

It was enough that things had been like this forever, it seemed, and certainly since long before Egiras had seen the Thousand Moons and lost her vision and her mind.

Some had called that Night of a Thousand Moons a hallucination, a trick of the Lord of Illusion. But Egiras was evidence, at least to her own intimidated household, that something occult had indeed taken place. For she had become a blind madwoman overnight, a silent remote being who did not respond to anything.

Egiras stared with unblinking eyes, never reacting when a candle flame was brought to linger before her face. Two handmaidens instead of one had to undress her at night and help her with her personal needs, because their now silent mistress seemed incapable of untying knots or adjusting her own clothing. No longer did she bother to make herself presentable, and her long black waterfall of silken hair was tangled from being worn loose and unbrushed. She never noticed it.

Egiras did not sleep at all that first night after the Night of a Thousand Moons. And the next night she slept briefly and fitfully, and came awake like a wild creature. Her eyes were glassy, filled with strange unseeing depths.

She cried out, and Nadir awoke immediately, rising from the chair in the corner where he had stayed with her to guard her sleep. He tried to soothe her with a light touch, but she snarled at him, as though in a waking nightmare, and beat him away with her fingers splayed like claws, scratching his arm bloody with her nails.

Physicians had to restrain her, and gave her a medicinal herbal draft, forcing it down her throat. It served not only to nullify pain but to take away her consciousness, so that the Princess fell back into drugged oblivion. But when she came awake later that morning she was once again a terrified alien thing, unseeing, and incapable of responding to soothing voices.

Old servants wept at the sight of their mistress, for though she had been cruel Egiras was still the one they had grown accustomed to serving. They loved not her but the symbol of her household and the security she represented.

"What is to be done, Lord Nadir?" they bemoaned, turning to the man who was her unwavering protector.

And the man who was named the lowest of the low soothed them all, saying, "We must wait."

Nadir's words were justified. As days passed, Egiras very tentatively regained a small amount of her senses. She was still fitful at night, and unpredictable; she would still snarl and act like a madwoman. But there were now times when her sarcastic clarity would return, and then a thin, cruel, perfectly rational smile would settle on her lips. Softly she would mutter words that none could hear properly, and which might have been remnants of her long-unused native tongue.

And eventually those muddled words too made sense, and they knew that she was calling for her homeland, asking to be taken back, far from this terrible city, to the place from where she had sprung.

"My Lady, it will be as you wish, and I will take you there," Nadir said then, in a voice that barely registered, but its softness for some reason had more of an effect on her than loud forcefulness. He added, drawing his face near hers, "What of your eyes? You understand when I speak, yet cannot see. Is that true? What do you see?"

The face of the Princess, with its delicate skin of pale yellow porcelain, remained immobile, and her slanted almonds of eyes did not move from their fixed position, the irises and pupils murky with a colorless dark.

"Moons, burning bright . . ." she muttered. "I see the whole world is burning. It is all around. Oh, take this brightness away! Deliver me!"

"I cannot . . ." whispered Nadir. "Oh, how I wish I could."

In that moment, for the first time in many days, her small cold hand gripped his strong dark one, finding it by touch.

Egiras turned to him, turned without seeing, and her gaze was blind and yet focused on that place that was him.

"Nadir!" she said fiercely, "Nadir, Nadir! Is it you? Speak so that I know it is you."

"Yes, it is I," he responded, heartened by her unexpected quickening. "I am here!"

"Why?" said Egiras then, an odd question—odd for it had no mockery and no taunt in it, only a sincere searching quality. "Why are you here with me? After all this time. . . ."

"Where else would I be, my Princess?" he said calmly, while his great hands trembled, betraying him.

But she did not appear to be aware of it, and instead her tone became remote again, abstracted, as she spoke.

"When will we go, Nadir? When will we return to the Kingdom in the Middle?"

"At any moment, we return."

"Then let us go now!" she exclaimed suddenly, and her greatly dilated eyes glittered. Yet they shed no moisture, not a single tear, although they appeared as though they must.

"Not immediately, my Lady, for we must tell the servants to pack your things, and to sell this House. . . ."

"No! Just . . . leave it. Leave all of it be."

Nadir frowned. For a moment, the woman before him shimmered and his own sight convulsed, as though a veil of Illusion had gently shifted between them, rippling in place for one instant. And then things came back, and he stared at her, wondering at this latest strangeness.

Egiras was still clutching his arm, and her grip had become painful, so that he had to gently extricate himself from her fingers. Where they had pressed his flesh had become a numb, bloodless place.

"We will need supplies as we travel through the desert," he said rationally. "And to equip a caravan with enough provisions and pack beasts and guards will require money. Because of that, we must sell your House."

"Then do it," she said fiercely, a pale shadow of her former commanding tone returning. Her empty eyes focused past him and through him, gazing upon an unseen distant horizon.

And Nadir lowered his head before her, even though she could not see it, and he said softly as a whisper, "It shall be done."

I glanced away from her eyes. Even then they were impossible to meet directly, roiling with darkness, so many layers of it. And yet for the first time I saw a difference in the overall lines of her face; a kind of new calm had settled upon her. Not peace, surely, for that was the one thing she would never have. But it was a stillness of some kind.

The one whom I knew as Egiras, my Princess, tormentor, sovereign, burden, was suddenly one other thing—a delicate being of agony. For the first time it had come to the surface, and I knew now that she was not perfectly invulnerable, but rather had been perfectly contained.

Egiras had been contained in an impenetrable shimmering veil of Illusion.

And pity came to stab me, to overwhelm, in that instant. I had always known it to be so, had always known she was one to be pitied, despite all, but it had never been sincere or real to me before, always on the bitter edge of hatred.

Until now.

And thus I did as she asked. I arranged to sell her city House and the dross bulk of her extravagant belongings, and hired an experienced caravan leader and trustworthy guards to take us far into the desert—all paid for by the revenues from that sale.

I also re-hired the most loyal of the servants to accompany us on this long journey into the unknown lands. Egiras would need her handmaidens to care for her person, especially now that she could not fend for herself. And the ones who would come on this journey had to do so without any qualms or fear for their lives.

For only the gods really knew where we were going.

"Yaro, Yaro, child of dust . . ." muttered the old woman, thinner and blacker than a dried-out twig, nearly blind, and draped in rags the color of the earth upon which she lay. "Where are you?"

"Here, mother," said a younger version of the old woman, equally dark and thin, and only a little less nearsighted, but with a straight back. She stood leaning against the outer city wall of stone, veiled in a poor shawl against the open wind of the desert.

The wind came to strike them both as it broke itself in fury against the city walls and the sparse earthen embankment that arose at the foot of the walls, the layer of soil that had been brought here from afar and deposited in a fine sediment to form the foundation of the city. Sand slowly encroached upon the earth, dunes rising like stilled waves of a petrified ocean. Whiteness mingled with sienna and deep umber.

"Do not go far . . ." said the old woman.

"I am not going anywhere. I only stand here so that I can see the road better, and the caravans that pass here. One of them will be ours."

"What caravan would take an old serving woman and her willful daughter who betrayed her mistress?"

"I betrayed no one . . ." bristled Yaro momentarily, her voice initially strong like an angry swell of surf and then again receding into dissolved humility. "And, yes, a caravan will take us, because it must. Because the sum of the whole world is justice, and it is at our disposal—at everyone's disposal—as long as we remember that we must give back what we take."

"What?" said her mother, "What kind of mad arrogant words do you speak, child of dust? Stop provoking the gods with your unending ramblings. It is not for the likes of us to use the things of the world, or to have opportunities come to us. We will die here in the sand, very soon. Or at least, I will die first, as I drink the last of our poor water, and then you will follow me, in the bright sun-whiteness that is desert death. . . ."

"Hush, stupid old woman! Take this instead and drink before you indeed go up in sun-flames. Look how burned and black you are!"

And saying that, Yaro squatted down at her mother's side and dug around in their one sack of possessions. Eventually she pulled out the old wooden bowl that she'd used to feed the old woman soup but which now held only water, for they had had nothing to eat for several days. She rummaged around some more and took out a water-flask, which she uncorked with difficulty, and poured a small amount into the very bottom of the bowl.

Yaro propped up her mother's head and tilted the bowl at her lips while the old one drank weakly, her turtle throat making swallowing movements. The old woman's shawl had come off her head, revealing white, tightly coiled hair close to her scalp, in sharp contrast to her midnight parchment skin.

When she was done, Yaro hid the bowl and the flask away again in the dim recesses of their bag, and used the corner of the old woman's shawl to wipe the glitter of sweat from her mother's forehead. Then she ran the cloth gently against the soft flattened nose and sunken hollow cheeks while the old woman sighed and closed her eyes under the touch.

The morning sun started its ascent towards the zenith.

And at the same time a caravan embarked from the city gates, with the soft clamor of pack beasts and the sounds of footfalls against the road near the embankment. Soon those too would fade as the road transformed into an ocean of silent sand. . . .

Yaro immediately sprang upright and placed her palm over her brows to shade her eyes from the wicked sun. She peered, squinting her eyes narrowly, putting all her intensity into the gaze, willing her blurred vision to focus the chaos of colored light and shadow and movement that was the world into distinct recognizable forms—which for a moment it did, granting her a brief scene.

There were pack-beasts cruelly loaded and fine horses bearing guards, stout wagons with wide-tracked desert wheels, and several covered sedans suspended from tall swaying camels. An altogether familiar sight: one more caravan exactly like a dozen she had already observed over the past days.

And yet unlike. For in that moment of intense squinting truth she recognized a large human shape atop one of the horses. She recognized him with her nearly blind eyes from a distance of several hundred feet.

She knew him merely by his manner of being. Not by the outline of his form or his bearing, but rather as one senses the position of all things in a single moment of homing—the distant horizon and the earth underneath and the sky above. She recognized him by his placement and direction relative to herself.

And, knowing who he was and whom he accompanied always, Yaro drew in her breath while a coldness came to slither into her, despite the heat of the climbing sun.

It brought cold, such cold, the act of knowing that salvation and destruction lay in the exact same place.

"Our caravan is before us, mother," said Yaro. Then she added, "Wait here, while I go to them and beg to take our former place. For it is the caravan of my former mistress the Princess Egiras, and with her is the Lord Nadir. One of them will condemn me and the other will insist upon mercy."

I trust mercy to prevail, Yaro thought.

But the cold continued. For, in order to be subjected to mercy, Yaro was about to destroy the last shreds of her pride.

As I moved forward to ride alongside the outer perimeter of the caravan—for we had just left the confines of the great city—with the white sands stretching in all directions immediately before us, I saw a human speck approaching from a distance.

Unbelievably, I knew who it was.

It came to me with a stab, the familiar frail slope of her shoulders, the thin hands hidden under layers of poor cotton, and paradoxically the quick energetic movements of power, the way she carried her shawl-covered head half-lowered and yet somehow defiant. Her skin, the same date-brown deep color as mine, or the color of the earth itself deep underneath the sands—umber, cool and dark and rich with unexpected moisture. . . .

A woman of my own race.

Yaro, the one who had brought the moon-mask to Egiras, just before the madness took over and made that festival night the Night of a Thousand Moons.

I watched her approach, walking with determination toward us, toward me, it seemed, then starting to run, leaving the solid earth of the embankment and stumbling over the resilient sands.

"My Lord Nadir!" she cried. "Please wait!"

I slowed my horse, falling behind the leisurely rambling gait of the caravan pack beasts, and sat in my saddle. I glanced once toward the covered chair that carried the Princess, seeing the curtains closed tight, and sensing nothing but stillness within.

Yaro had caught up to me by then, and she stopped before my mount. She was breathing quickly, and sweat was beading the black skin of her pinched face, her sunken cheekbones. Her shawl had slipped back to her shoulders, revealing the thick carpet of curls that protected her scalp from the deadly sun.

Her eyes were without any light and fathomless.

"Yaro . . ." I said. "What are you doing here?"

"I beg your mercy, my Lord Nadir," she said breathlessly, lowering herself to her knees. "My old mother and I have nowhere to go, and the blame is on me. . . . I know that the Princess has cast me forth from her side, and for a good reason. I have said things to her in proud thoughtless anger, disdainful impertinent things never to be uttered by a nothing like me. And yet I am here now, begging your kind mercy, not on my behalf but on behalf of my mother who suffers because of my willfulness. Her gradual fading into desert oblivion I cannot bear."

I stared down at her, watching the dark, tightly curling hair on the top of her head, the nape of her thin neck as she came to bow before me on the powdery sand. She was shaking.

"When have you and your mother eaten last?" I asked, my voice withdrawn somehow, controlled. It sounded cold and unyielding to my own ears.

She looked up at me—her eyes impenetrable because they were full of liquid, and were thus glittering in the sun—and said, "I no longer remember, my Lord. Several days ago. But we still have water. . . ."

I thought of what the reaction of Egiras might be to this. I imagined fury and raving madness and an instant banishment. And then I thought maybe it would be none of that. For Egiras was no longer aware of the world around her, and it was very possible she would not even notice the return of this serving woman unless someone pointed it out to her.

While I considered this, Yaro got up from her kneeling position and spoke again. "Please, my Lord," she said, "I no longer have any thought of pride or justice or even of what this means I am doing. If you would like me to grovel, I will gladly do it. I will prostrate myself at your feet, and at the feet of the Princess Egiras, and exult in whatever agony of punishment she may bestow upon me. I will take all humiliation, pain, mockery as the most supreme gift of the gods, nay, a blessing—"

"Enough," I interrupted. "You are delirious with sun."

And then, seeing the intensity in her liquid eyes, I raised my right arm and in a loud voice called out for the drivers to halt the caravan.

As the beasts and riders came to a noisy rolling stop before and behind us, I leaned forward from the saddle and stretched out my hand, large, powerful and leathered, to take her thin calloused one, encasing it completely.

I pulled her upward and onto the saddle in front of me, feeling as if I were lifting up a bag of bones wrapped in black skin and tanned cotton. She made no sound, and she felt like wind in my hands, before me.

"Where is your old mother?" I asked, speaking to the back of her head, just above her left ear, and smelling the desert. "Take me to her. She will have a place in the caravan. And as for you—you can be my very own servant, not the servant of Egiras. Thus the only one with the power to dismiss you, from now on, will be myself."

In the whiteness of sands that is the desert, time distorts into ripples of a roving dune, and hours, days and weeks blend into one.

The caravan bearing the Princess Egiras moved steadily and relentlessly toward the Eastern horizon. Egiras would say nothing, was a non-entity, seated in her sedan chair and wrapped from head to foot in billowing layers of pale fine cotton against the sun. In addition, the overhanging canopy cast her face into relative shadow, and the handmaidens who were carried at her side superstitiously glanced at their mistress often to ascertain that she was indeed there and not merely an empty veil filled like a sail with nothing but wind.

More than once in their progression of days they stopped at a minor oasis. The pack-beasts would be unsaddled and given rest while a small tent was rigged up for the Princess herself. At these times, in her blindness, Egiras seemed to pay no heed to a skinny black servant woman who might otherwise have seemed very familiar but who kept her head diligently lowered as she scurried about carrying things and doing relentless chores.

Yaro was unnoticed by all except Nadir.

Always at the side of the Princess, he would glance at the woman servant briefly and then intentionally ignore her, as though he feared that merely by looking at her he would mark her somehow, make others take note of her presence, and thus make her more real. If she were not real, she would not be noticed.

The old decrepit woman who was Yaro's mother had been concealed in one of the small covered wagons carrying supplies. She lay surrounded by sacks of grain and provisions, and covered by heavy burlap cloth against the sun. Yaro would come to check on her several times amid the day's chores, and when the caravan was on the move she would ride in the same wagon, sitting next to her mother and wiping her brow.

Every sundown, as cool relief came to the air even though the sands radiated stored heat like coals, the caravan stopped. Camels were relieved of their burdens, and came down crouching to sleep, while the other pack beasts were tethered to stakes driven deep into the sand. The servants and the guards went about the business of the evening meal and the preparation for sleep. It was then, while most were preoccupied and the handmaidens cared for the breathing marionette Egiras, that Nadir observed how Yaro silently and dutifully came to unroll his own meager bedding for the night.

The first time it happened, he was surprised, and stood up from his place in the vicinity of the cooking fire, where Egiras was being spoon-fed a warm stew that she barely managed to ingest past clenched lips.

"What are you doing?" he asked, coming up from behind Yaro like a silent giant shadow. Yaro started in nervous alarm, but then, seeing with her nearsighted eyes, up close, that it was only he, she inclined her head in respect.

"I am serving you, my Lord Nadir," she replied. The light of the remote fire flickered with liquid intensity in her pitch-black eyes as she met his gaze. Then she looked down and continued to prepare his bedding, shaking out the roll in case some harmful insects or scorpions had crawled in. Her slender callused fingers moved deftly, and her hands were steady, despite their alarming thinness.

"Thank you . . . ." said Nadir.

And then he did not know what else to say, and so he stood for several moments and watched her in peculiar silence before once again joining the group around the fire.

The next evening it was the same. Only this time, after Yaro had tended to his belongings, she brought food and wine to him as he sat resting before the fire, just a few feet away from the Princess.

"Where did you get this?" he said. "What is this?"

Yaro placed the cheese and thick warm stew on a large piece of flatbread and placed it on a spread cloth at his feet. She took the jug of wine and poured a cup for him, to the brim.

"This is from the pot, my Lord," she replied smartly. "And the cheese is from that large round serving bag near the Mistress. The wine I took from her servants also, telling them that it was for my Lord Nadir, since I am his one and only servant, and that, if they did not give it immediately, they would be invoking your great displeasure."

Nadir's brows lifted and he gave a soft laugh in the fire-lit dark. "I've never had such a servant as you before. . . ."

"You've never had *any* servant," Yaro said. "And it shows. My Lord needs to learn how to be a lord, for my Lord is too kind."

But Nadir continued laughing, so that the others looked their way, never having seen him even smile before; this was surely unprecedented.

"I have never needed a servant before," he said at last, taking a chunk of flatbread and dipping it into the stew, "because I am not a lord. But I find it a good thing to be served thus kindly by you, Yaro."

"Harumph!" said Yaro sternly, and not another word more. She then gathered herself up, quickly moving her dark spindly limbs, and was gone, disappearing somewhere behind the Princess's tent and the wagons.

Nadir ate the meal in warm silence.

More than seven days had passed, and there was no visible difference to the desert around them. Maybe it was simply that memory for such minute things is ephemeral, and all grains of sand look alike when they comprise one crumbling uniform ocean. The sun's sterile essence rained down impassively upon the world and brought apathy to all those who had to suffer beneath it.

The caravan steadily moved East in its journey.

Their stores of food and water were adequate, and yet grumbling was heard among the guards. And the handmaidens of Egiras whispered in displeasure that there was not enough water for them to wash their hands and faces properly, and that the constant sand dust had come to fill their hair and eyelids, despite the coverings of many veils.

Egiras sat propped up by a pillow in the suspended chair that carried her, her face swaddled and her nose and lips covered from the dusty wind. Only the cold liquid coals of her eyes were visible. She looked toward the East, and her gaze briefly rose, seeming to follow the movement of the celestial light overhead, before again fixing upon the horizon.

The delicate twin folds of skin over her eyes narrowed them into slits when the wind blew directly at her, but at other times she would look onward with glassy, fully open eyes. Sometimes her lips moved without a sound.

"What does Her Brightness see? Where does she strain at so intently? Her eyes are blind, yet why does she always *look?*" gossiped the handmaidens nervously. They were young and the idleness of the trip made them more susceptible to various forms of indisposition and restlessness. And the strange lack of demands upon their company by their silent frozen mistress made things even more unbearable.

In the previous days, before Egiras had become withdrawn thus, she would demand from them lively conversation, storytelling, singing of songs and retelling of court gossip. She would not allow them to rest. The handmaidens serving the Princess would be tense and fearful, ready to amuse her in any way in order to avoid quick punishment.

So who would have thought that it would come to this? They merely sat in their suspended chairs and embroidered with silk, or strung translucent glass beads in intricate arrangements upon fine cloth.

Egiras sat alone and motionless, her small pale hands held in her lap. There were no jeweled bands upon her wrists nor rings on her swan-delicate fingers, for she had demanded none, and the handmaidens never bothered with these details now that their mistress did not seem to care.

At many points in the day, as the sun traversed the pale celestial dome, the strange man they knew as Lord Nadir would pace his horse to walk near the swaying chair of the Princess Egiras and he would speak softly in greeting, then draw the curtains apart to make sure Egiras was well.

"Should we stop to rest, my Lady?" he would ask.

But for the most part she would not even turn her face to him, and only the tensing of her form would tell him that she knew he spoke.

Sometimes she would barely shake her head in response. He would then leave her be, and close the curtain between them.

At other times Egiras replied to him, her voice barely audible above the wind. "We go on . . ." she spoke. "Keep going."

It was at such times that Nadir would hear grumbling voices. When he turned to look, the servants would grow silent and withdraw behind the pack beasts. And then there would be strained silence in the caravan until the next nightfall when they stopped.

Such was the routine.

Until one morning the caravan woke up to a dull sky, and the dawn was obscured in a slate haze, while the wind sang louder than normal, in tumult. They proceeded to move onward, but with caution.

"Look at the horizon, Lord Nadir!" exclaimed a guard, riding back from up ahead to pause at my side. "See how blurred it is, and there is no line of sight between land and sky. A storm lies before us. This is a big one, and it will stir up the sands into a frenzy. We must stop and wait it out, or else we risk harm!"

I squinted and drew my hand over my brow as I stared East, blinking away the involuntary tearing in my eyes due to excessive dust. I looked back at the man, knowing him to be relatively trustworthy, and then I nodded. "I can see it. We'll stop, Patriq."

We became motionless, scanning the panorama of the desert around us, while the cooler wind of this overcast morning scraped our cheeks with granules of sand, made the ends of our cotton head-wraps flap uncontrollably, and billowed our travel robes.

I searched for any landmark, any sign of difference in the sands, such as an oasis or even meager shrubs—anything that would anchor us better in this desolation.

Nothing.

Resigned, I signaled with my hand and the caravan slowed, while the drivers and guards came to me, knowing without being told why we were stopping this time.

I spoke curtly and loudly above the wind, which was howling stronger with each moment. My voice rose above the clamor and became commanding. Rarely had I used this voice before, having learned it a long time ago in the days of my warrior training.

I told them to move the three wagons together to form an outer circle, and to bring the beasts around and allow them to crouch close together. The larger camels were to be on the outside, and the lesser pack-beasts in the middle. All were to remain laden, for the additional weight of their burdens would help them stay immobile against the wind.

In the very middle we ourselves would huddle, the guards and servants on the outside, the women in the middle, with the Princess Egiras at the very heart of us. Like solid veils, our human bodies would protect her.

Thus we would weather the storm.

As the household hurried to prepare for the ordeal, I dismounted also and, being taller than all and of greater strength than the guards, helped them disassemble the curtained chairs and fold and carry them to the wagons for safety. I then bodily carried the Princess Egiras to the center of our makeshift fortress, placed her upon a rug, and covered her like a child with additional cloaks and blankets. For a moment her slender fingers wrapped around my neck, and I felt her grasping me in terror, while her shadow eyes remained wide underneath the transparent veil that covered her face. In that instant of intensity, I almost thought she was staring at me, that the wildness in her eyes was visual comprehension.

And then I saw Yaro, quick as mercury at my side, as she brought more bundles of blankets and bedding, and together with the handmaidens and the other women servants she helped to arrange a tent over everyone's heads.

But then, instead of huddling closer with the women, Yaro dashed out of the tent like a madwoman, wind ripping at her poor clothing, and made her way toward one of the wagons.

"Yaro!" I cried. "Come back! Where are you going?"

"My mother!" she cried, without turning around. "She is in the wagon!"

I growled in anger, in sudden understanding of the inevitability of her actions, and then at the inevitability of my own actions that would follow. I was furious at myself that I had forgotten about the old woman even for a moment.

And so I went after her.

For the first time in these endless years, I was leaving the Princess in a moment of danger. That thought danced through my consciousness, flickering past the gale-level noise of the wind around us, as the edges of the storm came upon the caravan.

What am I doing?

But the answer did not come to me, not while my attention was upon the details of the wagon just ahead of me, only steps away past the backs of the huddled camels.

The air had grown dark, obscuring the faint sky altogether, and wind saturated with sand whipped angrily into my squinting eyes as I tore forward, seeing nothing but the thin woman's black limbs as she rummaged in the wagon, pulling up a lifeless bundle that looked like a sack but turned out to be the limp figure of an ancient woman.

Another second and I was at her side and taking over her light burden. I carried her mother back toward our tent, each step like quicksand through the thickness of wind, while Yaro came behind me and tried in her own way to help by holding a shawl against our faces as we walked.

Seconds stretched like days, and then we had reached the grouping where the household had gathered in and around the small tent, making a mass of burlap and cotton and swaddled bodies against the sand and wind. My Princess Egiras was inside.

I dropped on my knees before the tent, and, since there was no place within because all the womenfolk had been piled there, I placed the old woman down against the canvas and cotton blankets just at the edge. The blankets were already half-buried with airborne sand, but they were better than nothing. I turned around and grabbed Yaro's thin limbs and pulled her forcibly nearer to her mother, placing my great form against them both, shielding them like a wall.

Yaro struggled for an instant in surprise, but almost immediately went limp, for I was a giant compared to her, and besides she knew I was helping. And then, because the storm was now fully on us, even I was barely able to move despite my strength as I pulled up and drew with both hands a flapping blanket around us. With it I covered our three heads tight, swaddling us up to the necks in protective darkness and leaving only a small pocket of air so that we could breathe. And then I was falling motionless in the sand on top of them both.

While the maelstrom closed upon us with a sound that filled the whole world, I remembered another moment, this one a long time ago.

With a pang it came to me, the memory of myself as a small angry boy huddled over a young girl—her facial features forgotten now, a pallid blur except for her bright persimmon hair—Caelqua, my sister, and an old swarthy woman, my beloved grandmother whom I was later to know as Ris. . . .

And for the second time in my life we lay dying in the desert.

Yaro gasped, and her mind came flying back into her, or so it seemed. At some point during the storm she had lost consciousness, and had dreamed. Weightless, she wandered somewhere up high, as high as the clouds and oddly above the body of the storm. From her immortal's vantage point the world was a vista of cotton shades of monochrome. She saw the sun bright and unobscured searing from above—so unlike what it normally was in her poor vision—and underneath was the grey tumult of the sandstorm and the overcast haze of the desert.

A milky dream; nothing but a heady vertigo.

The cloth of the blanket was choking her, and she felt other limbs and bodies around her, and the pressing of sand.

There was also a strange silence.

Yes, it was that very silence that had brought her spirit back into her body, for the wind had died down and the sand granules rolled softly around her like strange warm water.

Yaro fumbled with the cloth around her face, moving slowly under the weight of sand, and then dug upwards, knowing the direction by instinct. Next to her she felt the movement of another body, and even closer she knew must be the skeletal form of her old mother.

Yaro dug fiercely, and then pulled the blanket away and was free.

Overhead, the sky burned. There was no sign of the storm-laden skies, and all around her the desert was smooth like barely rippling sand water. She had surfaced into desolation.

The realization of this utter solitude exploded within her. She reacted, digging wildly around her, feeling with her lower body the bodies of others nearby.

The sand went flying, and then just as quickly rolled back down upon her in a million granules even as she swept it away. And yet she managed to free the head and upper torso of the frail old woman, her mother. The old one still breathed, thanks to the protective covering of the blanket around her face, and was coughing weakly, unable to speak.

"I will get you water, mother. Don't be afraid!" whispered Yaro in a parched voice. The old woman nodded at her, then closed her eyes.

Yaro coughed and then, flailing, continued to dig in a wide circumference around her. Just behind them had been the tent with the mistress and her serving women, and nearby were all the rest. Off to the side somewhere were the camels and the wagons. And within were the precious sacks that held the caravan's water supply.

What a storm it had been that everything was covered up!

At that moment there was movement in the sand around her in several places, like the popping-bubble surface of a stew slowly beginning to boil. Others had come alive, one by one, and were attempting to extricate themselves also. Then from everywhere came the muffled braying of camels and the powerful snorts of other pack beasts as they dug themselves out, reaching up for air.

The sands shuddered very close, just behind Yaro, and Nadir's head emerged, blinking and snorting, and then the rest of him as he began to dig violently in the morass.

"Yaro!" he gasped. "Are you unharmed? Egiras!" And then he looked behind them to the place where the womenfolk had been confined by the sand and where there was now only a lump of smoothness.

Nadir freed himself and then began to work on freeing the Princess. He set to work digging up the area over the small tent, and soon others came wading through the sand to help. There were several of the guards, including their overseer, Patriq, who now gasped and spat sand and shook his beard free of the granules as he moved to Nadir's side.

"Dig here," said Nadir, breathing laboriously from the exertion. "This is the place."

"Gods help us . . ." muttered Patriq. "This is a nearly impossible task, for the sands are like ever-encroaching waves.

The more we throw off, the more they roll back down upon us. . . ."

"So talk less and dig more!" said Yaro sharply as she crawled toward the place where she last remembered seeing the wagons.

"Who is this woman with the tongue of an asp?" grumbled Patriq. "Is she not a servant of yours, my Lord Nadir?"

"I'll show you an asp!" cried Yaro, glancing over her shoulders and giving the man an incinerating glare while she crawled and pulled at the sands, digging in up to her elbows. "You just wait till I come back with a water skin, you'll feel it against your thick skull! If I can dig up a wagon, then surely you can dig up a tent!"

"Your mouth can indeed dig up a wagon, shrill wench!" cried Patriq, and then dug with his hands into the sand fiercely, making a deliberate show of ignoring her.

At that moment Nadir exclaimed that he had found the tent, and two men came immediately to his side. They battled the sand, having taken off their shirts and head-wraps and scooping it with the cotton. Finally they were met by feeble movement below, as the serving women beneath the canvas struggled to free themselves and their mistress.

Nadir pulled up the tent fabric and saw the familiar form of Egiras wrapped like an onion in blankets and coverings. At her side two young handmaidens sputtered and sneezed, and next to them other women servants wallowed and shook the dust and white powder out of their clothing. Everyone was unharmed, for the thick canvas had served them well, creating a pocket of air in which they had lain for the duration of the storm, and very little sand had come inside.

But the Princess herself remained motionless.

Something cold swept over Nadir as he stared at her swaddled figure. And then he saw the light movement of her, the movement of breath. He leaned forward and spoke urgently,

"Egiras!" while he moved the coverings and veils away from her face.

She lay with her eyes closed, short dark lashes of great thickness resting against her yellowish skin. She breathed just barely, like a drugged sleeper. And yet, with the first touch of warm air and sun upon her face, her eyes came open slowly, black and slanted, and then she blinked the glare away.

"Nadir . . ." she whispered, staring up into his eyes. "Are we dead? Is this the land of the dead?"

"Oh no, my Lady," said one of her handmaidens. "We have merely come forth from the storm that covered us with a mountain of sand."

"I see you are well, my Princess," said Nadir softly, smiling. "Then all is well. . . ."

Egiras sat up, and her women brushed the dusting of sand from her glossy blackness of hair.

"Oh, what shall we do?" wailed one of the servants, taking this opportunity to begin a rant. "The whole caravan is buried!"

"It was indeed a great sandstorm, the greatest I've lived through," whispered a guard.

Nadir ignored them.

"Now you must forgive me, Princess Egiras," he said, rising, "but I must leave your side yet again as we dig up the rest of our things, and the animals."

And then it suddenly occurred to him, and he froze. "Egiras," he said, his eyes intense upon her. "Can you see me?"

"Yes."

She spoke very lightly, and she stared back at him with her clear, suddenly familiar gaze. There was reason and understanding in her face.

"Gods be praised!" exclaimed a servant. "The Princess can see again!"

And at that point Yaro made her way toward them by scrambling and crawling through the sandy morass, dragging along with her a large water sack. Uncapping the stopper, she drew its neck forward and offered it to Egiras.

"Drink, my Lady, and then all the rest of you," she said breathlessly. "The desert saps away your life-water invisibly, and you must replenish it now."

Egiras slowly turned her face and looked directly at Yaro.

Yaro froze. The moment stretched and became immense and burning, like the heat of the sun, while sweat beaded on Yaro's brow.

But Egiras did not say anything, merely took the heavy water skin. She leaned forward and put her lips to the neck to drink several swallows. When done, she moved back with a trickle of water on her lips. Only then did she speak.

"Yaro. . . ."

That, and nothing else. Her fathomless black eyes remained impassive. Then Egiras looked away and wiped her lips with her hand. Her fingers lingered on the skin of her own face, outlining her cheek with possibly a tactile memory—one of masks and moons. She said softly, "I have drunk. Now, the rest of you, drink."

But Yaro continued to stare, also speaking nothing. She was frozen in a bizarre state from within which she was compelled to look without end even after the lock of their gazes was broken, having met the basilisk gaze of the Princess but once, until it also made her cold and vacant. Only when the water was being passed around did Yaro regain her senses enough to turn away, with an exercise of painful ripping effort. She then made her way toward her old mother, who sat with closed eyes, like an old sack herself, in the sands.

Yaro removed from the folds of clothing at her chest a small flask, which she had refilled in secret just moments ago, before she had brought the large water skin to them all.

"Mother," Yaro whispered hoarsely, putting her hand over the old woman's forehead. "Here, drink!"

The old woman gasped at the touch. The flask was put to her lips and she swallowed weakly, then pulled away. "*You drink . . .*" she croaked.

"I already have," Yaro lied.

"No, drink!" said the old one. And so Yaro took a couple of swallows, feeling the coolness go down her throat like balm, before stopping up the precious flask once again.

In the meantime, the desert was warming up.

The sun rode near zenith as the guards and servants labored to dig up their belongings and the wagons, to reclaim what was theirs from the clutches of the desert. Air began to warp with radiant heat, and sweat rapidly escaped from the skin, evaporating and leaving in its wake slow, parched exhaustion.

They had managed to clear away two of the wagons while the third still lay partially buried.

"We are wasting a precious day of water allocation and precious sweat. The gods must be willing for us to perish here in this merciless hell . . ." grumbled the servants and the guards, but mostly out of Nadir's earshot. Dark tired looks were thrown his way. But, seeing that Nadir toiled as hard as if not harder than any two men, their grumblings mostly died unspoken.

They paused to rest while the sun shone with its greatest fierceness. A couple of swallows each of water was given to the lesser pack-beasts, which huddled together, but not to the camels, who could do without for longer. The rest of the water sack was passed around and consumed by the humans.

After a short rest they resumed work. The third wagon was almost completely excavated, and camels were hitched to it with ropes to help free it of the morass.

It was at that point that the gods must have been feeling particularly bitter with these representatives of the mortal race. Because suddenly the wagon bed cracked from the weight of the sand, and two of the wheel axles came off.

The damage was repairable. But it would take at least another day, concluded Patriq darkly, as he crawled under the wagon.

Another day of wasted water.

"Then we leave this wagon behind us," said Nadir. "And we continue on our way right now."

"What of the load that this wagon carried?" said the guard.

"We leave it behind also."

"My Lord Nadir . . ." said Patriq, "That load is water. If we reallocated all the water sacks to the other two wagons, they would be too heavy to be pulled over the sands, and would slow down our progress considerably. And if we overload the pack beasts and camels, they will tire faster, and will have to take more frequent stops."

Nadir listened attentively. "We can relieve the other wagons of superfluous load, and also relieve the animals of things we can do without."

"True . . . But—"

Patriq lowered his head, as though afraid of what he was about to utter.

"What?"

"My Lord, there really is no superfluous load. We packed very tightly, like misers, in the first place. However, if I may suggest this—if we leave the sedan chairs behind, we could instead load the four relieved camels. The mistress and her women can ride with us, each one sharing a mount with one of the guards. That way we can carry all of the water. If we conserve the remaining water properly, we can manage—"

"Then, yes, we leave the sedans behind."

It was Egiras. She stood behind them, and had spoken in a soft yet inviolate tone of voice that somehow was her old self, and yet unlike her. Something was different, something. . . .

Nadir turned to look at her, looked earnestly, trying to fathom it, then inclined his head before her. "If you are sure that you will manage, my Princess, then it will be done thus."

"I will ride with you, Nadir."

"I will be honored," he replied, casting his gaze to the sand.

We moved forward once again, toward the East and the rising sun. I carried Egiras before me in the saddle. My horse was strong and great and seemed to feel no additional burden, maybe because the Princess was such an insignificant load.

She lay back against my chest, her veiled head resting lightly against me, and I could barely distinguish her breathing. At times she shifted slightly, and I felt the faint perfume of the precious rose oils that her handmaidens had used to anoint her hair. The scent carried on the wind and surrounded us and came with us on this journey in a living cloud.

Roses in the desolation.

There was something new about Egiras. I had sensed it from the first moment she had opened her eyes after the sandstorm. I had no words for what I saw there, but I suspected a strange calm wisdom had come to her together with the regained vision and reason.

Even now I was not sure. I was tense in her presence, afraid to properly hold her in the saddle, afraid to touch her—not because I expected the usual sarcastic putdowns and cruelty but rather because I knew they would no longer come.

Thus I knew not what to expect from Egiras. What I received was gentle silence.

The rest of the caravan rambled along. The two remaining wagons carried some extra weight, while the rest was redistributed among the pack beasts and the camels that no longer carried the sedans.

I had seen Yaro's old mother hidden once again in one of the wagons, and the young woman herself walked alongside her under the pretense of assisting the driver. I felt a momentary pang of something—a worry, a restlessness—when I saw Yaro's wiry, thin form struggling with each step as her feet sank in the sand. But she stubbornly said nothing and did not ask to be relieved of walking like the rest of the serving women.

Several of the guards were walking also, taking turns riding the heavily burdened horses and camels. The desert wind pulled at their long robes and entered their squinting eyes despite the protective wrappings over their faces. Their demeanor was grim when I caught their individual eyes.

It was then that I knew with my warrior's sense that something was not quite right.

Something dark was brewing.

We had stopped to rest for the night, and the animals were unburdened and given spare amounts of water. The tent was once again rigged, and inside it the women had arranged bedding for the Princess and themselves. Now, in the welcome indigo coolness of evening, everyone sat near the light of the small fire, eating cheese and old flatbread.

Egiras had refused the preparation of soup they would ordinarily make for her, and shared the simple road fare in silence, sitting cross-legged and somewhat slumped in her tent.

I knew by her drooping, bowed shoulders and her motionlessness that she was sore from the unaccustomed riding and that she was exhausted, possibly ill.

Sitting several feet away from the open flap of the tent, I watched her as I ate the food that Yaro had brought me, forgetting for a moment my own weariness and parched throat and the low underlying hunger.

"Eat, my Lord Nadir, and don't worry for the Mistress, for she will be fine," said Yaro, wrapping cheese in bread and handing it to me like a child, seeing that I was absent and remote. She poured water for me too, handing me a wooden bowl that I received automatically and drank from without looking.

The meal was quick, for everyone was so tired, and soon they all lay down to sleep. The handmaidens assisted Egiras, and the women now lay in the darkness of the tent except for Yaro who had crept silently to the wagon where I knew her mother lay.

Patriq and I put out the remains of the tiny fire by dousing it with sand, and then the guards and the rest of us stretched out in our blankets.

I was tired and yet could not sleep, instead lying on my back watching the infernal blackness of the moonless night, only a sparse casting of stars illuminating the airy vault overhead.

Eventually my eyes had grown used to the dark, and I stared into the darkness as I always had, alert to every tiny sound, hearing nothing but the occasional gusts of wind and the sleepers' breaths.

It served me well, that alertness, for I saw the shadows come when they did, obscuring the stars above me.

I moved quickly like a panther, rolling away by instinct as my trained muscles took over.

There were lunges behind me, and the dull thud of movement and the scattering of sand as someone fell, narrowly missing me.

I crouched, gasping, whirled around, blinking away the sand, dancing in the darkness while my temples pounded. I recognized the shadows as the forms of three of the guards.

Patriq was not one of them. I heard a low groan and saw him a few feet away, still in his sleeping blanket, as a shadow detached itself from right above him. There was the dull glint of starlight upon a blade. Patriq was motionless.

There was no time for regret, not even a single pang. In the terrible dark I moved, having drawn the curved blade that I always kept concealed at my side. I saw shadows and I struck true, feeling my blade violently meet then penetrate something, someone. . . . Once, then again.

A grunt, a moan, and a shadow fell only to be replaced by another, which fell in turn from my blade. In the dark my hands felt the warm spray of moisture.

I did not think. I threw myself in the direction of the tent where I had to protect Egiras.

E giras opened her eyes with a wild pang, for there was a hand against her throat and another against her lips to stop her screaming. Her body was held as in a vise.

She smelled sour breath and camel and darkness. . . .

"Silence, lie still, or you die . . ." came a whisper, and Egiras knew she had heard that voice before. It belonged to one of the caravan guards.

And so she grew still, in a weird timeless suspension, while they both waited. Egiras wondered about the other women who had been in the tent with her that night, but she could not turn, could not look.

She heard the sound of a quiet struggle outside, all footfalls muffled by the sand. Superimposed over everything was the hum of the night wind.

The tent flap moved and a slightly lighter patch of darkness appeared for an instant as someone entered from the outside.

The hand over the mouth of Egiras tightened. At the same time she felt the sharp prick of a knife at the nape of her neck, in warning.

But Egiras was beyond comprehension of warnings. Ever since she had awakened after the storm—shaken by its fury out of her eternal hypnotic nightmare of blazing glorious moons in a sky that was nothing but light—all things seemed dull to her, dull and soothing like balm, and her heart maintained one steady calm rhythm of remote indifference.

Danger was incomprehensible.

Pain was remote.

Sensation was—Egiras was not sure.

And thus, because it had meant nothing to her on a personal level, that warning of sharpness pressing at her vulnerable neck, Egiras took the moment and did what she needed to do without a moment of hesitation—just as it was natural for a scorpion to lash out and sting.

Egiras moved her face just a tiny bit, but enough to part her lips. . . .

And then she bit the hand that was pressed against her face.

She bit it as one would bite a birthing bit, in reflex fury, feeling her teeth crush through the resilient softness of meat into bone, tasting salty fresh blood. There was a cry of pain that was more a cry of surprise—

Whoever had entered the tent was now properly alerted, had heard the cry, the muffled movement, heard the *very sound of her teeth coming together*—or so she thought.

And whoever held her did not use the knife at her throat. Instead the hand was dropped and she was grabbed roughly, like a living shield.

Egiras was between the *two,* neither one of whom she could properly identify, though she at least suspected the identity of her attacker.

And then she was shoved down with an amazing invisible force from the opposite side, so that she was detached from the one who had originally held her, and she was lying on the floor of the tent, feeling its roughness of sand and burlap against her forehead, while over her head she heard the dull clash of metal, a clamor of movement, then a short cry of pain.

Then, someone had fallen on top of her, someone whose scent she recognized again, the sour-pungent smell of camels, and recognized the *feel* of the creases and folds of fabric that had been that one's clothing. And then that same body, now motionless, was displaced, and another took hold of her, picked her up. . . .

This other was great and all-encompassing, as if the night itself took on human form and carefully embraced her. And this one also was oddly familiar, but in a different way.

This one was holding her lightly like a precious parcel, and in reflex she clung back, leaning her head and cheek tightly against the place where she felt a chest and thought she heard a familiar beating heart.

And at the same time, hands came forth from the darkness on both sides of her, hands that wrapped around her gently and stroked her hair with warm, large, slightly trembling fingers.

"Nadir . . ." whispered Egiras, smelling the warm desert. "It is always you. . . ."

Yaro heard the footfalls of shadows as she lay next to her mother in the wagon. She opened her eyes wide and could just see *their* movements in the darkness as blurs, thanks to her nearsighted vision. She recognized them by their general outlines or maybe by some preternatural sense, never having heard their voices. These were the men that had worked in the caravan, the servants, the guards.

She knew it was a mutiny. They crept along the wagons toward the tent, never knowing she was there—or maybe not caring—and then she saw then heading toward the place where Nadir slept.

Terror rose up in Yaro's throat. Urgency. Her temples were ringing like city tower bells. She wanted to fly forth, to run toward them, to throw herself mindlessly between them and the quiet man who had taken her in and who would now be dead. . . .

But in that moment his form lunged from the ground, moving preternaturally fast, and with a triumphant relief Yaro knew he would not fall before this night treachery.

There was fleeting movement in the darkness—so fast she was not sure what happened. She squinted, needing desperately to see. Several shadows fell, then one detached from the rest and made its way to the tent.

Yaro was not going to leave things to chance. All reason indicated she should stay in place at her mother's side, hide in petrified silence and hope that the two of them would remain unnoticed. She had always been insolent in her courage. Recklessly she slipped from the wagon, fell to the cool night sand below, and then crept forward silent like a mouse and brave like a scarab beetle.

At one point stepping over bodies, she continued toward the tent.

Yaro paused near and listened. The night whispered unknown horrors in her mind, and she thought she heard the wind that hissed serpentine over the sands speak human words in a dry whisper.

Yaro, child of dust.

She ignored it, ignored the insistent whisper of fear, and instead strained to hear what was within. And then someone reached from behind her—maybe it was the night itself solidified—and took her firmly by the torso, while a hand was placed around her mouth. Her first instinct was to struggle, but the next instant she heard a real voice, not the wind, saying in her ear, "Peace, Yaro . . ." and she recognized Nadir.

In that moment from beyond the most distant wagon came the sound of roused camels. And then, in the living dark, she could see three of the creatures, barely corporeal pale ghosts against the night, obviously saddled and ready and indeed mounted.

They who rode the camels were fully equipped. And they pulled behind them two spare pack beasts, also fully loaded, as could be attested by the rounded bulky shapes crowning their backs.

"Gods!" breathed Yaro. "How can we stop them, or find them in this moonless night? The night is only halfway through! And what of the others? How will we survive the remaining hours of the dark?"

"There are no more others," replied Nadir no longer bothering to hush his voice. "I counted the fallen, both those I killed myself and those who were slain by the traitors. All are accounted for, the living and the dead. As for those three, we let them go."

"Nadir!" came a frightened soft voice from within the confines of the tent, and for a moment Yaro did not recognize it as that of her former mistress, Egiras.

"I am here," he replied. "Do not be afraid. It is over. Come, Princess Egiras, it is only Yaro here with me." And then he added, "Though it may be an uncertain thing we face in the morning."

Egiras came forth from the tent. In the obscuring darkness she was a mere silhouette of wispy pallor, a shade.

The shade stood at the tent's entrance in odd, stonelike resignation, without strength. Egiras said, "My women. They who served me. I could not see. I stepped on one of them—on her hand. And she just lay there, silent. They all—just lie. . . ."

I was the first to open my eyes, just as dawn colored the sands. I took in the first waking breath, hand gripping my sword by instinct, and then arose silently without disturbing Egiras or Yaro. Both of them lay sleeping nearby, directly on the cooled sand, and huddled next to Yaro was the old woman, her mother, whom we had brought forth from her hiding place in the wagon.

I stood, in that first moment not wanting to be alive, for wakefulness came to me with a pang of heavy truth. It struck me with a seething panic that I could never show, for I did not want to *know* what had come to pass in the night, did not want to face what was left to us.

It had been just as I thought. The camp we had made for the night, what was left of our already small caravan, was in devastation.

The remaining pack beasts and camels lay dead, their throats cut in the night. And in the wagon that held the water sacks there was further horror—all the sacks had been pierced, their water silently pouring out upon the sands in the darkness. Some of it had pooled in small shallow puddles on the bottom of the wagon, and traces remained in the sacks themselves.

But most of it had watered the desert.

I stood there while a cold inevitable knowledge came to me, for I knew now this was the end. The mutineers had managed to kill us with those two acts.

I understood it was not necessarily a malicious thing but a matter of self-preservation, removing all chances of pursuit by us. The men had lost trust for some reason, and wanted to return the way they had come. And they knew there was no other way they could break up the caravan. For it is known to all that, once embarked in the desert, a caravan is inviolate.

If only they had known me better. If only they had realized how much I valued lives, even theirs—I would have let them go and given them their share of supplies.

But they had not known me. And had not asked.

In the blooming of dawn, I salvaged as much as I could of the remaining water by pouring the dregs from the broken sacks into a larger clay vessel, one of the few containers packed in with the belongings of the Princess. It had been used to hold water for washing. I also swept up what was left in the puddles and thereby managed to add another cup or two of liquid to the jar.

When I was done, the vessel was more than two-thirds full, and I capped it tight to prevent further evaporation in the heat of the coming day.

I quietly surveyed the rest of the camp. Most of the dead were servants and guards who had come with us, including Patriq whose body I observed with an inner ache, remembering the moment of darkness when he had been killed.

In the tent lay the handmaidens of the Princess. All had been killed swiftly, professionally, which led me to believe that some of the hired guards had once been more than they appeared, military mercenaries.

What had been their motives? Why did they betray the caravan?

The answer remained unclear until I had examined most of the tent and noticed the rummaged contents of two small chests and the emptied jewelbox that belonged to Egiras.

They had taken whatever had been left of the Princess's fortune, several large ruby and opal stones and ropes of pearl and precious metals. It is possible they had been disappointed and expected far more, for Egiras was thought to carry secret riches with her.

But then Egiras always had that air of superiority, an illusion of the highest extreme nobility—even when she was reduced to nothing more than a quiet madwoman.

And the reason she herself had escaped with her life, I realized, was that they had planned to take her with them, possibly for royal ransom, not knowing that Egiras had no kin and there was no one who would care to pay for her release. Luckily I had interrupted their kidnapping.

As I continued moving through the camp, gathering the remaining things that might be of use to us—while my thoughts searched madly for a solution, for a shred of hope—Yaro woke and joined me.

"Tell me what I must do to help you, my Lord Nadir."

I looked into her earnest eyes and for a moment found a jolt of living energy there, that very hope I had lost.

"Go and gather cotton and rope and wood sticks," I said, keeping my expression blank, "and anything else you think may help from the wagons, in order to make a sling. We need something to carry your mother as we walk through the desert."

They had taken all they could carry, and bound things in bags to be slung over their shoulders. Since there was a greater stretch of desert behind them than before them, according to the days the caravan had traveled, Nadir had made the decision that they will continue onward toward the East.

Eventually the desert would end in plains, with possible sources of water, and then in the distance there would be mountains. Beyond those lay fertile land, and the trip from that point on would be survivable.

In secret, Yaro had looked into Nadir's eyes, however, and she knew that he did not believe they would come out of the desert.

The Princess Egiras was mostly silent, and she did not protest when given a small bag to carry. While the others got ready, she stood looking toward the East, her narrow eyes unblinking, hypnotized by the horizon. Her midnight black hair was tangled, moving in the warm gusts of wind, and her head was uncovered from the sun. She had to be told like a child to put her veils on and to shield herself from the incandescent sunfire.

"Leave me behind . . . please . . ." whispered Yaro's old mother as she was made to lie on a small cotton sling.

"Be quiet, stupid woman, or I will beat you!" snarled Yaro. A considerable sack of their food and belongings was attached to Yaro's thin back, and she fiercely picked up one end of the sling while Nadir took the other.

Nadir himself was loaded up like a pack-beast, and in addition he carried their precious jar of water.

"We go now. Come, my Princess Egiras!" said Nadir loudly, and Egiras obeyed his voice like a trained creature.

They started to walk, taking slow steps so as not to flounder in the thick sands.

Around them, the wind of the desert howled in laughter.

Their allotment of water was three sips for each of the four of them, twice a day. Nadir knew this was an unrealistic measure, and that they would not last long under these circumstances, no more than a couple of days. But the jar of water was all they had. And there was at least another week of travel left to them, if not more—now that they were on foot.

The first day passed in a white daze. They took frequent stops, and Nadir watched Yaro carefully, for she was not just overloaded but also carried the other end of the bed-sling. However, she seemed indomitable, her skinny figure filled with implausible strength. It was Egiras who stumbled most often as they walked through the burning sands.

"My shoes are torn . . ." said Egiras after their third stop. She was pale and serene. When they examined her feet, Nadir saw that indeed her expensive silk slippers had ripped apart, and the delicate soles of her feet had been scorched to bloody blisters by the heat of the sand.

"Let me bind your feet with salve and cotton, my Lady," said Yaro.

Egiras stared at her blankly, then nodded. Yaro rummaged in her bag, and came up with some cheap oil unguent, which she applied to the feet of the Princess, and plain rags which she used to create the simple wrap footgear of a pauper.

The rest of the day Egiras did not complain, and they walked onward, breathing hard, in silence.

Night was a blessed relief. After a quick meal of hard old cheese and flatbread, and their precious sips of water, they fell into delirious parched slumber.

A blink of an eye, and it was morning.

Yaro fed her mother and gave her water to drink, and herself took only two sips of water for every three that the others had. They took turns answering the call of nature, got their bags loaded, and were on their way.

The second day was more difficult. All pretense of hardiness was dropped, and everyone moved with a desperate stumbling gait as their feet sank in the crumbling sterile white powder. Breathing laboriously, they took each step with a group rhythm that had come about unconsciously.

Nadir walked with grim detachment, often throwing glances behind him at Yaro, seeing her breathe in shuddering gasps, her eyes averted, maybe in pride.

At around noon, Yaro stumbled and dropped her end of the sling. Her mother came down roughly and Nadir stopped and lowered his own end gently.

"Yaro," he said, watching her lie in the sand. "We will take a break now."

"No," she panted. "We go on, mustn't waste time. Let me catch my breath for a moment, my Lord. . . . Just one moment."

"Enough. I will carry the sling," said Egiras. The wind howled. They stared at her for a moment in incomprehension.

"Oh, no, my Princess," said Yaro, gasping and struggling to rise. "How can you do that? It is not right for you to carry the burdens. . . ."

"It is not right for me to perish in this desert," replied Egiras with a glimmer of her former sarcasm. "Therefore be silent, woman, and walk the best you can."

"My Princess—" began Nadir. But then, seeing her determination, he too grew silent, and nodded.

He picked up his end of the sling-bed, while Egiras took the other end in her slender pampered hands, with their delicate tiny fingers.

They resumed walking through the wind-blown sands.

The third dawn was parched agony.

Blinking, Yaro opened her eyes into searing pain, her eyelids red and sore from the endless dust that had collected on her face and had not been washed off for days.

Her throat was dry and scraped, and her innards hurt with desiccated constriction. She could feel her kidneys shriveling up and turning into stones within her. All movement was languid agony, and headache-induced dizziness came in waves as she tried to rise and felt herself immediately floating and detached from her body.

Early dawn, and the desert stood like an ocean of smooth dunes in bluish haze around her, while she could barely see the sleeping shapes of the others.

A thought came to her, *Today is the last day of my life.*

The wind swept her, and for a moment Yaro thought she flew.

She simply stood there, feeling herself soar, for long illusory minutes.

Eventually the others came awake, and then came the most important ritual: taking the three sips of water each to fortify themselves for the day's journey ahead.

They had stopped eating the day before. It was impossible to chew and swallow bread and cheese without water to wash it down. Indeed, hunger had become deadened and secondary to the ache of emptiness that was dehydration.

When her turn came, Nadir stood before Yaro, holding up the clay jar while she took one tentative sip of water, feeling it slip within her like a glorious miracle of the gods.

And then she took another sip.

"Go on," Nadir said, watching her intently. "One more."

"No . . ." Yaro said. "You take it, my Lord. Drink it for me, for you are larger, and you require more than me. Besides, I don't think I thirst all that much today. It must be a cooling of the wind. . . ."

But then came the voice of Egiras.

"I command you to drink. Else we go nowhere."

And Yaro had no choice but to obey.

They stopped at noon. The young women had been taking turns carrying the old woman in the sling, but it had become obvious she was dying, and so they paused, setting down their burden.

Yaro put her nearsighted face close to her mother's sunken chest and listened for her breath, lighter than a moth's flutter and coming in sporadic labored bursts. Yaro's expression contorted then, and she hid her face in the poor ragged cotton of the old woman's robe.

Nadir took out the clay jar and uncapped it. "Let the old one have the rest of my water for today . . ." he said softly, his own voice rasping and low.

Gently moving Yaro away, he tilted the jar and brought it to the old woman's black lips. The old one opened her eyes and stared back at him with quiet wisdom—nothing but eyes in a dry skull covered with shrunken ebony turtle skin.

She barely moved her head from side to side to indicate that she did not want the water. But Nadir continued nevertheless, and he managed to wet her lips with a couple of drops.

And then it came, the end of things. For as he tilted the jar vertically nothing more came forth from it. It was now empty except for a muddy thick residue of wet clay and moistened sand.

Indeed, as the dregs of sand poured forth, it was drying before their very eyes as the wind took away all that was not dust. . . .

They had run out of water, so much sooner than they had expected, and they had not even noticed.

But maybe not quite.

"Let me, my Lord . . ." Yaro whispered. "I have a small flask which I've carried on me in secret for all these days in reserve for such a moment, a moment of our end, and it is no longer any use to conceal it. Let me first give her a couple of drops from the flask, and the rest you can have, to share with my Lady Egiras."

As they watched, Yaro took out the hidden flask and reached into her pack for her old wooden bowl. She uncorked the flask and poured the small handful of liquid that it contained into the old worn bowl of polished faded wood. She took the bowl gently, with a timelessness of ritual, and brought it to her mother's lips.

The old woman sipped once, then closed her eyes.

Overhead, the sun burned at the zenith.

And Yaro, looking directly into the sun-blinded eyes of Nadir, offered him the bowl of water.

Nadir stared, then took the bowl from her and put his lips to it. It was the same bowl in which she had served him before at their nightly camp rests when the caravan had still been alive. He had held it, drunk from it, yet had not recognized it then.

But now it was high noon. And the sun glittered with sudden bright golden and persimmon fire upon the shallow surface of the water. . . .

Familiar fire.

Nadir felt the reflection of orange pierce him, strike his eyes with a sudden sharp memory of childhood.

He stared at the cup of water in his hands, and he *knew* it.

This cup was his, had *always* been his.

It was the cup of Ris, the same one that he had lost and had given to Egiras and lost again. . . .

More than twenty years ago.

"Where did you get this cup?" he whispered, looking at Yaro with an intensity that she did not understand.

"My Lord?" she replied. "It is my mother's old soup bowl. What do you mean? She's had it always."

"No!" exclaimed Nadir. "Where did she get this cup?"

And then the old woman parted her lips, barely croaking. "This is an old cup. I—picked it up many years ago, from the floor where it had been dropped and forgotten. I served the Princess Egiras long before my daughter Yaro served her. I served the father of Princess Egiras also, the late Lord Urar-Tuan. . . . It was in his tent I found it, on the day he died. In his tent, many years ago."

"Then this is *my* cup! The same one that my Grandmother Ris gave me, the one that used to hold boundless water, until—"

"Until I took it away from you," said Egiras. "I was a spoiled child and my dark will was to have the magical trinket. Except that, as soon as I had the cup to myself after my father had tricked you, poor little angry boy Nadir—as soon as it was mine, the miraculous water ceased. The cup became dry and useless."

Nadir stared into the mirror-bright water in the bowl, seeing in it the sun's double.

"Ris had taken away the wonder of it . . ." he muttered. "And yet here it is, after all the years—an impossible coincidence. Maybe if we pray to Ris she will show her mercy once again."

"I do not pray," said Egiras suddenly, rising behind him, a dark silhouette in the sun, coughing and speaking with peculiar energy. "And this is not a coincidence, simply the manner in which things came to pass. I remember the day of my father's death, and then later how you swore faithfulness to me, little brave Nadir. All that time I had tortured you so, and yet after all that, you still resigned yourself to my will. And in that one moment you truly gave me your prize possession, this thing of wood. I knew it was the very soul of you, and that's why I hated it and threw it from me. Because I hated you. Hated you because you served me so well. . . ."

But Nadir did not seem to hear her maddened speech. Closing his eyes tight, leaning his head forward, he mouthed silent words, his lips and breath against the wooden bowl's rim. And then he kissed it with reverence and took several swallows.

"You drink, my Princess," he said. "And then all the rest of you. Ris willing, there will now be water enough for all."

"Didn't you hear me?" she said.

But Nadir's face was transfigured. "Drink . . ." he said simply, and then smiled.

And thus she received the bowl from him and took two careful sips, then handed the rest to Yaro.

Yaro began to protest once again, but Egiras looked at her like a serpent. And Nadir stared with equal intensity, but one of a different nature—as if a sun were hidden within him.

Even Yaro's fading mother croaked something to the extent of insisting she drink.

And so Yaro drank.

She took one swallow, and then another, and then . . .

The wooden cup was empty.

The last drop had touched Yaro's lips, and already the desert wind was quenching itself on the surface of the bare wood, taking in the last remnants of liquid discoloration until the cup was pale and bone-dry once again like the well worn old utensil that it was.

It was then that Egiras began to laugh.

She laughed hoarsely, her voice scraped raw and wheezing, while the rest remained in silence, except for the hum of the wind.

In silence they remained, for there was no miracle of Ris to save them this time. And silence was the only thing left to those who respected the gods.

Meanwhile, the blasphemer among them, the woman whose nature had been bound from birth to the Lord of Illusion—who is also the Lord of Doubt—made noise and banished the quietude with her hysterical sound of despair.

"What did you think would happen, my poor Nadir?" she finally managed to croak after her outburst had settled down. "Did you think the cup would now replenish itself after you've muttered over it? Did you honestly think that you could call forth the gods themselves with your priestly lips? That Ris would deliver you, deliver all of us, for the second time?

"Truly, now that I think back, I hardly remember if it wasn't all a dream in the first place, if it ever existed—that original miraculous cup. When I was a little horrible girl and I played with the cup, just after taking it away from you, I don't remember if it was an illusion of water in it or if it was one of my sorcerous father's tricks.

"There was a god present, if I recall, a bound god whom my father was tormenting—indeed, my father had taught me well—tormenting the one called Tazzia, in the shape of a mortal horse.

"It was that marvelous horse that lured you to us, Nadir, was it not? Surely it was not our humanity. For you had newly come forth out of the desert, halfway a god yourself, and you were quietly insolent and angry and filled with dark energy that needed a release somehow. . . ."

As Egiras continued speaking, almost babbling, Yaro remained frozen in horror, holding the empty dry cup. Nadir meanwhile stood up and turned his back to them all.

The desert wind moved his pale cotton robes about him, and he stood dark against the light of the slate-white sky. His was a tall warrior shape, and yet the shadow he cast upon the sand was short and squat, for the sun had barely began to move from the zenith toward the West.

Looking at that crisply delienated dwarf shadow, Yaro thought she saw a flicker of something vaguely familiar.

And then she was sure. . . .

"My Lord Nadir!" she said faintly. "Do not move! Oh, stand still, my Lord, stand perfectly still. . . ."

And, while Nadir froze with his back to her in confusion, Yaro came up behind him, holding the empty wooden cup. She crouched behind him, and with one sudden movement dipped the cup into the darker shadowed area of the sand, just at his feet.

Then she arose, holding in her hands the cup, now filled with sand, and speaking like a madwoman. "I can see you! Oh, I know you, and I can see you, Illusion!"

To the others Yaro added, "This cup holds no sand, but true water. You can turn around, my Lord, but be careful not to step into your own shadow, for it is a small spring, and all around us is not dry sand but an oasis."

Nadir slowly turned around and looked directly at her. His expression was sorrowful, filled with kind pity.

"What do you say, Yaro, my poor one?" he said very softly. "Come, sit down, for we will not go any farther and it is easier that we die thus, as fast as possible, instead of lingering—"

"No!" exclaimed the skinny serving woman. "You don't understand, because you cannot see! And it is all because of *her!*" And Yaro pointed in the direction of Egiras.

"It is she!" continued Yaro. "She is a fount of Illusion, permeated by it. And all those around her also grow not to see, the longer they are with her, the closer they are."

"What a sad delusion, Yaro—"

"Not a delusion, but truth obscured!" retorted Yaro. "It is obscured in the same manner as it was on that Night of a Thousand Moons when I encountered *Him* for the first time in the shape of the Lord of Night. For he cast a glamour over my vision, allowing me to see clearly like I had never seen things in my entire blind life—for I am blind as a bat, my Lord Nadir, and that is my only true measure. I am *not supposed* to see clearly! And yet, though nearsighted, I can right now see each grain of sand, each tiny sharp outline of this desert for hundreds of feet around us! It is only at the horizon that things begin to blur naturally, as I am used to observing them. And therefore all of this must be not real."

"But to what purpose?" whispered Nadir.

"I know not," said Yaro. "Only that Illusion is her nature, and her purpose. Ask her yourself, my Lord. In the meantime, I will drink this water in the cup, even though you may think I am drinking sand."

And with that Yaro raised the wooden bowl to her lips, and swallowed hungrily, swallowed dry bone-white dust.

And then Yaro choked and began to cough.

"Stop," said Egiras, watching the sand granules spill from Yaro's face. "There is no water, Yaro. You have gone mad from the sun and the heat and the desolation."

"You lie!" exclaimed the servant, forgetting herself, and she again brought the cup up to her lips with trembling bony fingers, saying hoarsely, "I will see the water! Just as I saw the Lord of Illusion hiding in my Lord Nadir's dark shadow, as he always does, for that is how I knew! I saw a glimmer of water there, yes. . . ."

And to that Egiras replied quietly, looking at her with surprisingly straightforward sympathy, "I am sorry. It is nothing but a mirage, woman—possibly because we have remembered Tazzia the god of mirage, and thus called him to us briefly. And I regret myself that it is so."

Egiras looked at them all—at the wild-eyed dark young woman holding the cup, at her loyal Nadir standing like a monument to approaching death, at the old black-skinned crone who was even now taking her last breaths on the pallet.

And for a moment an odd sense came to her, a sudden feeling of constriction in the area of her chest or her lungs, or maybe a little deeper. It was a new feeling, for she had never sensed this before, this peculiar brief *connection* with others, with what they were sensing. . . .

Egiras looked at them and knew that they were all here in one way or another because of her.

Bonds of human servitude.

And a sudden thought came to her: what if indeed it was true, that she was herself so bound to Illusion that there were things being obscured around her, a whole world that she could not see except through the sterile filter of the dark one?

Egiras blinked, staring intensely, and for a moment the memory of the white moons standing with false brilliance in her vision returned with searing fire. . . . But she blinked it away.

And she looked at Nadir, and she saw his dark forehead which could no longer even produce sweat, and she saw that his eyes were so calm and resigned. Was that because of her? For he was here now and would be here up to the end, and he would die with her with just such calm silence, under a burning desert sun.

"Nadir," said Egiras, looking into his eyes, and then her voice broke and cracked, with something more than thirst. "Nadir. . . ."

The man looked at her, responding immediately to her call, as he always did.

"What is it, my Princess Egiras?" he said.

"Nadir, I want you to leave me, Nadir. Go forth. . . ."

In sudden attention he neared her. "What?"

"I want you to go," repeated Egiras. And then, "No, it is not I that want, not I—rather, you *need* to go. You must leave me now. All of you. It is not too late for you. I, meanwhile, will turn my face toward the East, and will walk alone for as long as I can."

"How can I leave you?" he said. "What nonsense! Where is there to go? We are all together now, and we will all die—"

"No!"

Her voice came as a screech, broken, jagged, inhuman, echoing in the windblown humming silence.

Egiras stood up straight and began to back away from them all—from the old woman and the dark skinny young woman, and most of all from *him.*

As she moved away, she felt an odd thing happening. It was as though an invisible ancient and permanent restraint were being drawn taut between them—between *her* and *him,* one on one—as though a rope of wind and dry sunrays stretched tight and began to constrict her throat and to pull at her innards. And the more she walked, putting distance between them, seeing the line between them stretch in her inner mind's eye, the more it hurt her inside, until the hurt became a sharp agony in her solar plexus and then in a place that she at last realized was her heart.

The rope of wind and sunlight pulled at her heart, and the other end of it was attached to Nadir's.

And then, as the agony grew utmost—so that she no longer sensed the heat of the desert, for it was brighter than the sun—

then Egiras cried with her last breath, "Be free of me! Go! I set you free! I will not look upon you or call you or need you, ever!"

With that, the rope of agony was severed—having been stretched to its utmost—and the world grew very dark, and at the same time it was very bright, beyond day.

I watched her crumple to the sands, like a puppet that has suddenly lost its strings. And as she fell I felt something break between us, a sudden sharp snap of acute pain. And I sensed a peculiar lightness that I had not felt since I was a little boy, walking alone on the streets of the great city that spawned me, long before I met Grandmother, who was Ris, and long before I entered the desert. . . .

With my old instinct I started to run toward her, but then stopped.

The urge of duty that had until now directed my actions was no longer there, and instead there was an emptiness. I felt light and calm and almost indifferent. I could simply leave her be, lying there in the scalding white sand, and walk away and never look back.

And then the next second I felt a stab of a different feeling rushing in, and in that moment I heard Yaro exclaim behind me. "Oh, My Lord Nadir! Oh, look! Water!"

But I did not look back. Instead, I walked forward and I knelt before Egiras, and I reached out with my shaking parched hands to hold her husk of a body, knowing that she was still alive but barely.

Sensing me in turn, she opened her dark eyes, and they were liquid. "Nadir," she whispered. "No . . . In the name of Ris, no . . . I have set you free, and now you will be able to see what you could not before, and you will be able to drink the water and live. But—only if you leave me. Get away from me, Nadir, for I stain you even now with the darkness of Illusion."

Yaro approached us, and she came down on her knees at my side. "Look!" she exclaimed, touching me, and I was compelled to turn.

I glanced and saw that she was holding the wooden cup, gingerly, and saw what was now *within* it.

The cup was full to the brim with clear water.

While all around us was a small oasis of prickly desert shrubs and hardy greenery surrounding, only a few feet away, a small natural spring.

"Take it, my Lord, and let her drink! We are saved!" whispered Yaro, a wild new expression in her eyes.

I released Egiras with one hand, with the other continuing to support her against my chest. And I took the cup from Yaro's trembling fingers. As I did so I felt a coolness come from it, like a breath of distant ocean, and with it a memory of childhood.

My heart began to race wildly as a maelstrom of hope surged into it, and I brought the cup to the lips of Egiras, dipping it forward.

But then I watched in growing horror. As the water came in contact with her flesh it immediately turned to sand, which crumbled down her chin and her throat.

"You see . . ." whispered Egiras to me with a strange smile of joy I had not ever seen in her. "I have set you free, Nadir. There is now a chasm between us once more, as it should be. I alone will die now, while the three of you will cross the desert. Even now, the desert is all around me. . . ."

And at her words it burst within me, something wild and uncontrollable that I had no words for. For the first time since childhood I wept.

Yaro watched Nadir as he shook with tears, his large smooth, features twisted, and she knew there was a new bond forged between him and the strange terrible woman whom he had so long served. And this time the bond was such that it was unbreakable.

For, while duty and honor and caprice and hatred had bound them previously with Illusion, in their place was now truth and warmth. Instead of cause and effect there was freedom. And with it, a choice.

"Egiras!" cried the great man, her former servant and henchman and loyal shadow. "I will never leave you, Egiras, how can I? You are like—"

"Go on, speak it," said Yaro. "She is like your very breath. She is the one closest to your heart."

And then the skinny woman sighed and put her hand to her brow, rubbing it thoughtfully, saying, "Tell me what I can do, and I will do anything I can. There must be something that can be done for her whom you love so much, my Lord. . . ."

"And surely there is, Yaro, child of dust," said her mother from the sling-bed.

Now the old woman arose, surprisingly hale, and stood up straight. And she walked toward them lightly over the sands, her footfalls effortless as the wind, those of a young woman.

Yaro's mother stopped, and they looked upon her and saw that her tattered beggar clothing had transformed into robes of brilliant white cotton. Her skeleton-parchment face was wrinkled still, and yet her eyes danced—young and mischievous and brilliant—and were distinctly no longer the eyes of a mortal.

"Mother!" exclaimed Yaro, her mouth falling open. "What has happened to you! Oh!"

"What do you think?" said the *one* before her with a smile.

"Oh!" continued Yaro, stuttering. "What—you are not— who are you?"

"Of course I am," replied the other, while Nadir stared, his dilated eyes filling with ancient recognition.

"I am still your Mother," said Ris to Yaro. And turning to Nadir she added, "And I am your Grandmother."

And then she moved between them and bent forward. She put her hand on the lifeless forehead of the dying Egiras and she said, "And as for you, daughter of Illusion, I have been nothing to you until the moment you decided to open your heart, and now I would like to make you mine also. For you carried me with your own hands."

There was a sudden rising of the wind around them, a wind that had come out of nowhere and wailed and stirred the sands.

Egiras opened her eyes with a snap.

Her eyes were roiling darkness, and they too were not mortal eyes now. "Ris . . ." she whispered, trembling. "I *see you*, Ris!"

And even as she spoke, a dark shadow began to form before them out of the swirling wind that obscured the very sun.

The shadow was translucent, like a malformed mirage, yet shimmering like air warping in the heat.

Only, he was cold, the Lord of Illusion.

He stood opposite Ris, and his eyes were not visible. Only his voice sounded, the whisper of a snake.

She is mine.

Is that so? Ris spoke forcefully, also in their minds.

Egiras arose in that moment, straining up, freeing herself from Nadir's arms, her eyes pupil-less. She stared upwards, between the shadow and the figure of corporeal whiteness of cotton.

"Choose!" exclaimed Ris. "This is your only moment of true freedom! Chose Him, or choose me!"

Come, Egiras . . . whispered the snake. *I have given you life, and I am a part of you always. Without me you cannot be.*

"Oh, I want to be with you, Ris, the Bringer of Stillness and Water, the Bright-Eyed Liberator, the Mad Sovereign of Wisdom!" sobbed Egiras. "And yet, He calls me, for He is my father also, my real father. . . ."

Choose!

And then the whole world came to a frozen silence. They all waited for her, even the granules of sand and the beams of the sun.

"I cannot . . ." whispered Egiras. "I cannot choose either one of you, for I contain both of you. I feel it now. Thus, I choose death, for I choose neither one of you, only myself, and I am dead already."

In reply, Ris laughed.

"A perfect answer!" said she who was the opposite of the shadow.

Agreed . . . whispered the snake. And then, surprisingly, the shadow began to fade, and the wind settled down.

Ris stood before Egiras, and she reached forth with a wrinkled yet preternaturally strong hand, and she helped Egiras rise.

"Where is that old cup of mine?" said Ris. "Here, give it to me, my children."

When Yaro placed the wooden bowl in her hands, Ris took the bowl and offered it to Egiras.

"Drink," said Ris. "Now you will be able to do so, for you are both his and mine, and thus your own. Death will claim you as it does all mortals, but not for quite some time. She was not invited to this feast, and she does not have any say today."

And Egiras took the cup and she put it to her lips, and indeed the water remained what it was while Egiras drank many great gulps, feeling the liquid balm pour inside of her. . . .

When she was done, she returned the cup to Ris, who handed it back to Yaro and then to Nadir. They also drank, and were filled with sudden coolness, as though their weeks in the desert had not been.

"Now then," said Ris. "Give me a hairpin, Egiras!"

And as they stared in confusion, Ris did not wait but pulled out one of the small metal pins that were stuck in the crumpled veils that Egiras wore.

"You think me mad, don't you?" said Ris with a grin in her eyes, looking from one to the other of them with mischief, as she fiddled with the pin, straightening it. And then Ris cast the pin on the surface of the water that was in the cup.

The pin spun, but did not sink, and instead floated. It was like a very familiar thing that they should all know but somehow didn't.

"Observe a desert compass," said Ris. "To help you navigate the ocean of sand. This needle points North, while its opposite end is South. Your journey, my children, lies toward the West, back where you came from."

"Will you come with us this time, Grandmother?" whispered Nadir, looking at her with luminous eyes.

But Ris sighed—if it is possible for a god to sigh—and then she smiled again, but with an odd bittersweet gentleness.

"Not this time either, my Nadir," she replied. "For I go with Egiras. We continue East, as is her destiny. And since the Cup is yours, I must walk at her side and give her My Water."

And then, like a chameleon, Ris brightened. "Come," she said to Egiras. "We must be on our way! But first you must kiss your beloved goodbye, this time in truth. For, although your hearts are bound now with true bonds of freedom, he is not yours, and neither are you his."

And as water began to come streaming out of her eyes, Egiras approached Nadir, and lifted her face to him. She stood and looked at him and into him and though him, and could neither blink nor turn her gaze away. Nadir in turn lowered his head, put his hands on her arms near the shoulders, and placed his lips upon her cool forehead.

Then he released her and turned his back to Egiras. And he remained standing thus.

It was the harshest gesture of his life.

"Tell me when they go, Yaro," he whispered, "for I cannot bear to look."

Thus Yaro stared directly East and blinked and watched in his stead. But before she could reply or describe the moment of their passing—if such a thing could be inscribed within a single moment—there was no one else with them, only the wind.

"They are gone, Nadir . . ." she said. "Look at me, my Lord."

And he did.

Silence and sunset.

"Not your Lord," he said. "But someone who will now walk at your side, if you will have it so."

Yaro stilled. Her face showed a succession of images and emotions as she moved through each and seemingly discarded them all, settling upon a blank expression.

"What side?" she said in a deadened voice, looking down at the sand. "I don't know what my Lord means. . . ."

When at last she looked up, in the warm glimmer of sunset, he could see that water was streaking her cheeks with reflected flashes of gold and persimmon fire.

"Yaro . . ." he said, putting his fingers against her thin cheek. "Oh, Yaro."

"Oh, Yaro what? Don't bother," she retorted with a snort. She scrunched up her features, and hastily rubbed the back of her hand against her dirty cheeks.

But Nadir could not help the involuntary curving of his lips, for here were the glimmerings of her former lively manner.

"Don't bother," she added, suddenly intense and once more serious, "unless you will have it so yourself. I am nothing, a child of dust. I can never be *her*, my Lord. You know that. . . ."

In reply, Nadir again smiled. He cast a final glance at the Eastern horizon, then did not look there again.

"If you are dust," he said, "then look around—you are the whole world. With me, you fill this Cup. Only together may we both drink."

Dream Thirteen

Caelqua's Spring

The desert spring drew the threads of her subterranean waters to her, picked herself up from the sands and became a woman.

It had been a long time.

Her name was Caelqua. Rather, it was hers once, a human name.

The woman stood considering, while water-memories surged into her mind, and time flickered in eddies of cool liquidity.

She had once been a young girl with persimmon hair, a garish flame. Now there was only the sand ocean in her tresses, skin taut with wind, and colorless eyes.

She was a husk. As though she didn't exist. . . . And yet she was something more.

Caelqua walked slowly through the scalding sands while the sky poured the anger of the sun upon her unprotected flesh. There was no sensation at the soles of her feet, and she felt no thirst.

She knew there was something she had to do.

But first she had to find it.

The North-bound caravan came to a stop before an oasis of several palm trees, and a small ancient well that was now almost dry. This had once been called Golden Livais, after a miracle of destruction had taken place here, a whole town being transformed overnight into solid gold.

It had been a miracle wrought of ignorance and tainted with greed. Legend said, they had tried to buy the favor of the gods with the bright clamor of gold in exchange for a replenishing of the water supply in a dwindling well.

But the gods only give you back more of what you offer up.

The gold had long since gone; fortune scavengers from all points of the Compass Rose had taken care of that. Not even ruins here. Only a new growth of trees remained, and the oasis persisted somehow.

But now a woman stood here, having come out of nowhere, with transparent eyes and hair like sand.

The caravan driver saw Caelqua from afar—or, rather, saw for a moment a bit of sun dislocated, a shadow of a candle flame.

Upon approach, it was no longer there. But observing her up-close, there came a blurring in his vision, a moment of times mixing.

"Who are you?" he whispered hoarsely, for his own throat was dry and he had not yet quenched his thirst by drinking from the well.

But, as he looked further at her, cool water stood before his eyes. And it occurred to him that this woman might be one of the supposed immortals.

"Are you Ris?" he asked carefully.

Ris. Bringer of Stillness and Water, the Bright-Eyed Liberator, the Mad Sovereign of Wisdom.

That name stirred something within Caelqua, another ancient memory.

"No," she replied. "But I have been touched by Ris and given a blessing of Water."

And speaking thus, Caelqua came forward and lifted her palms toward him, cupped together.

The air shimmered and her flesh became transparent, flowing.

He blinked, and now observed liquid dancing in the sun.

"Drink," she said. "And take me with you."

T he caravan took Caelqua through the desert. She came with them wordlessly and they shrank away in awe, knowing from the first instant that she was different, one of the divine.

The journey involved a number of days that all blended into one day of sun-spilled monotony, silence and the low hissing of the wind.

Eventually, a great city showed itself on the Northern horizon, and a road emerged from the sands.

They approached, blended with other rabble, and entered gates of iron past stone-faced guards into a place of living frenzy.

Here the caravan and Caelqua parted ways, for they would stop in the city for only two nights and then head farther North. She, by contrast, knew that her journey ended here.

Caelqua walked several hours through the urban chaos of agoraphobic marketplaces and claustrophobic alleyways. The city air was an astringent stew of garlic, human excrement and the perfume of roses.

But Caelqua's senses ignored the olfactory clamor and focused on one single scent.

She smelled water.

And thus she moved like a shade toward the heart of the city where stood a grand palace of white stone and garish gold.

Water was within.

And there was something very wrong.

T he tired queen with anemic skin looked down from her divan-throne past the barrier of veils and silk pillows at the woman with dull sand hair.

Caelqua stood before her like a stilled fountain.

"Who are you?" said the queen. "They told me you might help me. But I know that no one can."

"I am no one. And I am the only one who can redeem you."

The queen sat up with great difficulty and pulled the golden veils from her forehead. Her lips were white with approaching death.

"You bleed," said Caelqua. "Your woman's cycle has not ended for many moons now. Your womb is refusing to close up, and thus your life is running out of you in rivulets of darkness."

"Yes. . . . How did you know?"

But Caelqua said nothing. Instead, she stepped forward and touched the queen on the brow.

And the queen felt a rhythm of blood begin in her temples.

Guards tensed forward, but the queen stopped then with one weakly upraised palm. She stilled, and remained thus for a long span of moments beneath Caelqua's touch.

"I feel you. . . . An ocean. . . ." whispered the queen in vampiric ecstasy.

Caelqua released her hold.

"I require a sharp knife," she said.

"Do as she says!" said the queen. "You, give her your dagger!"

A guard stepped forward with suspicious eyes, and slowly drew forth his ornate weapon.

A moment of impossible silence.

Then Caelqua took the knife from him. And with it she slit her own wrist.

A spurting fountain of hueless water began to pulse from her vein, and she offered it to the queen.

"Take my Water and drink, for even Ris drank once from my wrist. For that act of quenching, Ris has given me Water in exchange for my mortal Blood."

The queen fell upon the hand in mindless hunger and pulled at the open vein with her succulent pale lips. She drank for a long span while the court watched in terrible wonder.

Finally she tore herself away, satiated, and there was a new, manic energy in her eyes.

"You have given me my existence, the one thing that was no longer mine," said the queen. "I feel it now, this new strength! My womb is closing even as I speak, and my flow has ceased. What miracle are you? I have everything, and will give you anything you ask!"

Caelqua looked into her eyes, and for the first time there was a smile on her face.

"I ask," she said, "for the Past."

There was an old place of stones and sand outside the city, a place where they buried their dead. The queen had given Caelqua a fine litter and servants to attend her, and a robe of ivory silk. Those, and a consultation with the temple Oracle, whose Voice had directed Caelqua here in her inexplicable search.

Caelqua walked past the ancient monuments and gravestones, looking for a specific one.

The Past was buried here, the Oracle had said, and it is what you seek.

And Caelqua looked for it now, her vision blurring with many waters, mindlessly taking in the sunlit expanse of white stone and sand.

She moved, drifting over the earth, and came upon a large antique tomb structure that was mostly below ground. Here, at the entrance, obelisks of cypress had sprung, reaching for the sky.

And here stood a man, his back turned to her but his skin showing him to be of a dark race, and his hair tight and coiled like snakes of midnight.

Something started to beat wildly in Caelqua's heart then, at the sight of him.

"Nadir!" she pronounced, her still voice cracking with emotion for the first time. "Nadir, it *is* you. But how you've grown!"

The man turned to face her, tall and muscular like an ebony god, with skin like dates, and warm eyes.

"Yes," he replied. "I am Nadir."

In response, Caelqua came forward with a wildness, her whole form wavering for an instant from flesh to a column of water and then back again. With one raggedly expelled breath she moved into his arms.

"I am Caelqua!" she said, shuddering against his chest. "Do you remember me, little brother? Remember how Grandmother—who was Ris—used to call you a little demon? Remember how we wandered together and how we suffered, and how you promised that you would grow up strong and fight injustice—and I can see that you have—"

The man called Nadir received her and held her close in silence, allowing the torrent of her words, and then whispered gently, "Yes . . . I remember. I know you now, my sister. Only— what happened to your bright fiery hair?"

"Ah." She breathed ragged bitter sobs. "It matters no longer, but my hair is now like the desert. For I have been one with it for many summers, as many as it took you to grow up from a child into the handsome man that you are now."

"How many summers has it been, indeed?" he said, his lips forming the sounds over her brow, while she could hear the rhythm of his strong southern heart.

She felt the flow of blood, the subterranean currents of it moving through his flesh, and her own waters responded in sympathy, surging within her and overflowing with intensity, bringing the excess of moisture to her eyes.

He turned her face to him gently and saw the tears brimming. "Why, Caelqua!" he said, stricken by the sight of the water. "You weep for your foolish younger brother?"

"Yes!" she cried. "Oh, yes! I weep for the moments of your life that I have missed, for your growth and the changing of your voice, for the strengthening of your arms, and the endless cycles of sunlit days that deepened the color of your skin, for the coming of force into your eyes. . . ."

He looked at her, taking her in, all of her. She was now stamped like an indelible afterimage of the sun in his mind's eye. And his mouth curved easily now with the receptiveness of love. "But you have missed nothing much, sister!" he said. "For I am all here, every day and moment that comprises me, every compounded breath that has marked the passing of time. You see the years before you rolled into one. Now, rejoice, for the Past is no longer a fleeting thing, and you have caught up with it at last. . . ."

And then he laughed, and once again drew her into his arms, saying, "Oh, there is so much I have to tell you! Come, you must meet my children, and their mother, the woman who is the joy of my heart! You must see the house in the city where we live—"

But as he spoke these things, Caelqua freed herself from his embrace very suddenly, growing still. She continued to look at him while the wind blew her desert-sand hair into a frenzy and the heedless sun scalded them both.

"Nadir," she whispered. "Little demon, apple of my eye. . . . Nadir. I cannot come with you, and both you and I know it. This is but a Moment. A Moment has been granted to me wherein I may reclaim a bit of my only love, which is yourself, and see in you the years made transparent and formed into one thing of flesh and blood."

"Sister . . ." he began.

But she interrupted him violently, like a drowning one grasping for a bit of flotsam, floundering. "Don't!" she said.

"This brief meeting has been a gift given to me, and maybe it has been a moment of equal wonder for you. But it must now come to an end. For—I now travel outside the normal flow of Time, and even now feel the beginning urge, the pull to return to my own state of being. While you—beloved brother of mine forever—must live out the rest of your life, and your children will grow, and their children, and the sands of the desert will move in, and this city itself will fold in upon itself and buckle under the weight of centuries. And maybe then, some day, I will once again be compelled to step into Time, and maybe your great-grandson or daughter in another Place will come forward also to greet me before proceeding with their own flow of personal eternity."

"Caelqua. . . ."

"I am now a being of Ris, and in me run her waters."

"Caelqua!" he cried, and for the first time his own dark eyes brimmed full with moisture.

But she drew her hand forward in an odd powerless farewell and took a weak step backwards, all the while her form shimmering and beginning to transform into a pillar of liquid.

It was dissolving already.

Nadir reached forward grabbing hold of transparency, crying out one last time as he watched the pillar start to sink softly into the incandescent bleached sands. And all around the place where she had stood the sands were discolored with the darkness that is born of moisture, discolored with life.

The wind stood still, and there was silence.

Nadir stood like a bereaved child or a very old man, and watched white powder cover the last trace of her, the very ghost. . . .

"You have done well," came a woman's voice. The queen herself stepped forth from the shadows of an ancient sepulcher to watch him. "You gave her what I promised."

Nadir started, then immediately lowered his face in obeisance and hung his head before the queen of this city.

"I have done as you asked . . ." he replied faintly. "The goddess of the spring mistook me for her ancient brother, my holy ancestor, the first man to bear our name. And as a result your promise to her has been fulfilled. Now the curse is lifted from your womb, my queen. I am happy to have served you so . . . well."

The queen only nodded to him with tired eyes, and motioned for servants to bring forward a heavy purse.

"Receive your payment," she said, turning away, glittering with golden veils in the sun.

Nadir bowed and took the weight of metal coins covered by silk. He could feel it, the weight of gold.

Gold for water.

And suddenly a memory came to him, one not his own. . . .

They had tried to create water from gold, but only gold comes from gold.

And now he would always have water to remember her by.

Nadir turned to the receding form of the queen and her retinue. He was still clutching the moneybag, and he could feel it clanking inside, solid smooth metal.

The voices of his ancestors clamored in his mind, crying to him. The wind of the desert started to rise once again, blowing the ever-present white dust of desolation.

You did not even see my children, ancient sister. Now that you've moved on from the Past into the Future, how will they remember you? Indeed, who *will remember you?*

But, as he stood in the silence of the desert, Nadir heard within himself a rhythmic heartbeat, a pounding at the temples.

Internal waters rushing though his veins. Through him. They would always be thus within him.

And he thought he heard Caelqua's laughter in his very veins, with each pulse. *You think you have given me a false gift, brother of my heart?* the waters sang. *Don't you know that, while you gave me the Past, I also gave you the Future? They are one*

and the same, with no end and no beginning, only a line of
waters running through it all, binding us.

The Spring of waters is Time.

And you and I will meet again and again, simply when one
of us chooses to Remember.

The purse of gold fell on the desert sand, slipping from his
fingers with a sound of bells. It lay there, and the wind
immediately carried fine grains to sprinkle the fabric.

Nadir walked slowly, his sandals sinking lightly in the
powdery whiteness. Ahead of him was the distant mirage city.
Behind, stretched the desert.

Within him was Caelqua's Spring.

Dream Fourteen

The Story of Time

L isten closely as I tell you the story of time.

Time is a spring of waters, a thought hurtling forward to shape its own footholds just before they land.

Time is the needle of the Compass as it is drawn to a point that is your future. For that is where you will be. Thus, *where* and *when* are entwined, and only the Compass Rose of your intent separates you from yesterday and tomorrow.

T he queen without eyes stood before an arched window overlooking a sea of gardens, in a grand city that was in the very middle of all the lands that comprised the world.

She was not a queen by birth, but rather by affliction. For at the moment of losing her sight at the hands of palace guards upon the *taqavor's* decree, she was taken by the eccentric son of the *taqavor,* Prince Lirheas, to be his bride.

It had been months, or maybe weeks, or maybe only days since her blinding. The blinding was a punishment for attempting to speak what she considered to be truth. And time seemed to have slowed down since.

She was a horrific sight, thought the servants who were made to attend her. An ugly cripple, a creature with two open sores in her face that refused to heal.

What made it even more intolerable was that the queen had once been a servant herself, attending the *taqavor's* House of Wives, and for lack of a true name had been called "you with the knowing eyes" by the *taqoui* and concubines for her clever perceptiveness and the ability to tell wise stories. They still remembered her in the House of Wives as the young woman who had filled the unmarked emptiness of their existence with bright swatches of wonder. They could still hear her words in the shape of living dreams that stood up and imbued languid evenings with a purpose.

And now, for obvious reasons, the designation "you with the knowing eyes" no longer applied.

"You with holes for eyes," some servants called her behind her back, upon first being assigned to her. Then they shortened it to "holes for eyes" and spoke it wickedly.

But not for long. The name persisted, but the wickedness itself transformed to pity. And as the cruelty was shed in its place grew a peculiar acceptance, as they who served her came to know her nature.

"Holes for eyes" was a being of gentle quietude.

When Prince Lirheas had first taken responsibility for her, she was reeling in shock and bleeding from the punishment meted out by the *taqavor.* Initially, the Prince had concealed her in his quarters and had called the palace physicians to attend her and heal and comfort her wounds.

The new queen's eye-sockets were filled with unguents, and her face bandaged with soft sterile gauze. The gauze—expensive, exotic, and delicate as filaments of silk—encircled her head in a band, blending with her light skin, but stood at cross-purposes with the plain darkness of her hair.

The queen was dressed in royal finery that she could not see, or appreciate except by tactile means, and she stood or sat or moved like a limp puppet, doing just as she was told and speaking almost nothing. In the same manner she lay in the Prince's bed, and her remoteness made him afraid to touch her.

And so he would lie equally frozen at her side, night after night. Not once had Lirheas put his hands on her after the first instant he had held her atrophied body, moments after the blinding, and watched the beast that was his father rant about "seeing without eyes."

It seemed the *taqavor* had forgotten her immediately, saying nothing to Lirheas in that moment when the son stood up to his father—as though it didn't happen. Or maybe the *taqavor* simply chose to pretend ignorance for the time being, and turned away, muttering to himself, to play.

He played with his current favorite toy, spinning the weighted wooden Rose of the great Compass that floated in a stone pool in the center of the palace—the same object of marvelous engineering that she had designed for him to represent his boundless *empirastan.*

The Prince's father, the *taqavor,* was a madman, it was clear now to all, and he was obsessed with truths and details of the world, such as the nature of the Rose.

The *taqavor* did not seem to notice his son's act of defiance. In truth, it might have been better for Lirheas if he had, if he had raged and threatened and opposed his son's decision to take the blind woman as his queen, for it would have forced the Prince to stay in his new course of courageous rebellion and to grow stronger. But as it was, Lirheas's single outburst was like the breaking of one great wave upon a cliffside, and when it was over the wave dissipated, while the cliff stood unaffected.

All things appeared to be as they had always been.

And Lirheas the silent Prince lost his nerve. He needlessly hid away in his own quarters and cloistered himself with the ugly blinded creature, her eyeless face thoroughly bandaged now and her lips immobile.

She was like a doll of flesh and silence.

At first he tried speaking to her in a soothing voice, saying gentle words to draw her out. But she was a dead weight. Her vibrant energy, the sense of purpose that had drawn him to her in the first place before the act of blinding, was all gone, faded.

Lirheas observed her immobility and terror consumed him, for he was no longer sure if he had done the right thing to take her thus, to refer to her as his intended consort. What a mockery indeed that he now called her his queen—when there had been no consummation. Such was the title bestowed upon the Heir's wife.

He was the Heir Prince of the *taqavor*. And she was but a shadow presence, not a wife.

For months before the blinding the Prince had been obsessed by her, watching the woman who had been nothing more than a servant now exalted to serve his father in the role of Master Artist and work with the artisans and engineers as she directed the creation of the Compass Rose. Lirheas had been at her side often, asking her questions and watching her reply with wisdom and explain to him the natural workings of the world. She had an answer to every question, and her logic was pure, glorious, and sunlike in its clarity.

Her eyes had been the most expressive features of her otherwise ordinary face. Through them he could just see something on the other side of this mortal world, something remote and nostalgic that filled him with a longing to soar, to search, to strive. . . .

Her eyes had been what had made him look forward to every moment that he spent with her. For in her presence time seemed to slow to an acute glacial intensity, colors took on a rich aroma, and the air itself was solid with thought.

Her blinding had come as a shock.

She had said something to the *taqavor,* something that made the madman react in a way that had cost her the most precious thing that Lirheas had finally admitted he loved her for.

And now she stood as she always had before a window of the Palace, her head turned sightlessly toward the open expanse. She must have felt the wind blow and the fresh air sweeping into the room, for how else could she know the direction of the open sky and the sun and the rest of the outside world?

Because the queen without eyes stood and *watched.*

A nd then one day the queen spoke.
    "What time is it?" she said suddenly. Her head was turned to the window as always, and her lips were slightly parted as though she were drinking in the breeze.

Lirheas—sitting nearby in his favorite place at the small work table and reading from an old parchment from his own library—started.

"Oh . . ." he said, confused at the very sound of her voice, "It is—I am not sure, some time after midday."

He arose in worry, and came tentatively to her side. "Is something wrong? Do you need something?"

Since she had no name, he was never sure how to address her. And calling her "queen" seemed a sad insult.

For the first time since her blinding, she laughed. It was a bitter, living sound, and he watched her lips curve.

"I need to see," she said simply, rationally, after her laughter had died away. She turned her bandaged face to him then, turned away from the window. "What is out there, my Prince?" she whispered.

Lirheas felt a pang of old agony. He dutifully looked outside and said, "I will look for you. . . ."

"Yes . . . look."

"I see gardens," he spoke, coming closer to stand at her side, so that his shoulder nearly brushed her head as he leaned forward in the open window. "I see beyond that the walls of the Palace, and they are pale gray stone. Some parts look rose-tinted under the sun, and others look bluish with the receding shadows. It is an old granite stone, originally brought here from a distant land."

"Yes, I remember," she said. "Look beyond the walls, and tell me what is there."

He stared, straining his eyes. "Beyond, I see the rooftops of the city. And then, the outside city walls, and then finally the desert. It is a brief stripe of creamy yellow, all that is on the horizon. Nothing beyond that."

The woman sighed.

"Yes," she said. "Nothing."

And although he tried to draw her out again, to speak to her, she was silent for the rest of the afternoon.

The *taqavor* wanted something, but he was not sure what it was. He was no longer a young man, but he was not so decrepit as to feel ailments in his body or to forget what it was like to desire.

But he was by now beyond the need for conquest, beyond carnal pleasures, and at the stage in his existence that demanded some acute mental experience.

The *taqavor* wanted to know the nature of all things, and to fathom the mortal world that he had conquered from end to end. He wanted to feel its very edges pressing against him inside his mind.

For, yes, there were edges and limits. To think otherwise hurt his head, and was thus unthinkable. He had blinded the woman who had dared to make him start to think *beyond* edges and limits, and anyone else who would ever again bring up such a thing would earn an even harsher fate.

The *taqavor* wandered the empty halls of his Palace, the fragrant gardens, and often lifted his face up to the sun and closed his eyes. Doing that seemed to make a difference to the nature of memories that seemed to haunt him more than ever now that he preferred the solitude of his own thoughts.

Cireive. . . . whispered the wind, in the ancient voice of a woman. He was not sure if it was the one who had birthed him and had sung to him her primeval songs or the one whom he had driven to the martyrdom of godhood by a singular method of destruction, or the one whom he had recently blinded.

He did not think of her much, that last one. And yet maybe once or twice she appeared on the periphery of his awareness, for she had been responsible in part for his insatiable curiosity.

Cireive. . . .

And for a moment he was nothing more than a small child, not worried about the nature of that whisper, hearing only what was safest, his mother's voice calling his name.

And for that one moment taken out of time, like a fragment of a broken mirror, Cireive the *taqavor* of the world smiled innocently and remembered. . . .

Fields of amaranth. They rose like crimson and green waves upon an anchored ocean as the wind swept clusters of feathered magenta filaments. The filaments stirred—tails of a peculiar animal of many limbs, with irregular fluid movement—and the rich grains remained hidden within the secret depths.

The world was covered from horizon to horizon, it seemed, with this growth. And he stood at the base of the hill rising just above the edge of the field and looked out, barely seeing over the tall stalks of many feet in height into a floundering sea. . . .

Were he to walk down and enter this field he would drown as stalks of amaranth closed far over his head, that of a young boy still only half grown.

"Mother!" he would often cry out. "Let's go inside and play! I want to hide under the red flowers!"

The musical voice—even in his memory, or maybe because it was but a memory—always came from behind. "Wait for a moment, Cireive," she would say every time. "You go on ahead and I will come after you, in just one moment. I dropped the basket."

And when he tried to turn and look for her, she would again say, this time with a peculiar urgency, "Don't wait for me! Go on, son. Hurry now! See how beautiful grows the amaranth. Go and hide inside and I will come to look for you! But you must be very quiet until I find you! When I count to three, you run!"

He heard her start to count off, and then he burst forward like a calf full of springing energy, running head-first into the red and green downy wonder. . . .

The amaranth obscured him immediately, but like all children of the plains he knew his direction well, and never got lost. Within minutes he would be able to retrace his steps if necessary. But not now, not this time.

Now they were playing a game. Stifling his welling exuberance and giggles he raced deep into the field with eyes closed to avoid the slapping leaves and brushing filaments, wanting to burst but holding himself back.

Soon his mother would be behind him, making a great deal of intentional noise like a crashing large cat of the plains.

He would hide by throwing himself to the ground, gasping for muffled breath, face against the rich soil in the darkness, his lips brushing the roots of the plant that he had rearranged and drawn upright overhead to obscure the path behind him.

He lay panting, his breath slowly stilling, and listened for her approach.

But after long moments there was only silence. The wind moved the ocean of growth over his head, and he heard the shimmering hiss as the filaments and stalks of the plants streamed in the breeze. . . .

Where was she? The little boy in him would suddenly grow impatient, but she had told him to stay and hide in silence, and that she would come.

She always came for him, and it would be no different this time.

And so he waited at the bottom of the living ocean of air and leaves and filaments until the silence became overwhelming, so that he could hear the slower beating in his temples, and time itself hung in the air between his cheeks and the scattered sun overhead.

At some point he thought there were distant voices, sounds of the unknown, lower, masculine and disturbing on some level he could not explain. He also thought he heard his mother's voice in the distance, and it was different also.

But then the wind came, blowing stronger, and he no longer heard anything except its hiss in the feather-filaments of amaranth.

After some long while of confused inaction, the boy Cireive finally decided to move, sucking in a breath that allowed his lungs to expand and his full consciousness to surface.

"Mother?" he said loudly, no longer interested in the game and instead feeling lost and claustrophobic.

There was no reply.

"Mother!" he tried again, this time yelling at the top of his young lungs. "Where are you, mother?"

The wind whistled against the blades of the plant all around him. Springing up too fast from the ground, he lost direction, just for a moment only, while his mind reeled. And then he ran back, arms ahead of him, slapping away angrily the endless growth that had now become the enemy. . . .

When he came out of the field there was no sign of his mother. Her basket lay abandoned, and several wild fruits and dirt-covered roots that she had gathered earlier had rolled out to lie nearby.

The boy Cireive stared at this, breath catching, while a cold of the unknown came to him. His lips mouthed the word that was not her name but which represented her.

And then he sat down at the foot of the hill in the shallow grass, with his back to the hill and facing the field. He sat thus in a trance of coldness, of inexplicable time distortion, until it had grown dark and it was more than time for him to return home—for *them* to return home.

Time spun from out and from under him, and Cireive, *taqavor* of the world, came awake to find himself standing on a shaded marble walkway. On both sides grew tall cultivated vines of exotic rose blossoms held up by a fine grillwork fence.

The blossoms were of a slightly magenta hue, and maybe it was their similarity to the feather wisps of the plant of his childhood that had triggered his reverie. He stood, suddenly feeling himself tiny, and the plants on both sides of him were tall amaranth, growing over six feet tall, obscuring the sky. . . .

Cireive's blond barely graying head trembled under the onslaught of the past. Rapidly he walked back into the cool darkness of the Palace.

Servants greeted him, but he cried out, in a high voice that cracked as though he were no older than twelve summers, "Cut all of them down, all the flowers of that crimson color! I want no red or magenta or other such abomination in my gardens! Cut them down and burn them!"

And because he was the *taqavor* of the world, the servants complied. Dozens of gardeners were sent to strip the gardens of all flower-bearing plants of a reddish hue, and the destruction that was wrought within an hour was such that dust arose in a cloud of pallor to obscure the once lovely gardens. Mixed in with the dust, were petals of crimson and torn bits of red. The wind swept them like rose snowdrifts, lifting their filaments up to the highest balconies of the Palace, and higher still, over the walls and into the world beyond.

Prince Lirheas noticed the crimson and dust swirling in desolation outside his window, yet he did not have the heart to tell the blind woman at his side what had come to pass.

But somehow she knew it. The blind queen turned her bandaged face to the wind and strained forward, breathing the tainted air.

"What is happening?" she said softly. "Tell me."

"I think they are burning the gardens," he said. "My Father's latest mad decree."

Lirheas neared her, and he touched her lightly on the shoulder so that she grew tense and motionless, instinctively not trusting anyone's touch.

"Please," he whispered then. "Forgive me . . . for not being there when it happened, when he—the beast—had this done to you."

His hand, the fingers that touched her shoulder gently, were trembling.

"My Prince," she replied, "you have always been there when you could. You are not like him at all, do you know? As though you are not his son."

And then she added, her voice infinitely gentle, "There is nothing to forgive when one is blameless. Tell me, did you ever know your mother? Was she like you? She must have been a kind woman."

"No. My mother died soon after my birth, I was told."

The queen's lips curved into a tired smile. "She was fortunate, then. The gods took pity upon her and allowed her to escape an existence with *him*. How did she die? Did they tell you?"

Lirheas frowned while his memories attempted to fly back to that obscured time, past all the dark things that had happened in the interim, dark things he did not want to recall.

There had been hushed whisperings in the Palace. He had paid little attention to them, but then he had been just a small child and did not know what was worth paying attention to; it had not interested him at that point.

There was little said thereafter about his mother. In fact, he did not even recall if her name had ever been spoken in his hearing.

But now suddenly, all these years later, with the sightless face of the blind queen before him, Lirheas was tormented by an urge to know. Who had his mother been? And, even more so, what kind of a peculiar creature was he that he had never wondered about this earlier?

"I don't know," he said after a long pause of stilled thought. "But I must now find out."

The *taqavor* was in his most beloved place, the central hall of the Compass Rose, when his son Prince Lirheas came to him with a question.

"Forgive me, my Lord Father," he said in a measured wooden voice, steeling himself for anything. "I want to know the name of the woman who had gave birth to me, my mother. What happened to her? How did she die?"

The *taqavor* tore himself away from the floating four-point star that pointed in the same direction always, a tendency he himself named "North."

He looked at his son with his earnest face, a younger man who had always been quiet and reserved throughout the years, and who now suddenly came into focus before him, out of nowhere, out of time.

"What's this?" said Cireive. "What do you ask?"

"My mother," repeated Lirheas. "Who was she?"

"How should I know?"

Lirheas strained to keep his breath even. "I am your son," he said. "Who else would know such a thing but my father?"

The *taqavor* raised one eyebrow, then his eyes moved away to look into nothingness. He then just as quickly looked back at the younger man, and approached him.

Lirheas wanted to step back from the sickly intensity of the gaze, but held himself in place.

"Who else?" said Cireive. "I am your father, yes. I am also your mother!"

And then the *taqavor* smiled and began to cackle, his voice sending up harsh echoes in the stone hall.

Lirheas looked at the madness before him, but he was now beyond caution, beyond fear, in a singular place of clarity, which required him to persist.

"What was her name?" he said. "You must tell me. Try to remember, please. . . ."

The bark that came in the next instant made the Prince's heart weak.

"Oh, I *remember,* do not doubt!" cried the *taqavor* in a shrill voice, again advancing on his son. "You think me insane, don't you, boy? Well, think what you will, but I remember it very well! It is the one thing that is with me always, and the one thing that I will never forget. Never. *Never!*"

The last word came as a scream.

"Then tell me," said Lirheas, with a false outer calm.

The *taqavor* laughed. He chuckled, then guffawed, then paused to listen to the macabre echoes he made and giggled, pointing with his hand to the sound as though it were something to be captured in the air like a summer fly.

"I will tell you," he whispered. "For she lives in my dreams. . . ."

Blue twilight had come to hang thickly over the amaranth field when the boy finally rose and walked up the hill slowly. He had left their basket behind and he was on his way home, which lay on the other side of the hill.

When he came to the row of outlying houses and the clearing where the well stood, he saw horses and strange men. They had stopped near the well, and there was loud talk and many foreign accents. Some of the townsmen had come out to barter, and now were discussing news of the outer lands.

Cireive walked straight ahead past them all, and several of the neighborhood boys waved at him and cried out bold greetings in their play language. But he ignored them all and continued forward.

His house lay within the confines of the town, and the room that he and his mother occupied was just next door to another family, sharing with them a thin wall and an outside entrance. To get to his own room, Cireive had to pass through his neighbors' one.

"Where is your mother, boy?" asked the old man who sat in his usual place at the entrance. He always asked that same question, but today Cireive paused before him and glared with all the intensity his small frame could muster.

"I've lost my mother," he said. "She did not come home? Did you see her enter, Grandpa?"

The old one scrunched a face that was already furrowed like a cracked jar of mud. "Where is your mother, boy?" he said again, for he was daft with time.

"Don't talk crazy, Grandpa!" said Cireive. "Did you see her, or not? Tell me! *Tell me!*"

But the old man shook his head, and began to mutter.

A young woman came out, dark-haired and smooth, probably his mother's age, carrying a heavy bowl. "What's wrong?" she asked. "Why are you shouting?"

And then she looked the boy over, saying, "You are a mess, Cireive. Your face is covered with dirt. Go on in and wash yourself, piglet. Where is your mother, anyway?"

And at that instant something burst in him, seeing this woman and hearing her say this, which somehow was such an ordinary thing. And yet it terrified him, seeing that these adults also did not know where his mother was. *Everything* suddenly became terrifying, because he knew that he was completely alone.

And Cireive bawled, huge tears rolling down his face. He wept in public for the first time in his self-aware life, not caring that he was a grown boy of six summers, and words came squeezed out of him, random and tattered words. . . .

"My mother is gone . . . she was supposed to go in and look for me, but she didn't, and I waited, and then I heard some strange men's voices passing by, and then I waited again, and then I came out and she wasn't there, and she is not here either!"

By now the neighbors had all come out, and the young woman of his mother's age took him to her and held him tight and rocked him against her. He was still sobbing, sobbing.

"Where is the boy's mother?" a man said. "Did she not come home tonight from the field?"

"I saw those strangers come riding from the same direction," said someone else.

And then they were holding Cireive and shaking him and questioning him. "Did you see the men come by?" they were asking. "Did these men talk to your mother, did they do anything?"

"I don't know!" the boy cried. "I did not see, I don't know!"

A crowd gathered. Tired, drawn, sun-burnt faces of grown men he knew, faces of stone frowning all around him, closing in, the swelling hum of the disturbed hive.

"We need to go look for the boy's mother!"

Twilight had grown heavy, and in the new darkness they lit torches.

Cireive trembled, holding onto the hand of the woman who was his neighbor, holding it as tight as a death grip.

"Show us where you last saw her, boy!" they were now saying. And he huddled further, covering his face against the cotton robe of this woman who stroked his hair.

In the growing darkness he was led forward through the center of town, and the woman walked with him, supporting him from the back and the shoulders while he continued to sob and tremble.

They walked up the hill and beyond it, torches flickering like angry orange eyes in the night, and within the hour had come to the edge where the blackness of the field stretched in all directions like an ebony sea.

The moon rose high, tumbling like a quarter of an apple across the abyss sky.

The men bearing torches had scattered, and they entered the field at the edges, like a necklace of light.

At some point someone found the dropped basket that Cireive's mother had left lying, and the tumbled fruits.

But there was no sign of the woman herself, though they searched the field in the vicinity, sweeping rows of growing amaranth methodically.

Eventually the moon began to sink to the horizon and drowned in the field. The search was abandoned for the night, and Cireive was taken home by his neighbors. The woman who was so like his mother pulled him along in the darkness, until they came to their communal dwelling. Here the boy was made to eat at the neighbors' table, and eventually put to sleep in his own room next door.

There was no one else in the room with him, which made the night uncustomary and terrifying. He fell asleep struggling against the dark evil which all children knew about, and which so obviously rushed in when the fire was extinguished and when others left the room. . . .

Evil, which preyed upon those who had lost their mothers.

L irheas watched his father rave, watched the memories being regurgitated, hearing things that were new, that he had not known before.

There was something that brought subtle unease, hearing the older man talk thus, something with a faint whiff of taint in the very telling of it, as though time itself were being filtered through a penumbra of illusion.

"Was she ever found, my Lord father? I am sorry.... I wish I had known my grandmother, seen her for one brief instant, just once. As it is, I see her only from this ancient story you tell."

The *taqavor* grew silent and stared at him. And then he smirked, saying, "You see nothing, boy. And you still do not understand. But then, you never can. Get out of my sight, for I grow tired of your stupidity and your questions."

And with that he turned his back on the Prince. He returned to his plaything in the stone pool of the Rose.

Lirheas could do nothing but stare in unfulfilled silence at his father's hunched back. Eventually he too turned away and left the hall.

The queen without eyes was in the same place he had left her. More and more she was like an inanimate thing, not a living being—pliable and yielding, and yet as remote as the horizon.

"I learned nothing of my mother," Lirheas told her softly. "But I learned something of his. I pity him because of it, and yet—"

"Look outside my Prince, and tell me what is out there," said the queen without eyes, apparently ignoring his words.

And when Lirheas moved to comply, wordlessly approaching the window, she suddenly reached out with her hand and touched him on his arm. Her fingers were cold, and he could feel their inflexible ice through the fabric of his sleeve. And yet his arm burned in that place with a sudden tunneling of the senses, a focus on nothing but her fingers, her light touch....

"Thank you," she said. "You have a strange ability to bend your will for the will of others. And I heard what you said, about your mother and his."

"Oh," he said, his arm still burning. And then, while the wind came in a fresh warm gust from the window, he put his arms around her and held her in a full embrace for the first time since that one time in the beginning. It was a touch which was light and tentative for fear of hurting her, but it was an embrace nevertheless.

In this butterfly-gentle embrace she became pliant. It seemed she melted into flowing water in his hands, her flesh a single warm current. He held it as it coursed, and he too felt his flesh melt and dissolve until the solid outlines that constituted his being were blending with hers in a peculiar moment taken out of time.

He looked up at the window, seeing the haze of the sunlit day, feeling the breeze upon his face, as he dissolved into her, and he said, "I see the horizon and—"

"And the yellow sands in the distance," she finished for him, speaking with a muffled voice, for her face was buried in his chest. "The sun rides halfway up, maybe less, the sky, and there is a shadow of lavender and indigo upon the right of the city walls. It all blurs into the distance. . . . And there is the fleeting shadow of a bird!"

"Yes!" he exclaimed. "How did you know?"

And the queen without eyes raised her bandaged face to him. Her lips curved into a perfect smile, and spoke eloquently as though they were her eyes.

"I can see everything now," she said softly—so lightly that he had to draw near her to hear the caress of her lips. "I see through your eyes now, my Prince."

The days were now languid and warm. Prince Lirheas walked gently at the side of the queen without eyes, along the sand-and-gravel path in the gardens. They passed by tall flowering blossoms, and when he looked the queen would smile and comment upon them, seeing exactly what he saw.

And yet it was clear that she saw even more.

"That green prickly growth that you call cactus, see the tallest, oldest one," she said. "Look upon its heart and see the flower that appears not once every seven years, as is the misconception of many, but only when, with the passage of time, it has reached its flowering age after which it will bear short-lived flowers every season. See the petals, colored a shade of rose and soft whiteness, see how the colors flow. They are more bright than any other living thing in the desert, because they have conquered time to appear and just as quickly fade away. It is a rare sight indeed."

"I never knew," he whispered, taking her hand.

At that touch she smiled, her lips curving generously, speaking more eloquently than eyes. And as he watched her smile, it occurred to Lirheas, with a stab of worry, that if ever he were not to be at her side, if ever she were to be on her own, how would she see? Who would be her eyes?

But the question faded inside him softly, for that possibility did not seem a part of their reality, did not seem to matter.

They walked farther, passing the House of Wives and the gallery of marble that was the courtyard. Here the fountain pools were silent like mirrors, for these days the *taqoui* rarely came out to enjoy the sun, and the *taqavor* rarely came out to enjoy them.

As Lirheas watched the calm surface of the water in the pond, smooth and without a blemish, the queen without eyes said suddenly, "He is getting old, you know. His time is approaching."

And the Prince nodded silently, knowing exactly what she meant, and not being sure how he felt about it. For the beast who was his father was an ever-present burden in the back of his mind. And yet pity now encroached in his perception, for Lirheas recognized madness and evaluated it in a different light.

But pity dissipated quickly, for the very next month there came a pronouncement that chilled his blood and the blood of many in the Palace.

Without any explanation, the *taqavor* had ordered a hundred and fifty-three coffins built—the exact number of *taqoui* and concubines that were left in the House of Wives.

P rince Lirheas came before the *taqavor* as bidden in the great central hall of the Compass Rose. He stood silently, watching his father pace back and forth. The *taqavor's* once blond hair was now streaked with whiteness, for it seemed that Cireive had aged overnight.

But his walk was undaunted and sprightly as he moved through the room, muttering.

"There you are," he said, seeing his son. "I want you to supervise the building of a marvelous structure. It is to have a great carved dome, marked North, South, East, and West, and within it, I will place their coffins."

"Whose coffins?" said Lirheas.

But the taqavor giggled, and said, "Why, the flowers, of course. The ones they burned in the gardens, the ones that were red and tall, and grew everywhere. I told them only to cut down the flowers, but they burned them too. And now there is no place to dispose of their ashes."

"My Lord Father," said Lirheas, "why must we bury flowers? Can we not toss their ashes over the earth, and grow new ones?"

The *taqavor* approached him, turning on his heel, and leaned forward, so that his face was inches away from that of his son. "What an idiot you are, boy," he said. "Any gardener will tell you that ashes improperly disposed ruin the fertility of the soil. As to why we bury them, I will tell you why. Because it is how it is done."

And then he drew away again, laughing, and said, "Now, go and build me a mausoleum for the flowers! And if you do so I will tell you about your mother. Don't you want to know?"

Prince Lirheas attended the area in the heart of the palace gardens where rose granite and marble from a distant quarry were piled in blocks, in preparation for the building efforts. Architects of the *taqavor* came to make measurements, and they all stared at the woman without eyes who stood at the side of the Prince, and who spoke quiet words of knowledge.

"You calculate the structural supports that will be required to erect the dome," she said. "Let me help you measure the curves of the arches of wood needed, in proportion to the weight of underlying stones."

"Your craft is great. And yet how can you assist us, o queen, when you no longer have eyes?" said one artist engineer who remembered her, for he had worked with her before in the creation of the Compass Rose, the single object that defined the *empirastan.*

"She has the use of my eyes," replied Lirheas. "And we will therefore proceed. I was told merely to supervise, but now I will also create."

And the architects and engineers obeyed, allowing the queen without eyes to approach their work, and with her the man who never left her side.

Over days and weeks the structure of marble grew like an exotic flower, and at the apex that held the dome were constructed rows of skylights to allow in the celestial lights during the day and the night.

For there was to be no other illumination within, nothing to disturb the pristine brass of the coffins, and the peculiar ashes they were to contain. . . .

There were no more blossoms of any hue left in the gardens. While the domed structure was being constructed by the engineers, the gardeners shook their heads in regret and continued to harvest the flowers of all living plants, on a daily basis, in order to avoid the anger of the *taqavor* of the mortal world.

For the *taqavor* walked the grounds pedantically every morning. And the more he looked the more new shades of rose or red he found, even when in fact they were not. But who was to argue with him?

"Amaranth," he was heard to mutter. "It is everywhere, red abomination. . . ."

"Of what does the Lord speak?" the gardeners said to one another. "What is this red flower that he names?"

"It does not grow here, although it could," spoke up one very old gardener. "And some think it is a weed, while others who know better plant it at the eve of summer and harvest it before the first cold for the wondrous grain and the leaves. It is a hardy plant that likes the burning desert sun and the cool forest and the mountains equally. Amaranth is sown and reaped in the land of my birth. Our Lord knows of it because the *taqavor* has traveled the whole world from end to end, which is his great *empirastan,* and in every place he must have seen it."

"You seem to know much of this amaranth," the gardeners persisted. "Tell us then why the Lord hates this flower so much?"

But the old one shrugged at that point, knowing in truth only as much as anyone, and regretting that he'd opened his mouth in the first place.

And so they continued to purge the gardens, and to whisper in fear among themselves. The piles of harvested blossoms of all varieties grew to be so big that even burning them had become a major chore, and there was no place to put the ashes. The Palace itself became a madhouse of anguished confusion, reeking of smoke and felled blossoms and ashes that were carried to the rest of the city on the fiery desert wind.

The coffins of brass were wrought by the most skilled metal-workers, and placed one by one in the central chamber of the round domed structure which was now complete. Each one of the coffins had been decorated with fine etchings including patterns that resembled a certain flower, according to the descriptions of the *taqavor,* who insisted upon this peculiarity.

The workmen who carried in the coffins made frequent warding signs against evil, for it was thought to be bad luck to mock the gods and death itself by using boxes designed for the dead to dispose of other things.

But in the end the deed was done. Then for several days gardeners and other Palace servants carried bags filled with ashes and filled the open coffins to the brim, packing them down as was needed, before going to bring more ashes.

There was no end to them, the ashes of the flowers. The plants seemed to grow back as quickly in the gardens as they were being cut down and burned. Very soon there were no gardens left but stumps of trees and uprooted holes in the shallow earth where rose bushes had once flourished. Underneath the disturbed earth, sand was soon revealed, for the gardens had been planted on top of soil brought here to the heart of the desert from other places.

The *taqavor* continued to walk along the gravel paths, on both sides of which were upturned earth and sand and wooden debris. And yet he looked about him as though he saw growing things, and his lips continued to mouth words that only he heard. Sometimes he would raise his hand and point to somewhere just overhead where he saw ghosts of swaying leaves and feather-light crowns of blossoms of a mauve and scarlet hue.

They continued to grow all around him, tall and thick and boundless, fluttering in the wind and invisible to all.

Dawn came upon the desolate palace grounds, and upon its first precarious light there came from within the House of Wives cries of terror and despair. There was the clangor of metal, the yells of guards, and the shrieks of women roused from slumber and herded outside in their fine silk and satin shawls.

The *taqoui* and the concubines and all their female servants were taken by armed palace guards to the domed structure of veined rose marble, smooth granite and delicate enamel hues in the center of the ravaged gardens.

"Why?" cried the first and oldest of the *taqoui* in anguish. "What have we done to deserve such treatment from our Lord, whom we love and worship with all our beings, and whose children we bear?"

But the guards who had brought the women here lowered their gazes and would not reply. Instead, the women were left alone in the semi-darkness of the structure while the doors were locked behind them.

And the *taqoui* and the concubines and the serving women cried and wept, many falling on the delicate tiled floor of cool marble, between the rows of open coffins filled with ashes. For hours they called upon the name of their Lord, the *taqavor* of the world, and they struck the doors with their fists. Others took the ashes that were everywhere and threw them over their hair and foreheads, wailing upon their knees, their faces turned to the floor, beating their chests and scratching their cheeks with their nails.

For that was the mourning ritual for the dead, and the women knew they must thus honor themselves since no one else would.

But the doors of the domed sepulcher remained shut, and no one came to heed their calls for mercy. Time flowed, and they watched through the skylights as the sky changed overhead from the whiteness of day to the indigo of evening and the ichor of night.

Thus ended their first day without food or water.

"How can this go on? Why do you endure him?" said the queen without eyes to the Prince, with barely controlled passion, as they stood in their usual place before the window.

Before them now lay a desolate world of burnt gardens and hazy air. From the distance came the weak moans and weeping of the women in the domed sepulcher. After three days the sound had become a constant, day and night, sometimes fading, sometimes resuming, as the voices of the slowly dying women were carried on the wind.

"What else is the son of the *taqavor* to do?" said Lirheas after a pause. "The mad one is my father."

"But he is not mine," she replied, her voice breaking. "And I must speak the truth, as I have spoken it always."

And with those words the blind woman turned and headed for the door, opening it violently without a moment of hesitation, knowing exactly where the handle was placed.

With a sudden sinking in his innards, followed by blind terror, Lirheas exclaimed, "Wait!"

And then he was after her, suddenly feeling himself moving like molasses, while the world and time itself seemed to grow still and stretch all around him. . . .

The queen without eyes walked with all the urgency of the sighted, and was soon within the central hall of the Compass Rose, which had become the *taqavor's* living place.

"My Lord *taqavor!*" she said to the hunched figure who huddled near the stone pool in the center. "Do you remember me, my Lord? You blinded me once for speaking things you did not want to hear or see, but I am again before you!"

The figure turned, fingers dripping from touching the water in the pool, and he was looking at her, at this woman with a bandage across her face. He remembered in a flash who and what she was, the memory surfacing out of the normal haze of his thoughts.

"You!" said the *taqavor*. "Oh yes, I know you now, woman! You built this Compass Rose for me, my very own Rose. But you spoke things that were not right. And thus I had your sight taken from you, for your will cannot go beyond mine, ever."

"Father!" said Lirheas, approaching from the back. "This woman is now mine; I claimed her in that moment when you said no one would. You may no longer harm her, for she is my queen." His forceful tone imbued his voice with ringing echoes, was almost unreal. For never had the Prince previously raised his voice before his Lord Father.

But his father laughed.

"No longer harm her? Why, I can do anything I like, idiot boy. But—what difference does it make?" said the *taqavor*, continuing his odd sequence of clarity. "She is a blind weight upon you, and you are impotent, boy. Not unlike your mother."

"My mother! Tell me of her, once and for all!" exclaimed Lirheas, approaching the older man, and standing taller and more threatening than he'd ever been in all of his life.

The *taqavor* took a step back for the first time, almost cringed, for he had to look up to meet his son's face, and he felt the invisible pressure from his thoughts.

And then clarity was gone.

The *taqavor* began to giggle, and he looked back and forth from his son to the woman without eyes.

"Those women of the House of Wives," said the queen softly, oddly drawing out her words, so great was the intensity she was holding back. "Why did you imprison them in a tomb for your . . . flowers? Even now, they live and they weep, and they call out your name. Let them out, show them mercy, for they are the mothers of your children."

The *taqavor* watched her sightless face, watched the expression of her lips. "I want to preserve them. While they are still like flowers."

"Nonsense. Your mind wanders," said the queen without eyes and without fear. "For the flowers are like ashes and not at all like women. Where is the logic in that? Ashes, flowers, women? Tell me why you do this. What do you plan? You are *taqavor* of the world, and your *empirastan* is boundless, and your truth is boundless also—is that not so? Then why make a mockery of it?"

"Stand away from me!" he cried then, Cireive the old man, in the voice of a dark petulant child. And then he began to chuckle, mumbling, "Come along, both of you, and I will release them. . . . Come with me. . . ."

He called his guards to him. The hall trembled under their running footfalls.

"I do not trust him," whispered Lirheas, "He—"

"He plans to make ashes of the women, that is clear," said the queen without eyes. "And then he plans to make ashes out of us."

But in the saying of that her lips curved into a smile.

Cireive walked along the desolate gravel path toward the domed tomb. At his sides came arrow-straight rows of Palace guards, surrounding him from all sides like stalks of tall plants with swaying crowns of red feather-lightness—no, he must not think that way. A few steps behind walked his son, Prince Lirheas, and next to him the queen without eyes.

They passed what had once been lush gardens seething with flowers but were now sparse stretches of empty earth and felled shrubbery, while the intermittent moans and cries from up ahead grew louder, carried here on the wind. And soon he was before the building.

The *taqavor* stopped in front of the ornate doors, and turned to face the others. In the fading daylight of this, the fourth day, his white hair was the color of dusk and his features were crenulated with lines. Only his sky-blue eyes remained young and sharp and brilliant with intensity.

"Enough, then. I will let them out," said Cireive, with a simple smile. "I will allow them to live, but you must promise to tell me the truth of the world, woman, for I know that you are the only one who knows it." He stared at the queen without eyes.

"What?" whispered Lirheas. "What do you mean by that, my Lord Father?"

But the queen smiled and raised her hand in a gesture to stop the words of the Prince. "I will do this, Lord *taqavor*, for I know this is what has been eating you always."

"Yes," whispered Cireive. "I knew you would understand. Now, tell me things. For each answer you give me, I will let one of them go. Guards, open the doors, but stand closely and do not let them run out in a crowd. Allow one only to pass at a time upon my signal."

"What madness is this . . ." muttered Lirheas. "Will there be a hundred and fifty-three questions and a hundred and fifty-three truths to impart? How in the world—"

"Silence, impotent humorless boy! Not madness but a game!" cried the *taqavor* in a high womanish voice. He began again to giggle, and pointed to his guards and the doors of the sepulcher, saying, "Proceed."

The Palace guards unbolted and unlocked the ornate doors of the domed structure, and then stood to block the dark entrance, from beyond which came wailing,. Many agonized female faces could be seen.

"Ah!" said Cireive, "I almost forgot. If there is but one question that you do not answer to my satisfaction, you will have to take the place of these women inside."

"No!" said the Prince. "Please, my Lord Father!"

The *taqavor* glanced at him briefly. "Oh, don't be afraid. I promise, you will join your blind queen inside. That is, unless you deny her now, and give up her worthless husk, and take another proper queen worthy of the Prince Heir. Do not think me daft, boy, that I have allowed you this nonsense of a marriage. I allowed it only to amuse myself at the spectacle of a blind beggar being made into a temporary queen."

"Enough! What is your first question?" said the queen without eyes. Her voice was strong and she was smiling.

And in response Cireive let out a peal of insane laughter and rubbed his hands gleefully. "At last, I'll see how truly clever you are," he said. "Tell me, why does the sun shine?"

"The sun shines because it can," replied the woman ruthlessly. "Now, let one of the prisoners out."

"Very well," said the *taqavor,* nodding to the guards. They in turn moved aside, and one trembling woman was taken by the shoulders and pushed out past the row of soldiers.

"Go quickly!" exclaimed Lirheas. "Go while you can!"

The *taqoui* took several tentative steps and then instead of running, came down on her knees, weeping in gratitude before the *taqavor* who ignored her.

"What is the purpose of dreams? What are the things that I see?" said Cireive to the queen without eyes.

She did not hesitate for a moment. "Dreams are created by you to protect yourself from the harsh truth, my Lord. Unlike the merciless reality of wakefulness, in dreams you see only that which safely shields you."

Cireive thought for a moment, then smiled. "Agreed," he said, and pointed once more to the doors of the sepulcher. Another of the *taqoui* was shoved into the fading daylight, as though she were a sack of bones. She came out swaying in weakness, and like her predecessor lowered herself on her knees.

"Ah, for goodness' sake, begone quickly, woman," said the queen without eyes in exasperation, *seeing* through the eyes of the Prince how the woman hesitated.

"Now then," continued Cireive, "tell me what is the number of directions from which the wind blows in my *empirastan?*"

"Simple," said the queen without eyes. "It equals the number of destinations where the wind arrives."

"What?"

"That would be your next question—for this one, you owe me another prisoner."

Cireive frowned, then opened his eyes wide, and nodded to the guards, and the third woman was released.

"Well then, explain," he muttered.

The queen smiled.

"When you speak of the wind, you speak of movement. Air moves from one place to another. For every point of its origin there is an end point of destination. Draw a line from the origin to the destination, and it will represent the direction. But it is rather useless to discuss it unless you have a specific stationary point in mind, because the wind never sits still but changes direction constantly and thus changes its point of destination. Thus, what starts out as a simple straight line ends up as an infinitely meandering sequence of ever-changing points. . . ."

"And what point is at the very middle of the world?" said the *taqavor* suddenly.

"From your relative perspective, it is you, of course," she replied. "But, in the absolute sense, every point on the surface of a sphere is the middle point."

"So then," the *taqavor* mused aloud, obviously pleased, "if I move, the middle of the world moves with me?"

"Of course," she replied, smiling softly once again. "If you choose to look at it that way."

Cireive chuckled, and motioned for the guards to release another *taqoui* from the prison of the tomb.

He never gave the *taqoui* a single glance, but immediately asked another question.

"I want to know the size of the world and thus the size of my *empirastan,* once and for all."

At this the queen sighed. "It is a very great number," she said carefully.

"Naturally it is a great number, I know that! But what determines this number?" the *taqavor* persisted. "Tell me, woman!"

"The gods determine it by designating for it a great place," she replied.

"How? And where is this great place that my *empirastan* is located? I would know!"

"Your *empirastan* is located on the surface of a sphere," replied the queen. "But that is the next question, so you need to release another one."

Cireive nodded to the guards absently, and continued to muse outloud, while an agonized woman rushed forth, and bowed before him like the other released prisoners.

"Tell me how is it that my *empirastan* covers a sphere? I would hear more of this impossibility," the *taqavor* continued.

The queen paused. After a moment she said, "The *empirastan* does not cover the whole of the sphere. It is great indeed, possibly the greatest of all. But it is less than the whole world, my Lord. I cannot lie."

In the growing twilight, Lirheas watched this insane game, and for the first time he knew that here was the end.

"I do not like your answer," muttered Cireive. "No, I do not. . . ."

"I did not think you would," replied the woman. "However, before you decide to be done with me, I offer you one more question and answer. Only this time, I raise the stakes, and offer a challenge. But first you must release all the rest of the women, and then you must enter the tomb alone with me."

Hearing that, Cireive let out another giggle. "Oh, you think you are clever enough to deceive me?" he said, shaking with laughter. "You want to lure me inside and shut the door? Is that so?"

"Of course," said the queen without eyes. "But I will come with you into the darkness. Are you afraid of being alone with me, a pathetic blind beggar, oh great Lord of the greatest *empirastan?*"

"Oh, no!" exclaimed the *taqavor,* no longer laughing. "I do not trust you for a moment, woman. I would never go inside with you alone. Oh, no, not ever. . . ."

And then he spoke to the guards, "I am tired of this game. Now take them both, this so-called queen, and my fool of a son, and put them inside. And take these women that I have just 'released' and put them back inside also. I had no intention of freeing them in the first place—"

"A pity indeed," said the queen without eyes. Moving preternaturally fast, she was at the side of the *taqavor,* and then she was at his back. She grasped him from behind and in the next instant, there was a long needle-sharp dagger of pale steel in her hand, and she was holding it at his throat while its razor-sharp edge was directly over his carotid artery.

Cireive went still in her hold.

The guards who had barely began to move, froze also, for it seemed she had moved outside of time itself, so fast she had been, so inhuman. They stood petrified, watching her. The *taqoui,* still on their knees, stared upwards in terrible wonder.

Lirheas felt an impossible cold intensity overcome him, and this moment crystallized, became the most violently urgent and yet stretched out moment of his life. . . .

"Lirheas," she said loudly, calmly, while the sun set on the horizon behind them. "Come to my side and open the doors of this prison wide. Release all of the women who are within. If anyone else moves, I will plunge this knife into your Lord father's neck."

There was a terrible fury in the face of the *taqavor.* But he felt the sharp point biting at his neck and so he hissed to the guards, "For now, do as she says. You will pay for this, bitch, and you also, Lirheas—"

The women of the House of Wives came forth like funereal shadows into the twilight. In the distance torches were being lit in the Palace itself and along the garden paths.

When the last of the women has been released, the queen without eyes directed Lirheas to stand between her and the guards. Then she moved, backing, taking the *taqavor* with her into the orifice of night that was the gaping doorway of the domed sepulcher.

"Close the door behind us," she said. "And do not unlock it unless I tell you so."

"What will you do? Let me come with you, my queen," whispered Lirheas.

But she made no answer, and for some peculiar reason he had no strength to follow her.

Prince Lirheas shut and locked the door behind them, and stood outside surrounded by a ring of guards while darkness fell completely upon the world.

In the darkness they were both equally blind, the *taqavor* and the woman whose eyes he had taken from her.

Cireive felt the sharpness of metal against his neck and he barely breathed, for fear had crept into him and then engulfed him, and he felt time dripping in precious globule moments, felt silence except for the blood rushing in his temples.

And then the terror increased.

For suddenly he sensed the rising sea of growth everywhere, the soft fluttering of leaves and the filaments of flowers rising from their desiccated ashes in the open coffins of brass.

The ghosts of the flowers were all around them, clamoring loudly in the silence, scarlet and vermilion and magenta in his memory, seething around him, amaranth. . . .

"Who are you?" he whispered, needing to hear the sound of his own voice, forgetting the fear of death and the biting steel— indeed, holding on as a consolation to the awareness of the sharp prick of pain and the grip of her hand against his neck. For these were mundane things, in contrast to all that was rising around them.

And then the moon came forth, and shone bright and pale through the skylights.

Cireive blinked, and thought he saw the ghosts of the flowers recede momentarily, but instead he saw her shadow behind him, the woman without eyes.

She had released him and moved out of his way, allowing him easy freedom. He could have bolted for the door in that moment, could have taken the sharp dagger from her hands and used it on her. . . .

But he stood frozen with the passing of time, and watched her stand there him in the brief illumination of the tomb. Without a word she raised her hands to remove the binding of cloth that covered her blind eye-sockets.

Untying the cloth, she let it drop to the ground, fluttering gently. He saw her face made soft and smooth by moonlight, and the pits of her ravaged wounds, still unhealed after all this time, her eye-sockets that refused to close, were deep with darkness in the twilight, seeming in their incidental shape suddenly to be like crowns of heavy blossoms, familiar to him, oh so familiar.

And suddenly, for a moment out of time, he recognized her.

"Mother . . ." sobbed Cireive, an old man in the voice of a little boy. "It *is* you, isn't it? Why did you come back now? Why did you leave me then?"

The woman stood watching him. He could see now that there were translucent ghosts of eyes in her empty sockets, and that this was the reason they could never close. Her ghost-eyes glittered, moist and soft and receptive.

"I never left you, my child," she said then, speaking for the first time since they had entered the tomb, and he recognized her afresh for he knew that voice, singing to him out of the depths of antiquity.

The woman took a step forward so that she was just before him, close enough to look into his own eyes. "How you've grown," she said gently, and he saw her form was fluid and shimmering with otherness. She reached forth with her hand and laid it on his cheek.

"My . . . Cireive."

And her ghost eyes were suddenly very liquid, so liquid that they pooled with richness, and the water came in a rivulet down her cheek.

"Remember what really happened, child. . . ."

Memories struck him wildly then, sharp images of the growing field of amaranth, tall stalks and leaves covering his head, and he was running, a small boy, running and crying for his mother.

Except he was not running in search of her. Instead he was running away, far away *from* her, leaves striking his face, running madly.

For he had left her there at the edge of the field, just as he had found her, quiet and dead at the bottom of the scarlet amaranth sea. He had sat down at the edge of the field then, with his back turned to it, and he had looked ahead and muttered to himself until dusk.

"How did you die?" whispered Cireive, the boy-old man in puzzlement, trying so very hard to remember. "What happened to you, mother?"

But the woman without eyes was again silent. Her form shimmered, and her ghostly eyes, now cloaked in a mantle of eternity, took on a deeper richness, the eyes of *another,* of a woman who was not a goddess and yet was not quite mortal, for she was suspended between times and she was unable to die, because of him, because of what he'd done.

"You!" cried Cireive, recognizing her suddenly, wildly—a woman whom he had seen coming forth from the field of amaranth many summers after he was a young man, in the same place where his mother had disappeared, carrying with her a small crying child that looked so much like himself and yet unlike.

He had almost forgotten. It had happened so long ago.

"Cireive," the strange woman had said to him, knowing out of nowhere his name. "I have stepped from time, and I am waiting for you, even as I hold *you* here, hold you back from the abyss of the bottomless well. . . ."

"Who are you?" he had said harshly, already a bitter man and a warrior. He heard the incomprehensible words, and he looked at her, seeing an old glimmer of something familiar, something that he should know.

She pointed to the child and then to himself.

"No!" he had exclaimed, taking an involuntary step away from her. "I do not know you, whoever you are, nor this brat! One thing is sure, it is not mine!"

But the woman stood watching him, and her eyes were in that instant impossible to describe, for the depth of ancient color they contained, showed times mixing in her pupils.

"I hold *you*, Cireive," she repeated. And then the next thing she said was a puzzle: "The soul is a flower, severed from its stem, bearing seed, planted at birth, reaped in death, but never discarded in the bottomless well."

And stricken by a sudden panic, he, who had not been afraid of hordes of armed men, ran from her, ran as he had so many years ago as a little boy. He turned around eventually, and looked down at the field of amaranth from the top of the hill that he had scaled in his frenzy.

She was not there.

Maybe she had never been there in the first place.

Cireive gasped for breath, surfacing in the here and now, where the wan moonlight of the tomb illuminated a woman with empty eye-sockets who stood like an upright corpse before him, waiting for something.

"Who are you?" he repeated, feeling the space of the large airy chamber close in on him as though he were in a cocoon of stems and leaves and branches, with filaments of magenta streaming just overhead.

"Wrong question," she said in that same peculiarly familiar voice. "Ask instead who you yourself are."

"Ah . . ." he muttered, taking a step back from her as the cocoon of ghostly flowers growing all around him began to close in even more. And then he cried, "I am Cireive, *taqavor* of the mortal world, and my *empirastan* is all this that you see around you! All of it!"

The woman smiled. "There are walls around you. Indeed, you are Lord of them, but nothing else, not even yourself. Don't you understand this, now of all times?"

Cireive frowned, his brow furrowing in effort. He stood considering, dislocated suddenly, and for a moment the world went dizzy.

"I am Cireive," he said. "And I have conquered the lands East, West, South, and North of the Compass Rose. The directions did not exist before I named them. I name all things. I name you!"

"And yet," she countered in a soft ghostly voice, "you cannot. For your names have no substance and are temporary designations. You named me 'you with the knowing eyes,' and then you named me 'holes for eyes.' You never named me at all, for you never learned my true name. Just as you have never known the women who serve you and for that matter the men.

"For, a true name is not given but observed and derived from the fabric of one's being. Look at me now and tell me what you see."

"Another game!" he exclaimed with false levity, while cold gathered about him, tightening the cocoon.

"If so, then play along with me, you who are *taqavor* of the world. Or are you afraid of a woman without eyes and without a name?"

Cireive lunged backward, but things were pressing on him from all sides, invisible things with stalks and wide leaves and filaments that brushed against his skin, making the hairs on the surface stand on end.

"Well then," she said. "What will you take away from me next? Strip me of my hair? Peel away the skin and then the flesh from my bones? Dig deeper yet, into the marrow, to seek the essence that comprises me, and which is still beyond your reach?"

She took a step forward, closer to him again, the bottom of her robe sweeping lightly against the intricate floor tiles strewn with ashes of the flowers. Ghostly eyes, brimming with liquid, once more filled her empty eye-sockets, and the liquid was overflowing. . . .

"Mother," he said, "what is happening? What am I? And what are you?"

"You have hungered for the truths of this world for so long," she replied. "All the while you have ravaged the world within your grasp. The oceans are overflowing with the blood of your conquest and creation of the greatest *empirastan* that spans the world. And yet the desert grows around you and around this city, and one day the ocean will close in, and you will be an island all alone. Indeed, you already are."

A knot was forming in his throat, even stronger than the pressing of terror. From the corner of his eye he saw the opened coffins filled with ashes, and pale shapes of growth rising, crawling vines reaching for him.

"You died, mother!" he exclaimed in the voice of a boy. "You scared me so much because you were so still and yet your skin was still warm. I was so scared, so cold and scared! You were warmer than me still, almost alive. And I wanted to shake you and yet I could not! I could not stand it, I had to run! Don't you see why—?"

The woman with the ghost eyes continued to weep before him as she said, "I had died, my child, and it was not your fault that I had, nor that you were frightened and that you ran. But don't you know that you kept me from the cleansing and renewing cycle of death, you kept me frozen in time, because of the injustice you had done in my name? Remember, Cireive! For that night you returned to the village alone, and you brought them back and they searched for me in futility. And the next day, when they came back again and found me at last, you lied to them, and blamed those strangers for my death!"

"No! No, mother!" muttered he, shaking. "No, I did not, no. . . ."

But the woman's words were now a river of time, flowing wildly and not to be contained. "And the people of our village believed you," she said. "Remember how the mob turned upon those innocent strangers who had stopped in our village to trade, and how they took them and stripped them, and lit torches from the bonfire of cut amaranth—do you remember now, my son?"

"No," sobbed Cireive. "I remember the flowers burning, the red feather tendrils curling into ashes, so pungent with smoke. . . ."

"They put me on that fire, Cireive, and my body—now truly cold—went up in flames, while my essence remained in anguish, for around me were the living cries of the innocents, the twelve men who did not properly speak our tongue and thus could not defend themselves, twelve who could do nothing but struggle against the ropes as they lay surrounding my body, being punished for a crime they did not commit. . . ."

"It did not happen!" he snarled. "No! It was so very long ago, but I remember it clearly, the flowers over my head as I was hiding, and their voices as they spoke to you, and you replied—"

"They spoke to me briefly, true, those foreign travelers," said the woman-ghost. "But, far from meaning harm, they only asked me for the direction of the village. They were kind men. While their skins were darker than ours and of an olive hue, their faces were warm and unthreatening, and they thanked me from their hearts before continuing on toward town.

"They were the last to speak to me in this life, Cireive. For after I watched them go, after I'd turned my back to resume our game and was about to go looking for you, I suddenly felt a sharp pain in my chest. It was so intense that I dropped the basket before I could even straighten myself. And then for a moment I still stood up, was still upright in spirit, while my body collapsed and lay on the ground at the edges of the great field.

"I had so wanted to run to you, my son! So intense was my desire, so much unfinished business, and yet my heart broke and then stopped its living pump, and my body was useless. Death with her shimmering scythe stood a few steps away, ready to take me by the hand gently, but I—fool that I am—shook my head at her and instead remained standing there near my still warm body."

In the moonlight, the woman's translucent eyes spilled forth a stream of tears, also ghosts. Cireive, weeping himself, watched with peculiar detachment their unreal passage, and wanted so much to put his hand there and feel their nonexistent moisture against his fingers, and to maybe feel the warmth of her cheek one more time after so many years.

"I was still there when you came back at last, my little boy Cireive. And when you saw me and when you ran in terror, I flew in spirit at your side, wanting to breathe warmth and relief into your being, but you never felt me, never heard my spirit cry. Instead, from great fear you sank into shock, and then into madness, and eventually, when twilight came, you returned to town. As you passed by the strangers, they had just began their trade with our people. An odd idea had come to you, and you somehow knew they had spoken to me, and in your denial of truth you wanted to cast blame upon someone. So, when the initial search for me was over for the night, you lay in bed, and I stood there at your side, and I saw a shadow approach you."

"It was *He,*" whispered Cireive, remembering suddenly a little boy's fevered imaginations of moving shadows in the empty lonely night. "*He* came to me in the evil darkness, called there by my fear. . . ."

The woman without corporeal eyes nodded slowly. "Yes, I know," she said softly. "The Lord of Illusion comes to us in our darkest moments, for that is when we are most vulnerable to a loss of reason and open to rebellion against the universe."

"He painted the Illusion so clearly in my mind's eye," said Cireive. "I could almost see how the strangers came to you and attacked you and beat you and forced you."

"Yes, you remember that version even now, even though none of it happened. It is the same thing you told our townspeople the next morning. And yet I cried out to you with all of my being, standing there between you and the Lord of Illusion, I cried and shielded you until dawn, and eventually *He* was gone, having done only partial harm, but *His* dark intent had taken root within you, and it was enough. . . ."

"Enough indeed," echoed the *taqavor.* He looked at the woman, and then his gaze slipped down to the hand in which she still held the long, thin, razor-sharp needle-dagger.

"All these years of compounded slaughter and darkness, my *empirastan,*" said Cireive. "What have I done, mother. What have I done. One long interminable . . . Illusion."

And, saying that, he reached across the space between them and took the dagger out of her unprotesting fingers, while she continued to stand before him, blind and yet all-seeing across time.

For a moment only, they looked at each other in silence.

"Will this free you, at last?" he finally said, raising the blade.

"No," she whispered and in her eyes there was utter anguish, while at the same time he swept the razor forward at an angle and then suddenly, swiftly, he returned it with an old warrior's skill, and struck it deep into his own chest.

Time blurred.

When next it focused, Cireive stood in the same place in the sepulcher with the moon streaming its bright radiance down through the skylights.

But now two shadowed forms stood before him. Directly opposite him was the woman without eyes. The other, just at her side, was a cloaked figure of interminable opacity, its skeletal silver hands holding a long staff upon which was a moon-shaped blade of unknown metal and rippling rainbows.

"You cannot escape this easily," said death in a voice of echoing nothingness. "The deaths of thousands are still upon you, and they weigh you down. I cannot carry all that weight of mortal agony and suffering that is your Burden, and thus I cannot take you."

And the skeletal one pointed with one bone-finger to his chest where was lodged a slim dagger of razor metal. Cireive looked down at himself, at the black stream of blood that had stained his chest. And all of a sudden he heard within himself the strange terrible resounding silence of a stilled heart.

What am I? he cried in madness. *Help me!*

"I cannot take you," repeated death. "Not like this. Lighten your burden first, and then I will come for you at last."

But how? he cried for the second time, realizing only then that he was unable to form words, for his dead lungs did not compress air, and thus the sound had emerged only in his mind.

But death had turned her back to him, and begun to walk away, shimmering into nothingness against the walls of the sepulcher.

Help me!

And the woman without eyes, without a name, who was and yet was not his mother, stood before him, ghostly tears streaming down her face.

Please, he whispered in his mind, *Mother, please don't leave me this time!*

And then he wailed, and howled, and it was not the sound of a human being, but of a peculiar unnatural beast.

Who am I? he growled and wept. *What am I that I cannot die, that not even death would claim me?*

Time was frozen around him, and he could feel its sterile walls pressing in, no longer empty red flowers born of Illusion, no longer the scent of ashes. Time stood choking him with its edges just outside of him, just at his periphery. . . .

He was in a walled cocoon outside the universe.

The bottomless well.

Who am I? the beast without a name whispered, reaching with its once human appendage forward, toward her. . . .

Mother. . . .

And the woman remained, at the edge of him. Her form shook with weeping, for she could do nothing now, even though she was so close, and she was *between* times.

I can see you at last, the beast spoke. *You are so real, and I can name you now. Your name is Amarantea, for you stand among the blossoms of the great field, as simple and unyielding and as beautiful.*

"I thank you for your beginnings of true vision," she whispered. "And yet that is not my name."

Who is she, then? his inner voice said, *For I know her somehow, and I know this name. Who is Amarantea? She is within you!*

And the queen without eyes and without a true name replied, "Amarantea was the mother of your son. The one who came forth from the field of red flowers carrying a child that you denied at first. He, that child, was the one who was never the son of your flesh, but then became the son of your conscience. All those years of darkness, he was the silent one who kept you back from the very edge. And you never knew it, just as he never knew."

I had no son, then, remembered the beast. *And yet Lirheas became my son, from the moment my eyes fell upon his little form. He reminded me of something.*

"He reminded you of yourself, of what you had been and could have been in innocence, had you not come before the sway of the Lord of Illusion."

Moments of silence. Moonlight began to fade in the skylights as the moon sank from its zenith.

The beast sank also, to its knees, and then lay forward with its head resting against the cold tiles of the floor of the sepulcher. It remained thus for long interminable flowing moments of time, muttering with inhuman lips against the stone, muttering words of regret and agony, and repeating the name "Amarantea."

The woman without eyes stood before it with infinite patience.

And then at last the beast raised its distorted face toward her, and it said, *She is gone, and I can never find her to beg her forgiveness, for I cannot even remember her, or remember hurting her. Such is the great power that Illusion has upon me. I do not remember. And yet I must remember her, Amarantea!*

"Then I will once again bring the purgatory of Remembrance to you," said the woman. "For you left Amarantea at the edge of that field—just another faceless woman, just as years ago you had left your dead mother—while you took her son away from her, and you ordered your soldiers to set the field to flames. The flowers burned as you watched for the second time in your life their red crowns and filaments turn to ash, and you observed Amarantea burning also, saw her scream in agony as she died while you held her infant son—crying and choking from the smoke—while silence and detachment were firmly lodged within you, and you felt nothing from beyond the first wall of Illusion.

I cannot remember any of this, uttered the beast, moaning.

"You now have all of eternity to remember," she replied. "All of eternity, or until the world ends, for you are now outside of time, and around you is the bottomless well. You yourself have chosen it to be thus. Your choice, to see not truth but through the veil of Illusion."

Help me!

"I cannot. The spirit of your mother lives within me even now, but briefly. And the spirit of Amarantea was in me for only a moment. And yet they are still both here, even now, for they are at your side, the only ones who will never leave you. I will not leave you either. For together we hold your soul at the edge of the bottomless well, we hold you tight and keep you from sinking forever."

The woman came to kneel before the beast, and, looking into its murky eyes, whispered, "We are your last hope . . . and we alone can see you through the thick layers of Illusion that now surround you. If you choose, look for us in return."

Then she rose and turned her back, and walked to the doors of the sepulcher where she knocked loudly, calling to be released from the night of hell.

Behind her, the beast was fading already, for only the gaze of her ghostly eyes upon him had kept him here, and now there was nothing left.

She turned around for a moment as the doors were being opened from the outside, and a shaft of pale dawn light came striking the stone floor and the old flower ashes. As she looked behind her, the beast came for a last time momentarily into view, and then its form curled in upon itself as it lay down, poised between death and time.

"Sleep . . ." whispered the queen without eyes. "And thus only will they see you. When you sleep, and when Illusion is weakest around you."

And then she walked outside, into the dawning daylight and the voices of nervous soldiers and into the arms of the Prince who loved her.

And thus I have told you the story of time.

The Prince Lirheas who married the queen without eyes, became a king and thus *taqavor,* and for many enlightened years he ruled the greatest *empirastan* that comprised the whole world—or so it was claimed.

The queen without eyes and without a name gave birth to three children over the course of time, and the first child, a girl, she called Amarantea. On that same day, the queen also took this name for herself, saying that it was in honor and in memory, and in hope.

Their great city stood like a blossom in the heart of the desert for many years, and in the Palace, in the center of a great stone hall floated a four-pointed star that was the world's first Compass Rose. Occasionally, when the dusk fell a certain way and shadows gathered, some claimed they saw the shape of a peculiar nameless beast hunched over the Rose, and muttering soft words that echoed through the hall. But then, it was all an Illusion, they knew, and in time even this legend was forgotten.

When the great *taqavor* and his queen Amarantea had died in their old age, much beloved by all, their heirs obeyed their last wishes, and opened a forgotten domed sepulcher in the middle of the Palace gardens.

Within were many old weathered coffins filled with dust and ashes, and not a sign of human remains. The coffins—since their purpose and true contents were unknown—were respectfully lidded up, and then three new coffins were placed in the center, all made of shining brass.

The bodies of the *taqavor* and his beloved *taqoui* were laid in the two outer coffins, while the middle coffin was left empty, as instructed, and its lid was shut over gaping nothingness.

That center coffin was thus a mystery.

But the children of the *taqavor* loved him so much that they did not question it, and simply closed the sepulcher tight, and, after grieving for the departed, went on with the business of living.

With time and with generations, it was rumored that in the empty coffin was contained the world's greatest evil. But of course it was nonsense, since many knew that it in fact contained nothing.

Only some very old ones—a decrepit grandmother of another great-grandmother who had lived so long ago—remembered that in their younger days things had been dark and bitter, things that had made the great *empirastan* what it was.

That coffin—they muttered, prompted to reminiscence by certain peculiar shadows in the corners under a certain light of dusk—that coffin is yet to be filled. It waits for someone.

The coffin waits for a soul which will one day step forth from the bottomless well outside the universe and back into the river of time to embrace death—for time is a cascading sequence of cause and effect, and death is the separator of memory of that sequence, the great delimiter.

But it will only be filled after the soul's choice is made to embrace the fullness of truth and to reject Illusion.

Thus it was spoken. But eventually even this legend too was forgotten.

Time swept through the *empirastan* and the great city, and with centuries the earth shifted and great oceans advanced to flood the desert. Around the city was formed an island, for somehow even the waters were unable to sweep this peculiar bit of land away in its entirety, as though something outside of time and the universe lay reposing here, some unfinished business.

The silver water sang, and waves came rushing softly upon an ashen ebony shore.

And with time the men and the women and all remnants of the great *empirastan* had left the island, and the once great city lay in ruins. While elsewhere in the world, it was said, new *empirastans* were created, and new vibrant things took root, in all the directions of the wind—North, South, East, and West of the Compass Rose.

The Compass Rose itself—who knows what really became of it? Very likely it lies still, no longer floating, but in a dried-up basin of a pool—truly, a great cup of water fit for a giant—in the center of a stone hall of a ruined palace, in an abandoned city, on an island of dreams that shimmers at the edges of time.

One thing is certain. As it stilled for the last time in the final moist dregs of the basin before this liquid too evaporated, the single lodestone-weighted point of the Compass came to rest in such a way that it still points North.

But maybe you will one day find out for yourself as you go searching for it, in search of your own directions, and lured forward toward wonder by the music that comes from your dreams and has no name, except as an ancient memory.

Amarantea beckons you thus, beckons all of us, and, if you do find it, then take a moment to refill the great cup of the pool and let the Compass Rose float free once again, fulfilling the next moment and the next in this neverending story of time.

The End

About the Author

Vera Nazarian immigrated to the USA from the former USSR as a kid, sold her first story at the age of 17, and since then has published numerous works in anthologies and magazines, and has seen her fiction translated into eight languages.

She made her novelist debut with the critically acclaimed arabesque "collage" novel *Dreams of the Compass Rose* (2002), followed by epic fantasy about a world without color, *Lords of Rainbow* (2003). Her novella *The Clock King and the Queen of the Hourglass* from PS Publishing (UK) with an introduction by **Charles de Lint** made the *Locus* Recommended Reading List for 2005. Her debut short fiction collection *Salt of the Air*, with an introduction by **Gene Wolfe**, contains the 2007 Nebula Award-nominated "The Story of Love." Other work includes the 2008 Nebula Award-nominated, self-illustrated baroque fantasy novella *The Duke In His Castle*, science fiction collection *After the Sundial* (2010), Supernatural **Jane Austen** Series parodies *Mansfield Park and Mummies* (2009), *Northanger Abbey and Angels and Dragons* (2010), *Pride and Platypus: Mr. Darcy's Dreadful Secret* (2012), *The Perpetual Calendar of Inspiration* (2010), and a parody of paranormal love and relationships advice *Vampires are from Venus, Werewolves are from Mars* (2012).

Vera recently relocated from Los Angeles to the East Coast. She lives in a small town in Vermont, and uses her Armenian sense of humor and her Russian sense of suffering to bake conflicted pirozhki and make art.

In addition to being a writer and award-winning artist, she is also the publisher of Norilana Books.

Official website:
www.veranazarian.com

www.ingramcontent.com/pod-product-compliance
Lightning Source LLC
Chambersburg PA
CBHW031033030726
47497CB00004B/1117